The Tarot Murders

An Isabel Sinclair Mystery

Lila Richards

Millwheel Press

Published by:

Millwheel Press Ltd

Eyrewell Forest, New Zealand

www.millwheelpress.co.nz

ISBN: 978-0-473-50202-7- softcover

978-0-473-50203-4 - Epub

978-0-473-50204-1 - mobi

When a series of bizarre murders based on major trumps of the Tarot rocks the usually staid city of Christchurch, the panel members of radio show The Psychic Connection are drawn into the case when it seems panel member James Myerson may be involved – or even the murderer. Detective Sergeant Declan Kelly returns to Christchurch, on sick leave after being wounded during a stakeout in Queensland, and adds his weight to the Psychic Connection panel's investigation of what the press is calling the Tarot Murders. The murderer's calling card, The Magician, left with each new victim, offers a sinister clue to the killer's identity – if only the panel can solve it in time to prevent the death of one of its own members.

CHAPTER ONE

The light from the fat, creamy candles flickered eerily, sending out a faint odour of beeswax as the three figures passed in front of them, their white robes swishing against the wooden floor. Three wooden stools had been placed in a row in front of the high altar, and they made their way to these. Before the altar, his face a shadow in the depths of the hood pulled down over his head, stood a tall figure in a scarlet robe. A slight movement of his arm told them to be seated. This they did, trying to appear calm and controlled, as befitted the rank they aspired to.

Behind the altar six more figures, also anonymous in matching scarlet robes, stood in a motionless semi-circle. At the back of the three seated candidates, their white robes gleaming faintly in the dim light, a number of other figures stood, more or less completing a ragged circle that enfolded the three candidates and the altar.

The altar itself was a double cube, eight feet long and four feet in height and depth. According to tradition, it should have been carved of a single block of stone, but the logistics of such an enterprise were beyond the skills of even the Brothers of the Second Order. Besides, such a large block of stone would have been impossible for the floor of the old second-storey warehouse to support, and they had no desire to have their temple accidentally exposed to the curious gaze of ordinary mortals. So, two wooden cubes—one painted black, one white, both inscribed with the appropriate symbols—had been constructed and placed in the precise position indicated by the radiesthetic skills of Brother Esto Sol Testis.

At the centre of the altar a candle burned for the Head of the Second Order Brothers, and behind it, in a semi-circle, glowed one for each of the others. Yet their faces remained in darkness, impassive rocks surrounding a golden pool of light. At one side of the white cube lay several unlit white candles, and beside them a number of scarlet cords woven of what looked like heavy silk. A silver chalice of intricate design stood at the other side, along with a straight, carved stick of some rich-toned wood, and a dark golden disk engraved with a pentacle. The black cube held a smoking brass censer and an impressive-looking sword, its ornate hilt encrusted with gems.

Above the altar, suspended from the dusty gloom of the high, beamed ceiling, hung a heavy brass dish-like object in which a flame burned, flickering slightly as air circulated among the rafters. This was the sacred flame of the Brotherhood. In an ideal world, it would have burned perpetually. As it was, however, it was the duty of whichever Brother was currently Keeper of the Flame to be sure he got to meetings before anyone else so it was always burning when they arrived. Naturally, everyone knew about this (apart from the newest of the neophytes who, by definition, knew nothing at all), but it was part of the mythos of the Brotherhood that they should preserve the illusion.

As soon as the three white-robed men were seated, the tall figure in front of the altar raised his arms high above his

2

head. The candle flames fluttered. Wild shadows went careering about the walls of the warehouse, so it seemed for a moment that the scarlet figures were themselves flames, leaping and flickering behind the altar like a wall of fire.

On his stool at the right-hand side of the row of aspirants, Brother Non Extinguar, of the Theoricus Grade of the First Order, felt his heart quiver with fear and excitement. In a few moments, he would know the results of his recent examination. Last time, he had failed to cross the gap between Theoricus and Practicus. He had been bitterly disappointed, naturally. But Brother Ex Flamma Lux, the tall figure now standing before them with arms raised in blessing, had advised him to continue his studies, and try again at the next Equinox. And so he had. He had worked very hard, and this time, he was certain, he would not be disappointed.

Brother Ex Flamma Lux slowly lowered his arms, sending the shadows dancing once more. From the depths of his scarlet hood, he addressed the assembly.

"The Council of Seven has deliberated with due care the examination material submitted by our three candidates for the First Order Grade of Practicus. Having reached our conclusions, it now falls to me, the Senior of the Seven, to communicate them to our three brothers in the usual way." The Senior Brother's deep, rich voice carried with the effortless ease of one used to addressing larger groups than were present today. It was a rich, cultured voice, with a slight, though definite, German accent.

With an unobtrusive movement of his left hand, Brother Ex Flamma Lux summoned one of the scarlet-robed brothers to his side. As he glided forward, he picked up the bundle of woven cords and held them at the ready.

The Senior's voice rang out again. "Brother Gaudet Luce, please step forward."

The candidate to the left of the three, a slight figure almost swamped by his voluminous gown, rose to his feet and moved to stand before the Senior. "Well done, Brother, you have attained the grade of Practicus by unanimous vote of the Council of Seven." The Senior tied the red cord about Brother Gaudet Luce's waist. Later, he would discard the white cord appropriate to the first three grades of the First Order, which until now had secured his robe. "Welcome to the Grade of Practicus. Honour it well." The Senior pulled a card from his robe, apparently from inside his sleeve, and handed it to the graduate. Such design as was visible suggested it was a Tarot card, the usual token given to graduates of their newly attained status. It would, of course, be the Magician.

With a slight inclination of his head, Brother Gaudet Luce acknowledged his new honour and stepped back to his seat.

"Brother Clariore Flammis, please step forward."

As the tall, slightly stooped figure moved to stand before the Senior, Brother Non Extinguar felt his chest tighten in expectation. He stared down at his tightly folded hands in an effort to calm himself, the Senior's words to the next candidate fading to a blur of sound as his heart began to thump against his rib-cage. With the tying on of the red cord, he would finally gain full authority to practise the rites appropriate to his grade—no longer just a learner, but a real magician. He was finally about to embark officially on the path to which he had, in that moment of clarity three years ago, dedicated his life...

"Brother Non Extinguar, please step forward."

Taking a deep breath to calm the blood pounding in his ears, the candidate did as he was bid.

"The Council of Seven is mindful of how hard you have worked towards this grade, and we commend you for this. Certainly none could fault you on your determination, and this is, as we all know, an essential quality for the practice of Magic."

Brother Non Extinguar tried to remain calm. After all, excessive pride was not conducive to the clarity of purpose needed by a magician.

"However, it is unfortunately also true that hard work alone is not sufficient."

A gasp leapt unbidden from the candidate's lips, and was immediately extinguished by the heavy silence that emanated from the other brothers like ectoplasm. His eyes widened in disbelief as the Senior continued.

"The decision was a difficult one, but after much deliberation, the vote was as follows: two for and five against. Once again, Brother, we commend you on your hard work." In a softer voice meant only for his ears, the Senior said, "Do not be disheartened, Brother. I will speak with you further on this." From his robe he drew a card.

Still in shock, Brother Non Extinguar took it and returned to his seat. Only later, after he had filed with the others down the narrow staircase that led past the storeroom on the first floor, and the health-food shop and natural-healing clinic on the ground floor, and had reached the rain-soaked pavement outside, did he feel able to look at it.

The Fool—again! Always the wanderer, the seeker, the innocent abroad. He had leapt willingly—gladly, even—into

5

the Abyss for God's sake! What more did they want from him! Or was it that they just didn't want him to be one of them? He had heard rumours of certain aspirants being excluded, not because they lacked ability, but because the Council of Seven considered them unsuitable in other ways. Maybe that was it. Well, he would just have to show them they were wrong. He would have to find a way of showing them he was a real magician, and not the fool they obviously thought him. Muttering rhythmically under his breath, Brother Non Extinguar tore the Tarot card to shreds and cast it into the brimming gutter, where it was swiftly carried away.

* * * *

As she brushed crumbs from the coffee table, Isabel Sinclair noticed a ring of spilt coffee. She was tempted just to throw the cloth over it, but she supposed she'd better give it a quick wipe with a damp cloth first. With a sigh and a flick of her long red curls, she hurried out to the kitchen. The telephone rang. She glanced at the wall clock. Still ten minutes before her tarot client was due to arrive. Time to answer the phone then.

"Oh, hello, Joss. I thought Luke had arranged for you to interview that woman about her haunted house this morning."

Joss Cherry, as a clairvoyant who was reasonably well known in certain circles due to her involvement, along with Isabel, in Luke Marriott's Psychic Connection radio programme, was called in from time to time to help people troubled by unwanted psychic phenomena. Since she was

6

also a journalist, every call could be regarded as a potential story, so she rarely refused such requests.

"He had," Joss replied, "but she rang and postponed it. She's got someone coming in tomorrow afternoon to do an exorcism, and she thought we might be able to work on her ghost together. She's already arranged it with the exorcist, so I'm going over earlier to see what I can discover about her ghost, and then get a first-hand account of the exorcism."

"That's great! Who's doing the exorcism? Anyone we know?"

"I don't think so. He only agreed to work with me on condition that he remains anonymous, so I'm not even allowed to know his name. It's all a bit cloak and dagger, but he's a lecturer at the university, apparently, and he doesn't want any trouble with his faculty or the university authorities. You know how conservative they can be. But according to Jean—that's the woman I'm interviewing—he's had a lot of experience with what she calls 'occult manifestations'. Comes very highly recommended, by all accounts, though she didn't actually say by whom. I must remember to ask."

"Luke will be thrilled."

"Oh, he is," Joss's voice sounded very dry. "His new flat-mate accidentally wiped the whole of this week's instalment of the history of the Golden Dawn last night, and he isn't going to have time to redo it before Wednesday's recording session."

"Oh dear," Isabel chuckled. "That'll teach Luke to leave his CDs lying around. Anyway, I thought he wasn't going to bother getting anyone else in after Philip moved out to the farm with Geraldine. It's not as though he needs the money."

"True. His parents left him almost indecently well provided for. And you're right; he wasn't planning to have another flat-mate. But this woman he knows who works in radio sound archives introduced him to a friend of hers who does psychometry. They got talking, and it turned out he was desperately in need of somewhere to live, and one thing led to another…"

"…and Luke's disc got wiped. Well I hope he gets a decent interview out of this psychometrist. Maybe he could give him a regular spot on the show. People could send in personal objects in plain brown wrappers, and Luke's flat-mate—what's his name, by the way?—could give them readings."

"Sounds a bit dicey to me. Who knows what vibrations they might absorb on their way through the postal service. I don't know the flat-mate's name. Luke didn't tell me. What he did tell me, though, which is why I rang in the first place, is that the annual radio awards are on Saturday week—all those wannabes and has-beens patting each other's backs and pretending it all matters. But Luke wants us all to go and hold his hand. That series of programmes he did on Bob Ferris and the Circle of Light is up for a couple of awards."

Isabel said nothing for a moment. Her mind went back to her own unexpectedly dramatic part in the exposure of the self-styled spiritual teacher. Her thoughts went also to Detective Sergeant Declan Kelly, and how their unlikely paths had crossed as he pursued Ferris from an entirely different direction. He was back in Brisbane now, somewhat reluctantly obeying the dictates of his job, but they were as close as ever in heart and spirit. She realised this each time he called her and she heard that deep, lazy voice… Her reflections were interrupted by the sound of the doorbell.

"Oh, Joss, I'll have to go. My client has just arrived. Tell Luke I'll be at the awards. Wild horses wouldn't drag me away. I'll see you when we record on Wednesday, anyway, if not before."

The bell shrilled again, and Isabel hurried to open the door. The young man who stood there looked nervous, in spite of the smile on his youthful face.

"I hope I'm not late," he said, in a quiet, eager-to-please voice.

"Not at all." Isabel smiled. "I'm Isabel, and you must be..."

"Um—Harry." The young man shook her hand and smiled again. His eyes were a grey as pale as a dove's wing, but disconcertingly intense. In his fair, even-featured face they seemed out of place, somehow, like a thorn unexpectedly encountered in a bunch of violets.

"Come on in then, Harry, and we'll get started." Isabel led him through to the lounge and quickly spread the blue silk cloth over the coffee table. The coffee stain would have to wait after all.

* * * *

"All in all, then—" Isabel pointed to the last card in the reading, then back again to the cross formed by the two in the centre "—I'd say you have a lot to work through over the next few months. It won't be easy, and you may even wish you'd never started. But you can achieve what you want, as long as you don't give up, and you're prepared to work through it, one step at a time."

Harry nodded his fair head thoughtfully. "Thank you. That's given me a lot to think about."

Isabel smiled. "Well, I hope it's been helpful."

"Oh, I think so." The pale eyes seemed to penetrate her like lasers as he shot her a glance before consulting his wristwatch. "But I must go now. I start work again in half an hour." He fished in his pocket and drew out the money for her fee. The bland smile he gave her as he stood up to leave seemed curiously at odds with the intensity of those eyes. Still, she thought with a slight shrug, as a professional Tarot reader she'd met stranger people than this.

She ushered Harry to the door, then drifted into the kitchen to put the kettle on. There was nothing like a cup of tea after an hour or so spent probing the depths of some stranger's psyche.

CHAPTER TWO

The new Law Department building, with its concrete facade swathed in bright blue strips, always reminded him of one of those mock-art deco movie theatres so typical of the fifties. Not that he had been around then, of course, but as an avid movie fan, he had been in any number of them. Tacky and tasteless they were, too, the lot of them. Not like the post-Edwardian grandeur of the old Regent, with its rococo balconies and curlicues, and the blue-black ceiling twinkling with tiny lights masquerading as stars. Now that was a theatre! And even that was up for modernisation now, worse luck. Still, you'd think they could have run to something a bit more dignified for the Law Department.

He turned from it in disgust, a slim figure with fair, wispy hair and a general air of being lost, and headed for the staff car park. It would be a relief, after a tedious afternoon spent setting up equipment for the first years, to get back to his bed-sitter. The library had finally managed to get that book for him on inter-loan, and he was eager to lose himself for a few hours in the words and ideas of Paracelsus, not to mention an era when life's complications did not centre around one-way streets and market forces.

"Hello there." The voice that hailed him was deep and rhythmic, with a hint of a German accent, and it pulled him back to the present with an unwelcome jolt. Brother Ex

Flamma Lux! Damn! Now he would have to pretend he was coping with the humiliation of his second failure to reach the grade of Practicus. Well, he was coping, damn it, even if not in the way Brother Ex Flamma Lux might expect!

Trying not to show his reluctance, he stopped walking and turned to greet his magical mentor. "Oh, hello..." He never knew quite how to address the Senior of the Council of Seven outside the clearly prescribed protocols of the Brotherhood. Although they both worked at the University, their worlds might as well have been in different solar systems, Brother Ex Flamma Lux being a Senior Lecturer, and he a lowly lab technician. It wasn't as though they were even in the same department. Which was why he had been surprised to hear himself addressed by the familiar voice.

Three strides were all it took for the tall Senior Brother to catch up with him. "Just finishing work?" he asked cheerily, his brown eyes twinkling in his thin, tanned face. Without pausing for a reply, he went on in a low voice, "I was hoping I might see you. I told you I would speak with you further about...a certain matter, and I feel it is important to do it sooner rather than later."

"I'm quite all right, thank you." Brother Non Extinguar kept his voice quiet and dignified. "Besides, I'm very busy—studying." It was impossible to keep a note of defiance out of his final words.

"Nevertheless," replied the Senior Brother gently, making it clear he had not failed to notice, "I would like to speak with you. I thought perhaps somewhere peaceful and neutral, where we can both come to grips with the situation, and decide where we should go from here."

The younger man said nothing, clenching his jaw tightly

to quell the anger he felt rising from his stomach. The amiably proffered suggestion amounted to an order, in any case. He had no real choice in the matter.

The Senior Brother rubbed his neat, grey beard reflectively. "I'm planning to go up to the mountains this weekend," he said, "to tramp, and enjoy the tranquillity. Why don't you join me there, and we can speak further."

Brother Non Extinguar felt himself relax as the anger subsided and coiled itself once more in the lair of his stomach. Perhaps it would be a good idea to discuss his spiritual development with the man who had power over it. It was not as if the city was jumping with other options, after all. He smiled and nodded. "All right. Thank you. When would you like me to join you?"

"I shall be leaving tomorrow after lunch—about one-thirty. I can pick you up if you like. You'll only need a sleeping bag. The hut is very well-equipped, and I shall have plenty of provisions with me."

"I don't finish work till four-thirty. But I can drive up there myself after that, if you give me directions."

The older man nodded in understanding, and rubbed his beard in a characteristic gesture. He took a notepad and pen from his briefcase and sketched a map, writing brief notes beneath it in a strong, angular hand. Looking at the neatly drawn map with its precise and detailed instructions, Brother Non Extinguar found himself wondering if the Doctor was as expert at explaining philosophy to his students. Not for the first time, he felt a pang of envy at not being one of them. Reading books was all very well, but sometimes he longed for a real debate, such as students of the Middles Ages apparently used to hear at the open-air universities of Europe, from the great scholars of the age. Well, perhaps the opportunity would arise during the weekend...

"I hope that's all clear to you." The Senior's voice cut through his thoughts like a well-aimed scalpel. He nodded. "Then I shall see you on Friday evening. I'm looking forward to it."

Another nod. "Thank you. So am I." At least he thought he was.

It was only later, gazing across the park that lay beyond the window of his bed sitting room, that it occurred to him to wonder about the more disturbing implications of Brother Ex Flamma Lux's words, 'decide where we should go from here'. They were still gnawing uncomfortably at the back of his mind when he finally laid Paracelsus aside and went to bed.

* * * *

Despite the misgivings still making intermittent attempts to attract his attention, he had to admit it felt good to be heading out of town on a Friday afternoon. The car—a slightly battered fawn Volkswagen—was running well, in its usual raucous way. Lucky he had decided to get the tune-up last week instead of waiting till the end of the month. Autumn was rapidly drawing to a close, as the paddocks that stretched either side of the road demonstrated in tones of gold and brown, relieved occasionally by swathes of misty purple that looked like thistles, though why anyone would be deliberately growing hectares of thistles was a mystery. Somewhere in the distance, a vast rectangle of yellow gleamed like a Van Gogh cornfield—minus the crows and the glowering sky.

The sky was sapphire clear and bright above the looming mountains, the first snows already trickling down their blue-tinged folds like cream on a plate of steamed pudding. As the little car crawled up the rising, curling mountain road, the effect became almost intoxicating. The blue of the sky intensified, seeming to take on an amethyst tone in response to the rich emerald of the giant pines thronging the valleys below. The snow on distant mountain peaks glittered like diamonds as the setting sun took one last, lingering look before shutting up shop for the night. Through the open window of the car, Brother Non Extinguar breathed in the rich air and felt his heart soar with the beauty of it all.

By the time he reached the climbers' hut, twilight was finally giving way to darkness, a thin line of greenish turquoise glowing above the black silhouette of the mountains. The hut was a small but sturdy wooden construction with a rust-coloured corrugated steel roof. It looked as though it had been built by someone who had once visited the Swiss Alps, but had lost all his photographs and been forced to build from memory a decade or more later. Nevertheless, a cheerful, flickering golden light spilled from the uncurtained windows on either side of the heavy door, and a thin line of smoke sauntered its leisurely way up into the thin, still air.

A dark grey Range Rover stood to one side of the hut under a clump of native beech trees. He parked his car beside it, feeling suddenly nervous. Beside the stolid bulk of the Range Rover, the Volkswagen seemed ephemeral and insignificant, and he was uncomfortably reminded of the difference in status between himself and the Senior of the Council of Seven of the Magical Brotherhood of the Flame. As he closed the car door, it was not the cool night air that made him shiver.

When he turned, sleeping bag and rucksack in hand, Brother Ex Flamma Lux was silhouetted in the bright doorway. "Hello there." The voice seemed disembodied. "Glad you could make it. Come in and get warm, and I'll make us some coffee." The silhouette moved aside to reveal a pot-bellied stove standing on a bed of roughly cemented bricks, greyish dried sticks crawling at its feet.

The inside of the hut was warm, and smelt faintly of pine resin, kerosene, and an indefinable but delicious aroma of food. A kerosene lamp hanging from a nail in one of the low ceiling beams cast its gaze over four bunk beds at one end of the long room, a sink and bench with cupboards beneath, and shelves above, piled high with the domestic remnants of a dozen second-hand shops, several aged and sagging chairs grouped around the pot-belly, and a scarred wooden picnic table with built-in chairs which stood in what seemed by default to be the dining area of the room. The floor was of wood, sparingly scattered with worn carpet off-cuts. The lamp light, however, cast a romantic glow, enhanced by the crackle and scent of pine logs in the pot-bellied stove.

Inviting his guest to sit down, Brother Ex Flamma Lux set a battered, blackened kettle to boil on a gas camp-stove on the bench, and came to join him, pausing first to stir a pot simmering on top of the stove. "First we shall have coffee," he announced, lowering his long body into a chair with admirable precision, "then soup. I hope you don't mind that it is from a packet. I have not had time yet to prepare any of the vegetables I brought."

Brother Non Extinguar thought of his own haphazard culinary habits and shook his head. "That sounds fine," he said. "Thank you." Now that he was sitting down in the warm hut, he felt suddenly tired, and oddly disembodied, as though he were watching everything from a long way off. When Brother Ex Flamma Lux spoke to him, his voice sounded like the distant roar of a crowd, and he looked up with surprise at the mug of coffee being offered. He must be tired from the drive.

The coffee, strong and aromatic, seemed to centre him once more in his body. He looked across at the Senior Brother, his faded corduroy trousers and blue checked shirt looking out of place beneath the precise angles of his tanned face and well-trimmed beard. His brown eyes, like the rest of him, seemed alert, but relaxed. Brother Non Extinguar realised with an unexpected surge of exasperation that he was going to have to work his way through coffee, stew, and probably more coffee, before he would be permitted to address the reason for his being there.

By the time these rituals had been performed to the Senior's satisfaction, the sky outside the windows was like black velvet, relieved only by the eerie glow of the snow on the high mountains, visible through the long window between the bunks at the end of the room.

Brother Ex Flamma Lux drew a pipe from his pocket and tapped it against the brick fireplace to remove the last traces of blackened tobacco. He carefully tamped fresh tobacco into place, taking his time over the process, concentrating as though it were the only thing in existence.

Brother Non Extinguar felt his chest tighten. It seemed as

though his lungs had suddenly contracted, yet, when he drew breath, it was like trying to fill a bottomless pit. He forced himself to breathe slowly, concentrating on his breath as it entered and left his body, imagining it as a stream of life-energy flowing along his veins and arteries, calming and centering him. Usually this worked, but tonight he could not rid himself of an unidentifiable feeling of unease.

Placing his pipe in his mouth, the Senior Brother lit it with a sliver of wood held for a moment against one of the logs in the pot-belly's red-hot bowels, puffing until the tobacco was properly burning. Then he fixed his dark eyes on Brother Non Extinguar's pale ones. Brother Non Extinguar had the impression of powerful car headlights turned deliberately to low beam.

"Now," he said, "to begin our discussion, I expect you would like me to explain to you more fully why I invited you here this weekend."

* * * *

It was a relief, for once, to be back at work. Here, he could lose himself in the humdrum routine, the sheer anonymity of it. As long as he did what was required, no one noticed him. Dennis, his supervisor, was only interested in the perpetual challenge of ensuring the lab equipment was set up in time for the students. His assistants were merely a means to this end. Not that he was unpleasant or unreasonable to work for. Far from it. It was just that his entire world seemed to revolve around setting up labs and making sure they ran smoothly. And that was just fine, since it meant he had not demurred at granting an early finish to the day once everything had been satisfactorily set up for the morning.

Brother Non Extinguar looked at his watch. Three forty-five. He looked both ways along the corridor. No one in sight. This was what he had been hoping for, deliberately choosing a time when most of the students and staff of the Philosophy Department would be in lectures.

Straightening the sheaf of papers under his arm, his excuse for being there should anyone happen along and ask him, he opened the door marked 'Dr R E Kleber' and went in, closing it softly behind him. Thank God it was unlocked. And, please God, let him find what he was looking for.

He stood for a moment with his back to the door, surveying the small office. Space was at a premium in most of the departments. Whoever had planned the new university had been woefully deficient in long-term thinking.

A good plan had not only to cover the foreseeable future, but to look well beyond it, taking everything into account, including the apparently impossible. He, himself, was becoming only too aware of that. Which was why he was here now, his eyes taking in the desk in front of the window, with four shallow drawers down one side, and three neatly stacked wire trays along one side of its top beside an expensive-looking laptop computer; the filing cabinet against the far wall on the other side of the window, strands of pot-plant spilling down its grey metal side with a fine disregard for order; the wooden shelf attached to the wall beside the door, its top cluttered with electric jug, jars of coffee and sugar, two hand-made coffee mugs.

Under the window was a pile of neatly stacked boxes, with more beside the filing cabinet. Hopefully he wouldn't have to look that far.

He turned and locked the door, then moved quietly to the desk. It seemed as good a place to start as any.

CHAPTER THREE

The Town Hall foyer was filled with chattering groups of people in evening dress. As Isabel stood there with Joss and Martin, gazing with interest at the colourful display of evening suits and extravagant designer garb, she wondered yet again whether her patchwork skirt and blue top (the ones she had worn that evening when Declan had taken her out to dinner, she remembered wistfully—the evening she had first admitted to herself that she might finally have met someone who could heal the scars left by Stephen, and that she probably wanted to let him)—weren't perhaps a trifle too casual for the occasion.

She glanced sideways at Joss, neat and elegant as always in a cream trouser suit that matched her hair. As though to confirm her self-assessment, a tall, blond man in a maroon evening suit and an extravagant pink lurex bow-tie made of the same material as his partner's figure-hugging mini-dress, veered in front of them, waving enthusiastically at a tiny, dapper man who stood alone on the edge of the crowd.

"Evan, you old fraud! What the hell are *you* doing here?" he cried with a well-practised sense of drama. "I thought you'd slunk back to your lair years ago!"

Since Isabel could imagine few people less fraudulent-looking than Evan, his reply promised to be, at the very least, interesting. Unfortunately, it was drowned out by Luke's arrival with Philip and Geraldine. Luke pushed his fair hair back from his face with a nervous hand, and fished in the pocket of his dinner jacket for the inevitable packet of cigarettes.

Joss, as usual, sighed pointedly. Martin bent and murmured in her ear, "Don't say a word. Can't you see the poor bloke's a bundle of nerves?"

"Thank you, Martin," said Luke. "You're a scholar and a gentleman."

"I'm not entirely sure it's possible to be both," Joss said tartly, gazing past Martin at nothing in particular.

This turned out to be one of the more flamboyant local radio personalities, looking unusually diffident in his expensive dinner suit as he steered a strong-featured woman, whose general appearance raised dowdiness to a veritable art form, towards the bar adjoining the restaurant. Presumably he was up for an award, too. He usually was.

She turned back to the others. "Let's get a drink, shall we? With any luck they'll be on the house."

They made their way across the front of the restaurant to where several dozen of those in the know were already lining the length of the bar, spilling out towards the small round tables. For some reason, no one much seemed interested in these, preferring to stand around in small clusters, grouping and regrouping in ever-changing patterns of swirling colour and sound. Swooping on a corner table, Luke and Joss took possession, beckoning the others across.

As Martin and Philip made their way towards the bar, Joss turned to Isabel. "You're very quiet this evening. What's up?"

"Oh, nothing really. I was just thinking how nice it would

be if Declan could be here. After all, he was part of it, too."

Joss gave her friend a shrewd look. Declan Kelly had returned to Christchurch just after New Year to whisk Isabel away on a well-deserved two-month holiday. It was apparent on their return that the initial attraction between them had deepened. But, once his leave had expired, he had had to return, albeit reluctantly, to being a detective in Brisbane. From what little Isabel had told her (and her reticence in itself was unusual enough to arouse suspicion), Declan wasn't exactly happy in his work, and hadn't been for some time. He also wanted to be with Isabel at least as much as she wanted him there. But so far neither of them seemed to have arrived at a viable solution to their dilemma, making do in the meantime with frequent phone and Skype calls from Declan to Isabel, and emails, mainly from Isabel, since Declan's undoubted abilities did not seem to extend as far as composing a letter. Joss reached out to squeeze her friend's hand in sympathy.

She glanced at Luke, who was leaning back in his chair breathing smoke into the overheated atmosphere, and gazing absentmindedly towards the spot where Martin and Philip had last been seen.

"Speaking of absent friends," she said, "why isn't James here this evening?"

At that moment, Philip and Martin emerged from the crowd at the bar with laden trays and made their way across to the table. It took a moment or two for the drinks to be dispersed to their correct recipients. Then Luke stubbed out the remains of his cigarette and looked at Joss. "Sorry," he said. "What were you saying?"

"James," Joss repeated. "I was wondering why he's not

here. It isn't like him to miss the chance to hobnob with the in-crowd."

"Or the chance of a free meal," added Geraldine. James Myerson's frugality with his far from slender means was notorious.

"He called this morning to say he wouldn't be coming." Luke sipped his whisky, grimacing slightly. Trust this lot to do things on the cheap. "A university colleague of his died recently, and James just heard about it today. He sounded pretty upset."

As Joss was about to comment, a superbly modulated male voice over the intercom signalled a general migration from the bar by announcing in seductive tones that dinner was about to be served.

The Town Hall Restaurant, which looked out onto ethereally floodlit trees and a fountain that seemed composed of giant, uplit dandelion seed-heads, was decorated for the occasion with bunches of red, silver and blue balloons and matching streamers. In one corner, a youthful quartet played meticulous but uninspired jazz in muted tones. Diners were offered a menu and a choice of wines which, while all perfectly palatable, suggested that broadcasting funding was not what it might seem. Noticing silver ice buckets on several tables, Luke made discreet enquiries, and ordered champagne. It was the least he could do for his supporters. So, by the time the Master of Ceremonies for the awards took the stage erected under a swathe of red and blue at one end of the restaurant, even Isabel was feeling suitably bubbly.

Luke's entry, the final episode from the series of three he had produced dealing with the background and dubious activities of self-styled spiritual guru Bob Ferris, had been submitted in both the Documentary and Special Interest categories. As usual with awards ceremonies, the entire programme was designed to lead up to the glamour categories involving such 'personalities' as the flamboyant DJ with the dowdy wife, who were seated two tables away from them, he attending to her every need and behaving generally in a manner totally at odds with his on-air persona, she smiling complacently as one who knew not only when she was onto a good thing, but how to milk it for all it was worth.

"Now we come to the Best Documentary category," the MC announced. Luke and the others pricked up their ears. The flamboyant DJ continued fawning on his wife. He didn't produce documentaries. "The entries in this category have been outstanding this year," the MC enthused, "simply outstanding! The task of choosing finalists was extremely difficult, however, we have finally narrowed the field down to three."

He turned to his female counterpart, a large but elegant woman who, having moved from star status on one of the big-city radio stations to a top job in administration—less glamorous, but infinitely more secure—was no longer a contender, and therefore ideal for the annual prize-giving. She fluttered a piece of paper in front of her designer-clad bosom.

"And this year's finalists for Best Documentary are...Jonathan Fleming, for Station Wives, from the series, Back-Country Life; Amiria Te Kahu, for Children of Earth and Sky, from her series, Maori Spirituality; and Luke Marriot for The Final Conflict, the third episode in his cult-group series, A Trick of The Light." She smiled at the MC, giving him his cue.

"And the winner is..." he announced, fiddling with the flap of a large envelope, making a production of it to increase the tension, "...Amiria Te Kahu!"

Amid enthusiastic clapping, Amiria, black hair swinging as she strode forward in wide black trousers and gold sleeveless top, went to accept her award. As she returned to her table, a brief out-take from her entry was played over the PA.

Throughout the announcements, Luke had been looking down at the table, fiddling with his cigarette lighter. He hadn't, realistically, expected to win this category, but being nominated at all inevitably created expectations that had little to do with reality.

"I can't handle any more of this," he muttered. "I'm going back to the bar. Wake me when it's over." He shoved the cigarette lighter back into his pocket, stood up and made to leave.

"I'll go with him," Philip volunteered. "Make sure he doesn't do anything he'll be embarrassed about later. You don't mind, do you?" he added to Geraldine.

Smiling, Geraldine shook her head. "Of course not. You go and look after him. Make sure he's in good shape for his next nomination."

When the MC announced the Special Interest category, where Luke's programme was also nominated, he and Philip had still not returned.

"I'll go and get them." Martin hurried off.

The three of them returned just as the MC was announcing, "And the winner is... Luke Marriot for The Final

Conflict!"

Luke, a stupefied grin transforming his face, made his way to the stage, to be congratulated by the MC and kissed on the cheek by Shona, the senior administrator. He made a nervous little speech of thanks, including the rest of the panel and Philip and Declan, then walked back to his seat, framed certificate clutched to his breast, as the customary excerpt was played.

The voice that was speaking, commenting on the trail of destruction Forster seemed to leave in his unwitting wake, was Declan's.

Isabel quickly stifled a gasp and looked at Joss. "It's his birthday on Sunday," she said, her voice suddenly bleak.

"Why don't you phone him?" Joss suggested. "I expect he'd like that."

"I can't—I don't know where he is." Isabel's deep voice was controlled enough to show Joss how worried she was. "When he called last week he was leaving for the Gold Coast on some major operation. I can cope with not being able to see him—I know that's inevitable. But I can't stand not knowing what's happening. Oh, Joss, I don't think I'm cut out for this. I should never have got involved with a detective." The tragi-comic tone in her voice didn't fool Joss in the slightest.

"Come over for lunch tomorrow," she said quietly. "The twins are away this weekend, and Martin's managed to get himself involved with a school outing, so the coast will be clear. Bring your cards over, and we'll see what we can find out."

Isabel smiled at her. "Thanks, I'd like that. I don't imagine I'll be able to pick up anything much, but if I can at least talk things through with someone other than myself, it'll help clear my mind."

The MC was already onto the next category. From the way the flamboyant DJ and his wife were paying attention, he must be one of the finalists. Resolutely focussing her mind on the present, Isabel leaned across to offer her congratulations to Luke.

CHAPTER FOUR

Isabel set down the last card and sat back to survey the layout. "I doubt if I'll be able to pick up much," she said to Joss. "I'm too involved."

The house, devoid of Martin and the twins, was unusually quiet. The only sounds were the twittering of two sparrows demolishing a crust on the patio outside, and faint snoring from under the kitchen table where Spock, the Cherry family's dog, lay sprawled as usual. Joss drained the last of her coffee and set the mug down beside her.

"We can but try," she said. "Anyway, I might pick up something myself. I take it you're doing the reading for Declan, not yourself?"

Isabel gave a snort of laughter. "I already know about me!" For a long moment she gazed at the cards, then let out a sighing breath. "Hmm... Those two in the centre, the Eight of Cups and Eight of Pentacles—they seem to be saying he's turning his back on emotional involvements, and starting a new job, or learning something new."

"It seems the reading is on the right track then," Joss commented, pushing her pale hair off her face. She was beginning to feel the familiar tightening in the pit of her stomach, which signalled the switch from normal to psychic perception. But for the time being, she said nothing to Isabel, preferring to allow her friend's own perceptions to surface first. In any case, the feeling had not yet resolved itself into anything specific.

Isabel looked up from the cards. "Turning his back on emotional involvements? I hope not!"

"If he's involved with an important job, I don't suppose he has much choice for the time being. Besides, there's nothing to say the involvement he's turning his back on is you. If he does end up moving to New Zealand, for example, he'll be leaving his family and friends behind."

"True. That's the trouble with doing readings for people I'm close to. I can read what the cards say, but I never seem able to get in touch with anything deeper. Maybe I should just not bother." She made an impatient gesture, as if about to gather the cards up again.

"No, no," Joss said. "Go on."

Isabel caught the slight edge of excitement in her voice, and looked at her sharply before continuing, "The underlying factors seem to be centred around some sort of power struggle—the Five of Wands, see." She pointed to a card showing five men with wooden cudgels engaged in a fight. "I imagine that's to do with the situation he's investigating. But since he wasn't in a position to discuss it with me, we're none the wiser. But the past here, the Lovers—I suppose that's pretty obvious. I don't like the look of this, though." With a worried expression, Isabel indicated the card at the top of the cross formation of the layout. It showed a blindfolded woman picking her way across a swamp between a number of swords stuck in the ground. "The Eight of Swords. That means danger, and unforeseen problems."

"Yes," Joss pointed out, "but it's only what may happen, isn't it? It's not inevitable." She smiled and reached across the table to squeeze Isabel's arm. Something like a mild electric shock tingled in her fingertips, another indicator that her psychic sensors were at work.

"That's true," Isabel agreed. "And the Four of Wands in the future shows things turning out well in the end."

The card she indicated showed people celebrating under a canopy decked with flowers and supported by four poles sprouting small clumps of new leaves. She turned her gaze on the four remaining cards, trying to look beyond the pictures themselves, to the deeper reality for which the cards were merely symbols. The cards, laid out vertically to the right of the cross formation, were the King of Swords, the Tower, the Star and, at the top, the Two of Cups.

"That's Declan, isn't it?" Joss asked, pointing to the King of Swords. It was the card she remembered from the reading Martin's old friend Terry Ryder-White—known to his friends as Tarot—had done for them when he had foretold Declan's arrival in the middle of their investigation of the Circle of Light group.

Isabel nodded. "Yes, it's in the position representing the self, so it must be. I'd say he'll need to keep his wits about him, whatever he's involved in." She pointed back to the Eight of Swords, and then at the Tower, which lay above the King. She shook her head, a slight frown creasing her forehead. "I don't like the feel of this at all."

"Mmm. It wasn't the best of omens in that reading Terry did for us, was it?" The feeling in the pit of her stomach was growing stronger, making her breathless. It was becoming harder to hold back the images that pushed at the edges of her awareness, like bubbles struggling to rise to the surface of a pool.

Isabel glanced at her sharply again and hurried on. "The Star here in the position of hopes and fears is pretty obvious—it's all about hope and faith. And the outcome certainly looks good—a reunion. Now, for goodness' sake, tell me what you've got. Your eyes have gone all funny. I know that look."

"Right." Joss took a deep breath. "I wanted to let you finish your reading first, and I must say it seems to have done the trick."

"What—?"

Joss put up a hand to stay her friend. "I think I'm in touch with Declan. He's in a car, near the sea. I think there's someone with him. Yes, I'm sure there is—a man with large freckled hands." She shrugged at Isabel's quizzical expression. Clairvoyance was always a bit of a lucky dip. "Oh, now I can see a building—it looks like white stucco, sort of Mediterranean style, but very run down. I don't think it's been lived in for a while." She paused, eyes closed, as Isabel waited impatiently. "Ah, I don't think any of that has happened yet. It's where he's headed for. There's going to be someone waiting for him there—or maybe someone he wants to meet." She opened her eyes and looked quizzically at Isabel. "And I keep getting a mermaid."

Isabel burst out laughing. "Oh, thank you very much! He's headed for a secret assignation with a mermaid—just what I needed to hear."

Joss shrugged, and threw up her hands. "Well, I don't pretend to know what it is I'm talking about. I'm a seer, not an interpreter. But, for what it's worth, I think you may see him again sooner than you think—sooner than he thinks, come to that. The house I saw is going to provide him with his way out of the police force, though don't ask me how."

At that moment, there was the sound of a car in the driveway, and seconds later Martin's bearded head appeared round the kitchen door. "Don't tell me you two are still picking through the goat's entrails. It's almost six o'clock."

"Good God, so it is!" Joss exclaimed. "Doesn't time fly when you're in touch with the infinite?" As Isabel gathered up her Tarot cards, Joss went to put the kettle on. "Why don't you stay and have dinner with us?" she suggested. "We're only having fish and chips anyway, since the girls are away. Meanwhile, let's have a coffee. It's almost time for the news."

As a journalist, Joss was an avid consumer of news in any form, and hated to miss the evening bulletin. Isabel, thanking Joss for the dinner invitation, carried her mug into the lounge where Martin, who seemed to regard television as an antidote to the rigors of teaching English and History to teenagers, was already sprawled in his favourite armchair. They watched through the main news stories, sipping their coffee, slipping in occasional comments on the day's activities. Martin had turned the sound down during a commercial break. As the two announcers returned to the screen, he turned it up again.

"In Christchurch," the female announcer was saying, "friends and colleagues are mourning the tragic death of missing tramper, Doctor Richard Kleber." Over film of the charred and smoking remains of a hut framed against a backdrop of snow-clad mountains, the announcer continued, "A Senior Lecturer in the History of Philosophy at the University of Canterbury, Doctor Kleber received international acclaim in the early seventies for his history of the Rosicrucian movement in Germany, which revealed new information about its connections with Hitler and the Nazi movement.

"He moved to New Zealand ten years ago after the death of his wife in a climbing accident in Switzerland. Now, in his mid-fifties, he has become the victim of a bizarre accident in which the hut where he was spending the weekend burned down. The remains were discovered yesterday morning by two women tramping in the area. Police say they don't suspect foul play. A full report is expected later this week, but investigations so far suggest the fire was caused by a kerosene lantern, which may have been accidentally knocked over. A strong northwest wind that blew up over the weekend is thought to have caused the fire to swiftly engulf the wooden hut."

"What an awful way to die!" Isabel said with a shudder.

"Mmm." Joss looked thoughtful. "I wonder if he was the reason for James not turning up at the awards. Come to think of it, he seemed abnormally quiet and subdued at last Wednesday's recording session. I suppose he must have known then that Doctor Kleber was missing." A calculating look crossed her face. "Maybe I should give James a call."

"Joss!" Isabel sounded horrified.

Martin said, in long-suffering tones, "She's a journalist, Isabel. They're trained to abjure all human feeling in the interests of a good story. After a while, they can't help themselves. They stop being mere newshounds, and turn into veritable hounds of hell. They even hunt in packs. Surely you've heard of 'Night of the Living Journalist' and 'Nightmare on Fleet Street'?"

Isabel laughed, in spite of herself.

"Nevertheless, dear," Martin addressed his wife sternly, "I do feel you should wait a decent interval before sinking your fangs into poor James." As Joss bowed her head in not entirely mock contrition, he continued, "As a penance, you can go and get the fish and chips. Meanwhile, Isabel and I will fill the gap caused by your absence with dry sherry and 'Wheel of Fortune'."

"Ah, thank you, my sweet. As you see, we've not been idle in your absence." Martin took the proffered fish and chip packet and handed Joss a glass of sherry. He refilled his and Isabel's glasses from a cut-glass decanter. "I like this sherry much better than the last lot. What do you think?"

"Mmm," Joss replied vaguely through a mouthful of fish. "I didn't realise how hungry I was. Pass me the sauce, dear."

"Philistine!" said Martin. "Too many press functions, that's your trouble." Martin, however, had developed a hearty appetite during the course of an afternoon spent showing local history to fifth-formers, so it was some time before he announced casually to Joss, "Oh, by the way, Luke phoned while you were out. He wants you to call him back."

"Was it urgent?"

"You know Luke—he manages to make everything sound life or death."

Joss laughed. "I'll go and put the kettle on, and call him while it's boiling."

When she returned with a tray of steaming mugs and a packet of gingernuts, she announced, with a smug glance in Martin's direction, "I was right. Doctor Richard Kleber is, indeed, the very colleague who deprived us of James's scintillating company last night."

"Surely," said Martin with a lift of his eyebrows, "even Luke wasn't crass enough to ask James about him."

"No," replied Joss, handing a coffee mug to Isabel and offering her a gingernut. "Hell-hound he may be, but even Luke is not entirely devoid of tact. Jean, the woman with the haunted house, phoned him after the news item. Apparently—and this is really freaky—not only is Doctor Kleber James's colleague, he's also the exorcist I worked with at her place the other week."

Isabel dunked her gingernut in her coffee and bit into it quickly, before the soaked piece fell off into the mug. "So this Doctor Kleber is not only a close colleague of James's, but also an experienced exorcist, even though he's not a priest. I wonder what he *was* trained in, then?"

"Well," said Martin, "the news item said he wrote a book on the Rosicrucian movement, and they were pretty heavily into magic, weren't they?"

"They were," Joss agreed, "Kabbalistic magic, mostly."

Isabel looked thoughtful. "Masonic stuff, too. So he could have had links with the Freemasons. Or the Golden Dawn, come to that. They were basically an offshoot of the Rosicrucians, at least in the beginning. As a matter of interest, I seem to remember reading somewhere that one of the big-wigs of the Golden Dawn in Britain moved to New Zealand after it started to fall apart there, and established a temple in the North Island somewhere."

Joss's blue eyes narrowed slightly as her mind processed the information. "We can't question James about it just yet, and I have a feeling he wouldn't tell us anything anyway..."

"Always assuming," Martin cut in, helping himself to another biscuit, "that there's anything to tell. He was only

James's colleague, after all."

"Ye-es." Joss conceded the point. "Still, I'm intrigued. I think I'll see what I can find out at work. There's bound to be something, even if dear Barry hasn't seen fit to print it. I've got a couple of contacts at TVNZ, too. I'll look into it tomorrow."

"Okay," said Isabel. "And I'll see if I can track down that book of Doctor Kleber's in the library. If nothing else, it might provide some good material for that series Luke's been working on. A New Zealand connection always pulls in the punters, and it'll tie in with your haunted house. Besides, it'll help keep my mind off things until I hear from Declan again."

Seeing the query in Martin's face, Joss explained the situation to him. "So Isabel can't even wish him a happy birthday," she concluded.

"Well," said Martin, reaching across to give Isabel's arm a squeeze, "there's no reason why we can't celebrate on his behalf. And hang the expense—I'll go and get that bottle of Grand Marnier I've been hoarding!"

CHAPTER FIVE

"Right!" Luke flicked the last switch on the control desk and reached for his cigarette packet. "That's that for another week. Who's for a coffee?"

Isabel and Geraldine agreed enthusiastically. James had been fiddling even more than usual, not only with his exquisitely stylish tie, but with his pen as well, scribbling strange doodles on the back of an envelope. He nodded, but it was clear his heart wasn't in it.

Joss said, "I'd love one, Luke, but it'll have to be quick I'm afraid. I have an interview to do in—" She consulted her watch "—just over an hour, but it'll probably take a good twenty minutes to get there. You know what the traffic's like at this time of day."

They all made their way along the hall, Luke hurrying ahead to put the kettle on.

"What are you working on at the moment? Anything interesting?" Geraldine asked Joss. Now that she was living out of town with Philip, she rarely saw the other panellists except at recording sessions.

"Yes, as it happens," Joss replied. "You may have heard about that chap who died up on Whitewash Head a few days ago?"

"The one who went over on his motorbike?"

"That's the one. Leo Hart. He ran a business out at

Sumner, designing and manufacturing furniture. I had a call at work yesterday from his boyfriend. He seems to think it might not have been an accident. So I'm going to interview him to find out why he's so doubtful."

They had settled themselves in Luke's sitting room by now, and he was already setting down a tray of steaming coffee mugs on the carved wooden coffee table. James had been squirming unhappily on his usual perch on the piano stool, a little apart from the others. Now he looked at his watch and stood up. "I'm real sorry, Luke," he said, the broadening of his American accent betraying his nervousness, "but I've just realised I'm supposed to be somewhere in five minutes. I won't be able to stay for coffee after all. I do apologise. Really." He strode abruptly from the room.

Luke shrugged at James's retreating back. "What's up with him?"

Joss shook her head slowly. "Correct me if I'm wrong, but it strikes me that James hasn't really been himself for several weeks now. Not since the radio awards, in fact, and that's almost a month ago."

"Well, I know he hates to miss out on his share of any glory that's going," Luke said with a laugh, "but he should have got over it by now, surely."

"Maybe this Leo Hart was a friend of his, too?" suggested Isabel.

"Two friends dying in bizarre accidents in one month?" said Joss. "Not very likely. Besides, James is pretty conservative, even for an academic. Somehow I can't quite see him mixing socially with a gay furniture designer."

"He mixes with us," Luke protested, "and we're not

exactly normal."

"Speak for yourself," retorted Joss.

"Nevertheless—" Geraldine uncurled her long brown legs from the sofa "—I haven't seen James for a while, and he looks distinctly worried to me."

"I'll have a chat to him sometime soon," Joss said. "He's pretty reticent, as we all know, but he'll usually talk to me."

"Meanwhile—" Luke leaned forward to stub out his cigarette, pushing his fair hair back with his other hand "—why don't you give us the inside story on this Leo Hart. Did he fall or was he pushed?"

Joss laughed. She wound her long scarf about her neck, flicking out her blonde hair with one hand in an unconscious gesture as she stood up. "No time now, I'm afraid. I have to go and interview his boyfriend. I'll let you know, though, if I turn up anything interesting."

Luke shrugged, making another fruitless attempt to control his hair. He pointed to James's unused mug of coffee. "Does anyone want that," he asked, "or can I have it?"

* * * *

Simon Drawbridge, Architect, was not in his office. His receptionist, an elegant redhead of indeterminate age, assured Joss in a voice so cultured it might have been grown in a Petri dish, that he'd just popped out for a moment. Would she like to take a seat? The seat, like all the others in the pastel blue reception area, was an avant-garde creation in flesh-pink leather and chrome. It was surprisingly comfortable. Joss wondered if it were one of Leo Hart's designs.

Although she saw no one enter or leave the deserted reception area, within five minutes the receptionist said, "Mr Drawbridge will see you now," and ushered her along a short corridor of a subtly different shade of blue, and through a pale wooden door.

Simon Drawbridge's office was spare and spacious, with a huge window overlooking the river. Its walls were painted in the same pale flesh tone as the chairs, and boasted several carefully placed large paintings and a graduation certificate in a silver frame, but little else—just a large bookcase against the wall behind his desk, neatly stacked with books and glossy magazines. Even the desk, a curiously rounded affair in whitish polished wood, bore nothing other than a large white pad, a silver pen and ruler, a pale-grey telephone with an intercom, the inevitable computer, and a strange little globular metallic object for which Joss could imagine no obvious purpose. Surprised to see no tools of his profession in evidence, Joss glanced around the office. There was a door behind the desk next to the bookcase. Perhaps that led to a workroom of some sort.

As she entered his office, Simon Drawbridge stood up. He was, perhaps, in his mid-thirties, of slightly less than average height, and as pale and refined as his office. His hair, cut stylishly short, was even fairer than Joss's, with the colour and soft sheen of a pearl, an effect enhanced by his round, creamy, smooth-featured face. Even his eyes were almost devoid of colour. What colour there was, was an odd mixture of grey and pale brown. He seemed to have no eyebrows at all. His dove-grey trousers and expensive-looking white shirt, however, were unexpectedly enlivened by a red, tartan tie and braces. The grey jacket hanging on the door showed a glimpse of matching tartan handkerchief.

Joss introduced herself and held out her hand.

"Simon Drawbridge. Lovely to meet you," the designer said in a soft, low, surprisingly penetrating voice that made Joss wonder if he'd had theatrical training. He leaned across his desk and shook her hand with a smooth, firm grip. "Do sit down. I'll get Edwina to bring us some tea before she leaves for the day." He pressed a button on the intercom and made his request.

He busied himself dispensing tea and biscuits until he heard the outer door close, then smiled at Joss. "Thank you so much for coming."

Joss thought she detected a slight hesitancy beneath the smooth manner. Not surprising, really. It must have been bad enough to discover his boyfriend had died in an accident, but if he now believed it might have been no accident after all, he must be feeling confused to say the least.

Joss smiled back in what she hoped was a reassuring manner and voiced a query that had been in the back of her mind ever since Drawbridge had called the 'Sun' and asked to speak to her. "Before we go any further, there's something I'd like to clarify."

"By all means." Drawbridge's smile was gracious.

"If you suspect Mr Hart's death may not have been an accident, why contact the press and not the police? I presume you haven't contacted them?"

Drawbridge sipped his tea then set the porcelain cup carefully back on its saucer. "The police," he said, "are convinced it was an accident and, quite frankly, I have no real reason to doubt them."

"But obviously you do. Why?"

Drawbridge took a deep breath. "I'm not entirely sure why. That's why I haven't been to the police. But I feel absolutely certain in my own mind that Leo's death was not just an accident."

"Okay," Joss said, pulling her note-pad and pen from her bag. Presumably, since he had contacted her, he felt able to handle any tricky questions she might throw his way. "Let's go through this from the beginning. As I understand it, Mr Hart's body was found with his motorcycle at the bottom of the cliff at Whitewash Head." Drawbridge nodded. "What was found at the top of the cliff?"

Drawbridge breathed deeply again as though steeling himself for the task ahead. "From what the police told me, they found skid-marks that were obviously from the bike tyres, and some scuff-marks they believed were from his boots on the ground and on a couple of small rocks. There were some boot-prints on the ground as well, but they were very unclear. They said it looked as though Leo skidded while riding near the edge of the cliff-top, and his bike went out of control. The scuff-marks and so on were apparently made as he tried to regain control."

"Hmmm." Joss stopped writing and tapped her pen thoughtfully against her chin. "Have you ever been up on Whitewash Head?"

Drawbridge nodded. "Leo and I go—used to go––walking there quite often. Leo grew up in Sumner, and he'd been in the habit of going there ever since he was a boy. He liked looking at the sea and the sky—said it helped him to clear his mind."

"Did he have something on his mind then?"

"Not that I was aware of. Though he had just signed a big export deal. It would have been worth a great deal of money, enough to pay off the loan he took out last year to expand his business. So I suppose he may have been looking for inspiration there. Leo was very intuitive in the way he worked."

"Hmmm," Joss said again. "Can you tell me who gave him the loan?"

"Well yes, I think so, but..." A dubious frown creased his smooth forehead.

Joss hastened to reassure him, "I don't want to pry and, of course, you aren't obliged to tell me anything you don't want to. But if you're right about Mr Hart, you're going to need information if you want to prove anything, and it occurred to me that money, especially in large quantities, is often a motive for foul play. Assuming that's what you suspect."

"Ah, I see. Well, his bank was a small, private one, the Phoenix, but I'm fairly certain the loan was a personal one. I can check the details at home and get back to you." He frowned again and smoothed back his pale hair. "I hadn't quite thought of it like that, but I suppose I am rather suggesting foul play, aren't I?"

Joss nodded. "Unless you think it was suicide?"

"Oh, no!" Drawbridge shook his head vehemently. "Whatever it was, I'm sure it wasn't that! Suicide would have been totally contrary to Leo's entire philosophy of life. He would have regarded it as an act of cowardice—cowardice of the worst sort. No, no, I'm sure it wasn't suicide."

"Okay." Joss consulted her notes. "So, apart from possible foul play, we're back to the theory that he skidded while riding along the cliff-top."

Drawbridge began toying abstractedly with the small metal object on his desk. "I've known Leo for a good seven years now—we've been living together almost five—and although he's been a motorcycle enthusiast for all that time and longer, I've never known him to do anything even remotely dangerous. He was an expert rider, and a very careful person by nature, and I just cannot believe he would have been riding that close to the edge of a cliff-top that's known to be dangerous. Besides, he'd barely had the bike a year, and it was his pride and joy—a Triumph Bonneville he'd restored. There's just no way he would ever have risked damaging it." He shook his head as though to emphasise his point, and ran his hand through his hair again. Looking up suddenly, he said, "There's something else that's been bothering me, too."

Joss finished scribbling in her pad and waited. If journalism had proved anything to her, it was the truth of the old adage, 'All things come to he who waits'. Though, of course, it also helped if one went looking for them.

Drawbridge went on, "If Leo had been riding his bike, he would have been wearing his helmet."

Joss felt a familiar prickling at the back of her neck as she asked, "What makes you think he wasn't? Where did they find it?"

"They didn't. As far as I know it hasn't been found at all."

"That's odd. If what you say about Leo is true, it should have been found with him. Could it have come off when he fell and been washed away on the tide, do you think?"

"Not unless he was wearing it unfastened—after all, the whole point of a cycle helmet is that it shouldn't come off in a fall. And, knowing Leo, I just don't believe he would have been riding his bike without wearing his helmet correctly."

"Have you said that to the police?"

"Yes, more or less. But their view was that, since there was no evidence to suggest Leo wasn't on the cliff-top alone, and since no one has come forward who saw any of what happened, they have no choice but to accept the Coroner's finding of death by misadventure." He shuddered. "What a ghastly expression!"

Joss looked at him with genuine sympathy. "This must be very difficult for you. I appreciate how you feel, but I'm not quite sure what you think I can do about it."

A long sigh escaped Drawbridge's lips. "Neither am I," he admitted sadly. "I suppose I was hoping you might be willing to – investigate. I asked for you in particular because I'd heard your name in connection with that Circle of Light business."

Joss laughed. "Oh, that! Thank you for the vote of confidence, but I'm not entirely sure it's well placed. We didn't exactly go into that expecting foul play. And we certainly weren't dealing with suspected murder."

Drawbridge gave a slight shudder. "I suppose it was a bit of a long shot. Still, I can't get rid of the feeling that it wasn't just an accident. Look, thank you very much for coming to see me. I'm sorry if I've wasted your time."

Joss stood up and held out her hand. "Not at all," she said. "I'll certainly scout around a bit and see what I can come up with. If you don't object, I'd also like to run it by my friends on 'The Psychic Connection'. They might have some useful ideas. And if you'd like to get back to me with the name of the person who gave Leo that loan, I can certainly go and talk to him."

"Thank you. By all means talk to your friends. I expect there's nothing in it, but I can't stand just doing nothing. I feel so helpless."

He put the ornament he had been toying with back onto the desk in order to shake Joss's hand. It rolled over, and she saw that the other side of what had appeared to be a globe was, in fact, hollow, and contained a tiny ornate gold cross with a red enamelled rose at its centre. The cross surmounted a stylised representation of flames, enamelled in scarlet and gold. The prickling at the back of her neck became stronger.

She picked up the object, turning it over in her hand. The feeling was now like a strong electric current running through her fingers. She was no psychometrist but, if she needed any convincing that Drawbridge was right to be suspicious, it was here in this strange little ornament. She swallowed, and said to Drawbridge in what she hoped was a casual tone, "This is unusual. Is it a paperweight?"

"That's what I use it for," Drawbridge replied. "Leo gave it to me a couple of years ago. He said it would bring me luck, or protect me—something like that. Like a Saint Christopher medal, I suppose."

Since Drawbridge seemed unaware of the true nature of the symbolism, Joss decided not to enlighten him for the time being. "It's lovely," she said. "I don't suppose you happen to know who made it?"

Drawbridge shook his head. "I don't think Leo ever said. But naturally we both know—knew—a lot of artists and craftspeople."

"I suppose so," Joss agreed, making a rapid mental note.

Drawbridge thanked her again and showed her out to the

reception area. He returned to his office saying he had work to catch up on, and promising to get back to her soon with the name of Leo's banker.

Joss made her way thoughtfully back to her car.

CHAPTER SIX

"You're quite sure it was a Rosicrucian symbol?" Martin moved his arm upwards a fraction and ruffled his wife's hair affectionately. They were leaning back against the padded headboard of their bed drinking their after-dinner coffee while Kate and Rachel commandeered the lounge and the television to watch the evening soaps and their favourite comedy show before being despatched off to bed. Through a process of trial and error, this had proved the most painless way of bridging the cultural ravine dividing their own viewing tastes from those of the twins.

Joss smoothed her hair down again. "Oh, yes, that's what it was all right. Though I've never come across a depiction of it with flames underneath."

"Makes you wonder what Leo Hart was into, doesn't it?"

"Mmm." Joss gazed, apparently blankly, into the middle distance, sipping her coffee. Martin recognised the look. Far from indicating mental vacuity, it meant her mind was working at top speed, testing linkages between various items of information, scanning for possible patterns. Quietly sipping his own coffee, he waited.

Her eyes still fixed on some imaginary distant object, Joss said, "Leo Hart's business was apparently doing well—he'd just signed a major export deal. And he doesn't appear to have had any other worries. According to his boyfriend, he wasn't the type to go riding on the edge of a dangerous cliff at all, let alone without his helmet. Yet no helmet has apparently been found, at the site, his home, or his work. And he gave his boyfriend a Rosicrucian symbol as a talisman, which suggests he understood its significance, even though his boyfriend didn't. Or said he didn't. I think we ought to—"

Her musings were cut short by the shrill of the telephone in the hall, closely followed by the thud of heavy footfalls. Then Kate's voice called, "Mum! It's Isabel," and the footsteps thumped back to the lounge.

Joss put down her coffee mug, and went out to the hall, ruffling Martin's hair in retaliation on her way past.

"Oh, good," said Isabel's voice in reply to her greeting. "I was hoping you wouldn't be working tonight. I'd like to come over for a while, if that's okay."

"Of course," Joss told her. "I wanted to talk to you, anyway, about this afternoon's interview. But what's up?" She thought she had discerned a note of anxiety in Isabel's voice.

"I'm not sure." Isabel definitely sounded worried. "I've been feeling quite strange since about two this afternoon. I was reading that book by Richard Kleber, but it wasn't that— though I must say he managed to discover some very peculiar goings-on in the Nazi Party, both before and during the war. I was quite engrossed in it, completely oblivious to the outside world..."

Joss nodded to herself. She shared Isabel's ability to lose herself in whatever she was doing at the time. It could be extremely annoying to others (such as Martin), but it certainly had its uses.

"...then, all of a sudden, for no apparent reason, I started thinking about Declan. I couldn't even read any more, it was so strong. Fortunately Dominic came home for a while, and the feeling receded while he was there. But he went out again after tea, and it's come back again, stronger than ever."

"Does it feel good or bad?" Joss asked.

"I'm not really sure, though the fact it's happening at all is a worry. I almost never have premonitions except through a medium like the cards."

"Mmm." Joss knew this was true. "Well, come on over, and we'll see what we can make of it."

"Thanks. And you can tell me about your interview. I want to hear about it, anyway, and maybe it'll take my mind off things." Maybe, thought Joss, and went to put the kettle on again.

By the time Isabel arrived, the coffee was ready to serve, the twins' programme had just ended, and Martin was doing sheep-dog duty herding them off to bed.

"The lounge is clear now," Joss said, pouring boiling water into the gigantic coffee mugs that were a Cherry family trademark. "Let's go through there, shall we?"

At Isabel's request, Joss re-capped her interview with Simon Drawbridge. "I was just saying to Martin when you phoned," she ended, "I think we ought to go and have a look around up on Whitewash Head."

Isabel nodded, grasping her bottom lip thoughtfully with her teeth. "I wonder if it's possible to get down to the bottom of the cliff," she said.

"It must be possible," said Martin. "They got Leo Hart's body out, and his motorcycle. The question is whether you could do it without a full-scale search-and-rescue operation.

Anyway, what do you hope to find there?"

"Oh, I don't know. But there might be something. We might even find his helmet."

Joss shook her head. "If Drawbridge was right about his boyfriend—and I imagine he knew him pretty well after seven years—we won't find it at the bottom of the cliff, or even washed up along the coastline somewhere. If it wasn't on his head when he was found, I think we can take it he wasn't wearing it at all when he went over."

Isabel's grey eyes sparkled with excitement. "So he can't have been riding his bike when he went over the cliff. And if Drawbridge is right that we can count out suicide, that means he may well also be right that Hart's death was no accident."

"Got it in one!" Joss's china blue eyes gleamed with the thrill of discovery. "Look, let's try and picture what Leo Hart might have been doing up on Whitewash Head that day. Drawbridge told me he liked to go there to look at the sea and contemplate."

"If he was into Rosicrucianism or something similar," Martin suggested, "maybe he went there to meditate, or perform some kind of ritual."

"Mmm," Joss said, "could be, though a lot less likely, I should think. Whatever it was, let's assume he would have taken his helmet off. I mean, would you wear a motorcycle helmet to sit and contemplate the sea and the sky on a cliff-top?"

"I certainly wouldn't," Isabel agreed. "I'd want to be able to hear the sound of the waves, and the wind in the grass."

"Exactly! So Hart would presumably have put his helmet down beside him. It's years since I've been up there, but if I remember rightly, there's a sort of park bench that looks out over the sea, kindly placed there by the powers that be specifically to aid in the comfortable contemplation of the elements."

"There are rocks there, too, I think," said Martin. "He might have preferred one of those to sit on."

"Or he might have sat on his motor-bike," Isabel suggested. "I suppose it's just possible, if he did, that the bike might somehow have gone off-balance and fallen over the edge, taking Hart with it. Come to think of it, he most likely secured his helmet onto his bike. I've seen lots of bikes parked in town like that. They use those chains with padlocks. But if that's the case, his helmet should have been found with his bike at the bottom of the cliff. And it wasn't." She gave an exasperated sigh.

"Well," said Joss, "whatever he chose to sit on, wherever he put his helmet, even if he walked around with the thing stuck underneath his arm like Anne Boleyn's ghost in the Bloody Tower, one thing seems more and more likely—he didn't meet his death at the bottom of that cliff alone and unaided. There are too many things that don't add up."

"You do realise what you're saying here?" said Martin. "Are you sure you're not just jumping to conclusions?"

Joss gave him a pitying look. "Of course I'm not. But you have to admit that, barring suicide which, as I said before, we can pretty well rule out, the Coroner's verdict is beginning to look just a little unlikely."

"If you're right," said Martin, "don't you think you ought to go to the police? It's their job to look into potential murders. Yours is just to write about them afterwards."

The look of pity became positively withering. "They seem

to have made up their minds already. Besides, what can I tell them that'll make any sense? However—" she smiled beatifically at Martin "—if we were to find something the police had missed, like a motorcycle helmet, for example..."

"All right, all right," Martin said. "Whatever you say, dear. I know that look only too well. Just be careful, that's all."

"Thank you, dear. Now, would you be a sweetie and make us some more coffee? The news is on in a minute and I want to watch it because I missed the earlier bulletin." As she spoke, she reached for the remote control.

"Don't push your luck," growled Martin. But he dropped a kiss on Joss's forehead as he passed her on his way to the kitchen.

The lead story on the news was, as usual, political. Joss, as usual, watched avidly. As she turned down the sound for the commercial break, she glanced across at Isabel. Isabel was twisting a lock of hair tightly around her fingers. Her face looked pale and tense, her eyes staring unseeingly at the screen.

Joss reached across and squeezed her arm gently. "Are you all right?"

Isabel shook her head slightly as though to clear it, and let the lock of hair fall loose. "I think so." She took a deep breath, and slowly let it go. "I just felt odd again all of a sudden, as though all my perceptions are on hold, waiting for something to happen."

Joss recognised the feeling. It had preceded some of her strongest clairvoyant visions. But before she could say anything, Martin reappeared with the coffee. "Turn the sound up," he said. "The news is on again."

The presenter was saying, "A report has just come in from

Australia, where one police officer was killed and another injured in a shoot-out late this morning near Mermaid Beach on Queensland's Gold Coast. We take you now to an on-the-spot report from our Australian correspondent, Amanda McQueen."

Isabel leaned forward, fists clenched with both fear and excitement. As the image switched to show an ambulance and police cars outside a long, white stucco house, Joss said, "I think that's the house I saw when we did that reading."

On the screen, the reporter began to speak. "Things are normally quiet at this time of year here at Mermaid Beach, just kilometres south of Surfer's Paradise. But, according to bystanders, all hell broke loose here just three hours ago." The camera followed Amanda McQueen to a middle-aged man, presumably one of the aforementioned bystanders, who confirmed this was, indeed, a very quiet neighbourhood usually, and no-one had been more surprised than him to realise that the couple who'd moved in next door were mixed up in child pornography and drugs. They'd seemed such a nice couple, had Ken and Evie. Kept pretty much to themselves as a rule, but always pleasant to talk to... He shook his tanned, balding head at the perplexity of it all.

"Ken and Evie," Amanda continued, "are, in fact, Kevin Brent Patterson, forty-three, and Elaine Judith Walters, thirty-six, not a married couple at all, but ring-leaders in a million-dollar pornography and drugs business that had operated for the last year out of Brisbane, with the help of some corrupt members of the local police force.

"This corruption came under investigation three months ago and, as a result, several of those involved, including two senior police officers, were arrested last month. Patterson and Walters fled to Mermaid Bay, intending to lie low under false identities until it was safe to return to New Zealand, their original homeland, with what they had managed to salvage from the 'profits' of their operation, believed to amount to around half a million dollars.

"However, two weeks ago, police in Brisbane learned of their whereabouts, and undercover police arrived to keep the house under surveillance. It seems Walters and Patterson themselves received a tip-off yesterday, and were getting ready to leave when the police moved in. They initially refused to leave the house, and began shooting as police tried to talk to them. An initial burst of fire killed one police officer. This seemed to frighten the pair, as they stopped firing at this point. The other officer was wounded soon afterwards when he surprised Walters as she attempted to leave the house alone by the back door. Both Patterson and Walters have now been arrested, and police are confident this effectively spells the end of their operation."

Footage was shown of the pair being escorted to a police van, then of two stretchers being carried to waiting ambulances. As the second stretcher was being lifted into the ambulance, Isabel gasped sharply and clutched at Joss's arm. "Bloody hell! Did you see that? That was Declan!"

Joss released the breath she had unconsciously been holding. "I do believe you're right," she breathed, not wanting to proceed to either of the next logical conclusions.

Isabel looked at her, eyes wide. "Are you thinking what I'm thinking?" Her voice was little more than a whisper.

"I'm not thinking anything," Joss said firmly. "No names were given, so we don't know which of the two is Declan—if it was Declan. It was only a brief shot, and not exactly a close-up at that. We mustn't jump to conclusions."

"But," Isabel insisted breathlessly, "that was the house you saw. And the mermaid. That must have been Mermaid Beach."

Martin leaned forward and set down his coffee mug with a firm thump. "Why don't you," he said quietly to Joss, "phone the paper and see if they have more details?"

"Of course!" Joss cried. "Someone's bound to have been writing it up for tomorrow's paper. I'll talk to Gwen. She'll know all about it." She jumped up and hurried out to the hall.

"And you, my dear," Martin said to Isabel, "are going to have a stiff drink. No, don't argue. You don't have to drive home. You can stay here tonight if you like. I'm sure the cats will manage without you till morning, and I doubt if Dominic will notice your absence, even assuming he comes home at all. Besides, whatever may or may not have happened, a good night's sleep never goes amiss."

When Joss returned, she was waving a piece of paper. "Here's what I've got so far. The officer who was killed was a Detective Inspector Joseph Russo, and they haven't released the name or details of the injured one yet, because they haven't notified his next of kin. But he's been flown back to Brisbane for treatment."

"It *is* Declan," Isabel said, her voice tight with anxiety. "I know it is. I've been thinking about the time difference, and the time that reporter said it all happened ties in exactly with the time I started thinking about Declan."

"I expect you're right," Martin said. "You two usually are. But really, there's nothing more any of us can do until the morning."

"Martin's right," said Joss. "I'll go and make you up a bed in the study. I don't think you should be at home alone while you're feeling so anxious."

"Thanks," Isabel said with a bleak smile. "I'd like to stay here. Though I doubt if it'll stop me worrying."

"Of course it won't." Joss smiled. "But at least you won't be worrying on your own."

CHAPTER SEVEN

She was fighting her way through a dense, black cloud, making frantic swimming motions with her arms, as much to stop the stuff—which was as acrid as smoke, though cold and damp and clinging like fog—from choking her as to keep moving. It seemed ages since she'd heard the sharp crack and the cry, and the cloud had suddenly swirled around her, blocking her view in all directions. Frantically she had fought it, knowing she had to get to him. But the more frantic she became in her efforts, the thicker it seemed to become, cutting off sound as well as vision, drifting into her eyes and ears, seeping into her mouth and down her throat.

Suddenly she could fight it no more. Closing her eyes and mouth tightly, and placing her hands over her ears, she drifted in the acrid murk, forcing herself to breathe slowly. Gradually her heartbeat slowed and became quieter, and she realised a voice was coming to her faintly through the fog. Lifting her hands from her ears a fraction, she heard the voice calling her name, "Isabel," softly at first then again, more strongly, "Isabel."

"Yes," she called back, excitement mounting as she recognised the voice.

"Isabel," called Declan, "listen to me. It's all right. You can open your eyes now."

Isabel hesitated. "Go on. You can open them now," he

insisted. Slowly, Isabel opened her eyes. The dark cloud was drifting away into the distance, its ragged edges disintegrating as it went, and she found herself sitting on her lawn at home, blinking in the bright sunlight. Above her head, a tiny silver aeroplane was circling. It must be going to the airport, she thought, and the thought was strangely comforting.

Then she woke up, and saw the desk looming over her camp bed, with Joss's computer monitor gazing solicitously down at her. A fly was buzzing around somewhere near the ceiling. As she sat up, shaking her red curls off her face, she remembered last night's television news, and the glimpse of that unconscious face she was sure was Declan's. Then her dream drifted back into her mind in snatches, and she heard his voice again, saying, "It's all right." And somehow, contrary to all expectations, she was sure it was.

She looked at her watch. Bloody hell! It was almost quarter to ten. She must have slept soundly after all, to have missed the twins and Martin getting ready for school. Yawning, she put on her clothes and rummaged in her bag for the large-toothed comb she needed to remove the inevitable morning tangles from her hair. After a quick wash in the bathroom next door, she made her way to the kitchen where she could hear Joss moving about.

Joss looked up from the sink as Isabel entered. "Oh, hello. I was wondering when you'd finally surface."

"I certainly didn't expect to sleep so well," laughed Isabel. "I had the strangest dream, too."

"Well, put the kettle on, grab yourself some bread, and you can tell me all about it over toast and coffee."

As Isabel ate her breakfast, she described her dream to

Joss. As she finished, Joss grinned, "Who says you don't have premonitions!"

"I don't, usually. But I must say, I feel so much better, I can only assume that's what it was."

"Either that, or a message straight from the horse's mouth, if you'll pardon the expression." Joss swallowed the last of her coffee, stood up, and gathered up the two coffee mugs and Isabel's empty plate, stacking them neatly in the sink. "Speaking of which, I thought we might pop into the newsroom this morning and see if there's a cable update."

"Oh, yes please!" Isabel said. "As long as we can drop by my place first to feed the cats."

The Sun newsroom was like a cross between a warehouse and Father Christmas's workshop the week before Christmas. One long, cream wall was entirely taken up by pigeonholes stuffed with papers and shelves filled with files. The rest of the large room held ranks of desks, most with computer monitors, in various states from severely tidy ("That's Neil's," Joss told her. "If he runs his home like he does his desk, I'm glad I'm not his wife, much less one of his kids.") to overflowing with wire trays disgorging lengths of computer printout, papers covered in cryptic shorthand, USB drives, and the ubiquitous dog-eared dictionaries and copies of 'The New Zealand Style Book'. Some of the desks were empty, while at others various men or women sat or sprawled, engaged in a variety of activities, some of which might conceivably have been related to newspaper production. Joss exchanged greetings and banter with her colleagues, most of whom seemed surprised to see her.

As they passed by one of the messier desks, Joss said,

"That one belongs to Marnie Freeman. You'd never think it to look at that, but she's never missed a deadline in the ten years she's been here, and she writes so well she wins prizes all over the place for her stories. And she looks and dresses like an international model. No one can figure out why she hasn't left us years ago. Any of the glossies would snap her up—and pay her more for the privilege into the bargain."

Isabel shrugged. "Maybe she's got a fabulous man in her life who refuses to leave this fair city, and she can't bear to live without him."

"You haven't met her husband!" snorted Joss. "Even on a good day, Maurice Freeman has all the charm and charisma of a used condom."

"Joss!" Isabel's remonstration was rendered pointless by her giggles. "Anyway, I wasn't necessarily talking about a husband."

"Now there's a possibility I hadn't considered. Ah, here we are. Through here."

They had reached the far end of the newsroom. Joss knocked, then led her through a glass door covered with taped-on cartoons, snippets of news items, and computer-generated graphics, mostly containing scurrilous comments about politicians and other leading figures on the world stage. The office it led to was quite large, but so cluttered with papers, books, cabinets, two computers, a printer on a metal trolley, an assortment of wilting pot-plants, and a large Japanese kite that hung, faded and dusty, from the ceiling, that it looked claustrophobically small.

At first, it seemed the office was empty, then a tiny woman with a brown, wrinkled face and grey hair making its triumphant escape from the confinement of a bun on top of her head, peered out from behind one of the computers. "My God, you're keen!" she said to Joss. Her voice sounded as dry and wrinkled as her appearance. "I thought you weren't due in till tonight."

"Don't worry, Susie, I'm not," laughed Joss. She introduced Isabel to Susie Powers, Overseas Sub-Editor, and explained why they were there.

Susie riffled through a pile of teleprinter printouts produced, apparently, out of thin air, and extracted one. "I think this is what you want," she said, waving it at Joss. "Take it away, for God's sake. This office can do without any more clutter. Just bring it back when you've finished with it, yes?" She vanished back behind her computer, already oblivious to them, before Joss could answer.

"Let's go and get a coffee," said Joss, "then we can read it at my desk."

The printout confirmed what they had already heard, but added nothing new.

Joss noted Isabel's disappointed face. "I'm sure he's all right," she said. "If it was him."

"It was him—I'm certain of it. I just wish I knew where they've taken him, so I could at least get a message to him."

Joss said, "Do you have a phone number for the station he works from in Brisbane?"

"No, just his home number."

"Hmm. Look, we're recording this afternoon, and if we're going to get to Luke's place on time, we'd better go and get some lunch now. Come back to my place. If we hurry, you'll have time to call Directory Service. I'm sure you can track him down later, if you don't mind one or two toll calls."

Isabel shrugged, and gave a short laugh. "Live now, pay

later," she said. "Come on. Let's not waste time."

* * * *

Declan opened his eyes—slowly. Just as slowly, they closed themselves again. For some reason, his eyes seemed unwilling to obey his brain's message. Not that his brain was making much effort either, come to that. Maybe it was something to do with the mist drifting round his head. Best not to try... not to worry... not... to...

Gradually, he became aware of sounds. A metallic clatter from somewhere in the distance. A soft rattling sound. Voices. Voices getting closer. Beside him a soft movement, and a voice, strangely distorted, like a record played at too slow a speed, saying, "I think he's starting to regain..." Then it all swirled away again into the mist.

When he woke again it was dark in his room, though he was aware of yellow light spilling in through the open door. Problem was, it was the wrong door. He certainly couldn't remember installing any door with a window in it, and a shiny metal plate instead of a doorknob. And when the hell did he buy that picture with the pink and mauve flowers and the artist's name blazoned across the bottom in large print? Come to that, why? He must have been out of his mind! And, in the unlikely event that he had bought it, surely he would have had more taste than to have it framed in that metal frame.

Frowning, he pulled himself to a sitting position, and was suddenly overcome by dizziness and nausea. Quickly, he lay back down and the feelings receded. He became aware that his bed had shrunk. The mattress felt different, too – harder, but saggy in the middle. What the hell was going on? A movement from outside the open door caught his eye. He turned his head and caught a glimpse of a woman dressed in white and walking swiftly. Maybe he was dreaming. Fascinated, he kept his head turned in the direction of the door. Before long, another woman in white passed, followed by two men in green coats pushing a metal trolley.

Something pushed at the back of his mind. A memory. More memories. Quite suddenly, it came to him that he was in hospital, and also why. Relieved, he pulled the bedclothes up and went back to sleep.

In his dream, he was talking to Isabel. He couldn't see her, because of a dark, heavy fog, but she seemed distraught with worry, and he was trying to reassure her. He thought he had succeeded, but it was impossible to be sure. If only he could touch her, but she seemed so far away. It was all very puzzling...

Far too soon, he was woken again by the soft clatter of a trolley out in the corridor. A middle-aged woman in a blue overall, with a cheerfully worn face and an aggressive perm, came bustling in. "And how are you this morning?"

Feeling unequal to the task of hazarding a guess, Declan smiled. It seemed the question was purely rhetorical in any case, as the woman merely deposited two plates on the trolley at the end of his bed, rolled it towards him, and bustled out again. This time, he managed to reach a sitting position without passing out, but his head hurt a lot more than he would have preferred, and so did his left leg. None of which was conducive to eating...

He was still sitting there contemplating his next move when a nurse came in. "Good morning, Sergeant Kelly. How are you this morning? Not feeling like eating yet?"

Declan looked at her. She seemed almost ridiculously young, with a sprinkling of freckles on her smooth face. The long red hair twisted up under her cap reminded him of Isabel. Suddenly he felt more lonely than he could ever remember.

"Are you all right?" The nurse was standing beside his bed now, looking down at him with a small, worried frown. Her eyes were the wrong colour grey—much too pale. Which didn't help a whole lot.

"My leg hurts—and my head." He put his hand to his temple where the throbbing was worst, and was surprised to feel gauze and sticking plaster. He didn't remember anyone hitting him.

The nurse said, "I'm not surprised, after what you've been through. I'm sure we can do something about it. I'll go and have a word with Sister." She smiled down at him with sympathy, and what looked embarrassingly like admiration. "Look, you don't have to eat yet if you don't want to. Think you could manage a cup of tea?"

"Make it coffee, strong, milk, no sugar, and I'll give it a go."

Before his coffee, came the woman with the perm, clicking her tongue in mild reproof as she whisked the plates off his trolley, then the sister, with the mercy of a shot of some painkiller. Whatever it was, it was highly effective.

"Sorry to be a nuisance," he told the red-haired nurse when she returned with his coffee, "but you couldn't run to a couple of pieces of toast, could you?"

"Sure. What do want on it? You've got a choice of Vegemite, jam, or honey. I'll do you one of each, shall I? Oh,

66

by the way," she turned in the doorway, "this just arrived for you."

Onto the bed beside him, she tossed an envelope. In it was the printout of an email. From New Zealand. How the hell...? His heart was suddenly racing as he unfolded the paper and read:

'Stop chasing other women! Bad for health – Mine! Miss you. Take care. Will write. Love Isabel'

Later that morning, Police Constable Carol Anderson called in on her way back to work, and was immediately struck by the huge grin engulfing Declan's face. "You're looking very cheerful for a man who's just had his kneecap shot off," she remarked. "Whatever it is they've got you on, reckon you could get me some too?"

"Not a chance. That stuff's reserved for us heroes." The irony in his voice belied his words.

"Well, hero," Carol's tone carried irony to the brink of sarcasm, softened by her smile, "the Chief asked me to drop by and remind you he's going to want a report on the incident, ASAP. Oh, and he said to tell you 'Get well soon'."

"Bloody good of him!"

Carol grinned. "Well, what he actually said was, 'Tell him he's already had more paid leave this year than anyone can reasonably expect.' But I think that was just his way of letting you know he cares. And I wouldn't take the bit about the report too seriously. The case seems to have got itself all wrapped up very nicely, thanks to you. Oh, by the way, we had a phone call for you yesterday afternoon. Came in just as I was finishing my shift." The grin became a teasing smile. "You didn't say anything about having a lady in New Zealand."

"Contrary to popular opinion," Declan told her, "I'm not a complete idiot."

Carol grinned again. "Seems you made the TV news over there. She wanted to know what hospital you were in. I didn't think you'd mind if I told her. So I guess you'll be hearing from her."

"Yeah," said Declan, making no attempt to control his own grinning face. "Any idea where my cell phone has got to?"

"None whatsoever."

"Reckon you could get me some paper and envelopes, then? And some stamps?"

CHAPTER EIGHT

"Right," said Luke, stubbing out his cigarette with a decisive flourish, "what are we going to do now?"

They were gathered in his sitting room—Joss, Isabel and Geraldine, James not having arrived yet—trying to settle on material to record for the following evening's programme. So far, however, apart from this week's edition of the regular, pre-recorded series on the history of the Order of the Golden Dawn, and the usual fifteen-minute phone-in, inspiration seemed to have deserted them.

"It looks like we've still got half an hour to fill in," Luke persisted. "Since you lot won't let me mention that bizarre murder in this morning's paper, how about you come up with something we can use instead." With an aggrieved sigh, he pulled another cigarette from his pack and reached for his lighter.

"I must say, though," said Joss wistfully, "it's a pity we can't discuss the murder. It's not every day you come across a body hung upside down from a tree and trussed up like the Hanged Man."

"Not to mention the Tarot card that was tucked into his belt," said Geraldine. "That must have been the murderer's calling card."

"Mmm," Isabel agreed. "The Magician. There's got to be a clue in there somewhere. What a pity we don't have access to the police file on it. I'd love to know if they found any fingerprints, or hairs, or clothing fibres, you know, like they do on television."

Luke blew a cloud of blue smoke towards the ceiling and tapped the ash off the end of his cigarette more savagely than was strictly necessary. "Look, since you've already managed to convince me we can't talk about it on the programme, would you all mind not rubbing salt into the wound by going on about it ad nauseam when we've still got half an hour of programme to record, and not an idea between the lot of us."

"Sorry, Luke," Joss said contritely. "Haven't you got anything else at all?"

"Well, only this strange commercial James asked me to play. It looks like some sort of coded message, though God knows who it's for."

"Where is James, anyway?" Joss demanded. "Even he isn't usually this late."

"Oh, he called in earlier, just to leave his message, and to say he wouldn't be able to be part of the panel today. Something's come up, apparently. Sorry, I meant to tell you."

"So what is this strange message?" said Joss. "Let's have a look at it."

Luke pulled a piece of paper from under his notepad and gave it to her.

Joss read aloud to the others, "'Those who enter the light need never fear the flame, but he who uses the flame to do harm shall find himself in darkness. His flame shall be extinguished'."

"That's weird!" said Isabel.

"It must mean something," said Geraldine, "but what?"

"I don't think it's a commercial at all," said Joss. "I think

70

he's trying to tell someone something—someone who listens to the programme."

"I can't handle any more of this," said Luke. "I'm going to make some more coffee. Here." He stood up and thrust his notepad and a pen into Joss's hands. "By the time I come back, I want a list of useful ideas."

Two hours later, as they all trooped from Luke's studio back to the sitting room, Joss threw her arm round Luke's shoulder. "There," she said, "it came together all right in the end, didn't it?"

"I suppose so," Luke admitted grudgingly, "though it was hardly one of our more inspired programmes."

Joss gave his shoulder a squeeze and grinned mischievously. "If you ask me, all this award winning has gone to your head."

"Just as well I didn't ask you then, isn't it?"

"Smile, when you say that, stranger."

Isabel gave a laugh, part amusement, part exasperation. "Will you two please stop bickering? I've just had a very interesting thought about the Hanged Man murder."

"Sounds like the title of a book." Joss smiled. "But let's hear your interesting thought."

"Coffee first," said Luke, "please!"

Ten minutes later, he set down a tray laden with steaming mugs of coffee and a plate of the afghan biscuits for which he was justly renowned. "Now," he said, settling himself in his chair and rubbing his hands together in anticipation, "I'm all ears."

"Ah, that explains it," Joss observed, her carefully bland expression failing to hide the gleam in her eyes. "You've had a haircut!"

As Luke's arm went out towards the couch, Joss ducked reflexively, but he merely picked up his cigarette packet, tapping one free as he said to Isabel, "Ignore her. She probably can't help it, but one mustn't encourage her. Please go on."

"Well," said Isabel, with a chuckle and a flick of her red curls, "this chap McNaught's death was made to look like one of the Tarot major trumps, right?" Nods of agreement from the others. "But Leo Hart's death also fits one of the major trumps—the Fool." She took an afghan and bit into it.

"Come to that," Joss said thoughtfully, "what about James's friend, Doctor Kleber?"

"What do you mean?" asked Luke.

"Well, a teacher on a mountain with a lamp. What does that put you in mind of?"

"The Hermit!" exclaimed Isabel. "But his death was definitely an accident. He was alone in that hut."

"Was he?" Joss asked mysteriously.

"The police certainly thought so," Isabel replied. "And surely, if anyone else had been there, there would have been some evidence. Like tyre tracks, or footprints or something."

"Well," said Joss, "the police seem sure Leo Hart's death was an accident, but his boyfriend doesn't think so and, after talking to him, I'm more than a little inclined to agree."

"Have you heard back from Simon Drawbridge yet?" asked Isabel.

"No. I meant to call him this morning. But what with Luke being such a slave-driver, it completely slipped my mind."

"I make no comment on that slur on my good nature," Luke said. "Like the Buddha, I shall maintain a noble silence."

"That'll be the day!" Joss responded. "Anyway, before I do, I think it's about time we got round to making that trip up to Whitewash Head. We should have gone last week, really. Let's hope such evidence as there might have been is still there."

"Well, at least we haven't had any rain for a change," said Isabel.

"It's too late to go today," said Luke, glancing at his watch. "It's nearly five o'clock now; it'd be almost dark by the time we got there. Too dark to see properly, anyway."

"And I've got to drive back out to West Melton," said Geraldine. "I've got a horse to feed, not to mention Philip, who'll be as hungry as one by the time he gets home."

"Surely Philip hasn't regressed to complete helplessness in the few months he's been with you?"

Geraldine laughed. "Of course not. He's a wonderful cook, as well you know. But it's my turn to get dinner tonight. We take it in turns through the week, and on Saturday night we dine out or buy takeaways. All very egalitarian and civilised, I assure you." She uncurled herself from the couch and pulled on her camel-hair jacket. "Anyway, I really must be going."

"If we go up to Whitewash Head tomorrow," said Joss, "I suppose you won't be able to go with us?"

"Sorry, I'm working all day tomorrow. But you can tell me all about it next week."

"Oh, well," said Joss, after Geraldine had left, "the rest of us can still go."

"I have a client in the morning," said Isabel. "Can we make it after lunch?"

"Suits me," said Luke. "I'll have the programme in the can

by then, so I'll be able to give my full attention to the matter in hand. I'll pick you both up if you like. No sense in using more than one car."

Joss and Isabel exchanged glances. They had both experienced Luke's driving before. "All right," Joss said. "We must be insane, but we'll put our lives in your hands. Pick us up about one."

* * * *

"Oh, just look at that!" Joss was standing near the edge of the cliff, looking out across the sea. The day was crisp and bright, a brisk north-easterly wind chasing wispy clouds across the sky like a flustered sheep dog attempting to herd recalcitrant sheep, which managed to elude it by constant shape-shifting. The sea far below was a gigantic mosaic of lapis lazuli stretching to infinity straight ahead, broken at the edge of vision to the left by the long, pale brown finger of the South Shore spit crooked around the estuary where the Heathcote and Avon rivers met the sea.

Following the sweep of Joss's gaze, Isabel looked down to where the incoming tide lashed the rocks at the bottom of the cliff, giving them the appearance of wet lignite. The narrow beach was thick with driftwood, broken shells and bloated-looking seaweed, as well as the usual detritus of modern life bobbing there incongruously. She thought of Leo Hart, his body lying lifeless and broken, washed about by torn plastic bags and blue plastic packaging strips, tiny balls of polystyrene strung about his body like pearls. She thought of Declan, lying wounded by the dilapidated white house at Mermaid Beach. How alone they must both have felt. How terrible to be completely alone at such a time. But perhaps, in reality, one always was alone in moments of extremity. Maybe that was what it meant to be an individual...

"You can see why Leo Hart came here to contemplate, can't you?" Joss's voice beside her saved her, thankfully, from her own contemplations.

Isabel shook her head slightly, expelling her breath as though her sombre thoughts would leave with it. Before she could respond to Joss's question, Luke called out, "Come and look at this." He was squatting by a small group of low rocks, brown and pitted, encrusted with patches of pale green lichen, clustered about three metres from the cliff edge. Isabel and Joss hurried over.

"Look." Luke pointed at one of the rocks. Its top was about half a metre across, rounded and flattened by centuries of wind and weather. All along one side, lichen had been dislodged and lay, like flaked enamel paint, on the grass at its base. The grass itself, scrubby and brown from the summer sun and salt-laden wind that even now was whipping across it with the stinging force of a slap, had been dislodged in places, exposing the hard, dusty earth.

Joss noticed several more areas where the dried grass had been either dislodged or flattened, all of them within a radius of about two or three metres, including the rocky outcrop.

"Looks like something happened here," she commented, gazing thoughtfully around.

"A scuffle, maybe?" Luke suggested.

"Maybe. Look, let's go back to the scuffmarks nearer the edge. The ones the police told Drawbridge about." Joss led the way to where the tyre tracks of the motorbike could still just be seen in the hard, dry soil. Beside them were gouges of varying depths, which were presumably where Leo had attempted to stop his motorcycle from running over the edge of the cliff.

"I wonder," said Isabel, rescuing a strand of her hair from the wind and chewing on it thoughtfully, "why the marks are only on the left side of the tyre tracks. It looks to me as though he was wheeling the bike, rather than riding it. And why would he be wheeling it towards the edge unless..."

"Maybe," said Joss, "Drawbridge was wrong about Hart killing himself."

"Or maybe," Luke suggested, "it wasn't Hart wheeling the bike. What if there was someone else here with him—someone who killed him, then pushed him over the cliff and the bike after him? That would account for the marks on the ground by the rocks back there, and the lichen being knocked off."

"But the police must have had his body examined," Joss objected, "as well as checking out this whole area. And they obviously didn't find any signs of foul play. No, I'm more inclined now to favour suicide as an explanation, whatever Drawbridge thinks."

"Mmm, I suppose you're right. It's not surprising his boyfriend doesn't want to believe he committed suicide. I remember how guilty I felt after Mother and Dad died. It was a plane crash, so there was no question about it being an accident, and there was nothing I could have done about it in any case; but it was over a year before I stopped blaming myself for encouraging them to take that trip after Dad retired."

While they were talking, Isabel had wandered back toward the clump of rocks, following the scuffmarks and flattened grass that formed a vague and meandering trail between the tyre tracks and the rocks. Just as Joss reached out to squeeze Luke's arm in sympathy, they heard her call out in an excited voice, "Come and look at this! I think I may have found something!"

She was crouching beside another low rock about a metre away from the others. Smaller, and perhaps less weathered, its pitted surface formed a number of jagged little points. Isabel's gaze was fixed on a point at its base, where she was busy scrabbling at the dirt with her fingers.

"What is it?" Joss knelt beside Isabel and looked where she was pointing. In the dirt by the rock lay more of the pale green curls and frills of dried lichen, some with clusters of faded orange dots of spore still clinging to them. And in amongst them, something metallic gleamed. Isabel picked it up carefully and held it out. It was a small oval badge. Its black enamel was scratched and dusty, but a single word, in black italics edged with gleaming silver, was perfectly clear: Triumph.

"Oh my God!" Joss's voice was breathless with excitement. "That must be Leo Hart's! Drawbridge told me his bike was a Triumph Bonneville."

"I don't want to be a killjoy," said Luke, "but it doesn't actually prove anything. We already know Hart was here. The badge could easily have fallen off during the course of either an accident or a suicide."

Joss sighed. "I hate to admit it, Luke, but you're right."

Isabel, meanwhile, had been staring at the rock and the earth beside it in apparent fascination, running her fingers over its rough surface and down its side. Now she looked at the other two and said, "I'm not so sure. What do you two make of this?"

The rock was the same grey-brown as the others, pitted all over, jagged cracks and grey-green lichen here and there on its surface giving it the appearance of a diminutive desert landscape. Down one side, where Isabel's finger was pointing, the rock was streaked a darker brown, the lichen brownish instead of dusty green. It looked as though someone had tipped a small tin of red-brown paint—about the size used for painting models—over one side of the rock, and it had run down the crevices onto the ground below, forming tiny pools where the soil was too hardened to absorb it, eventually drying into a blackish brown glaze like egg-white burnt onto an overcooked pie-crust.

Luke squatted down beside Isabel and Joss and peered closely at the stains. "No—it can't be!" he said at last, doing his best to convince himself.

Joss, who had been turning the badge over in her hands, said, "Don't be too sure. Look at this." She held it out, showing them the back of it, where the bent pin hung loosely awry. A small splash of the same reddish brown was encrusted there.

"It's dried blood, isn't it?" said Isabel.

Joss nodded. "I think it is."

"Then it's evidence," Luke stated. He pulled a handkerchief from his jacket pocket and held it out to her. "This is clean. Wrap the badge in it. If it turns out to be Hart's blood, we might just be onto something."

Isabel stood up, smoothing down her jeans, shaking her legs to ease the circulation back into them. Looking once more at the grassy area between the two rock outcrops, she said, "Maybe we should take a bit of the rock, too, or some of the stained dirt. If these stains really are blood, then all this flattened grass, and the lichen scraped off the rocks, could indicate a fight took place."

"It could indeed," Luke agreed, "between Leo Hart and... well, person or persons unknown. Isn't that what the police say?"

"Don't look at me," said Isabel. "I only know one of them, and it doesn't sound at all the sort of thing he'd say." She rubbed her hands together, thrusting them into the pockets of her jacket. "Is there anything else we should check out, or can we leave now? This wind is freezing."

Joss scooped up a little of the stained earth, and wrapped it in one corner of Luke's handkerchief. The badge she wrapped in the opposite corner, then placed the handkerchief carefully in the pocket of her parka and zipped up the pocket. "I think we'd better have a meeting in the next day or so," she said, "to discuss where to go from here. In the meantime, I want to have another chat with Simon Drawbridge. After all, this might not be Hart's badge at all. We might be on the wrong track entirely."

Luke looked dubious. But he said, "Okay. I'll drop you two back home, and get in touch with Geraldine and James this evening to find out when they're free. I've a feeling there's going to be a great story in this." He pushed his hand through his hair in a characteristically futile attempt to prevent it from flopping over his eyes. His boyish features took on an air of pain. "God, I'm dying for a cigarette!"

CHAPTER NINE

Joss braked her Fiat Bambina at the stop sign and glanced up the hillside to where Simon Drawbridge's white house perched like a gigantic albatross ready for flight. Thank God there's a side road up to it, she thought, eyeing the multiple flights of steps that led up to expensive-looking houses nestled at varying levels on the hill. As a gap in the traffic presented itself, she swung the little car round the corner and began to coax it up the steeply curving road past banks crowned with great clumps of blue-purple spiky blooms, pink and red geraniums, and ice-plants with white and yellow flowers spilling like foam down their sides.

As she trudged up the final flight of steps to the house, she thought breathlessly that if being filthy rich required this sort of stamina, she was quite content to be moderately well-off and living in a reconstituted nineteen-forties bungalow on the flat, thank you very much. At least one didn't need crampons and an alpenstock to get to it.

Simon Drawbridge was waiting for her when she finally halted, puffing, on the grey tiled terrace that fronted what seemed like an acre of faintly tinted glass looking out over a spectacular view of rock-rimmed sea. He was wearing light blue jeans and a matching chambray shirt, which imparted a faint seawater tinge to his eyes. Braces, Joss decided, must be his trademark. The ones he wore today were floral, in pinks and mauves that admirably set off the muted tones of chambray and denim. "Hello," he called, his well-bred voice echoing slightly as though astonished—as Joss was—at the grand scale of everything. "Good of you to come. I hope you didn't find the ascent too daunting."

"Well," gasped Joss, "it's certainly not what I'm used to."

Drawbridge gave a gentle laugh. "One does get used to it. And it's worth it for the privacy—not to mention the view. Anyway, come on in and I'll make us some tea. Or would you prefer something cold?"

"Tea will be fine, thanks," said Joss, and followed him through the vast, airy, tiled foyer (one couldn't call it a hall) and into a surprisingly cosy-looking sitting room. Curved fawn leather couches (more of Leo's designs?) were placed to give the best view of the sea stretching out beyond a colourful tumble of hillside growth to the pale pink gauze of the horizon where a crescent moon hung just above a ragged streak of dark clouds.

"It is spectacular, isn't it?" Drawbridge said, observing Joss's expression. "We've—I've—lived here for four years now, and it still takes my breath away. Look, do take a seat. I'll be back in a minute."

Tea was served in fine porcelain cups of a quietly spectacular red edged with gold, and accompanied by fingers of shortbread. In the face of such evidence of taste and breeding, Joss hardly liked to broach the subject of Leo's financial arrangements, so it was a relief when Drawbridge went over to an antique walnut sideboard and came back with a black box file.

"These are Leo's papers," he said, "going back to when he started his business, six years ago. You can look at them if you like. I'm sure Leo wouldn't have minded, and I certainly don't."

"Thank you." Joss opened the lid of the file. It was almost filled with neatly bundled papers. "Would it be all right if I took it home for a day or two? I think it may take some time to go through all of these."

Drawbridge nodded his head. "Be my guest. But you wanted to know who gave him his loan, and I can tell you that now. It was a personal loan, as I thought, but the lender was Arthur McNaught, his bank manager."

"But that's..."

Drawbridge nodded again as Joss gasped in astonishment. "Yes, I know. I read about it in yesterday morning's paper. What a bizarre thing to do. And what a bizarre coincidence."

Joss pushed her hand through her fringe and took a deep breath, expelling the air through her teeth with a whistling sound. "I'm beginning to wonder if it was just coincidence." She explained to him about Isabel's 'tarot' theory, and their discovery on Whitewash Head. She took Luke's handkerchief from her pocket and carefully unwrapped the badge.

Now Drawbridge gasped. "That's Leo's!" he exclaimed. "At least, he had one just like it. He belonged to a motorcycle club—no, not that sort," he chuckled, seeing the look on Joss's face. "We were very different, I suppose—a queer couple in more ways than one, but... no, it was a group who all owned or were interested in Triumph motorcycles—the Canterbury Triumph Riders, or something like that. Most of them weren't like Leo at all, strapping great mechanics and the like." Joss thought she detected a hint of grudging admiration in his voice. "But Leo got on well with them.

Common interest, I suppose. Not one I shared. But then Leo wasn't interested in Scottish dancing, either." He smiled to himself, remembering.

"Is this their club badge then?" Joss asked.

"I don't think so. I don't think they had one, as such. But he may well have got it through the club."

Joss pulled a notepad from her pocket and wrote down the club name. "I'll check it out later," she said. "But, tell me, what do you make of the possibility that Mr Hart's death fits the same Tarot pattern as this Arthur McNaught's?"

Drawbridge leaned forward, elbows on knees, and gazed out across the sea vista, rubbing his chin with the fingers of one hand, apparently weighing up the pros and cons of the matter before pronouncing judgement. Suddenly, he sat up straight, a gleam of insight lighting his eyes. "Do you know, I believe you may be right!" he exclaimed. "He never said anything to me directly, but about two and a half years ago, he started going to regular meetings, once a month, sometimes more often, of some group or other. Come to think about it, I believe it was shortly after that he began banking with the Phoenix. I did ask him about that, but he said he wasn't allowed to say anything. I respected that, of course, though I have to admit I teased him sometimes about funny handshakes and so on. It became a bit of a running joke with us. Even before I met him, Leo had been interested in the Masons, and that sort of esoterica. He used to meditate, too, on a regular basis—claimed it inspired his designs." He gave an eloquent shrug and picked up a piece of shortbread.

Joss pushed a hand through her hair again and wondered how much she should say to Drawbridge. She decided, on balance, she might as well be as open with him as he had been with her. "That's extremely interesting," she said, "because there may be another connection as well. Just over a month ago, a Doctor Richard Kleber, a university lecturer, died, apparently by accident, in a trampers' hut up in the mountains."

Drawbridge nodded. "I remember reading about that."

"Then you may also have read that he wrote a book in the seventies about the Rosicrucian movement in Germany and the Nazi Party's involvement with it."

"Yes, I believe I did, now you mention it. Mind you, I didn't take much notice. Those sorts of rumours have been around for decades. I can't see that they contribute anything useful by way of explanation of the rise of Hitler or the Nazis, much less an excuse for what they did."

"I agree, totally. The thing is, though, that paperweight you have in your office..." Joss paused briefly as Drawbridge nodded again, a puzzled frown creasing his brow. "...the cross with the rose in the centre is a Rosicrucian symbol. Actually, it's *the* Rosicrucian symbol."

"Ye-es, I can see that," said Drawbridge thoughtfully. Then, with a swift grin at Joss, "One doesn't make one's way through nine years of private schooling without acquiring a fair amount of Latin. One's pronunciation may want accuracy, but not one's understanding."

Joss grinned back. Having been to a very traditional girls' secondary school herself, she knew exactly what he meant. "It might prove interesting," she suggested, "to know who made that paperweight. Did Mr Hart keep receipts and the like?" She indicated the box file hopefully.

"He was pretty organised as a rule," Drawbridge told her,

"for an artist. There's another file as well as this one. You're welcome to take that as well, if you like. I'll just go and get it for you." He left the room, returning moments later with an identical black box and a large ring-bound folder with a maroon leatherette cover.

Placing the box on top of the other one, he held the folder out to Joss. "I thought this might interest you, too. Leo was a great hoarder of memorabilia. This is his photograph album." He opened it near the front. "This is Leo on his Triumph. It was taken shortly after he'd finished restoring it, about five or six months ago." As Joss took the album, Drawbridge turned away abruptly and went to stand by the window.

The picture he had indicated showed a man aged around thirty, sitting proudly astride a great black and silver motorcycle. His close-fitting black leather trousers and jacket showed him to be slim. His height was not easy to guess, but from his general build, Joss thought he was probably no more than average height. One hand grasped the cycle's handlebar, and the other held a white cycle helmet in front of him on the fuel tank. On the front of the helmet was a small insignia in what looked like red and gold, but it was impossible to make out what it might be. His tanned face, an attractive mixture of toughness and vulnerability, was framed by thick, light brown hair, cut short and spiky on top, longer at the back. The total impression was one of tough, energetic good humour, very different from Drawbridge's reserved, languid manner.

"As I said, we were very different in many ways." Drawbridge might have been reading her thoughts as he turned from the darkening seascape and came to stand beside her. "Leo came from what these days would be called a disadvantaged background. While I was being financed through a degree in architecture, he was busy broadening his education by learning how to relieve people like my father of their unneeded material possessions." Drawbridge gave an ironic little laugh. "Luckily for him, before he could end up in prison he was sent on a training scheme where he was taught furniture making and upholstery. The aim was to teach him some useful skills—and, I imagine, to keep him busy while they tried to make him see the error of his ways. What it did do was give him access to a wonderful creativity that must have been there all the time, just waiting to be discovered." Drawbridge's expression clearly showed his admiration for his former partner. "After that, he never looked back. He even went back to school and finished his education, and then on to a business course at the Polytechnic. I met him some years later at a domestic-design exhibition. My sister was showing some of her rugs there. I was attracted immediately by his energy and his earthiness—and I was intrigued by the contrast with his designs..." Drawbridge broke off, obviously affected by his memories. He shook his head slightly to clear them from his mind. He did not, however, Joss noted, apologise for his display of emotion. "Please take these," he said, taking the album and placing it with the box files. "Keep them for as long as you need them. But you will keep me informed, won't you? I loved Leo very much, and I want to know the truth about his death."

"Of course," Joss told him. "I'll be in touch the minute I find out anything." As she began to wrap up the badge once more, a thought occurred to her. "The stain on the back of this...we think it's probably blood. If it is, it'll be vital to know if it's Leo's. I expect I could find a way to get tests done, but I was wondering—I thought it might be easier..."

"Of course! I'm only too happy to do anything in my power to find out how Leo died. I'm just so grateful you've agreed to help me."

Joss finished wrapping the badge and left the handkerchief with him. As she made her way back down the steps to the driveway, the slim curve of the moon was finally engulfed in cloud.

* * * *

As things turned out, neither Geraldine nor James were free before the following week's recording session. Now the five of them were gathered in Luke's sitting room for their usual post-recording coffee and de-briefing. Geraldine was curled up in her favourite corner of the leather couch, her long maroon skirt wrapped around her legs. Her high boots of dark brown leather lay collapsed on the carpet beside a matching shoulder bag. James was perched, as always, slightly apart from the rest of them on the piano stool by Luke's beloved baby grand piano. Unusually for him, he was not wearing a suit and tie, but a dark brown casual shirt and brown tweed jacket. He seemed moodily engrossed in the mechanics of his silver fountain pen, his mug of coffee unnoticed and untouched beside him.

He appeared equally oblivious of Joss watching him shrewdly over the rim of her coffee mug. As she sipped, she was trying to work out just what it was that seemed different about James. Reserved and conservative by nature, he was always fairly reticent about anything that didn't involve his professional opinion as a lecturer in psychology. But lately, he seemed, somehow, pre-occupied. Yes, that was the word for it. But why? Once or twice she had tried, tactfully she thought, to broach the subject, but James had very skilfully managed to avoid admitting to anything beyond the usual pressures of work, at the same time making it politely clear that further enquiries would be regarded as an unwelcome intrusion.

Suddenly, Joss put down her coffee mug and broke the silence they had all fallen into. "When I spoke to Simon Drawbridge the other day, he seemed very interested indeed in your 'tarot' theory about the recent deaths," she said to Isabel.

Isabel, who had been gazing absent-mindedly out of the french windows, twisting a lock of hair round one finger, looked round. "Yes? What did he say?"

"He got quite excited when I told him. Said it was quite possible, because Leo had belonged to some group that he thought was Masonic, or possibly Rosicrucian. He didn't really know anything about it, though. Leo had told him he wasn't allowed to tell him."

"Ah," said Isabel knowingly, "a secret society."

"So it would appear. And when I told him about Doctor Kleber and the book he wrote, Drawbridge immediately made the connection with that silver paperweight he has in his office. He's given me Hart's files to look through, and a photo album. I'm hoping, among other things, to find out who made the paperweight."

"I'll give you a hand if you like," Isabel offered.

"Me, too," said Luke.

Geraldine also offered to help them, provided she could fit

it in between work and exercising her horse.

"What about you, James?" Joss asked, with another shrewd glance in his direction. "You know, many hands make light work, and there are two big fat files to go through, as well as the photo album."

James regarded her with an unfathomable expression. "No, I really don't think so," he said stiffly. "I'm very busy just at present. Besides, I must say I find the whole idea just a little ridiculous. The two earlier deaths were quite clearly accidental, so how can there be any connection between them, let alone with the most recent one, which was just as clearly a murder? Really, I think you're letting your success with that Circle of Light business go to your heads. If there were anything suspicious in these deaths, I imagine the police would be aware of it, don't you?"

Before anyone could respond to this speech, James stood up and made to leave. As he did so, he turned as though suddenly remembering something. "Oh, Luke," he said, "I owe the station for that advertisement I placed with you last week. Will a cheque be okay?"

"Oh, um, yes." Luke sounded startled. "That'll be fine. Make it out to the programme though, to avoid any confusion."

"Sure." James wrote rapidly in his chequebook, then tore off the cheque and passed it to Luke. "Thanks for the coffee," he said. "I really must go now. I still have term papers to mark, and a faculty meeting to prepare for."

"What's up with him?" asked Geraldine, as James retreated rapidly down the hall. "Did you manage to find out anything, Joss?"

As Joss ruefully shook her head, Luke said, staring at the

cheque in his hand, "You didn't happen to say anything to him about McNaught being the one who loaned money to Hart for his business, did you?"

"No, why?"

"Or about McNaught being the manager of Leo's bank?"

"No, he never gave me the chance. For goodness' sake, why?"

"Look at this." Luke handed Joss the cheque. Along the top were the words, Phoenix Banking Corporation Limited. The logo beside them was a black, crested bird rising triumphant from scarlet flames.

"I think," said Joss quietly, "we'd better get together as soon as possible, and not just to look through Hart's files."

CHAPTER TEN

"Come in, Brother. The others are already here. Glad you could come at such short notice."

"Not at all. I've been aware for some time now of the need to take urgent action."

Deliberately ignoring this mild reproof, the taller man turned on his heel and led the way down the long, elegant hallway. He was just over six feet tall, but his slim build gave him the appearance of greater height. His dark, sardonic good looks added to the effect, so that he seemed to tower over others by the sheer force of his presence, and his abrupt way of speaking did nothing to dispel the impression.

His guest, walking behind him, wondered briefly whether his habit of invariably dressing in black was a deliberate attempt to create an ambience of power and mystery. The Lord alone knew what his clients thought of him. Or perhaps he had created yet another persona for their benefit. He wouldn't put anything past Brother Esto Sol Testis, he thought, running a hand over his smooth, dark hair, and nervously adjusting his tie as they entered the study where the others were waiting.

The study, like the rest of the meticulously restored Edwardian villa, was spacious and high ceilinged. Such areas of its walls as were not lined with rimu bookshelves, or taken up with the long, narrow, green-curtained window in the far wall, were papered in dark green. The plaster ceiling was alabaster-pale, providing maximum contrast with the ornate ceiling rose, which had been painted metallic bronze. From it a heavy, opaque-glass lampshade hung on three brass chains. Such light as there was, however, came from the candles in two silver candlesticks, one on the mantelpiece above the green-tiled fireplace, the other on the massive leather-topped desk. The effect was highly atmospheric. The atmosphere was oppressive.

Three high-backed chairs upholstered in dark green leather had been placed facing a similar, but larger, chair in front of the desk. The taller man sat down in the larger chair, motioning his guest to a place beside the two earlier arrivals. One of these was a stocky, muscular man in his forties, with an air of controlled aggression. His grey hair, close-cropped and spiking up from his square head, gave him the appearance of a middle-aged Action Man. The other was younger, probably around thirty, thin and ascetic looking with stooped shoulders. With his owlish, metal-rimmed glasses and prematurely thinning hair, he seemed the archetypal scholar. He was, in fact, a civil engineer of some note.

"Since you all know why we're here," Brother Esto Sol Testis said abruptly, "let's get on with it. We have a great deal to decide, and no time to waste. Our first order of business is to choose a new Senior for the Brotherhood."

Brother Fulget Virtus shuffled slightly on his chair and straightened his tie. "May I suggest," he said, "that we base our selection on strict seniority. It seems fairest, and should obviate the need for lengthy discussion."

Murmurs of "Hear, hear," and "I agree," came from his

two companions. Brother Esto Sol Testis said nothing.

"So," Brother Fulget Virtus looked at the others, his smooth features carefully devoid of expression, "are we agreed, then, that Brother Esto Sol Testis, as the Brother who has longest held the Grade of Adeptus Major, should become our new Senior—subject, of course, to his acceptance?"

Nods and murmurs demonstrated unanimous agreement.

Brother Esto Sol Testis rose to his full height and executed a slight bow. "I accept, and shall strive at all times to be worthy of the honour," he said, then sat down again, his dark eyes belying the humble words of his formal speech of acceptance. Brother Fulget Virtus inwardly heaved a sigh of relief. Like the others, he knew perfectly well how difficult life could have been for them all had Brother Esto Sol Testis not received what he considered to be his due.

The thin, ascetic-looking brother, pushing his glasses further up his nose, stood up. "I'd like to propose," he said, in a high, nasal voice, "that in keeping with his position of seniority, the grade of Adeptus Exemptus now be conferred upon Brother Esto Sol Testis."

A flicker of emotion lit the new Senior's dark eyes, but it was veiled before the others could interpret it. "Thank you, Brother Solem Fero. I'm honoured. But what do the others think?"

"Strictly speaking, of course," said the stocky Action Man, his gruff voice a thinly-disguised challenge, "this should be subject to the usual examination."

"Perhaps, under the circumstances, Brother Ferro Comite," Brother Solem Fero replied, "we might waive that formality?" It was spoken as a request from one reasonable man to another, but Brother Ferro Comite was not to be deflected. An ex-military man, he took the view that established procedures were there to be followed—to the letter. He was also the only other Adeptus Major amongst them.

"The Senior Brother," he said stolidly, "must not only take responsibility for the Brotherhood, he must, surely, be seen by everyone as having proper authority to do so."

As he felt the others' eyes on him, Brother Fulget Virtus stopped fiddling with his tie and tried to look decisive. Brother Esto Sol Testis, having already indirectly indicated his willingness to accept the higher grade, would take no further steps to settle this threatened dispute. Direct action was not his style in any case but, as Senior, he should not be seen to be taking sides. That way lay confusion.

Which was, of course, exactly what Brother Fulget Virtus was now feeling. Direct action was not his style, either, and he had always had an intense dislike—some would say fear—of altercations. Swallowing hard to clear his throat, he spoke with considerably more calmness than he felt. "The difficulty, of course, due to the untimely—ah——passing of Brother Ex Flamma Lux as well as the other two, is that we now have no one with the seniority to examine the Grade of Adeptus Exemptus. We do, however, have the literature to determine the attributes and abilities pertaining to that degree. So perhaps, if Brother Esto Sol Testis agrees—and the others, of course—we could confer the degree pro tem, and arrange for him to be formally examined at the next solstice, by which time we'll have had time to consult the literature and meet again to discuss it. That way he can act with proper authority in what I feel sure we all agree is a very difficult situation."

"A judgement worthy of Solomon himself," Brother Ferro Comite pronounced with heavy irony. But he agreed to the suggestion, as did the others.

"Thank you, Brother Fulget Virtus," said the Senior, taking charge once more. "Now we need to elect three brothers to replace those so tragically lost to us. The rules of our Order state that the Council of Senior Brothers shall at all times number seven."

After a mercifully brief and harmonious discussion, three were chosen who met the requirements of the other four, namely, that they had reached a sufficient level of attainment, and could be trusted. Their formal induction—subject, as always, to their acceptance of the honour—was set down for the winter solstice, some three weeks away.

"That," announced the Senior, "concludes our formal business. Brandy, gentlemen?" He went to a small cabinet behind his desk and took out a crystal decanter and four matching glasses on a silver tray. He wiped them fastidiously with a clean white napkin, poured a measure into each glass, and presented the tray solemnly to each in turn. In his black suit and matching shirt, relieved only minimally by a dull red tie, he looked every inch the master of magic. It was, indeed, rumoured that he privately practised rituals far in advance of his official status in the Brotherhood. There were even those who believed he had been inducted into the Secret Chiefs of the Third Order during a business trip to Europe the previous year. If he had, he had not divulged the secret, even to his fellow Adepts. Not directly, at any rate.

As they sipped their brandy, he broached the subject that had been on all their minds. "Two tragic accidents in as many months, and now a third brother murdered. A terrible coincidence indeed, brothers." He looked at the others, a steely glint in his heavy-lidded eyes. "However, as we all know, on the inner planes there is no such thing as coincidence. Therefore, we must take steps to discover the true meaning of this apparent accident of fate."

"The way Brother Dabunt Espera Rosas's body was tied and hung to look like the Hanged Man," said Brother Ferro Comite in his blunt way, "suggests the murderer has knowledge of our teachings."

"If so," said Brother Solem Fero, sipping delicately at his brandy, "it would seem he was intended as some kind of sacrifice."

"Perhaps." The Senior seemed doubtful. "But what about the tarot card—the Magician, I believe—that was left with the body? I wonder if that might be a clue to the murderer's identity?"

"Could be." Brother Ferro Comite helped himself to another brandy. "Accidents are one thing, but when a brother is murdered, we need to know who did it. We certainly don't want to be harbouring a traitor in our midst. The matter should be dealt with, swiftly and decisively, and as soon as possible."

Into the murmurs of approval from the others, Brother Fulget Virtus, thinking of comments heard elsewhere earlier in the week, said quietly, "I wonder, is it possible that none of the deaths are as accidental as they might seem? Of course, as you so rightly said, Brother—" he nodded in the Senior's direction "—there is, in reality, no such thing as coincidence. But it may go further than that. The death of Brother Nobilis Est Ira Leonis could be said to resemble another Major Trump, the Fool. And even our former Senior could be seen in the guise of the Hermit. Not only has he been a mentor to me and others in the Brotherhood, but his death itself, on a mountain, with a lamp, could be seen as significant, don't you think?"

The others, clearly struck by this interpretation of events, were silent. Finally, Brother Solem Fero removed his glasses and painstakingly wiped the lenses with a corner of his handkerchief. Settling them back on his thin beak of a nose, he said, "If you're right, there may be forces at work on other levels." He pronounced the last two words with a heavy, portentous air, gazing around him as though to see what effect it might have had.

"But why, for heaven's sake?" Brother Ferro Comite sounded impatient. "And if they were all murdered, why weren't tarot cards left with all the bodies?"

The new Senior, clearly recognising an opportunity to demonstrate his suitability for promotion, resolutely downed the last of his brandy and placed the glass back on the tray. "We must take steps, on all levels," he pronounced with authority, "to discover the answers to these questions. Once we know the truth, we can take appropriate action to restore balance and harmony. I propose, therefore, that we meet at the Temple tomorrow night, which, fortuitously enough, is the night of the full moon. I shall see that all is in order for a scrying. That should take care of the inner planes. Then we can decide what needs to be done on the outer."

CHAPTER ELEVEN

"The trouble is," said Isabel, "there are too many things happening at once. Every time we start following a trail, something else comes along that needs immediate attention, and by the time that's been dealt with, we've forgotten where we were up to on the original trail."

"Okay, Hawkeye," said Luke, "what do you suggest we do?"

Joss placed the last mug of coffee on the tray and carried it across to the table. Outside, a light but persistent drizzle drifted across the patio like smoke, but the big kitchen, where the four panellists, as well as Martin and Philip, had spent the morning going through Leo Hart's files, was warm. "I think," she said, "to continue the analogy, we've reached a point where we can't see the wood for the trees. What we need to do is make a list of all the points to be considered. Then we can discuss what we want to do about them."

"Good idea," Geraldine agreed. "That way we'll be able to see the pattern, if there is one." Joss reached down to where her bag leaned against the wall under the window. She took out a pen and a large jotter pad and began writing. "First," she said, "Leo Hart's files. File One – Business. No luck with finding out who made the paperweight. We'll need to decide what, if anything, we want to do about that. File Two – Personal. Very little in that, and certainly nothing helpful."

"Isn't that a bit odd," said Martin, "for someone supposedly keen on memorabilia?" He took another gingernut from the packet on the tray and dunked it in his coffee. "I mean, not even any old love letters—just a few theatre and art show programmes, and the papers for his motorbike."

"Well," Joss countered, "until fairly recently, it could have been quite tricky, legally, to have love letters from another man lying around—always assuming there ever were any, of course. And some people don't keep that sort of thing, anyway. Some people consider it soppy."

She looked pointedly at Martin, who grinned, and blew her a kiss. "Still," Joss continued, "I agree it does seem a bit odd. It's probably not significant, but I'll make a note of it as something we might want to pursue. Next, there's the photo album. Nothing of note there either."

"Well," said Isabel, "he'd hardly keep snapshots of his magical mates, would he? But there was that photo of him on his motorbike. We should at least recognise his helmet if we come across it."

"I can't really see what we can do about finding it," Joss said, "but it is a significant factor in all this, so I'll put it on the list."

"And the badge," said Philip, "what's happening about that?"

"Good point." Joss wrote it down in her neat, square writing. "Simon should get back to me early next week about the blood-test results. I assume he was able to get them done, otherwise I would have heard from him by now. I'll phone him on Monday, anyway." She made another note. "Then, once I get the badge back, we can get in touch with the president of the Triumph Riders. Ah." She wrote again. "We'll have to find out who that is."

"I can do that," Philip offered. "We've got a list of sports clubs at work somewhere. Jacko'll know where it is. I'll let you know first thing on Monday, so you can go and talk to the president."

"Thanks," Joss said, "but there's not much point talking to him until we've got the badge to show him. I'll make a note to ask Drawbridge about that, too."

Luke stood up and stretched his arms above his head. "I need a cigarette," he said. Patting his shirt pocket to make sure his cigarettes and lighter were there, he pulled on his jacket and started for the door, glancing dubiously out of the window.

"Use the back porch," Joss called after him. "Even I don't expect you to smoke soggy cigarettes. I'll make some more coffee while you're gone. I think we could all do with a break."

"Have you heard any more news of Declan?" Geraldine asked Isabel, as they all milled around the kitchen stretching arms and legs.

"I had another letter a week or so ago. He was bored out of his mind with being in hospital—said he'd even resorted to writing the report his boss had asked for, since there was nothing better to do. I deduced from that," she concluded drily, "that he was feeling better."

Geraldine laughed. "I'm glad. It must have been very worrying for you, especially being so far away and unable even to contact him." She glanced at Philip. "I don't think I could cope if it was me." Isabel said nothing to Geraldine about what she had also deduced, reading between the lines, of Declan's deep loneliness, and the doubts about his job which, during his enforced period of inactivity, had begun to surface more strongly. Neither did she mention her own distress at not being able to be there for him.

"I don't exactly have any choice," she said. "A plane fare is out of the question, and I can't phone him. Still, they should be letting him out soon."

"You make him sound like a caged animal," Philip said.

"If his letter was anything to go by, I'd say that's a pretty fair description."

Luke reappeared just then, and Joss refilled the coffee mugs and took them over to the table.

"What's next on the agenda?" asked Luke, hanging his damp jacket over the back of his chair.

"It's probably a good idea to consider any possible links between the three deaths," Isabel suggested. "We know already that Hart and McNaught were linked, if only through the Phoenix Bank. So why don't we assume, just for argument's sake, that there's also a link to Kleber, and see where we end up?"

"Okay," said Joss, writing furiously. "The way McNaught's body was tied up, and the tarot card left with it, both suggest the murderer has knowledge of the tarot."

"And," said Isabel, "that he may be using it to give some sort of message."

"Mmm. Who to, I wonder?" Joss wrote another note.

"That's a good point," Luke said. "If the murder, or at least the tarot aspect of it, was meant to tell someone something, that certainly suggests a link to at least one other person."

"Well," said Isabel, sipping her coffee thoughtfully, "we

already have reason to suspect Leo Hart had links to some sort of esoteric organisation—Rosicrucian if that paperweight is anything to go by—and we also know Doctor Kleber was an expert on the Rosicrucians. What if all of them, including the murderer, were involved in the same group?"

"Whatever that may be," said Luke, frowning. Suddenly, his brow cleared. "Hang on a minute!" He flicked back his hair, which, as usual, fell forward again immediately. "We're forgetting James."

"Of course!" exclaimed Joss. "The Phoenix Bank!"

Martin looked at Joss over his coffee mug. "Are you saying James is involved in all this?"

"Well, why not?"

"But," Martin objected, "there must be thousands of people who bank with the Phoenix. You can't say all of them are involved in some sort of magical murder plot. That's ridiculous."

Joss sighed. "Of course I'm not saying that. But you have to admit James has been acting very strangely of late, not least at the mention of the three deaths."

"That's true," Luke said. "In the case of Doctor Kleber, it was understandable. But, as far as we're aware, he doesn't even know the other two. So why get so touchy whenever we mention them?"

"Yes, and what about that strange advertisement he gave you to play?" said Geraldine, with a nod at Luke. "It was like some sort of weird coded message."

"Slow down a bit, I want to get all of this down. I have a feeling it may be important," Joss said. Then, "Okay. Can you remember what was in the message, Luke?"

"Not word for word, but wasn't it something about someone's light being extinguished if they misused the flame—or was it the fire? Oh, I can't remember," he broke off with a grimace of annoyance.

"Not to worry," Joss told him. "You can always check it up when you get home."

"Extinguishing someone's light sounds a bit ominous," said Philip. "Sounds like a threat to me."

"Mmm," Joss agreed, and wrote down, 'possible threat? From? To?' She scanned what she had written so far, then looked up at the others, flicking her fair hair back from her face. "We've got a definite link between Hart and McNaught—and James, come to that—though we don't yet know if it has any significance. And we have a postulated link between them and Kleber. I wonder what we can do to prove that one?"

"Break into his house?" Luke's face was carefully bland, his eyes widened in an expression of innocence.

"Oh, ha ha!"

"No, hang on a minute, Joss," said Martin. "That's not as daft as it sounds."

"Investigation is one thing," Joss told him scathingly, "but I draw the line at burglary."

"I don't mean literally. But it might be possible to get into his office at the university. That would be a start."

"Ye-es, but how? We can hardly just waltz in and say we want to look through Doctor Kleber's papers to see if he belonged to some esoteric society."

"True," Luke said, "but I did my philosophy degree there and, as far as I know, old Prof Hartigan is still Head of Department. Also, Doctor Kleber was a guest on the Psychic

103

Connection a year or so ago, remember? What if I told them we'd been working on a series or some such before his death, and he'd promised me some information, but he died before he could get it to me?"

"Do you think that'll work?" Joss sounded doubtful.

Luke shrugged. "Well, it can't do any harm, can it? Tomorrow's Monday. I'll call the Professor in the morning. I wonder if he'll remember me?"

"How could he possibly forget?" murmured Joss.

* * * *

Professor Hartigan was one of those people who, having reached a certain age, seem to stop the clock of their ageing. He was, perhaps, a little shorter than Luke remembered, though that might merely be due to the foreshortening effect on his perspective of his own advance in age from late teens to early thirties. The Philosophy Department looked smaller, too. The Professor, who must by now be in his late sixties, still had the same shock of dark hair sprinkled with grey, still the same promontory of a nose under piercing blue eyes, still the same rascally grin. And his voice retained, as doubtless it always would, the remains of an Ulster accent as he greeted Luke as though he were the prodigal son returned.

"Marriott, my dear boy! Grand to see you again after all this time! Come in, come in. And what are you doing with yourself these days?"

In the place of fatted calf, he poured coffee for them both from the coffee maker in his office. Luke told him, diffidently at first, but with increasing enthusiasm as Professor Hartigan showed a gratifying degree of interest, about the programme. From there it was but a short step to his real business at the university.

"Ah," said the Professor, shaking his shaggy head, "that was a bad business. And a great loss to the Department, I can tell you. It's not every day a University in this neck of the woods is able to acquire someone of Kleber's calibre. I can't imagine how we're going to replace him." He shook his head dolefully again. Then his eyes snapped open and focussed sharply on Luke. "However, you didn't come here to listen to me rambling on about university finances. The thing is, my boy, I'm afraid I can't really help you. I'd be more than happy for you to look at Richard's papers, but they aren't here any more. Someone from his lawyer's firm came soon after the accident and cleared everything out. Apparently there's a niece back in Germany who's his closest surviving relative, and they wanted to make an inventory of his estate to send to her. Besides, his office would have had to be cleared out sooner or later. The University can't afford to be turning it into a shrine, now can it?" He gave a short, ironic laugh.

The two of them chatted for a while longer, but eventually Professor Hartigan, with a glance at his watch, told Luke he had a lecture to give. Luke had been racking his brains for some time for a way round this latest setback. It wasn't until the Professor was gathering up his lecture notes that an idea came to him.

"I don't suppose you'd be able to give me Doctor Kleber's home address?"

"Not off-hand," the Professor said, "but I do remember the name of his law firm. How could I forget? Bentham and Locke." He gave a rumbling laugh.

"How, indeed," Luke agreed, sharing the joke. "Which one

is Doctor Kleber's?"

"Locke, I think, though I wouldn't swear to it. But I do know the name of the young man who collected his things. It was Longford-Brown—Peter Longford-Brown."

"Thank you." Luke shook the Professor's free hand. "You've been very helpful."

"Don't mention it, my dear boy. I've enjoyed chatting with you."

Thanking him once more, Luke pulled his cigarettes and lighter from his pocket and made his way back to the car park.

Half an hour later, he stepped out of the ancient lift into the vault-like reception area of Bentham and Locke, Barristers and Solicitors. Peter Longford-Brown was unavailable, but the receptionist, after consulting the computer on her desk, was able to confirm that Mr Locke was, indeed, taking care of Doctor Kleber's estate. He was free at the moment. Would Luke like to speak to him? Luke would.

Hamish Locke was fiftyish, his sandy hair just beginning to show flecks of silver-grey. He walked with a slight stoop, probably, thought Luke, from long years of manoeuvring himself through doorways no taller than he was without sustaining brain damage. He led Luke along a narrow, panelled corridor and into a panelled office cluttered with an antique wooden desk and a number of oak filing cabinets, all piled with boxes, and bundles of files tied with red tape.

Luke, ad-libbing frantically, explained that Doctor Kleber had phoned him only the day before he died, to let him know some historical material he had been preparing for him was ready. Unfortunately, before Luke had been able to pick it up the following Monday, Doctor Kleber had died. Naturally, he hadn't wanted to pursue the matter after that until a decent interval had elapsed. And now he had been told all Kleber's papers had been removed from his office by his lawyer.

Locke clicked his tongue sympathetically, peering around at the mess that was his office. "I know it's here somewhere," he muttered. Eventually, his gaze came to rest on one of the taped bundles on top of a filing cabinet. "Ah! I think this is the one." He pulled it down. A brief inspection confirmed his suspicions. "Yes, here we are. We would have brought his things here, but as you can see, we simply don't have room." Luke nodded, controlling the impatience that, as always, threatened to overcome him. Unfortunately, his usual strategy for dealing with it was not an option here. Apart from any other consideration, smoking in this environment would constitute a definite environmental hazard. He had no desire whatsoever to be responsible for razing the entire building to the ground, and himself with it, so he gritted his teeth and waited.

"It seems my colleague, Peter Longford-Brown, took them to Doctor Kleber's apartment."

"Perhaps I could look at them there," said Luke hopefully, "if you could give me the address?"

"I could, but it won't help you much. The apartments are managed by a firm of estate agents. Kleber's lease still has another three months to run, so in the meantime they're continuing to take care of things. Apart from the fact that his remaining family is in Germany, we don't anticipate any complications, so we're hoping to settle his affairs before the lease runs out. Now, if only you'd come last week, while Peter was still making an inventory, he could have helped you. But now, while the will is awaiting probate..." His voice trailed off as he gave a helpless shrug.

Luke said nothing, trying in vain to come up with another option. It was obvious that Locke, cautious as lawyers invariably were, had no intention of divulging the name of the estate agent. "How long is that likely to be?" he asked at last, though he knew from experience it could be months.

"Well, as I said before, we're hoping to settle his affairs within three months at the latest, and we don't, at this stage, anticipate any difficulties..." Again his voice trailed to nothing. Again he shrugged. In the resulting silence, Luke made up his mind.

"Thank you very much for your time," he said, and held out his hand.

Locke shook it. "I'm sorry I couldn't help you more," he said. "Would you like me to get in touch once we've received probate?"

Luke assented to this. It probably wouldn't do any good, but then it wasn't likely to do any harm either. His stomach told him it was nearing lunchtime. The antique wall-clock in the reception area confirmed this. Well, he could do with a break. Besides, he was going to need sustenance before tackling the problem of what to do next.

CHAPTER TWELVE

It took no more than a cigarette and a cup of coffee for Luke to realise Kleber's address would almost certainly be in the telephone book. Not surprisingly, there was only one Kleber listed, at Apartment 4, Carrington Court, 15 Carrington Crescent, Ilam, Christchurch. Well, Luke thought, that sounded about right. The university itself was in Ilam, so it made sense for him to live nearby. It was probably one of those up-market, modern apartment blocks that were nowadays scattered amongst the homes of the nouveau riche professionals in the outer—and newer—suburbs of the northwest. The sort of suburbs that Luke, whose forbears had practised law in the city virtually since its establishment, regarded with unconscious—and unwarranted, in view of his chosen lifestyle—snobbery as beyond the pale in every sense of the term.

Still, he could see how such an apartment would suit Doctor Kleber's lifestyle. It was close to his work, and doubtless offered a minimum of maintenance and a maximum of security. The problem was, how to track down his estate agents and persuade them to let him past that security. Short of simply phoning every one of them, however, nothing came to mind. And that was a job he didn't fancy tackling on his own.

Joss was at home when he called. "I see what you mean,"

she said with ready sympathy. "Probate can take months." Then, after a moment's thought, "Look, why don't I call Kleber's lawyer? I'll tell him I'm writing a feature article on Kleber for the paper, and I'd like to see his home, and any material relating to his life and work. It's amazing the places you can wangle your way into with a press card. And I may be able to avoid waiting for probate by pleading urgency. I'll tell him that since Kleber has no family here, I didn't know where else to go."

"Thanks a million, Joss. I knew I could count on you."

"Don't get too enthusiastic just yet. It may not work."

Just over an hour later, however, Joss phoned back to say the lawyer had agreed to her looking through Kleber's papers, provided the cousin in Germany, as his sole surviving relative, agreed. He would send a fax to her office in Hamburg, and get back to Joss when he received a reply.

* * * *

Joss had still not heard back from Kleber's lawyer two days later when Simon Drawbridge phoned with the frustrating news that the blood tests had revealed nothing helpful. The blood samples were the same blood group as Leo's, but since it was O positive, the commonest type of all, this information hardly constituted solid proof of anything. He had requested DNA testing, but it could be a month or more before these results were available. Even then, it all hinged on hospital records relating to an accident Leo had had three years ago, after which he had needed a blood transfusion. And it didn't seem likely they contained sufficient detail for a useful match. He was terribly sorry, but there really didn't seem to be anything more he could do at this stage.

Joss made sympathetic noises and explained that she, too, was waiting for further information. So perhaps in the meantime, if no one else needed it, she could have the badge back so she could pay a visit to the president of the Triumph Riders' Club. Drawbridge was only too happy to oblige. She could pick it up from his office next day, if that suited her.

The following morning, Joss collected the badge, now ensconced in a small, transparent plastic bag. From Simon's office by the river, she walked in the pale sunshine and sharp air of an early winter morning the few blocks to the sporting-goods shop where Philip worked. There was no hurry, she decided. The president most likely worked during the day, and she'd have to wait until evening to call him. She might as well take advantage of what might well be the last burst of autumn gold for the year. She bought a coffee at the cafe next door and sat at one of the outdoor tables where she could listen to the young man in the red and yellow Pied Piper outfit, who was wandering about nearby playing ethereal tunes on a bone flute. At this time in the morning, he was the only one of the usual melange of performers to have arrived at the mall, so he had the field to himself. Though, by the same token, his audience was correspondingly small. His brown felt hat lay on the ground, one or two coins glinting in its battered depths as he drifted between the little round gardens enclosed by wooden benches. He seemed oblivious, completely engrossed in his music.

As she listened, she ran through what they had learned so far. It was a very short list, and it contained nothing that would be likely to persuade the police to change their minds about Leo Hart's death, let alone Doctor Kleber's. If only they could find Hart's helmet. Though, even then, they had nothing more than Drawbridge's word for it that Leo never rode his bike without his helmet. Really, she thought, moodily stirring the remains of her coffee, if she had any sense she'd tell Simon Drawbridge she couldn't help him. It was probably the truth, anyway. Oh well, in for a penny, in for a pound. She swallowed the rest of her coffee and went to see Philip.

"Hi, Joss," Philip's dark, handsome face and ready smile greeted her. "I found that list for you. Come on out the back and I'll photocopy the page with the address you want." He led her through a narrow doorway into a cluttered room that seemed to serve as both office and tearoom. A young blonde woman in jeans and a t-shirt was poring over a pile of invoices, the computer in front of her displaying what looked like a mailing list.

As Philip and Joss entered, she looked up, a frown on her tanned face. "Do you know what this is supposed to mean, Phil? I can't make sense of it at all."

Philip looked at the offending document. "Nope," he told her with a shake of his head. "I can't make it out either. Must be a doctor. Just use the initial—the surname's clear enough. Have you seen that list of sports clubs? I thought I put it over here."

The girl, now busy with the computer, waved vaguely in the direction of a set of metal shelves bolted to one wall. "Sorry. I thought you'd just left it lying around. I put it back with the others."

Philip found the list and flicked through the pages. "Ah, here we are. Canterbury Triumph Riders Inc." He photocopied the page, then returned the list to its shelf.

"Thanks, Tracy, much obliged." Tracy waved vaguely again and began to scroll rapidly through the computer display.

* * * *

The home of Tony Stone, president of the Canterbury Triumph Riders, looked reassuringly ordinary—a cream wooden bungalow with an oiled paling fence, a neatly trimmed lawn, and a quantity of well-pruned shrubs amongst which roses seemed to predominate. A thoroughly respectable house, in fact, in a thoroughly respectable suburb. In the driveway stood a red van with several ladders on its roof rack.

Stone himself proved to be thoroughly respectable, also. He came to the green panelled door, thirtyish, solid and tanned, with short brown curly hair. He was wearing grubby blue overalls and socks. "Just got in from work," he apologised. "Last job took a bit longer than I expected. Come on through. Pauline'll make us a cup of tea while I get myself cleaned up."

He took her to a large kitchen-dining room with french doors leading to a concrete patio at the back of the house. The room looked as if it had once been two smaller rooms, presumably the kitchen and panelled dining room of a typical forties bungalow. The french doors had been added later, presumably to create more light, as well as access to the added patio. Beyond the patio stretched a long section with a large vegetable garden, a revolving clothesline, a child's blue plastic slide, and two small and battered tricycles lying on their sides among the neatly pruned fruit trees. There was no sign of any children, however.

By the time he returned, in jeans and a pale blue shirt, Pauline, a plump and cheerful woman, tanned like her husband, also in jeans and a shirt, had made a pot of tea and set a biscuit tin beside it on the Formica table. "Help yourselves," she said, pushing the tin towards them.

"Thanks, love." Tony took the mug of tea from his wife and turned to Joss. "I heard about Leo's accident, of course. We're all going to miss him. He was a great bloke—real good value. But how can I help you?"

"It's not so much me," Joss said, wondering how delicate she was going to need to be, "but Simon Drawbridge, his—um—friend."

"It's okay," Tony grinned. "We all knew about Leo. One or two members were a bit bothered at first, but not once they got to know him. What's Simon's problem?"

"Well, he doesn't think Leo's death was an accident, and he asked me to look into it for him." Briefly, she explained Drawbridge's concerns, adding, "I'm a reporter," in response to Tony's unspoken query.

Tony nodded, rubbing his face with one strong, weathered hand. "I must say, it doesn't sound like Leo to go riding along the edge of a cliff. Without his helmet, too. Man'd have to be a bloody fool. And Leo wasn't that. No way."

"If it wasn't an accident," asked Pauline, with a sharp glance at Joss, "then why aren't the police looking into it?"

"They seem to have made up their minds it was an accident and, really, there's nothing concrete to suggest it wasn't. Simon asked me to do a bit of investigating—because I'm a journalist, I suppose. Anyway, to cut a long story short, a couple of friends and I went up to Whitewash Head to have a look around. And we found this." She pulled the badge from her jacket pocket and placed it, in its plastic bag, on the table. "Simon said Leo had one like it, and he thought he probably got it via the club."

Tony picked up the packet. "Yeah, Leo had one of these. One of our members, Jeff Weatherby, sold us a bunch of them—about thirty, I think—at mate's rates. I don't know where he got them from, but he's a Pom, so maybe he has contacts in the UK. I know Leo bought one, because he didn't have any cash on him, and he wrote a cheque for three dollars fifty." He gave a short laugh, shrugged, and handed the package back to Joss.

"When was that?"

"Oh, not long ago. About a couple of months, I think. I can find out if you like. I'll have the docket in the club file."

"No, don't go to any trouble. I only wanted a rough idea. You've been very helpful. I won't keep you any longer." She turned to Pauline. "Thanks for the tea and biscuits."

At the front door, Tony said, "I hope Simon's wrong about Leo. He was a good bloke. It's hard to see why anyone would have it in for him. Unless it was because he was—well..."

"I don't think it was that. But look—" She pulled out her notepad and wrote down her work and home telephone numbers "—if you think of anything that seems as though it might be useful, do give me a call."

Tony took the page from her. "Yeah, okay, I'll do that. But I wouldn't hold your breath."

"I won't. Anyway, thanks for talking to me."

"No problem."

Joss wasn't so sure. If Simon was right, there was more to Leo's death than even he imagined. What it might be, however, was a mystery. So far all the vital pieces of the puzzle still seemed to be missing.

* * * *

"Oh, hi, Mum." Rachel poked her head round the bathroom door as Joss opened the front door. "You're back early."

"Mmm. We didn't have much to record today." Rachel's long, pale hair swung out as she nodded her head. Something about the expression on her face, something in those cornflower-blue eyes, so much like Joss's own, aroused in Joss a vague feeling of suspicion.

Before she could pursue it, however, Rachel said, "Someone phoned you earlier. I can't remember his name, but he left his phone number. It's on the pad there." She waved briefly in the direction of the hall table, and disappeared back into the bathroom.

For a second, Joss contemplated going to the bathroom to investigate. Then she saw the phone number. It was Hamish Locke, Kleber's lawyer. Locke had gone home for the day, his secretary informed Joss, but she relayed the message that a reply had arrived from Hamburg, and she could pick up the fax whenever she liked. She looked at her watch. Almost quarter to five. No time now—not if she was going to get dinner organised before work. On the other hand, she could always pick up some fish and chips on the way back from the lawyer's.

At that moment, both twins emerged from the bathroom. Rachel came first, then Kate, a towel wrapped, turban-like, about her head. The feeling of suspicion was no longer vague. They were definitely up to something.

As Joss strode towards them the twins retreated across

the hall to their bedrooms—actually one large room Martin had converted into two private spaces by means of folding doors. She reached the door before they were able to close it. Rachel had flung herself on her bed and was peering out through hands held over her eyes. She looked as though she couldn't decide whether to laugh or cry.

Kate was framed in the gap between the folding doors, her blue eyes wide with a mixture of guilt and rebellion. The towel slowly unravelled from around her head and her hair, long and straight like her sister's, fell damply to her shoulders. No longer were she and Rachel identical twins. Kate's hair was now a purplish black.

With a deep sigh, Joss resigned herself to the fact that the fax would have to wait, now, until tomorrow. No fish and chips, either. Gazing balefully at the twins, she said, "I'm going to get dinner on. Your father will be home any minute now. We'll discuss this then. Meanwhile, don't either of you move from this room." The twins, who recognised the steel behind their mother's quiet tone, did as they were told. Joss sighed again, and went to put the kettle on.

CHAPTER THIRTEEN

He had heard it all before. Heard it twice, in fact. But he forced himself to look as though he found it as interesting as the others obviously did. To be fair, it was interesting. Almost as fascinating as when he had first heard it. The trouble was, he had long ago passed the level these others were at. It was only politics that were holding him back. But he was dealing with all that. Had it all under control.

At first he had been frightened. Once he had had time to reflect, however, and to meditate on the matter, he had realised that was only because the first one was an accident, and took him by surprise. He kept his face carefully impassive as his mind went back to the scene. The screams had terrified him. He had not been expecting that. What had he expected, he wondered? Not the wave of fury that had washed over him. Not the strength it had given him, either. And certainly not the results. He recalled how he had crouched there afterwards, breathless and panting, utterly amazed at what he had done, those half-forgotten words from Tennyson running through his mind over and over like a mantra: 'He has the strength of ten because his heart is pure.' He had truly been in touch with his superconscious mind. How else could he have known in time to get out before the flames engulfed the hut?

The flames had been incredible. The sight of them had

lifted him to heights of ecstasy unlike anything he had felt before. Not even that other time—he must have been about fourteen then and, to this day, no one but he knew what had really happened. God, people were such fools! They lived their lives half-blind, half-dead, little more than zombies. But he had been granted the power to see—not, like them, as through a glass, darkly, but face to face. Only a glimpse, so far. But it was enough. Enough to show him the way.

So it was hardly surprising the second time had been so easy. At the time it had seemed like a lucky chance but, on reflection, he was convinced he had been guided. How, otherwise, had it happened that he had been in the right place at the right time? How, if not by guidance, had exactly the right words been uttered to produce in him that righteous anger that led to such superhuman strength?

The high had not been as good the second time, and this had puzzled him. Afterwards, he had gone home and purified himself, and prayed, asking for guidance, kneeling before the little altar at the end of his bed. It had taken time and concentration, and finally, at the prompting of his superconscious, the performance of a tantric ritual. He had never tried this before, because he had always assumed he would need a magical partner. But, just days before, he had read how it might be done. The result was amazing—beyond his wildest imaginings! As he had made the sacred offering to the High Ones, he had finally caught a glimpse—only a glimpse, but oh, how glorious it had been, radiating pure power!—of the One who was his Guide and Protector. And then he knew exactly what to do.

The next one had been planned to the last, tiniest detail, just as his Guide had told him. He would never have believed how much better it would be. The ecstasy was beyond anything he had ever known. Not even the sight of those flames had come near it. And this time, it had lasted for weeks. It was the reward given by his very own High One— reward for a job well done, and promise of what was in store if he obeyed instructions.

So he had listened, and he knew what to do now. And once it was all accomplished, he would go to his holy place and purify himself once more, and be granted the full companionship of his Holy Guardian Angel, for ever and ever, Amen.

"Brother Non Extinguar?" The reedy voice of Brother Solem Fero pierced his thoughts. It was an effort to quell the anger that rose up in him, but he succeeded in banishing it from both eyes and face, presenting a bland face as he looked up. "Perhaps," the class tutor said, "you could explain to the others the importance of a firm purpose to the practice of magic."

Oh, yes, he thought, I, of all people know that. He nodded and began to speak. But it was only words. His secret mind was occupied with real magic, because now he knew how to become a real magician.

When the class came to an end, the brothers left quickly. It was not the custom of the Brotherhood to waste time or energy in idle chatter, either before or after classes or rituals. The teaching insisted that energy be conserved for matters of genuine importance--spiritual matters. Brother Solem Fero lingered only to douse the candles on the altar, then he, too, filed down the stairs after them, carefully locking the door behind him. The tall, dark form of Brother Esto Sol Testis, the new Senior, passed him on the stairs. Another surge of anger almost took Brother Non Extinguar by surprise, followed, to his astonishment, by an overwhelming desire to laugh. He quelled them both, using the mind technique he had been taught. Such feelings must not be allowed free reign now, but their time would come.

He heard the Senior's voice. "Ah, thank you, Brother." There was the soft chink of metal as Brother Solem Fero handed over the keys. Then the Senior's deep, resonant voice again. "If I might have a moment of your time. I've been thinking since we last met about the deaths of our three brothers." Brother Non Extinguar had been about to step through the door at the foot of the stairs, and out into the cold, gloomy evening. But now he shrank back into the shadows behind the open door.

Brother Solem Fero had stopped on the little landing between the second floor, where the temple was, and the first, where a door led off to the storeroom where stock for the shop was kept. Brother Esto Sol Testis stood beside him, leaning against the storeroom door. He could see them both clearly in the dim light that shone through the skylight on the landing. But he was sure they could not see him. Was it chance or the prompting of his superconscious that had led him to wear dark clothes this evening?

No time for speculation, however. Brother Esto Sol Testis was speaking again. "In the light of what we discovered at the scrying, I'm becoming more and more convinced that all three met their deaths by the same hand."

There was the sound of an exhaled breath, and then Brother Solem Fero spoke. "I'm very much inclined to agree. Unfortunately, it's too soon to contact their departed spirits with any reliability, but the readings for all three had a very similar pattern. Do you think—murder?"

"Not necessarily, though I wouldn't rule it out. However, I was speaking earlier today with Brother Fulget Virtus. You'll remember he heard through that radio programme he's involved with that Brother Nobilis Est Ira Leonis was not wearing his motorcycle helmet when his body was found. And so far it appears no one else has seen it. The police are, as you know, convinced his death was an accident. But apparently that architect fellow he lived with thinks otherwise, and he believes the missing helmet is significant. He's asked that reporter woman on the radio panel to look into it. According to Brother Fulget Virtus, she and the others were up on Whitewash Head the other day snooping around."

"They haven't found the helmet." Brother Solem Fero might have been voicing a statement or a query.

"No, of course not. I don't think we'll have any problem there. But what does concern me is that they've apparently made a connection between the symbol on an ornament Brother Nobilis Est Ira Leonis gave the architect, and a group he told them our dear brother belonged to, the symbol being the Rosy Cross."

"But that isn't exclusive to us."

"No, but it was our version—the one with the flames."

Brother Non Extinguar heard a sharp intake of breath, but when Brother Solem Fero spoke, his voice was calm. "Is there anything we need do?"

"Not at this stage. There's nothing to connect us with the ornament, so I think the less said or done about that, the better. And I believe Brother Fulget Virtus is best placed to deal with the matter of the helmet, working, as he does, at the university. I'm expecting to hear from him again tomorrow in any case."

Brother Non Extinguar slid silently through the open door before the other two turned to descend the stairs. By the time they had reached the door and locked it securely, he was in his car and on his way. There was no time to lose.

Fortunately, traffic was light, and he reached the university with half an hour to spare. He parked his car in the visitors' car park closest to the buildings, and ran across the grass and through the courtyard beneath the closest lecture block. On the other side, he slowed and forced himself to walk. No sense drawing attention to himself. The trick was to remain invisible, not to stand out from the crowd. Or, in this case, the trickle of students wandering to or from their evening lectures. He glanced at his watch. He still had a good twenty minutes, and he had almost reached the library.

Just for a moment, he stopped walking and closed his eyes. It was all right. The feeling was still there, the sharp, fluttering energy coursing through him. If he didn't know better, he would probably mistake it for panic.

He opened his eyes again and walked up the steps and into the library foyer. He could feel his heart beating as he made his way past the pigeonholes where the students left their bags, and the pegs where they hung their coats. The peg he wanted was at the far end. Ah, there it was. Someone had hung a coat on it. He felt a momentary surge of—what was it? Fury? Panic? It didn't matter. That must be the helmet, that bulge under the green padded jacket.

Looking around, just to be sure he was alone, he lifted the jacket. It was the wrong helmet! But this was where he'd left it. He was sure of it. And it was inconceivable that Brother Fulget Virtus had got there before him. They had told him it was safe, and they would never lie to him. Not him. Never! It must be here somewhere. Someone must have moved it. Yes, that must be it.

Another swift glance told him the foyer was empty. He walked along the rows of pegs, lifting coats and jackets and bags. Then he looked into each of the pigeonholes. The helmet was not there. It was impossible, but it was gone.

Brother Non Extinguar found he was breathing very quickly, and his mind was beginning to fill with images. He must do something—now! But not that. No! He forced the images back into his subconscious, muttering the prayer he had devised, over and over under his breath. Gradually the images subsided, and he felt calm enough to walk back to his car.

In the car, he leaned over the steering wheel, his head on his hands, and sought guidance. It was not long before the answer came. The helmet had been there for over a fortnight now, and he hadn't thought to check on it for almost a week. Obviously one of the students had stolen it. He sent a prayer of thanks to his Holy Guardian Angel and drove home, his heart singing and his body pulsing with power.

CHAPTER FOURTEEN

"So what did you do in the end?" Isabel deftly foiled Dali's leap onto the bench with her left hand while pouring milk into her coffee with the other. With an air of injured dignity, the little black and white cat strolled to the doorway, sat down with his back to her and began to wash himself. Isabel took the two mugs of coffee across to the table.

"Thanks. Well, first of all," Joss said, "I put the vegetables on for tea. I doubt if we've ever eaten such well-scrubbed potatoes! By the time Martin arrived home I'd calmed down quite a bit. We left the girls to stew while we discussed it over a coffee. In the end I realised it wasn't so much the fact that Kate had dyed her hair as that she'd done it behind my back—well both of them did, really. God knows how long they imagined they'd be able to hide it from us. Anyway, we've put them both on slave duty for the next month."

"Oh dear!" chuckled Isabel. "I hope I never have the misfortune to cross you. Just as a matter of interest, would you have said yes if she'd asked you?"

"Good God, no!" With a look of horror, Joss gave exactly the answer Isabel had expected. Isabel refrained from the obvious comment, that that was doubtless precisely why Kate hadn't asked. "Oh, I know I'm hopelessly conservative," Joss added. "I'm sure you wouldn't have batted an eyelid. Anyway, what I came to tell you is, I've just been to Kleber's lawyer to pick up the fax from his cousin in Hamburg. She's had a look at the inventory they sent her, and she's more than happy for me to look through his things."

"Great! So when do we go? I take it it's okay for me to go too?"

"Technically, probably not. But I didn't get to be the hotshot journo I am today by observing technicalities. I'd better call Luke, as well. He'll never forgive me if I leave him out."

"I should think not, after all the hard work he put in ferreting out the original information."

"Hard work my foot! Prying and subterfuge are breath of life to Luke."

Isabel smiled, her eyes glinting with mischief. "I suppose that's how he got to be the prize-winning broadcaster he is today," she said sweetly.

"All right. Touché." Joss grinned back at her friend. She drank the last of her coffee and took both mugs and placed them in the sink. "Can I use your phone for a minute? If Luke's free, we can all go now. Oh, and I'd better phone the estate agent, too, and arrange to pick up the keys on our way."

"We'd better take my car then," Isabel called after her. "I don't want to end up with cramp."

An hour and a half later, Isabel pulled her station wagon in to the kerb beside a high concrete-block wall bearing a large number 15 in flowing wrought-iron italics. Behind it rose the matching terracotta walls of the four two-storey apartments that stretched the length of a narrow section a little less than halfway along the tree-lined, lawn-edged elegance of Carrington Crescent. "Right," she said, turning the ignition off, "let's go and see how the other half lives."

"I already know," Luke said, with a flick of his hair.

"You're not the other half," Joss retorted. "You're in a category all your own."

"Mmm." Luke smiled smugly at her. "Unique."

"They certainly broke the mould when they made you—fortunately."

"Are you two going to sit there all day bickering," said Isabel, "or are we going in to have a look at these famous papers?"

"Spoilsport," muttered Joss. But she and Luke climbed out of the car and allowed Isabel to lock it.

There was a long driveway to the left of the apartments. Along it were four garages, evenly spaced, and next to each a high wall above which could be seen the tops of bushes and clotheslines. "Those must be the back yards," Joss commented. "No way in there except through the garage." So instead, they walked along the paved pathway that ran like a narrow lane along the other side of the apartments. It was bordered on one side by a varied selection of youngish trees, and on the other by a long, high wall into which was set a wrought-iron gate for each apartment. As they passed each one, a glimpse was visible of a small wrought-iron balcony, garden furniture, shrubs and plants in terracotta pots, and, on one miniature lawn, a tiny white dog that rushed, yapping, to the gate as it saw them.

"Ooh, look at this!" Isabel had gone on ahead, and was standing outside the gate of the end apartment. As the others caught up with her, they saw that, instead of the plain wrought-iron gates of the other apartments, this one boasted a design of flames, leaping above a row of what might have been stylised roses.

"At a rough guess, I'd say we've come to the right place," Joss commented.

"It's pretty amazing, though, isn't it?" Luke was clearly impressed.

Joss nodded agreement. "I wonder if it's a Leo Hart original?"

"Come on," Isabel said, swinging the gate open briskly. "We're not here to admire the scenery. And before either of you say any more, no, it won't fit in the back of the station wagon."

The arched front door of the apartment opened onto a square entrance foyer with off-white plaster walls and a plush fawn carpet. A staircase rose from its right-hand side, and at the end stood a plainly styled, elegant little table holding a telephone and two directories. Two doors, both closed, led off the hallway.

Luke opened the door to his left. This revealed what was clearly intended to be a bedroom. Apart from a small settee upholstered in brown tweed fabric, however, it had been set up as a study, with a large wooden desk by the window, and built-in bookshelves lining one wall, every shelf crammed with books and magazines, all neatly stacked. A small filing cabinet stood beside the desk. On the desk was a computer along with a closed black briefcase and the usual array of office stationery.

"This could repay further investigation," Joss remarked.

"Let's check the rest of the place first, shall we?" Isabel was already halfway across the hallway. The door she opened led into a spacious, high-ceilinged living room with the same dark beams as the bedrooms. The room was long, the far end narrower, its plaster walls painted to match the rest of the apartment, and with the same luxurious carpet. At the far end of the room, a large window showed a small walled courtyard with two shrubs in large terracotta pots. In front of the window stood a round dining table with curved brass legs and a black glass top. At the near end of the room two fat armchairs and a couch, all covered in soft black leather, surrounded a low coffee table with the same curving brass legs and black glass as the dining table. Along one wall, an arrangement of black shelving contained a small television set and a quantity of expensive-looking stereo equipment. There were no ornaments, but several rows of compact and digital discs, both audio and video.

Luke immediately went to inspect these. "Hmm. Mostly classical by the look of it. Beethoven, Mozart, Bach. Nothing like supporting the home team. Hang on, though, what have we got here?" He had been scanning the backs of a row of DVDs. Now he pulled one out for closer inspection. "Look at this." He held it out to the others. On its back was a plain white peel-and-stick label. The writing, done with a black marker in a neat, old-fashioned hand, said, 2006 – AE, Walp, WS, SE, AH, SS.

Joss ran a hand through her hair with a puzzled look. "A home movie of some sort, by the look of it, or something Kleber copied from another source. I wonder what the abbreviations stand for? I'd love to have a look at it." She and Luke looked speculatively at the DVD, then at each other.

"We can't take it," said Isabel firmly. "Apart from anything else, the lawyer has an inventory. They'll know if anything goes missing, and they'll know it was us."

"True," said Luke, "but there's nothing to stop us having a

look at it while we're here. I'll set it up."

"While you're doing that," Joss said, "Isabel and I will have a look around."

The two women walked to the dining area. A wide archway on their left led to an ultra-modern kitchen, as scrupulously clean and tidy as the rest of the apartment. "I wonder where the bathroom is?" mused Isabel.

"Probably upstairs, with the bedrooms," Joss said. "And this is probably the laundry." The door she indicated led, as expected, to a laundry with a small toilet off it. At one end of the laundry, one door led to the garage, another to a small, paved back yard with a hideaway clothesline and very little else. Just then, they heard Luke's voice in the lounge saying, "That's odd."

They hurried back to where he was standing, remote control in hand, staring at a screen blank except for occasional flickers of white. As he heard them he looked round. "There's nothing on it," he told them. "I've run it through on fast forward, and it's completely blank."

"Perhaps he never got round to copying whatever it was he intended to put on it," Isabel suggested.

Luke shrugged. He turned the disc off and removed it from the machine.

Joss picked up the disc's cover and looked thoughtfully at the label. "I think I might just know what it was meant to be, though," she said. The others regarded her with interest as she pointed at the 'Walp' on the label. "It was this that made me realise. I think it's short for Walpurgisnacht, which is German for—"

"Beltaine," Isabel broke in. "May Day Eve. So the others must be..."

"Autumn equinox, winter solstice, spring equinox and so on," Joss resumed, pointing to the initials on the label. "I think it was supposed to be a DVD of seasonal rituals."

Luke took the cover back from her and slipped the disc into it. "None of which helps us at all," he said with a sigh, replacing it on its shelf.

They wandered back into the lounge again, all three of them beginning to feel disappointment. "Those must be the things from Kleber's office," said Isabel, pointing to a number of boxes of various sizes stacked neatly against the opposite wall. Above them hung a large painting—an impressive abstract in sombre blues and greys. Isabel stood looking at it, wishing Declan was there to enjoy it with her. Wishing Declan was there, full stop. Most of the time she managed to avoid dwelling on how much she missed him, but it was always there, lurking at the back of her mind, waiting to take her by surprise with a sudden stab of memory.

"I suppose we'd better get started then," Joss said. "By the look of that lot, we've got quite a job on our hands."

Isabel dismissed her feelings sternly, and turned to the task at hand.

However, since the boxes contained only books and papers relating to Kleber's university work, it took them less than an hour to determine they were no further ahead than when they began. Luke stood up, stretching his arms and rubbing his back. He reached into his pocket for his cigarettes.

"Not in here," Joss said. "We're lucky enough to be allowed here at all. You can't go smoking the place out."

Luke threw her a long-suffering look. "I'll wait for you

outside then," he said with a pointed sigh.

"I'm so glad I'm not a drug addict," Joss murmured after him.

Luke made a rude gesture behind his back as he left the room.

"Poor Luke. You really are rotten to him," said Isabel.

"We're friends," Joss said by way of explanation. "Come on. Let's have a look upstairs."

At the top of the stairs was a small landing with three doors leading from it. As expected, one of these proved to be the main bathroom, with another toilet off it. Isabel opened one of the other two doors. Looking in, they saw more off-white plaster walls and a high, sloping ceiling with dark-stained beams. A double bed with a plain dark wooden headboard stood against the far wall. Its two matching bedside cabinets each held a lamp with a heavy pottery base whose dark green abstract design echoed that of the heavy, unbleached cotton bedspread. The dressing table opposite was of the same rich-toned wood as the bed and cabinets. There was no other furniture, but a large built-in wardrobe occupied most of one wall.

Isabel opened its doors and peered inside. "Only clothes in here," she reported.

"Hmm." Joss stood looking around the room, a slight frown on her face. "I wonder where he kept his personal things—wallet and cheque book and so on."

"Wouldn't he have had them with him? I expect they got destroyed in the fire."

"I suppose so. But people usually keep old chequebooks and so on, at least for a while. I know I do."

"Mmm, me too. What about in here?" She strode to the

dressing table and began opening drawers. They contained only underclothes and toiletries. "So much for that theory."

"What about the bedside cabinets?" Joss opened the door and the small top drawer of the one closest to her. They were empty.

"Not his side of the bed, presumably," Isabel commented, pulling open the drawer of the other cabinet. "Aha! Look what I've found!" She held up a black plastic chequebook folder. She could tell by its feel that it was empty, but inside was a white business card. It displayed the logo of the Phoenix Banking Corporation and the name of Arthur McNaught. With a look of triumph, she pocketed the folder.

The second bedroom was much smaller, and completely empty apart from a single bed and a small dressing table that doubled as a bedside table. "Guest room," Joss surmised, opening and shutting drawers, "assuming he had guests. Nothing in these, anyway."

Isabel had opened the door of the wardrobe. It was also empty. "Let's go and have another look at the study," she said.

At the foot of the stairs, Luke met them.

"Feeling better now you've had your fix?" Joss asked with an exaggerated air of concern.

"Get knotted," Luke replied cheerfully. Then, with a nod towards the stairs, "Anything up there?"

"Only this," Isabel said, showing him the folder. "Let's go and check out the study." She had sensed the beginning of another round of the mock-venomous badinage Joss and Luke seemed to enjoy. Usually, she could either enjoy it with them or ignore it. Right now, however, she was not in the mood.

The desk drawers revealed nothing more interesting than further stationery and two boxes of unused computer discs. Joss fiddled with the clasp on the briefcase and managed to get it open. Inside were two copies of the quarterly magazine of what seemed to be a German philosophical society. Underneath these lay a large box of tissues, half-empty, and a number of letters, some in English, some in German.

Joss flicked through them. "There's nothing useful amongst the English ones," she said to Isabel. "They all seem to be business letters. I don't suppose you know any German?"

"Auf Wiedersehen," Isabel said.

"Ich liebe dich," added Luke.

"You're a great help! However, it's probably reasonable to assume they're to do with his work, and therefore not what we're after. Let's see what's in that filing cabinet."

"What about the computers?" said Luke. "I'll check them out and you look through the filing cabinet."

Joss was fiddling with the heavy wooden drawers. "Damn! They all seem to be locked."

She looked round at the others with a sigh of frustration.

"Never mind. Come and see what I've found." Luke had opened a laptop computer on a table by the window, and turned it on. He had found a plastic box of CDs, inserted one, and was now rapidly tapping keys. "I think this is what we want." The miniature screen showed what looked like a mailing list. The others crowded round to peer at the tiny print as Luke scrolled through the names and addresses.

"Are you sure it's the right one?" Isabel gazed doubtfully at the screen. "You've passed M and there's no sign of James."

"Mmm," Joss said. "And most of the others seem to be university people, judging from their titles."

Isabel had turned to the box and was flicking through the discs. She pulled one out and held it out to Luke. "How about this one?"

Luke looked at the label. On it was written in the same neat hand as the other DVD, 'BOF.' With a shrug, he switched discs. Immediately the screen displayed a heading, Brotherhood of the Flame, and underneath it a list of items:

1. Rules and History of the Order
2. Rituals and Observances
3. Membership List
4. Minutes of Meetings
5. Miscellaneous

"Bingo!" Luke cried, grasping Isabel's arm in excitement. "How did you know this was the one?"

Isabel shrugged. "I didn't, but it was the only one that didn't have its contents spelled out in full, so I figured it might be something he wanted kept secret."

"Good thinking, Sherlock." Luke grinned. "Now all I need to do is make a copy."

"There are some boxes of unused discs in here." Joss opened the desk drawer. "I wonder if they counted them for the inventory?"

"I doubt it," Luke replied, reaching across to extract one. "Besides, they might easily have made a mistake." He turned on Joss and Isabel one of his well-known innocent expressions.

"Besides," said Joss, emulating his expression, "our need is greater than some cousin's in Hamburg."

As Luke set about copying the disc, a fiddly business with

only one disc drive, the others made a rapid search of the rest of the room. The wardrobe, they discovered, was full of camping and sports equipment, including a pair of skis, but apart from what might be in the inaccessible filing cabinet, they found nothing else of interest.

"Right, that's done," announced Luke, pocketing the copied disc and closing up the computer.

"All we need to do now," Isabel said, "is find somewhere we can look through the thing."

Joss, who had been gazing thoughtfully out of the window, said, "We haven't checked the garage. We should do that before we go." They all trooped back through the apartment to the laundry. Joss unlocked the door to the garage and turned on the light. It was a spacious double garage but, apart from a can of engine oil, a large metal petrol can, a hand lawnmower and some gardening tools, it was empty.

"He certainly didn't go in for extraneous possessions," Luke remarked, gazing around.

"No," agreed Joss. "Everything in the place looks extremely expensive, but there isn't much of it."

"Maybe it was one of the rules of the order—the Brotherhood of the Flame," said Isabel.

"Maybe." Joss sounded doubtful. She locked the garage door and they made their way back to the front of the apartment. Joss closed and locked that door too, and they went back to Isabel's station wagon.

As they turned the corner out of Carrington Crescent, Luke pulled the disc from his pocket.

"I wonder where we can get a look at this?" he said, turning it over in his hands with a speculative look.

"We can do it at work," Joss said, glancing at her watch, "but not today. We'll just about have time to get the keys back to the estate agent's before they close. Then I'll have to get off home. I've got work this evening. And no," she added, laughing at the looks the others gave her, "while they're paying me, they expect me to work for *them*. You'll just have to be patient until tomorrow."

CHAPTER FIFTEEN

The following morning, as soon as the twins had left for school, Joss went to phone Isabel and Luke. She was about to pick up the receiver when the phone rang.

"I'm so glad I caught you," said a cultured male voice. "I would have called you last night, but I remembered you told me you work at night." It was Simon Drawbridge. Beneath the urbane sophistication, Joss discerned a note of suppressed excitement. "Something rather strange has happened," he continued. "Last night when I got home—it was quite late; I'm working to a rather important deadline at the moment—I found Leo's helmet."

Joss felt a tingle run up her spine and spread out into a prickling sensation across her scalp. At the same time she was aware of something significant that remained frustratingly just beyond the bounds of her psychic perception. She filed it mentally on her list of things to be dealt with later, and asked, "Where did you find it?"

"On the terrace by the front door. It was in a plastic supermarket bag."

"Ah. So we can eliminate the possibility that Leo had just mislaid it or left it somewhere?"

"I suppose it is remotely possible that a friend, or even one of the neighbours, found it and dropped it off." There was silence for a moment as Simon thought about this. Then he said, "I can ask around, if you like." His voice expressed his doubt of any real point to this course of action.

Intuitively, Joss was inclined to agree with him. However, since it seemed a pity to leave any possibility unexplored, she told Simon she thought this would be a good idea. His next words, though, left her rather more dubious.

"I was thinking perhaps I should take the helmet to the police. I've been careful not to touch it, because I thought there might be fingerprints on it—apart from Leo's, I mean."

"Perhaps," she suggested, hoping Simon would agree with her, "it might be best to check with your neighbours and so on first, in case something else comes to light. The fact that the helmet was left as it was means someone took it there. But it could be as simple as Leo leaving it at a friend's place and the friend finding it and bringing it back."

"You're right, of course," Simon said. "Shall I get in touch with you again, then, when I've made some enquiries?"

"Thank you. I'd appreciate that. In the meantime, I've been able to have a look at Kleber's papers and so on, and there's something I want to follow up today. So, with any luck, I'll have further information myself." Joss left her statement carefully neutral. No point in raising either of their hopes unnecessarily.

"Oh, well I'll let you get on then. I'll call you as soon as I can, though I doubt if it'll be today. I really must get some work done now." He gave a slight laugh.

"Of course. Thank you for letting me know about the helmet. I'll wait till I hear from you, then we can decide what we want to do next."

As Joss made her calls to Luke and Isabel, arranging to meet them later that morning, she was aware of something still nagging at the periphery of her mind. It was something important, she was certain of that, but she couldn't quite catch hold of it.

* * * *

"You sunlighting again?" Susie Powers paused en route to her cluttered office to push a strand of wiry hair off her face. "They won't pay you any more, you know."

"I don't doubt that for a minute," Joss grinned. "We've got something on disc we want to have a look at. It's unofficial at the moment but, with any luck, there'll be a humdinger of a story in it before long."

"Oh, well, in that case, be my guest." Susie's words trailed into silence behind her as she swept into her office and closed the door.

Joss took the disc from Luke and fed it into the computer. Seconds later, the three of them were clustered round the screen as it displayed once more the menu under the heading, Brotherhood of the Flame.

"What do you think we should look at first?" Joss looked up at the others.

"I'm extremely tempted," said Isabel, "by the rituals and observances. But I suspect the membership list will prove more to the point. And then, maybe the minutes of meetings."

Luke nodded agreement, so Joss clicked on the number 3 and began to scroll slowly through the list. Suddenly Luke pointed at the screen. "Take it back a bit, Joss. I think I saw something."

Joss scrolled back. "A bit further. There, look. I thought

so." The others looked to where he was pointing. They saw Leo Hart's name. "Let's have a look at the rest of them now."

Slowly, Joss scrolled through the list, and, in alphabetical order, they found the names and addresses of Richard Kleber, Arthur McNaught, and James Myerson. They also saw the names of several well-known local business and professional men.

"I think," Joss commented ruefully, "it might pay us to forget those others. But at least we've established a connection between the three deaths. Regardless of whether or not they died by accident, they all belonged to the Brotherhood of the Flame."

"Presumably," said Isabel, "some sort of magical organisation. I wonder what kind of magic they're into?"

Joss shrugged. "Most likely some derivative of the Golden Dawn. They usually are. Magicians on the whole seem to be remarkably unimaginative."

"I take it you've never read any of Aleister Crowley's books then," Isabel remarked.

"Yes, but I didn't mean that kind of imagination. I meant that, whatever they do, it's almost certain to be based on the Kabbalistic magic of the Golden Dawn, with maybe a bit of Enochian stuff thrown in if they've read Crowley."

"And Rosicrucian," Isabel said, "seeing their erstwhile leader wrote a book on it—not to mention that ornament Leo Hart gave to Simon Drawbridge."

"The Golden Dawn was Rosicrucian, to all intents and purposes," Joss said. "The main thing, though, is that we've now discovered another connection between the three deaths."

"We've also discovered why James has been acting so

141

strangely." Luke was grinning smugly.

"Mmm." Isabel sounded dubious. "I think it might be better if James didn't realise we know, though."

"Why?" Luke's crestfallen expression was almost comical.

"Because," Joss explained carefully, "appealing though the prospect might be, we're not trying to upset James's equilibrium, merely to help Simon Drawbridge find out more about his boyfriend's death."

"I suppose so." Luke did not seem entirely appeased.

"Besides," said Isabel, "some of the people on that list are pretty powerful, and they might not like the idea of a bunch of amateur detectives poking their noses into their secrets."

"True," said Joss. "Remember that enquiry into the Freemasons overseas? Some very nasty things started happening to people. I seem to remember one of them was found hanging dead under a bridge."

"Oh, for heaven's sake!" Luke's expression hovered somewhere between exasperation and amusement. "Don't tell me we're not even going to be able to look at their rituals."

Joss gave him a withering look. "Don't be daft! Of course we are. Just don't say anything to James, that's all."

"Minutes of meetings first, though," said Isabel. "If we're looking for possible reasons for Leo's death—or the others, come to that—I should think we're more likely to find them there. Groups like that have a tendency to form factions and, if this one runs true to form, there should be at least a hint of it in the record of meetings."

The minutes were, on the whole, brief, but they covered almost three years, and consequently would take some time to read in full.

"I've got plenty of time," Luke said, "how about you two?"

"I haven't," Isabel said with a glance at her watch. "It's almost two o'clock now. I've got a client at three, and I wouldn't mind a bite to eat before she arrives."

"I've got to go now, too," Joss said. "We can always come back again, though. Come down this evening, if you like. Come to think about it, why don't you come and do a printout of the whole thing? Then we can study it at our leisure. I'll be busy with other things, but I expect there'll be a spare computer somewhere if you can make yourself inconspicuous."

"That sounds like a challenge." Luke grinned. "How can I refuse? What time do you start work?"

"Seven. I'll meet you here then." Joss slipped the disc out of the computer and into her pocket. She turned to the others. "I almost forgot. I had a call from Simon Drawbridge this morning." She told them about the helmet.

Isabel groaned. "Another puzzle! This whole business is getting more and more like one of those ghastly metal things with all the interlinking bits that are dead easy to take apart and utterly impossible to put back together again. Every new piece of information just seems to add to the confusion."

Joss gave a sympathetic grimace. She stood up, shrugging on her jacket which she had draped over her chair.

As they were leaving, Luke said, "I've just thought how we might be able to solve one bit of the puzzle—Quincy."

Joss gave him a quizzical look. "I thought that was another name for tonsillitis."

"No, no," said Isabel, "that's quinsy. It's a fruit—small and sour, but supposedly good in a jam."

Struggling to curb his laughter, Luke leaned against his

car. "I grant you," he spluttered, "he can be a bit of a pain in the neck, and if the way he wiped my disc is any indication, I wouldn't want to rely on him if I were in a jam. But he's really quite sweet, once you get to know him."

"Aha!" exclaimed Joss. "Enlightenment dawns! You're talking about your new flatmate."

"The very same! Quincy McCarthy. He's supposed to be a pretty mean psychometrist, according to Thea Harrow, who introduced him to me, so why don't we put him to the test on Leo Hart's helmet, now it's turned up?"

"What a brilliant idea! You ask him and, if he agrees, I can ask Drawbridge when he gets back to me. He said he'd check with his neighbours in case any of them saw who left the helmet on his doorstep."

"I'll ask Quincy tonight when he gets home from work," said Luke. "I'll be able to let you know when I see you this evening."

"Great. Meanwhile, I'd better get you home, Isabel. Can't have you doing tarot readings on an empty stomach."

* * * *

Saturday morning in the Cherry household was rarely relaxed, and today was no exception. Kate, her hair still disconcertingly plum-coloured, was rummaging frantically in the bottom of the wardrobe. Her voice issued from its depths, raised in a wail of frustration. "Mum, I can't find my purple trainers!"

Joss, putting more bread in the toaster, raised her eyes in exasperation. "They're probably under your bed."

"They're not. I've already looked there. I bet Rachel's

taken them."

Joss silenced Rachel's impending reply with a look. "Don't be ridiculous," she called out to Kate. "If you can't find them, wear something else. If you want Dad to take you to Poppy's place, you'll have to be ready to go in ten minutes at the very most. So, unless you fancy carrying your bass on your bike, you'd better get a move on."

At that moment, the toast popped and the phone began to ring. As she raced to get the phone, Martin emerged from the bathroom. "Your toast's just popped," she said to him, and in the same breath, "Hello," into the receiver.

"Hi, Joss, it's Luke. I hope I didn't catch you at an awkward moment."

"No, no, just the usual Saturday morning mad house."

Luke laughed. "Oh, well, I won't keep you out of your element for long. I just wanted to let you know I've spoken to Quincy. He's happy to see what he can pick up from Leo Hart's helmet, only it'll have to be either today, during the day, or sometime tomorrow. He works most nights as well as during the day."

"Some people just don't know when to stop. What does he do?"

"He's a shipping clerk with an import-export firm, but he has an evening job as well. He's saving up to go to Ireland to visit his long lost relatives."

"Ah. Sort of Box and Cox."

"Well, no, more Jekyll and Hyde, really." There was a pause, as though Luke were deciding how best to express himself. "He's an exotic dancer. He's doing strip-o-grams at the moment. Don't laugh. It's a perfectly respectable profession!"

145

"I can't wait to meet him," Joss chuckled. "I'll phone Drawbridge, shall I, and see if I can arrange something for this afternoon?"

"That sounds good. Quincy should be up and about by then."

"Okay. As soon as I've got Martin and the twins off my hands, I'll give him a call. I'll call you back when I've got a definite time."

No sooner had Joss replaced the receiver than the phone began to ring again. This time it was for Martin.

"That was Mitch," he announced a few minutes later. "I hope you don't mind, but I said I'd go along this afternoon and help him supervise the kids who're setting up the science display for the school fair next week. It's not really my thing, but I dare say it'll be mainly a matter of making sure none of the little horrors gas or poison one another."

Joss exhaled a sharp sigh of resignation. It seemed forever since she and Martin had been able to spend an entire day in each other's company, much less a weekend. "No," she said, with a shake of her head. "That's okay. If things go according to plan I'll be out myself this afternoon." She explained what she and the others proposed to do.

"Sounds fascinating," said Martin. "You can tell me all about it this evening. Meanwhile, I suppose I'd better go and round those girls up or they'll never get to their practice." He kissed Joss then strode out to the hallway, where he could be heard mustering Kate and Rachel together with their instruments and herding them out to the car.

As silence fell on the house, Joss heaved another sigh. She made herself a large, strong coffee and went to phone Simon Drawbridge.

CHAPTER SIXTEEN

Joss led the way up the picturesque steps leading to Simon Drawbridge's house. Luke and Quincy followed her, Luke complaining about the unaccustomed exercise and trying vainly to keep his hair out of his eyes. From her position at the rear of the cortege, Isabel noticed Quincy was taking the ascent, literally, in his stride, moving with the lithe grace of a trained dancer. He was of no more than medium height, but somehow contrived to appear tall, perhaps due to the way he held himself. His body was muscular, but in a slim, wiry way rather than the overblown bulk of a body-builder. As he walked, his hair, which was dark and straight and would probably reach almost to his waist if released from the narrow black velvet ribbon that tied it back, swung heavily against his black leather jacket with each graceful stride.

Quincy McCarthy, as had been readily apparent when they had met him at Luke's place half an hour ago, possessed in full measure all the charm traditionally attributed to the Irish. In his late twenties, he was not exactly handsome. But with his strong features, pale olive skin, and large blue-grey eyes that somehow managed to convey both boyish enthusiasm and the promise of something considerably more manly, it was easy to see why he was in demand as an 'exotic dancer'. And, by all accounts, he was, though he was quick to add that he regarded it as merely a means to the end of visiting his relations in Ireland. Isabel had not been surprised to hear the family seat was near Blarney Castle.

Thinking of Ireland led inevitably to thoughts of Declan, still, as far as she knew, languishing in hospital in Brisbane. Though languishing, she mused, was hardly the right word. Straining at the leash would more adequately describe the tone of his latest letter, which had arrived two days ago. As usual, it was a very short letter. Obviously Declan's forbears had never been near Blarney! But, as always, the poet in his heart had filtered through. Somehow (he didn't say how), he had managed to acquire, golden and perfect, a leaf, which he had tucked into the letter, because, he had written, it looked like a heart.

They reached the top of the steps and the grey tiled terrace at the front of the house. "Oh, wow! Isn't that amazing!" exclaimed Quincy, taking in the entire seascape with an elegant sweep of his arm. "Wouldn't it be great to live up here?"

Luke, struggling to regain his breath, regarded him with a look of undisguised loathing.

"You shouldn't smoke. It's bad for your health," said Quincy primly, though with an ironic gleam in his eyes.

"So," observed Joss, as Luke made a lunge at Quincy, "is telling him about it."

Quincy, with a dramatic twirl, removed himself adroitly from Luke's immediate vicinity. Joss grinned at him and rang the doorbell. Simon appeared almost immediately, and ushered them through to a small courtyard at the rear of the house, where Joss performed the introductions.

"Make yourselves comfortable," said Simon, indicating a number of chairs that looked as though they had been fashioned out of driftwood and canvas sails. "I've made a pot of coffee, but I can make tea if you'd prefer it." Having ascertained that coffee would be fine, thank you, he disappeared back inside the house.

The seats proved surprisingly comfortable, and the sheltered terrace gave an uninterrupted view across hillside rooftops to the rocky shore with its sea wall and boat club marinas. It was as intimate as the view from the front of the house was vast and impersonal.

Simon reappeared with coffee and biscuits on a large tray. They sat in silence for a time, savouring their coffee and enjoying the view. Then Simon said to Joss, "In case you were wondering, I've done a bit of asking around about the helmet, and I'm afraid I'm none the wiser. It seems no one of Leo's circle of acquaintance brought the helmet here, and none of the neighbours seem to know anything about it either. Sorry."

Joss shrugged philosophically. "Oh, well, never mind. Let's hope Quincy can tell us something." Quincy, across the table from her, gave a smile she would have found devastating had she been fifteen years younger and not already met Martin.

"I hope so." Simon turned to Quincy. "Actually, I'm looking forward to seeing you in action, so to speak. I've never seen a psychometrist at work before—or any other kind of psychic, come to that."

"Well, you've plenty to choose from here." Luke put down his coffee cup and pulled out his cigarettes. "Apart from Quincy, Joss is a clairvoyant and Isabel reads tarot cards."

"And you?"

Luke gave a self-deprecating laugh and shook his head.

"I'm afraid I'm just the mechanic."

Joss noticed Drawbridge's puzzled look. "He's the technical wizard," she explained. "Without him at the controls, we wouldn't have a programme at all. Not to mention all the research he does."

"Well, I must say I'm full of admiration. I must admit I don't normally listen to your show, but Leo was a great fan. I think he knew someone on your panel."

"Mmm, that would be James," said Isabel. "They both belonged to the same—ah—organisation." She had realised as soon as she spoke that she might be divulging information best kept to themselves at present. The way Quincy pricked up his ears reinforced the feeling. Somehow, Quincy did not strike her as the discreet type and, even from their very brief acquaintance, it seemed clear his friends and associates were legion.

Fortunately, Joss realised what had happened and stepped smoothly into the breach. "Quincy, would you rather do your psychometry out here or inside?"

Quincy looked around him at the view. "I don't think it'll make any difference, and it's so beautiful out here."

Simon stood up, gathering cups onto the tray. "I'll just take this lot inside, then, and get the helmet."

A moment later he was back, carrying a yellow plastic bag. "I haven't touched it. Because of fingerprints, you know." He spoke to Quincy. "I dare say you'll need to, though."

"You're still planning to take it to the police then?" Joss asked.

Simon nodded. "I think I'll have to. I don't want to be accused of withholding evidence."

"I suppose not."

"It's not a problem," said Quincy, with another dazzling smile. "I can always put my hands on the inside of it, where it's padded. They couldn't take fingerprints there, anyway."

"Brilliant." Simon handed him the bag and Quincy carefully slid one hand inside the helmet and drew it out of the bag. It was white, with a transfer of a tiny red lion on the front. Quincy held it carefully with both hands inside it, balancing it lightly on his lap. He closed his eyes. As the others waited there was silence, apart from the occasional buzz of a bee amongst the last, fading flowers of autumn, and the faint murmur of the sea far below. The sea, under the windless grey of a cloudy sky, was like a sheet of grey-green plastic, slightly crumpled and apparently motionless. Everything seemed to be holding its breath.

At length, Quincy began to speak. "I'm by the sea, but it's not here. It's on top of a cliff. The grass is mostly brown, and there are rocks. Not big rocks, small ones sort of sticking up out of the ground. There's a man there, sitting on a motorbike—a big, black bike. I can't see his face, but he's got sort of spiky brown hair, and he's dressed in black leather, and he's just sitting there, looking out at the sea." Quincy was silent again.

Joss glanced at Simon. His pale eyes were wide with amazement.

Quincy gave a sudden gasp, as though in pain. "Oh, shit! It's all happening so fast!" He broke off, panting.

"It's all right. Just breathe slowly, then go on." Joss spoke to him calmly and quietly.

Quincy, his eyes still closed, did as she suggested. When he spoke again, it was in a quiet monotone, and using the past tense, as though he had deliberately stepped outside of what he was describing.

"This other guy arrived on foot, and began talking to the guy on the bike. I couldn't see him clearly, but he looked thin, not short, but not tall either. He suddenly got really angry, and pushed the guy on the bike. He sort of jumped off the bike, and it fell over. Then there was a fight. They were rolling around on the ground. I couldn't see it too clearly, because I was in it, but I could feel it. The grass was all dry and prickly, and the ground was hard."

Joss spoke quietly again. "Did you feel any emotion?"

"Anger... anger and confusion. I think the guy on the bike was confused. Then I felt a tremendous pain, here." He placed his hand on his head. "And then..." he paused for a moment, and seemed to be staring at something, though his eyes were still closed. "Now I'm looking over the edge of the cliff, and the guy and his bike are both lying at the bottom of the cliff. And I feel—this is weird—I feel this great surge of excitement, and sort of sick, too."

For a long moment, Quincy said nothing. There was a slight frown on his face, as though he were faced with some perplexing puzzle. "He doesn't know what to do with it. He's picked it up off the ground. He's going to throw it over the cliff. No, he's walking away with it. Now he's getting into a car with it." Quincy shook his head, still, apparently, perplexed.

"With what?" Joss asked for them all.

Quincy opened his eyes and stared at her like someone waking from a strange dream. "The helmet."

"Did you see what the car was like?"

"Not really. I got the impression it was small and light coloured, but I didn't really see it. Hang on, I think there's something else." He closed his eyes once more and sat quietly for a moment. "It's the helmet again," he said. "I can see it hanging on a peg. There's a whole row of them, with coats and bags and other helmets hanging on them. It looks like it might be a cloakroom. Something like that." Again he was silent, giving the impression of listening or watching for something. Then he shook his head and slowly opened his eyes. "That's all I can get."

With a huge sigh, he slid the helmet carefully back into the bag. For a few minutes he sat breathing deeply, holding the bag on his lap, then he handed it to Drawbridge with a smile. "Could I have a drink of water, please?"

"Of course." Drawbridge got to his feet. "Are you sure you wouldn't prefer tea or coffee?"

Quincy shook his head. "No thanks. I've found water helps the most."

Drawbridge nodded, his smooth hair glinting palely, and turned to the others. "Can I get you some more coffee?" They signalled their assent and Drawbridge went inside, taking the helmet with him.

Luke pulled a cigarette from the packet he had left on the table, lit it and drew deeply. "That was pretty damned impressive," he said to Quincy through a cloud of blue smoke. Quincy turned out his hands with a non-committal shrug, saying nothing. He looked drained.

The water seemed to revive him somewhat. As they drank their coffee, Simon said, "Thank you very much for that, Quincy. I really do appreciate your giving up your time to help me."

"I only hope I was some help."

"Oh, I think so. I'm convinced it was Leo you saw, and the

other man must be the one who killed him."

"It could still have been an accident, though," said Luke, playing devil's advocate. "There's nothing in what Quincy saw to suggest it was deliberate."

"Then why didn't whoever it was go to the police about it?" asked Joss. "If I'd killed someone accidentally, that's what I'd do. Wouldn't you?"

"Perhaps he was scared."

"Mmm, I suppose so." She turned to Quincy. "Pity you didn't see him more clearly," she said, adding hastily, "not that I mean to criticise. I know what it's like. You see what you see. It can be very frustrating at times."

"Don't I know it! But for what it's worth, the feeling I had was that the guy was really pleased to see Leo dead, even if he didn't mean to kill him."

Drawbridge had turned even paler than usual, and was sitting with his hand over his mouth, in an attempt to control his emotions. His eyes looked like two ink blots in the parchment of his face.

Joss, seeing this, said quickly, "I'm sorry. This must be very upsetting for you."

Visibly pulling himself together, Drawbridge said, "No, no. As I said when I first contacted you, I felt all along that Leo's death was not a simple accident. I'm quite sure of it now, and I'm really very pleased to know. It just takes a bit of coming to terms with, that's all."

"Of course," Joss said. "Look, would you rather we went? We've taken up quite a lot of your time, anyway."

Drawbridge passed a hand across his forehead, smoothing back his hair. He nodded. "I think perhaps I'd like some time alone. But thank you all again so much for your help."

They got up and Drawbridge led them back to the front of the house. He was about to open the front door when the doorbell rang, startling them all. Drawbridge opened it. A thin, middle-aged man in white shorts and a pale-blue collared t-shirt stood there, the breeze blowing off the sea ruffling what remained of his greying hair.

"Oh, hello, Chris," said Drawbridge. Chris looked hesitant, his gaze taking in the group standing behind Drawbridge.

Joss let her professional persona take over. "Thank you very much," she said briskly to Drawbridge. "Give me a call if anything else comes up."

"I will." Drawbridge smiled gratefully. "And thank you all again."

"Wonder who that was?" Luke was in grave danger of falling down the steps, craning his head to see what was happening. But Drawbridge and his visitor must have gone inside, for there was no sign of them.

When Joss arrived home, the house was still uncharacteristically quiet. Even Spock must have wandered outside somewhere. The sound of his snoring was conspicuous by its absence. There was a note from Rachel on the kitchen table, telling Joss she and Kate had gone for a drive with Poppy and her parents, and had been invited to stay the night. Would Joss please phone Poppy's place if this was not okay. Gleefully, Joss crumpled the note and tossed it in the kitchen tidy. Cheered at the thought of having Martin to herself for once, she put the kettle on, then began to rummage through the drawer where she kept her recipe books.

She was sipping coffee and flicking through the books looking for inspiration regarding half a kilo of steak that lay thawing on the bench, when the telephone rang. Downing a quick mouthful of coffee, she went to answer it.

"Oh, hello, Joss. Sorry to bother you again so soon, but there's something I thought you'd want to know." It was Simon Drawbridge. "The man who arrived just as you were leaving—Chris Allen—lives over the road. He was away yesterday when I was asking around about the helmet. But another neighbour mentioned it to him last night. Anyway, what I wanted to tell you is that he saw the man who delivered the helmet here."

Joss's heart gave a thump of excitement.

"Well," Drawbridge went on, "he only saw the back of him, but he was definitely carrying something in a yellow plastic bag."

"What did he look like—what your neighbour could see of him?"

"About medium height and build, straight dark hair, and he was wearing a dark suit."

Joss's heart sank. The description didn't really add anything significant to what they already knew. Drawbridge went on, "Chris did get a good look at his car, though. He noticed it because it was a BMW, almost brand new, and he's been thinking about buying one."

A tiny tremor of excitement seared through Joss. "What colour was it?"

"A light metallic grey, Chris said. And he thought the registration was G-H-eighteen-something. He didn't remember all of it, but he thought it was a short number, only two or three digits. The car wasn't there for long. Chris didn't actually see whoever it was leaving, but when he looked again, about fifteen minutes later, it was gone. I don't know if that's any help, but I thought you'd like to know."

"Yes. Thank you. I think it may have been very helpful indeed." Though helpful, she told herself, was perhaps not quite the word she was looking for. She needed time to think about it. "Can I get back to you? I don't want to say too much at the moment, in case I'm jumping to conclusions."

"Of course." A slight note of disappointment was just noticeable in Drawbridge's voice, but, courteous as ever, he merely said, "Just call me whenever you want to, at home or work. In the meantime, I've decided to take the helmet to the police, and the badge you found. I really wouldn't feel right if I didn't."

It was Joss's turn to stifle her disappointment and say, "Of course. I'd be interested to hear what they say."

Simon promised to let her know. Joss went back to the kitchen, her good intentions for dinner forgotten. Absent-mindedly, she gulped down her now cold coffee, then sat staring unseeingly out at the patio. The sense of something important nagging at the back of her mind grew stronger as she sat, resolving into a specific thought. But it was ridiculous.

When Martin arrived home over an hour later, she was still sitting there, staring at the darkening garden. At the touch of his hand on her shoulder, she looked up, startled.

Martin looked down at her solicitously. "Are you all right?"

Joss nodded, then shook her head as though to clear it of unwelcome thoughts. "It just doesn't make sense," she said.

"Would you like to tell me about it?" Martin pulled out a chair and sat down beside her, crossing his arms and leaning forward on them to look into her eyes with interested concern.

Briefly, Joss told him what Simon's neighbour had seen. "I'm damned if I know what to make of it," she concluded, shaking her head again, "but I'm ninety-nine point nine per cent certain it was James who took Leo Hart's helmet back to Drawbridge."

CHAPTER SEVENTEEN

"I thought you might like this." Luke handed Joss an oven dish covered with a flamboyant red and yellow tea towel.

Joss lifted the cloth slightly and peered under it. "Ooh, Luke, you darling! A quiche! Come on in. Isabel's already here."

As they entered the kitchen, Isabel was at the bench, pouring boiling water into three coffee mugs. Joss showed her the quiche, saying, "We may as well have our coffee first, though, then I'll pop this in the microwave."

"Luke, you truly are a marvel!" Isabel set a mug on the table in front of him. "I'm amazed someone hasn't snapped you up years ago and transformed you into a house-husband."

"Fat chance!" Luke grinned. "Anyway, I'm hell to live with. Just ask Philip. The first time an available woman crossed his path, he moved out. Talking of which, have he or Geraldine contacted you yet about his birthday party?"

"Not me." Joss shook her head as she tucked herself into a chair beside him. "Mind you, I haven't been here a lot lately."

"There was a message on my answer phone last night," Isabel said. "It's a couple of weeks away, on the solstice, isn't it?"

"More or less. Philip's birthday is the twenty-first of June but, seeing that's a Monday, they're having it on the Sunday night. It's not really a party, but a mid-winter dinner. Some work contact of Philip's has donated a chunk of venison, and they've invited half a dozen of us to share it. Geraldine's already made a plum pudding, and I've baked a fruitcake. I'm going over earlier to help them deck the halls with boughs of holly, and so on."

"I'll come and give you a hand in the afternoon, then," Joss said. "I have to work Sunday night, so I'll miss the dinner. What a pity. I could really do with a mid-winter rave-up."

"We'll save you some goodies," Luke promised.

"Oh, that reminds me." Joss got up to put the quiche in the microwave. An hour later, replete with soup and quiche, the three of them took mugs of coffee through to the lounge where the fire in the log-burner warmed the bleak afternoon, and large windows made the most of what little light was managing to filter through a dull grey blanket of cloud. Joss took a thick sheaf of papers from the built-in sideboard and placed it on the coffee table around which they drew their chairs. It was the printout of Richard Kleber's computer disc of the Brotherhood of the Flame.

"I had a look through the history and rules section," she said. "I thought it might save time. It's definitely based on Rosicrucian and Kabbalistic ideas. I'd say the Brotherhood itself was founded by Kleber, based on an organisation he was involved with in Germany. I don't remember the exact name off-hand, but it translates roughly as 'The Brothers of Light'."

"So it was another all-male outfit," said Isabel.

"Yes. I got the impression it had links with some obscure German branch of the Freemasons."

"That figures." Luke leaned back in his chair, crossing one leg over the other, and ran his hand through his hair. "I wonder what led him to set up a group here? I mean, surely he wouldn't just put an ad in the paper for the hell of it?"

"It has been known." Joss smiled. "Remember that ad that ran in the personal column for months a year or so ago, which the police thought was a cover for a pornography ring, but which turned out to be some bloke trying to start a Gardnerian witchcraft coven?"

"In other words, a pornography ring," Luke interjected, with a cynical look.

Joss laughed. "In Kleber's case, I think it was after he got to know James, and they discovered they had, shall we say, 'interests' in common."

"Yes." Luke leaned forward again, uncrossing his legs, and picked up his coffee mug. He took a mouthful, grimacing slightly. At home, he never drank anything but ground coffee, so the bitter aftertaste of the instant coffee gave offence to his taste buds. "They would. I seem to recall James mentioning he'd been a Mason. Probably still is, in fact."

"I didn't realise that," said Joss, "but I had wondered how he knew so many wealthy businessmen. One of them, a chiropractor called Trenberth, or something like that, was one of the founding members, along with James, and Kleber himself, and someone he referred to as the Colonel."

"Not Trenberth—Trenwith," said Isabel, who had been scanning through the printout. "Jonah Trenwith. His work address is listed here as The Hermes Centre for Holistic Healing. That's in High Street, isn't it?"

Luke nodded, placing his empty mug back on the coffee table, then leaned back once more. "It's down near the bottom end. There's a big health-food shop next to it. I think that's got a Greek name, too."

"That's right, it has," said Isabel. "'Demeter's Garden.' I've a feeling Dominic went to school with someone called Trenwith, too—Clive Trenwith I think it was, or maybe Clyde. It's an unusual surname, so maybe this chiropractor chap is his father."

Luke, who had been fidgeting uncomfortably for some minutes, conducting apparently unsuccessful experiments with body position, suddenly stood up. "I've got to have a cigarette," he declared. "Must be all this talk about health products."

"Withdrawal symptoms, more like," said Joss scathingly. "You go and have your fix, then. I'll make some more coffee, and then we'd better make a start on those minutes. All this history is fascinating, but I think Isabel was right. The most likely place to find out what we really want to know is in the record of meetings."

By mutual consent, they began with the most recent meetings of the Brotherhood. The Brotherhood of the Flame held its committee meetings once a month, on or about the date of the new moon. By cross referencing with the mailing list, they established that the committee, or the Brotherhood's equivalent to it, numbered seven, usually referred to as The Council of Seven, or simply The Seven. In order of rank these were: Richard Kleber, the leader, or Senior, of the group until his death; Jonah Trenwith, who succeeded him as Senior; Colonel Campbell Murdoch; Arthur McNaught; Sebastian Foorde; James Myerson; and Leo Hart.

"It says here—" Looking up from where she was leaning

over them, Isabel stabbed a finger at the notes that lay on her lap "—that according to their rules, they always have to have seven Senior Brothers." She flicked back her hair, which had tumbled forward, partially obscuring her view. "It seems they plan to appoint three new ones at the solstice."

"Does it say who?" Joss looked up from the notes she had been poring over.

Isabel shook her head. "Presumably they hadn't decided yet. They seemed to have enough trouble sorting out their new Senior. Listen to this." She read out a passage.

As she finished, Luke gave a snort of laughter. "Sounds like there was a bit of a power struggle going on between Trenwith and the Colonel, with the Colonel fancying himself as the natural successor to Kleber."

"Yes," said Joss. "I got the distinct impression it was a continuation of an earlier rivalry between Trenwith and Kleber, with James, as usual, trying to pour oil on troubled waters. You know what a wimp he is when there's any trouble."

"Which is why I find it hard to believe he's a murderer," Luke said, alluding to an argument he and Joss had had earlier, when she had recounted her telephone conversation with Simon.

"Especially," said Isabel with a grimace, "when you consider the ways they died. Even if we assume Kleber's death was an accident, it now seems likely that Leo's wasn't, if what Quincy saw was genuine. But can you honestly see James rolling around in the dirt in a scuffle?"

"I dare say, though," Joss countered, "that's what they said about Doctor Crippen."

"I never knew Crippen was given to scuffling in the dirt

with his victims," said Luke.

Isabel heaved a sigh. "In his case, it was drowning his wives in the bath, but you know perfectly well what I meant. Still, it does seem unlikely."

"What about McNaught, then?" Luke said after a pause. "He was found hanging upside down from a tree in his garden, trussed up like the Hanged Man, but surely it wouldn't be possible to have actually killed him like that. I mean, wouldn't he have had to hang by his neck or something?"

"Don't you read the papers?" said Joss. "He was stabbed in the back of the neck first, presumably severing his spinal cord, and then tied up and hung from the tree."

Isabel grimaced again. "Surely that proves my point. I can't see James even knowing how to do something like that, let alone doing it. Can you?"

"Well," Joss replied thoughtfully, "he might just have the anatomical knowledge, having studied psychology. But I have to agree with you, I can't see him actually doing it. He's far too squeamish."

"There's also the matter of why," Luke pointed out. He indicated the papers lying on Isabel's lap. "What about Colonel What's-his-name? He seemed to be the one opposing Trenwith and, if he's been in the army, he'd presumably know any amount of good ways to kill someone."

"Good point," said Joss. "And I don't imagine he'd be bothered by a bit of a scuffle, either."

"Nevertheless," Isabel said, "what little we have in the way of hard evidence all seems to point to James. He was the one who returned the helmet to Drawbridge, and if he hadn't been up there on the cliff with Leo, how would he have had it in his possession or, come to that, known it had any significance?"

"He'd have heard us talking," Luke said. "He knew Drawbridge had contacted Joss, and I imagine it wouldn't have taken him long to put two and two together. Anyway, I need a cigarette." He stood up and stretched. As he reached the hallway, the phone began to ring. Luke answered it, calling back, "Joss, it's Simon Drawbridge."

Ten minutes later when Luke returned, he found a fresh mug of coffee waiting for him, and the remains of a packet of shortbread biscuits. Isabel and Joss had already made heavy inroads into devouring them.

"What did Drawbridge want?" Luke asked, biting into a shortbread and savouring its buttery sweetness as it melted on his tongue.

"He took the helmet and badge to the police this morning and made a statement," Joss told him. "They're going to fingerprint them, but it seems they're still pretty dubious about his theory of foul play. Simon suggested we go and tell them what we know about the Brotherhood of the Flame."

"Do you think we should?"

Sipping her coffee, Joss thought about this. Finally, she set the mug down in front of her. "I don't see how we can, really. All we've got to go on is Isabel's theory of the deaths being based on tarot cards, Quincy's psychometry, and a few ideas about rivalry in some supposed magical brotherhood. They'd most likely laugh us off the premises."

Luke nodded. "Only the other day I heard a police representative on the radio stating quite categorically that the police had never had any success at all with psychics as sources of useful information."

"Yes," said Joss, "I heard that, too. Mind you, he was speaking at the annual convention of the Skeptics' Association, so it probably wasn't exactly an unbiased opinion. Still, I take your point. If we're going to approach the police we need solid evidence."

"We've got these," Isabel said quietly, pointing to the computer printout, "and a copy of the disc. Surely they constitute proof of something at least worth investigating."

"Mmm, but I still don't like it. For a start, how do we explain how we came by our copy of the disc? We're probably infringing intellectual property laws, not to mention just plain theft. Besides, one of the blokes on that membership list is a pretty high-ranking police officer. I think if we did mention our theories, we'd soon find cold water being poured on them from a great height."

"I think you're right," said Luke. "It seems to me we'll just have to go on making our own enquiries for the time being."

Joss nodded somewhat gloomily, and swallowed the remains of her coffee. "What a pity Declan isn't still here. At least he's one cop who'd listen to our theories without laughing at us." Realising suddenly what she had said, she turned to Isabel. "Oh, sorry, Isabel. That was really thoughtless of me."

Isabel gave a wistful smile and shrugged. "Obviously, I wish he was here, too. There's no point in trying to ignore the fact that I miss him, but I don't mind you mentioning him. I'm just waiting for the rest of your prophecy of the other week to come true. However, I agree it's probably not a good idea to go to the police just yet. But before we wrap this up for today, how about getting something down on paper—a summary of what we've come up with so far from these." She pointed once more to the notes. "I don't know about you two, but I'm starting to feel swamped by having all this information, and not knowing quite what to make of it. Maybe some sort of list will help us see things more clearly."

"Good idea." Joss went to the sideboard and took a notepad and pen from one of its drawers.

Twenty minutes later, with the help of Isabel and Luke, she had produced a neat list:

1. Power struggle, at least six months, between Trenwith and Kleber.

2. Trenwith – apparently supported by James and Foorde – becomes new Senior after Kleber's death.

3. Kleber – supported by McNaught and Colonel Murdoch. NB. Murdoch may have wanted to replace Kleber as Senior.

4. No indication which side Hart on. Assume neutral for now.

5. POSS SUSPECTS –

a. Murdoch – Prob ability, but no known motive for killing Hart, definitely none for killing Kleber, McNaught.

b. James – supported Trenwith, therefore prob opposed Kleber (and McNaught). (NB. Enough to want them dead?)

– Knowl of helmet suggests poss involvement with Hart's death, or knowl of it. (But what motive?)

Poss motive for getting rid of Kleber, McNaught.

Kleber. Where was James when Kleber died?

(NB. Upset at Kleber's death, poss not genuine.)

– McNaught. James poss. knows how to kill him, but would have needed help to hang him—eg. Trenwith?

c. Trenwith – Poss motive. Poss ruthless (i.e. Takeover bid).

NB. See if Dominic knows anything about him.

Joss handed it to the others. "We certainly need to find out more about this Trenwith character," she said. "He seems to have at least as much motive as James."

"More, really," Isabel said. "After all, he's ended up as their new leader, which is what he seems to have been after all along. Besides, if we have to suspect someone, I'd much rather it was him than James."

"Me, too." Joss stood up, flexing her arms and fingers. "You see if Dominic knows anything about Trenwith, then, and I'll see if I can find out any more about McNaught's death while I'm at work this evening. There might be something I've missed."

Luke got to his feet and peered dubiously out of the window at the glowering sky. He pulled on his padded ski jacket and zipped it up. "You know," he said ruminatively, "I haven't had a chance yet to let James know about Philip's birthday dinner."

Joss laughed. "He won't be able to go. That's when they'll be having their swearing-in for Trenwith, and whoever they choose to replace Hart and McNaught." She threw Luke a conspiratorial wink. "Still, by all means give him a call."

CHAPTER EIGHTEEN

Isabel drove her station wagon into the carport and turned off the ignition. As she got out, two dark forms came running to rub themselves round her legs. She bent to pat Madame George, her gargantuan tabby cat, and Dali, her small, slightly scruffy black and white companion, then went to unlock the front door, the cats trotting silently at her heels. Overhead, stars glittered like ice crystals in a sky faintly glowing with the reflections of city lights, and the grass, silvered with the first frost of winter, crunched beneath her boots.

The night felt doubly cold after an evening spent feasting with friends in the cosy farm cottage Philip and Geraldine rented at West Melton, just beyond the edge of the city. It had once housed farm labourers' families, in the days before larger farms had been divided up to provide farmlets—or 'lifestyle blocks' as the real-estate agents liked to call them—for wealthy professional people to play at farming.

Now it provided a home for Philip and Geraldine, and grazing for Geraldine's horse, while the actual farming, such as it was, was carried out by Geraldine's friend Penny, who lived with her stockbroker husband in the colonial-style red-brick house with which they had replaced the rundown old original farmhouse. It was an idyllic situation, thought Isabel, surrounded by grass and trees, with the Southern

Alps as a backdrop, and the nearest neighbours a mile down the road. Geraldine and Philip were clearly in their element there, stoking up the coal range and whipping up batches of scones for their guests. For herself though, Isabel suspected she'd miss the instant access to city amenities.

Still, she couldn't help wondering, yawning as she fumbled the key into the lock, whether she might have been wiser, after all, to at least have stayed with them overnight. She knew she would have been welcome, and she certainly didn't have to worry about Dominic—he was more than capable of looking after himself. Besides, now he and his band were finally getting gigs on a regular basis, he was coming to seem more and more like an occasional guest. But even as their antique clock had struck one and Geraldine and Philip had repeated their offer, she had known, with that utter certainty she had long since learned to obey, that she had to make the drive home. And following Orion the Hunter, standing on his head above the eastern horizon, his two dogs loping overhead at his heels, for some reason she kept thinking of the King of Swords.

As she opened the door, warm air wafted out to meet her, along with a faint aroma of some perfume she could not quite recognise. Dominic must have been home earlier with some of his friends. And, sure enough, as though to confirm her suspicion, there in the soft glow of the hall light was his message on the whiteboard above the hall table. She peered at it, trying to decipher the illegible scrawl. It couldn't possibly be what it looked like, surely: 'Well nut behave tonight'. With an exasperated shake of her head, Isabel turned her back on the cryptic communication. A glance at her watch told her it was just after half past one in the morning. Whatever it was Dominic had been trying to convey, it could wait. What she wanted now was a nice cup of tea, and then bed.

She was on her way to the kitchen, where the cats were hovering hopefully by their food bowls doing their usual skilled impressions of terminal starvation, when she noticed a dull orange glow through the half-open door of the lounge. Damn Dominic! He must have left the heater on again. No wonder the place was so warm. Isabel went into the lounge. Sure enough, the heater had been left on. She was just straightening up after switching it off when she heard a slight sound behind her. Instinctively, she froze. Then Madame George's solid form scudded across the floor at the edge of her vision. Breathing a sigh of relief, Isabel turned to leave the room.

But there it was again—a soft groaning sound this time. There was someone in the room. Slowly, she turned in the doorway, her eyes scanning the darkened room. On the dark bulk of the couch she could just make out a darker shape. As she looked, it moved slightly. Then a sleepy voice said, "Isabel? Is that you?"

Isabel flicked the light switch and there, rubbing his eyes and blinking in the sudden glare, was Declan. For a moment, Isabel just stood there staring. Then she flew to the couch. "Declan! What are you doing here?"

Declan hauled himself into something approximating a sitting position and ran his hand through his thick, curling hair, his mouth twitching up at one corner in a lopsided smile. "I thought you might be just a little bit pleased to see me."

"Don't be daft, of course I am!" Isabel's shining eyes

corroborated this. "But I wasn't expecting you. Why didn't you let me know, then I would have come home earlier?"

"I didn't know myself till this morning. I got out of hospital a couple of days ago, with strict orders to take it easy for the next month. After a month in hospital, you can imagine how I felt about that! I did try going in to work, but Voodoo took one look at me and told me I was no use to him in my condition, and besides, he wasn't going to be held responsible if anything went wrong, so he didn't want to see me again till I had permission from the doctor. Mind you—" Declan gave a rueful grin "—he was absolutely right. I was completely knackered, just climbing the stairs to my apartment. So there I was, to all intents and purposes under house arrest, without even a halfway decent book I hadn't already read. Then early this morning, lying in my lonely bed, I had this brilliant idea..." Declan's arm went around Isabel to pull her close. He grinned his crooked grin again. "I did try and call you—twice. I phoned from Brisbane before I left, but there was no answer. Then I called again from the airport this evening when I arrived. That would have been about seven. Dominic was here. He said you were out visiting someone, but he didn't think you'd be back too late. He took off himself not long after I got here—said to tell you he won't be back tonight."

Ah, thought Isabel, that explains the message.

Declan continued, "I hope you don't mind, but I helped myself to some food and a shower. Then I fell asleep. What time is it, anyway?" He winced slightly as he sat up to look at his watch.

"Oh, your leg!" exclaimed Isabel. "Does it hurt a lot?"

"Not all the time," Declan replied with a wry twitch of his

mouth. "Tell you what though..."

"Mmm?"

"I reckon it'll feel a whole lot better after you kiss me."

Isabel threw her arms around his neck and complied with his request. It was good to feel his arms around her and, even better than she had remembered, to feel his lips against hers, and to smell the warm scent of his skin. His face, Isabel noticed, seemed thinner, more lined, than she recalled. Her hand went up to stroke his cheek. "I'm so glad you're here!"

"Me too." His arms slid beneath her jacket to hold her closer.

At length, Isabel looked up at him. "It must be really late by now. Shall we go to bed?"

"That's the best offer I've had for months!" Declan pushed himself to his feet, wincing as he straightened his leg.

"Are you going to be all right?"

"Well, I reckon I might have blown my chance of making it to the tap-dancing finals this year."

Isabel laughed, and squeezed his arm. "Oh dear, you must be devastated!"

"Oh, I am. Still—" Declan put his arm around her waist and kissed her "—I might just manage to console myself, with your help."

Isabel looked at him. "Are you sure you can—I mean, won't it be...?" she stammered to a halt, looking down to hide her embarrassment.

Unexpectedly touched, as much by her confusion as her concern for his welfare, Declan kissed the top of her down-turned head and murmured, "We're both pretty resourceful. I'm sure we'll think of something."

From habit, Declan woke early. With its blue curtains closed, the room was like an underwater grotto in the half-light. For a while he floated in its depths, gradually surfacing to a realisation of where he was. He pushed himself up on one elbow and looked down at Isabel sleeping beside him. Her long red hair flowed around her head, covering her pillow, curling over one shoulder and the soft curve of her breast. The blue light dulled its colour to a muted bronze, at the same time giving her fair skin the soft gleam of moonlit snow. Suddenly, he wanted desperately to cry.

The feeling confused him. With an effort, he pushed it back down to whatever recess of his mind it had arisen from. It was not something he wanted to explore just now. He wasn't entirely sure he wanted to explore it at all, though he suspected he would have to before long. Very softly, so as not to wake Isabel, he slid out of bed, pulled on his jeans, and padded out to the kitchen.

When Isabel awoke, the first thing she saw was Declan standing by the bed. On the bedside table stood a tray containing the teapot and two mugs, and a large plate of hot toast.

"Hi, sweetheart, hope you're hungry." Declan sat down and leaned across to kiss her.

"I am. And thank you. I can't remember the last time I had breakfast in bed."

"Then it's been too long." He placed the tray between them on the bed, and poured tea into the mugs.

For a while they ate in silence. Declan moved the tray back to the bedside table. He pulled Isabel into his arms, and they lay together, holding one another and talking quietly. Declan felt the tears welling up again, and this time there was no stopping them. Isabel held him and stroked his hair, making small soothing noises, but saying nothing.

Then to his amazement, before he'd had time to think about it, he found himself telling her about his injury. "I was such an idiot! By sheer chance I happened to see the woman—Walters—trying to sneak out the back way, and I just ran down the driveway without thinking. It never occurred to me she might be armed, and it bloody well should have. It's not like I'm a beginner, for Christ's sake! I didn't even bother to get my own gun out. It was sheer luck I happened to knock her down, too, when I fell, and now they're talking about giving me a bloody commendation. I don't deserve it, Isabel! I'm no hero. The whole operation was a mess from start to finish. It wasn't planned properly. I didn't want to go, and neither did Joe. And now he's dead." Overcome, Declan buried his face for a moment in Isabel's shoulder, then all his doubts about his job, and his life in general, came pouring out.

Isabel said nothing. She guessed it was a very long time since he'd spoken like this to anyone, and she had no intention of doing anything to stem the flow. She stroked his forehead gently, smoothing back the thick, dark curls, feeling him gradually relax as fears, anger and anxieties welled out along with his tears.

At length, he looked at Isabel and smiled his crooked smile. "Sorry. I didn't mean to lay all that on you. I hope I didn't make too much of a fool of myself."

Isabel kissed him, saying, "You obviously needed to tell someone, and I'm glad it was me. Anyway," she added, her voice taking on a gently teasing note, "it's not so bad to be a fool sometimes. You never know what you might find at the bottom of the cliff once you take the plunge."

"Oh, Isabel!" Finding himself unable to say any more for fear of bursting into tears again, Declan pulled her close and hugged her very tightly.

Much later, they were sitting talking, Isabel leaning back against Declan while he idly made tiny braids in her hair, when the doorbell rang.

Declan stopped plaiting. "You expecting anyone?"

Isabel shook her head. "I'd better go and see who it is, though." She reached for her dressing gown and began to pull it on.

"Tell them to go away and come back later—like next week." Declan grinned up at her. Isabel turned in the doorway and blew him a kiss.

When she opened the door, Joss was standing there, a folded newspaper tucked under her arm. "What, not up yet? That's not like you. I rang earlier and left a message. Obviously you didn't get it."

"No." Isabel grinned sheepishly. "I, um, turned the volume down last night—well, this morning, really."

"Ah. I take it you had a good time at Philip's party, then?"

"Oh, yes, it was great. Look, come in. I'm sorry, I'm not really with it yet."

"It must have been quite a night. What on earth have you done to your hair?"

Isabel put her hand to her head, suddenly remembering the plaits. "Oh, um... Look, can you go and put the kettle on? I'd just like to have a quick shower."

Joss looked at her quizzically. "Do you want coffee or tea?"

"Um, coffee'll be fine, thanks. I won't be long." Isabel

disappeared into the bedroom.

"I guess it's time to get up, huh?" Declan grinned up at her.

Isabel nodded. "It's Joss. I think there might have been a new development in this thing we're working on."

"Sounds interesting."

"Mmm, it is. I'll tell you all about it when I've had my shower. D'you want me to leave the water on for you?"

"Thanks. Of course, we could save time and shower together."

"What on earth makes you think that would be quicker?" Isabel made it through the door just in time to avoid the pillow.

"Hello, Declan, this a surprise. It's good to see you again." Joss turned to Isabel. "I knew you were up to something. You looked—furtive."

"Me? Furtive? Surely not!" Isabel blushed slightly and pointed to the still folded paper. "Anyway, what's up?"

Joss spread the paper out in front of them. The lead headline, in large type, said, 'MUTILATED BODY FOUND IN ROSE GARDEN'. "It looks like another tarot murder," said Joss. "The news came through last night while I was at work. I didn't want to bother you while you were partying, so I rang first thing this morning, at which time you were obviously otherwise engaged." Isabel smiled. "Anyway, read the rest. It gets even stranger."

Isabel and Declan read:

The bizarrely mutilated body of a Christchurch businessman was found yesterday evening in the Rose Garden of the Botanic Gardens. Caretaker Roger

Popplewell found the body after hearing a noise while returning from locking the gates.

His investigation found no trace of any intruder, but the body of a middle-aged man, lying beneath the sundial draped in a black cloak and wearing a cardboard death mask. One hand and one foot had been completely severed and were lying near the body.

Also found near the body were a scythe, and a white rose taken from one of the bushes nearby. A tarot card was found on the face of the sundial weighted down with a stone.

Police have identified the body as that of Jonah Trenwith, well-known chiropractor and owner of the 'Demeter's Garden' chain of health shops.

A police spokesman said last night that the 'Magician' tarot card found with the body was identical to that found with the body of recent murder victim, bank manager Arthur McNaught. However, at this stage he would not say definitely that the two murders were committed by the same person. Both murders are currently under investigation.

Police would like to speak to anyone who was in or near the Rose Garden area of the Botanical Gardens between approximately six and eight pm yesterday.

"Jesus Christ!" exclaimed Declan. "Don't tell me you two are mixed up in this?"

Joss gave a wry smile and looked at Isabel. "I suppose we'd better fill him in."

Isabel nodded, and the two of them told him of their investigations so far.

As they finished, Declan emitted a long, whistling breath.

"Holy Mother of God! You don't really think James is responsible for this, do you?" He stabbed the paper with a forefinger. "From what I remember of him, I can't see it."

"Up till last night," said Joss, "based on what little evidence we've managed to dredge up, he did seem the most likely candidate. But now..." She broke off with an expressive shrug of her shoulders.

"If he did do it," said Isabel, "we can't have been right about the motive. This Jonah Trenwith character was the one James supported." She sat for a moment, thoughtfully twisting a damp strand of hair round her finger. "Anyway," she added, "there's one way we might be able to find out. With both murders, the tarot card left with the victim was the Magician, so it seems reasonable to assume whoever left them could have bought two decks of tarot cards recently. And, since there are only a few shops in Christchurch that sell tarot cards, it shouldn't take too long to check them out."

"He might already have owned more than one deck," Joss said. "You do."

"True, but not two identical ones. Besides, my guess is he'd most likely take cards from a deck he didn't want to use afterwards. I still think it's worth checking out. It would make things a lot easier, of course, if we could find out what deck we're dealing with, and whether the cards were new ones." She turned a beseeching gaze on Declan.

Laughing, Declan put his hands up, and shook his head. "Oh, no you don't! I'm way outside my jurisdiction here. Besides, I'm not allowed to do anything strenuous. Doctor's orders."

Isabel said nothing, but pursed her lips and continued her gaze, a gleam in her grey eyes.

"I wonder," said Joss, looking from Isabel to Declan with amusement, "why that doesn't sound a very convincing argument?"

"I really can't imagine," Declan said with an attempt at innocence.

Isabel grinned. "It's a terrible argument!"

"Quite right, dear. I really haven't got a leg to stand on—um—so to speak. But as it happens, I do have one or two contacts here from that Circle of Light business. God knows what sort of yarn I'm going to spin, but I can probably find out what kind of cards this bloke was using. That's if you really want to go on with this investigation."

"Of course we do!" said Isabel. "Why shouldn't we?"

Declan looked at her and sighed. "I thought you'd say that. I take it you realise you're probably dealing with a nutter?"

"I take it *you* realise you're not going to put us off by bombarding us with technical jargon," Isabel replied tartly.

Declan sighed again, but the look he gave Isabel was one of admiration. "I'll just go and make a phone call then." Looking back from the doorway, he added, "and I wouldn't say no to another coffee."

CHAPTER NINETEEN

"Right." Declan lowered himself into his chair and gratefully took the coffee Isabel had made him. His knee was beginning to throb, and he really ought to be resting it, not aiding and abetting some hair-brained, and possibly dangerous, amateur investigation. "I can go in and talk to this bloke—Constable Johnson..."

"The locksmith." Isabel smiled, remembering how he had opened Ferris's safe for Declan.

Declan laughed. "Yeah, right. Thing is, I can't see him till this afternoon—one o'clock, he said, when he gets back from lunch. By all accounts the station's fairly buzzing with talk about these murders. They've never had anything quite like them before."

"I can imagine!" said Joss. She ran her hand through her hair, shaking her head. Slowly, her fine, fair hair floated down to fall against her head like floss silk. She closed her eyes for a moment, thinking. "Since we're all here," she said at last, "perhaps we should have another look at what we've got so far. I brought this." She pulled the computer printout from her capacious leather bag. Joss's bag was famous—a home away from home, Luke called it.

Declan finished his coffee and put the mug down in front of him. "Look, don't you think you should leave this to the police? Christ knows what sort of madman you're dealing with. We already know he's capable of pre-meditated murder, and his technique is gruesome, to say the least. Don't you think he might get just a little bit resentful if someone starts coming between him and his crazy plans?"

"But we aren't planning to confront him directly," Isabel objected, a stubborn look on her face. "All we're trying to do is find out what his plans are. We're convinced the deaths of Doctor Kleber and Leo Hart are somehow tied in with the two murders. We just want to find enough evidence to take to the police, that's all. I can't see how that's going to put us in any danger."

Declan sighed. "Okay. As long as that's all you're doing, I guess I'd better tag along and keep an eye on you. I reckon you're going about it back to front, but. The first thing you need to look for is the motive. Once you've got that, you're halfway there."

"Mmm." Joss looked thoughtful. "We thought we had a motive. There seems to have been a rivalry building over several months between two factions among the leaders of the Brotherhood—the Council of Seven. It looked like one faction was getting rid of the other, and everything seemed to point to James as the murderer, though we found it as hard as you did to see him as a killer."

"He could have hired someone," Declan suggested.

"I hadn't thought of that. But in any case, since the latest victim is the leader of the faction James supported, I think that fairly much puts paid to rivalry as a motive."

"Do they really take their mumbo-jumbo that seriously?" asked Declan. His expression made it clear he found it difficult to credit.

"Who knows?" Joss shrugged. "Though I would have

expected them to use some sort of magic against one another, rather than plain old-fashioned murder."

Isabel nodded. "You seem to think the murderer is insane," she said to Declan, "so maybe we should be looking for an insane motive—something illogical."

"Insane people don't necessarily lack logic," Joss pointed out. "It's just their own kind of logic, based on their own set of rules."

"Bloody hell!" exclaimed Isabel. "That could be anything!"

"So," said Declan, "we look for a pattern, any pattern."

"Well, there's the tarot cards," said Isabel, "though they only apply to the last two deaths. We need something that applies to all of them, otherwise the first two still look like accidents."

"Oh, I don't know," said Joss, an edge of frustration in her voice, "maybe we've been wrong all along. Maybe the first two were accidents. Maybe they're completely unconnected with the murders."

"They were all members of this Brotherhood, but," Declan said.

"Senior members at that," said Isabel, "members of the ruling junta."

Declan pushed a hand through his hair. "I guess that means they made all the decisions, then?"

Joss nodded. "That sort of group is invariably pretty hierarchical and autocratic. I don't see why the Brotherhood would be any different."

"So, there'd be plenty of scope for resentment in the lower ranks?"

"I suppose so, though I don't remember any mention of it in the minutes."

"There wouldn't be," said Isabel, "at least, not necessarily. The row between the senior brothers was there, because inevitably a large part of it was carried out through their meetings. But if the group is as hierarchical as we're assuming, there might not actually be any official way for anyone in the lower echelons to air grievances. So, as far as the Council was concerned, they wouldn't exist, unless they got to a point where they had to be dealt with at Council level."

"Good thinking," said Joss. "Though it does mean we probably won't discover anything helpful by going through these again." She tapped the sheaf of papers on the table.

"No." Reluctantly, Isabel agreed. "The frustrating thing is, there may well be a full record of the group's activities somewhere—some sort of equivalent to the Book of Lights and Shadows kept by witchcraft covens, quite possibly written by hand." She turned to Declan to explain, "Traditionally, they're supposed to be. Unfortunately, we're never likely to set eyes on it. Since we've no way of knowing whose job it is to write it, we wouldn't even know where to start looking."

"But aren't those kinds of records kept by individuals, rather than for the group as a whole?" Joss asked.

"Both, I should think."

"I'd love to see James's." Joss grinned.

"Fat chance! Anyway, none of this is any help to us. Our best bet for now is to check out these tarot shops." She glanced up at the wall clock. "It's just after twelve, so I don't suppose we've got time to have lunch first."

"God, is that the time?" exclaimed Joss, jumping to her feet. "I've got to interview someone in twenty minutes. I'm afraid you'll have to hunt tarot decks without me." She picked up the computer printout. "But come over later, if you like, and tell me how you got on."

"Okay." Isabel nodded. "See you later." She turned to Declan. "You hungry?"

Declan, who for some time had been trying unsuccessfully to ignore the pain in his knee, said, "Tell you what. I've got some pills in my bag for this wretched knee. If you'd like to get them for me, I'll shout you lunch in town after I've spoken to Johnson. We can go to that cafe in the Arts Centre, where we went before. How does that sound?" Isabel was already halfway to the bedroom.

There was a cheerful fire in the great stone fireplace of the cafe, and Declan had found them a seat beside it. The pain in his knee had all but gone now, though the medication had made him slightly drowsy. He watched Isabel walking towards him, gracefully picking her way through the crowded tables. She was wearing a long straight skirt of scarlet wool, and her black boots. A red tartan scarf peeped out from the collar of her dark green jacket, which was made of some soft, heavy woollen material that swayed about her as she moved. Above it, her hair moved in counter-rhythm around her face, falling forward as she bent to place the tray on the table and enveloping him in her sandalwood perfume.

Isabel sat down and removed her coat and scarf. The gold geometric brooch on her black top pointed like an arrow to the pale skin revealed by its V-shaped neckline—as if he needed reminding! It was all too much for Declan. "How do you expect me to concentrate on eating, with you looking like that?" he said.

Isabel glanced down at herself, puzzled. "Like what?"

Declan laughed. "Isabel, you are wonderful! If I promise to be good and eat up all my lunch, can we go somewhere nice and quiet and...?"

"Declan!" Isabel tried to look stern, but a smile curved her lips as she poured milk into her coffee and stirred it. "Anyway," she said at last, "now we know both of the Magician cards were from the Waite deck, and that they were both brand new, we have to see if we can find out who bought them. What did you tell Constable Johnson, by the way?"

Declan rubbed his temple with one forefinger. His mouth twitched up at one side. "Well, since I'm in town for a few weeks, I just dropped in to say hello. I was surprised, naturally, to hear about the tarot murders—that's what they're calling them, by the way. Then Johnson remembered I'd been mixed up with a bunch of people from that Psychic Connection radio programme when I was here before. Next thing I knew, he was wondering if they'd be able to shed any light on the case. So I said I'd see what I could find out, and get back to him." He looked at Isabel over his coffee cup, his face expressionless.

"I trust he was suitably grateful?"

Declan's face creased into a grin. "Tell you what he did say that was interesting. The latest victim, the bloke who was found in the Rose Garden—"

"Jonah Trenwith?"

"Yeah. Johnson said he was stabbed in the back of the neck, same as the other one."

"So our murderer has a knife, and knows how to use it. Isn't that a slightly unusual method for a premeditated murder?"

Declan shrugged, and swallowed the piece of blueberry muffin he had been chewing. "I guess so but, on the other hand, most city people don't own a gun, much less know how to use one. Generally, people use what they're familiar with, or whatever they've got to hand."

"If the murderer is part of the Brotherhood," Isabel said thoughtfully, "and we're pretty sure he is, then he might well own a knife, for ritual purposes. Bob Ferris did, remember?"

Declan nodded, grimacing. He remembered all too well.

"At the very least, he'd be aware of the concept, so I suppose that's what he'd think of using."

"He must know a bit about anatomy, too," Declan said.

"What do you mean?"

"Well, if you were planning to stab someone, what's the first place you'd think of?"

Isabel thought for a minute. "The heart, I suppose."

"Yeah, so would most people, because they know that's what keeps you alive. But it's not really the best place to stab someone. For a start, it's messy. The heart's nothing but a blood pump, after all, and a fairly well protected one at that. Unless you know exactly what you're doing, there's always the risk of hitting a rib by mistake. And the victim can see you coming. But if you stab someone in the back of the neck, you're attacking from behind, so you can take them by surprise. And you can sever the spinal cord, which means instant death. It doesn't bleed much, either, and the wound isn't too obvious. If you put the knife in just above the hairline, it can't be seen at all, without a search."

Isabel had been looking at him with a slight frown, indicating by minute movements of her head and eyes an elderly couple sitting at the next table. Following her movements with his eyes, Declan saw that they were staring at him with expressions of mounting horror.

"I think we'd better leave," said Isabel in a strangled whisper.

Declan managed to keep his face straight long enough to pay the bill and get outside, where they both collapsed against one another in gales of laughter. "How many shops have we got to go to?" he said at last, wiping his eyes with his sleeve.

"Three. Two of them, New Directions and The Aquarius Bookshop, are only a couple of blocks from here, so we may as well go to them first. The other one, Vision Quest, is on the other side of town." Isabel glanced at Declan's knee. "We can take the car if you like."

"Let's check out the two nearest ones first. We may not even need to go to this Vision Quest." Declan took Isabel's arm and tucked it under his. As they walked he said, "Where on earth do they dig up these fancy names?"

Isabel shrugged, "New Age people are nothing if not imaginative. How else could they believe some of the things they do? New Directions and Aquarius are fairly self-explanatory, I suppose, but I imagine Vision Quest comes from a ceremony some of the Native Americans had. It was part of the puberty rites for their young men, I think, where they'd fast and go out on their own to seek a vision to guide them in their adult life. Some of them used sacred drugs as well, then when they came back, the shaman would interpret the vision for them, and reveal their personal totem and their secret name."

"You're a real mine of esoteric trivia, aren't you?" Declan

said with a grin.

"Well, you did ask."

Declan detected a defensive note in her voice. He kissed her on the cheek and said softly, "Don't be upset. I never did go for brainless bimbos."

"Is that what you had before?"

Declan gave a snort of laughter. "No, far from it. But I reckon I didn't appreciate what I had before. I've learnt a lot since then." He leaned closer to murmur in Isabel's ear, "And I definitely appreciate what I've got now." By the time Isabel had regained her composure, they were standing outside the wide glass frontage of The New Directions Bookshop.

CHAPTER TWENTY

The New Directions Bookshop was large and modern. Rows of shelves set at angles to one another held books on subjects as diverse as Astronomy, Alchemy, and Art. A row of smaller shelves held a diversity of greeting cards, some handmade, some displaying art prints. Next to these were calendars with themes ranging from Mediaeval and Renaissance paintings to garish science fiction fantasies. Opposite the long, curving counter, there was a tall glass display case in which rested numerous decks of tarot cards, several types of rune-stones, and a small crystal ball. Isabel looked, as she always did, to see if there were any new additions to the large and seemingly ever-increasing range of tarot cards available. When she had first become interested, there was a choice of three decks: the Ryder-Waite; the BOTA, or Builders of the Adytum, a Kabbalistic group along the lines of the Order of the Golden Dawn; and a so-called Tarot of the Egyptians. Now, some thirty years later, the discerning buyer could choose from a bewildering range of mythologies and New Age symbolism. For herself, she preferred the Kabbalistic symbolism she had learnt from, and long ago internalised.

"Can I help you?" At her elbow stood a thin, pale young man wearing square, gold-rimmed glasses, a ponytail of sleek black hair, and a hopeful smile.

Isabel looked helplessly at Declan. They hadn't decided on

a campaign plan, and it now dawned on her with some force that they had no convincing reason for asking questions about the shop's customers.

Declan, however, rose to the occasion. "I wonder if we could speak to the manager," he said quietly, glancing meaningfully towards the open door behind the counter, through which he could see what looked like an office.

"Um..." The young man looked in the same direction, then back at Declan. "He's not here at the moment, but if it's an enquiry...?" His thin young face took on a professional determination.

With an ironic twitch of his mouth, Declan fished into his jacket pocket and drew out his police badge. He allowed the young man a glimpse sufficient to divulge its general nature, but not to give the game away completely. Within seconds, they were seated in the office. The young man, having assured them the manager would be back directly, scurried back to fiddling with the computer on the counter.

The office was just large enough to contain a small desk, a chair, and two stools, a small filing cabinet, and a wall full of shelves. On these an apparently haphazard selection of books and boxes stood, sprawled, or lay supine. Further piles of books vied for space on the desk with a computer and a pile of dockets on a spike. The top of the filing cabinet apparently did double duty as a coffee bar. It was all in stark contrast to the tasteful arrangement of the shop itself.

"Just as well you had your badge," Isabel said to Declan. "I couldn't think of anything to say that would have sounded convincing."

"Never leave home without it." Declan grinned. "I reckon it's accepted in far more places than American Express."

At that moment a large, amorphous form darkened the narrow office doorway, and a deep, rolling voice rumbled like distant thunder, "Marcus Trotter. How can I help?" They looked up to see a balding, red-faced giant who, in vast jeans, with an open-necked plaid shirt stretched across his paunch, looked more like a professional wrestler than the proprietor of a New Age bookshop.

To Isabel's relief, Declan took charge, again allowing a brief glimpse of his badge. "Detective Sergeant Kelly," he said, holding out his hand, "and this is my assistant, Detective Constable Sinclair." Isabel gulped, and nodded at Marcus Trotter in what she fervently hoped was an official-looking manner. Declan continued, "We're trying to trace someone we believe recently bought two identical decks of tarot cards, and we need to determine where they were bought, and by whom."

"Ah," rumbled Trotter. "The tarot murders. Thought someone would be in here sooner or later. I don't suppose you happen to know what sort of deck we're dealing with?"

"Yes," Isabel said, "the Ryder-Waite deck."

Trotter scratched at his beard, which, like his fast-vanishing hair, had probably once been a sandy blond. Both were now liberally sprinkled with silver. "Let's see." He seated himself at the desk and turned on the computer, rapidly tapping keys until he found the display he wanted. He turned and looked up at them, blinking his pale, greenish eyes. "What sort of date are we looking at?"

Declan looked at Isabel and raised his eyebrows in a query. Isabel made a rapid mental scan of recent events. "Probably late May or early June," she said, "possibly a little earlier."

Trotter scrolled through the computer display, his huge hands surprisingly agile on the keys. "Ah, here we are," he said at last, then, dashing both their hopes, "No, sorry. Only decks we sold around then were a Merlin and a Marseilles. Unusual, that. These days people tend to go for the ones with the fancy art-work."

"Could you try a little earlier?" asked Declan. "He may have bought them a few weeks before the first murder."

Trotter obliged, but found nothing. Isabel and Declan stood up. "I suppose it was too much to expect success first time," Declan said, "but thanks, anyway."

Outside, Isabel turned on Declan, eyes flashing. "Thank you very much! You could at least have warned me what role I was supposed to be playing."

"Sorry. I guess we should have sorted it out before we went in."

"Detective Constable Sinclair!" Isabel snorted, her curls dancing as she tossed her head angrily. "I ask you! Do I look like a Detective Constable?"

"Not a lot," Declan admitted, trying hard not to smile, "but I had to think of something. Besides, this was your idea in the first place. As I recall, you insisted on it, against my advice and my better judgement."

"Just don't you dare say 'I told you so'." But her grey eyes were smiling. The storm had passed.

Aquarius was a much smaller shop, nestled cosily between a designer clothing boutique and an up-market coffee bar. Just inside the door stood a notice board covered with posters heralding talks by luminaries of the New Age lecture circuit, and advertisements for astrologers, tarot-card readers, and assorted New Age practitioners. The shop itself was narrow, its walls lined from floor to ceiling with packed shelves. A double row of shelves also ran down the centre of the shop, leaving customers just enough room to sidle between them and the walls. Just now, however, no one was sidling.

Cornered behind the miniscule counter opposite the notice board stood a tall, slim woman at the younger end of middle age. Her light brown hair was drawn up into a half-hearted bun from where its escaping strands wafted about a pointed face dominated by large, pale blue eyes. Her cotton dress, worn over a black high-necked jersey, was layered in pink and purple, and over it she wore a hand-knitted jacket in a pale, leafy green. With her slightly stooped stance, she reminded Isabel of a runner bean that had split open.

Turning her pale gaze on them, the woman smiled vaguely. "Hi, can I help you?"

"I hope so," Declan replied, repeating his trick with his badge and explaining their quest.

The woman bent down and fished under the counter, pulling out a large exercise book. "Let's see," she said, flipping through its pages, "I think... yes, here we are. I thought I remembered him. Quite a nice young man he seemed—very polite and quiet—still, you never can tell. He bought two decks of the Ryder-Waite cards. That's still our most popular one, you know."

"Why did he want two decks?" Isabel wondered.

"He said they were presents." And so they were, Isabel thought ironically.

Declan smiled at the woman. "What did this young man look like?"

The woman thought, absent-mindedly poking a strand of

hair back into her bun with one thin forefinger. "Slim," she said at last, "with fair hair, I think. He was quite ordinary looking, nothing unusual... oh, apart from his eyes. Very intense they were. Grey, I think," she spoke slowly, trying to remember, "and very pale." She made another attempt to deal with her hair. On one of her fingers, two amethysts glowed like droplets of methylated spirits in an ornate silver ring.

"I don't suppose you'd have a record of his name?"

"Sorry, I haven't. He paid cash."

"Oh, well." Declan closed his notepad and put it back in his pocket. "Thanks. You've been very helpful." He turned to leave, and Isabel followed him.

"Wait," the woman's thin voice drifted after them. Isabel and Declan turned. "I've just remembered, he originally wanted three decks, but he said they all had to be the Waite deck, and I only had two in stock. He'd already been to New Directions, and they were waiting for new stock, too, so I suggested he try Vision Quest. Do you know where that is?"

Isabel smiled. "Yes, we do. And thank you very much for your help."

Back on the tiled footpath, she turned to Declan, her eyes shining. "This is exciting!"

Declan put his arm round her and gave her a squeeze. "You can assist me any time you like!"

"Ooh, does that mean I get to drive the car?"

"You've been watching too much television."

Vision Quest was not really a shop at all, but a large stall in an indoor market that seemed to specialise in cheap jewellery, plastic novelties, and clothing and accoutrements for dope-smoking motorcyclists with a conspicuous lack of taste. It also boasted, ensconced in one corner, a gaudily curtained booth advertising a palm reader. At the very heart of all this lay Vision Quest, draped in mauve and pale blue muslin, sprinkled with silver stars and hung about with a rainbow of crystals that swayed gently in the breeze blowing from the open doorway. A tiered display case on the milky way of its muslin-swathed counter held a selection of tarot decks, and a number of other divination aids, including silver-tipped wands in small, medium and large.

The stall appeared to be unmanned, but as they stood gazing in wonder at the mind-boggling variety of items on offer, from brass statues of dubious heritage to woven rugs, candles, incense, cheap jewellery, and 'smoking paraphernalia', two batik bedspreads hanging at the back of the stall parted, and through them stepped a diminutive, olive-skinned young woman swathed, apparently, in remnants from the stall's draperies, and carrying a paper cup on top of which a paper plate of some vaguely oriental-looking food balanced precariously. Her long, dark hair was swept up at the sides and held by ornate matching silver combs, and when, after carefully setting down her refreshments on the counter, she smiled at them, her teeth were such a dazzling white they seemed artificial. She certainly looked the part, thought Declan.

"Hi," she said, and waited, eyeing her paper cup with a speculative air. When Declan pulled out his badge, however, she flashed an uneasy glance behind her before fixing him and Isabel with a carefully neutral gaze. Declan explained why they were there. Her face cleared, and with almost palpable relief she said, "Hang on, I'll just get the book." She ducked behind the bedspreads again, reappearing a moment later clutching a dog-eared exercise book. "It'll be in this one," she told them. "I only finished it yesterday."

She flicked her hair back over her thin shoulders and began to riffle through the pages. Finally, she pointed a petite finger. "Here it is. One Rider-Waite tarot deck. I seem to remember the guy saying he needed another one and the other shop he went to had run out."

"That sounds right," said Declan. "Did he pay cash?"

"Yeah, he did. If it'd been by cheque I'd have written the number down."

"Okay. Thanks, you've been very helpful." He flashed her a smile. "I don't suppose you remember what he looked like?"

The girl picked up her paper cup and sipped thoughtfully. "Not really. Sort of average, I guess." She put down the cup and turned her attention to the plate, picking it up and removing the white plastic fork, which was sticking out of the mound of noodles. She rotated the fork slowly, winding noodles around it, and bent forward, the better to convey them to her mouth. Declan thanked her again and he and Isabel made to leave. "Except," the girl mumbled through her mouthful of noodles, "he had really weird eyes."

Declan turned back to her. "Weird?"

She swallowed the noodles and wiped her hand across her mouth. "Yeah. Sort of spaced out. Looked like he was on something, y'know?"

"Yeah." Declan's mouth tipped up at one side in a conspiratorial smile. "I don't suppose you recall what colour they were?"

The girl shook her head slowly and began to twirl her fork in her noodles again. Declan was about to thank her and leave, when she said, "They were kind of pale, I think." She screwed up her own eyes in the effort to remember. "Yeah, pale. Definitely light-coloured. Grey, I think." She shrugged her thin shoulders. "That's all I can remember."

"Thanks again." Declan gave her a smile. "You've been very helpful."

The girl shrugged again and turned back to her food.

They wandered back through the mounds of garish merchandise and out onto the pavement. The sky had completely clouded over and a cold wind was blowing from the southwest. Declan pulled up the collar of his jacket and zipped it up. "I could do with a coffee," he said. "I'm not used to this cold wind."

Isabel didn't reply immediately. Something was pushing persistently at her awareness, demanding recognition. She was certain a new piece of the puzzle had just been presented to her, but she couldn't quite see where it fitted. Maybe she needed more information to see its place in the picture. With a shake of her head, she banished the frustrating feeling. "Let's go to Joss's," she said, "we can get some coffee there."

* * * *

"Come in. I was wondering if you'd make it over here. The twins are at band practice, so we've got about an hour and a half before they and Martin descend on us." Joss took them through to the kitchen and switched the kettle on. The big, airy kitchen was warm and bright, in contrast to the wind-whipped, leaden sky that threatened rain outside. She poured boiling water into their coffee mugs, "So, how did you get on?"

"We've got a description of sorts," Isabel said, "but no name, unfortunately."

Joss placed a steaming mug in front of each of them. "You were right about the tarot decks, though?"

"Looks like it." Isabel sipped her coffee gratefully. "Only it was three decks, not two, all bought on the same day by a man answering the same description."

Declan had taken a small bottle from his pocket and shaken out two capsules. He was tired from walking, and his knee had been throbbing badly for some time. He washed the capsules down with a generous mouthful of coffee. "Maybe we'd better start at the beginning," he said and, between them, he and Isabel recounted their afternoon's activities.

"I can see you're going to be an asset to this enterprise." Joss smiled at Declan. "Good thing you brought your badge with you."

Declan looked dubious. "I'm still not sure any of this is a good idea. Unfortunately, I'm a sucker for redheads with English accents. I just can't help myself." Isabel found herself blushing. She was still unused to Declan's compliments.

Outside, a few large drops of rain fell, forming dark splotches on the tiles of the patio. Joss got up to turn the light on, then went to the bench and switched on the kettle. "More coffee?" Declan and Isabel both nodded, and Joss spooned coffee into the mugs and poured on boiling water.

"I meant to tell you before," she said, "Simon Drawbridge called just before you arrived. He's got the results of the DNA tests, and it's definitely Hart's blood on the badge. Unfortunately, there were no clear fingerprints on the helmet. Either our murderer or James must have wiped it clean."

"That was very considerate of them," Isabel observed. "Still, Simon should be pleased his intuition has been vindicated."

Joss nodded. "He is." She took the mugs of coffee back to the table and set them down. "Did you manage to find out anything more about Jonah Trenwith from Dominic?" she asked Isabel.

"I haven't seen Dominic for the best part of a week," Isabel said, a hint of annoyance in her voice. "I know he's been home once or twice. He was there when Declan arrived on Sunday, and he's left the odd cryptic message. But I haven't actually seen him and, naturally, he hasn't told me where he's staying. He's not answering texts, either."

"Ah," said Joss, "same old Dominic." It wasn't like Isabel, she thought, to be upset about Dominic's unpredictability. He'd been that way as long as anyone could remember, a trait apparently inherited from his father, though in his case redeemed by his scrupulous honesty.

Declan had also noticed Isabel's swiftly concealed flash of emotion. A sudden thought struck him. "He's not staying away because of me, is he? Because if he is—"

"No, it won't be that. I expect it's just that his band is getting quite a few gigs now and, when they aren't performing, they seem to spend most of their time practising. I should call Phoebe's mother. She's their drummer—Phoebe I mean, not her mother. They mostly practise at her place, because the drums are the hardest instrument to move. Besides, it's such a madhouse round there the extra noise goes virtually unnoticed."

Declan flashed her a smile of relief. "That's all right, then. I'd hate Dominic to feel uncomfortable in his own home."

"It's hard to imagine Dominic feeling uncomfortable anywhere," laughed Joss. "Besides, anything he might know about Jonah Trenwith has probably been superseded by events, now."

Declan put his coffee mug down and looked at the others. "How many did you say were on the committee of this brotherhood?"

"Seven," said Isabel. "Why?"

"And how many of them are dead?"

"Four. Why?"

"It's just a thought, but it's beginning to look like someone's trying to get rid of all seven of them."

"The guy who bought the tarot decks?"

Declan pushed a hand through his hair. "He does seem to be the obvious choice. I just wish we could find out what his motive is."

"Joss," said Isabel thoughtfully, "do you mind if we borrow the computer printout? I can give it back to you at Luke's on Wednesday."

"No, of course not. What do you want it for, just as a matter of interest?"

"I'm hoping maybe if Declan and I look through it he might pick up something we've overlooked. Something that will point to a motive for all these deaths. I realise it's not much of a hope, but at the moment, it seems to be about all we've got."

CHAPTER TWENTY-ONE

The light from the candle on his altar flickered, just as he
knew it would, although the door and window were tightly
closed against the cold and the rain. He sat motionless,
waiting until the flame was once more still, balancing atop
the candle like a droplet of pale gold. Again, he sent out the
thought. Again, the flame flickered. A slow smile of
satisfaction stole across his features. But he remembered to
give thanks to the High Ones and, in particular, to the One
who had come to him to be his guide. He had not yet been
granted more than a glimpse of his protector, but he could
sense His presence, dark and still, like the centre of a storm,
coming and going at His own ineffable whim. And when He
was there, it was as if he himself were taken over by that
irresistible presence. Then, all doubt and fear were banished.
Then, anything was possible. Had he not proved that, yet
again, only yesterday? His mind went back to it, lingering
lovingly on every detail, so clear and sharp in his memory he
might have been there now.

It had all fallen into place so perfectly, in a way he could
never have planned alone and unaided. The anger, which
had begun that night when Brother Esto Sol Testis had
passed him on the stairway from the temple, had not, as it
usually did, dissipated over the next few weeks. It had
stayed, burning like a fire in the pit of his stomach, fuelled

anew each time he saw those dark, mocking features. Gradually, he had come to see that this was, in fact, a message from his guide. *Do not forget,* He was saying with each new burst of heat. *Never forget that a wrong done to you is a wrong done to Us. A wrong that must be avenged.*

Then had come the news that Brother Esto Sol Testis was to be the new Senior. How angry he—and They—had become then. His guide had come to him that night as he lay in bed, and he felt the familiar sensation constricting him until he could scarcely breathe. But by now he knew what to do. Struggling from his bed, he had lit the altar candles and the incense—real church incense; nothing less would do. Without the music, it was harder to force his mind to that necessary point of concentration, but he dared not make a sound in case the other tenants heard.

One day, he promised himself, he would have his own house out in the country, where he could work Their Holy Will without hindrance. In the meantime, he felt sure They would understand.

And, of course, They did. The feelings They had granted when he made the offering proved it. And afterwards came the calm, silent stillness into which They had whispered his instructions.

Getting the equipment together had not been easy. There was more of it than before. And he was aware that Brother Esto Sol Testis was a different proposition entirely from Brother Dabunt Aspera Rosas. He was at least ten years younger and, as the owner of a string of health shops, he naturally prided himself on being fit and healthy. And, as a chiropractor, he must have developed strong arms and shoulders. He was strong-willed, too, and capable of ruthlessness; this was well known among the brothers. It was why the likes of Brother Fulget Virtus made such a point of placating him. Doubtless it was the reason they had chosen him as the new Senior—or thought they had.

But justice had to be done, and his guide had whispered to him over and over again that Brother Esto Sol Testis must not become Senior. For how could he be considered worthy when he had so little insight into the true nature of things? Brother Esto Sol Testis, like the other four, had shown no awareness of the great value placed by the High Ones on effort and steadfastness, the very qualities required of a true magician; for would not the Great Ones themselves provide the necessary teaching to those who did not fail them? No, this lack of insight was not to be tolerated.

They had told him the best time—the night of the solstice, when the energies of the universe were held in balance, on the very brink of change. The following night would be too late. By then the balance would have tipped—only slightly, but enough for error to be set in place.

All of Saturday he had been on edge. At first he had thought he was afraid. To calm himself, he lit a candle and some incense, and listened for a while to the soft, pure music They liked so well, the music of Mozart. Then, sure of himself once more, he had made a survey of his equipment. Yes, it was all there. Everything was in order. So he waited, feeling the sensations welling up in him, but not allowing them to overwhelm him. Not yet. That time would come.

He had kept vigil all that night, both unable and unwilling to sleep. At dawn, skin taut and eyes prickling, he had crept to the bathroom along the hall to purify himself. He must not be seen by anyone—success depended on it. He had pulled clean clothes on over skin almost unbearably sensitive. But this was good, he reminded himself. It meant his guide was near. Then he carried the equipment down to his car. Most of it, being small, fitted into the boot, but he had to drive leaning slightly towards the door, to avoid the big blade curving over from the back seat. The other blade was safe in the leather sheath he had made for it, hanging from his belt underneath his jacket. He reached down to feel it, and the sensation as it moved against his thigh was an exquisite foretaste of things to come.

Driving through the quiet morning streets, he went to his favourite spot near the gardens where the willow trees, now almost bare of their leaves, dipped the tips of their branches into the slow-moving river. There he awaited instructions. He was hungry, but he had promised Them he would eat nothing this day until he had accomplished his task. He would let the hunger of his body for food be a metaphor for both his and Their hunger for justice. Gradually, an idea came to him. He turned it over in his mind, searching for flaws, but there were none that he could see. Smiling, he turned on the ignition and drove. It was just a matter of time now.

And that was exactly how it had turned out. He had merely to wait near the health shop until the woman had come to open it. Fortunately, she had no idea who he was— she knew nothing of the Brotherhood—so it was simplicity itself to ask her if she could please phone an urgent message to Mr Trenwith, asking him to meet Mr Myerson at ten o'clock at the clinic, upstairs. They had told him, through his inner senses, that Brother Esto Sol Testis would read this coded reference correctly.

And so it had proved. At five minutes to ten, the Senior elect had arrived in his black Jaguar, parking it outside the shop. It had not been possible to overhear his brief conversation with the woman in the shop, but he had done what was required. After a brief glance up and down the street, he had unlocked the door that led up the narrow staircase to the temple, and gone upstairs.

Unnoticed by the woman in the shop, who was busy re-stocking the shelves, Brother Non Extinguar had slipped up after him. The tall brother was pacing in front of the altar, checking that all was in order for his formal induction the following night, glancing once or twice at his watch. He suspected nothing, however. Brother Fulget Virtus was not known for his strict punctuality.

Brother Non Extinguar stood silently in the shadows near the door. With the sacred flame and the candles unlit, the temple was virtually in darkness. The row of windows set high in one wall had long ago been painted over. It took a moment or two for his eyes to adjust, then he looked carefully about him for a suitable weapon. He had been aware from the start that Brother Esto Sol Testis would need to be dealt with in some cruder fashion before the final, exquisite thrust of the knife. And, though it offended his sense of honour and justice, he would have to be dealt with from behind. He could only hope a glimpse of recognition would be possible before...

As he edged his way silently along the deeply shadowed wall, his eye caught sight of the heavy candlestick glinting dully on the altar. How wonderfully appropriate. He sent a swift prayer to his guide, whose presence he could feel hovering near him like a dark cloud. His prayer was heard.

Brother Esto Sol Testis stopped pacing to stand before the altar, his head tilted as though listening for the arrival of Brother Fulget Virtus.

The dark cloud descended upon Brother Non Extinguar, suffusing him with a terrible power. It was only afterwards that he realised he had suddenly darted forward, seized the candlestick and brought it crashing down on the back of Brother Esto Sol Testis's head. His tall form crumpled without a sound.

Brother Non Extinguar looked down, amazed. He saw the head turn slowly, a look of horrified recognition lighting the eyes for a second before they closed. Oh, yes! Thank you! This was perfect! Sternly quelling the ecstasy that began to creep through his body, he looked quickly about him. He had not thought to bring rope. They had not told him he would need it. Then he remembered the cords. A bundle of them had been placed on the altar in readiness for tomorrow's ritual. Swiftly he bound the hands of the unconscious brother, then the feet. Finally, choosing a scarlet cord, he bound it tightly several times around his mouth. Then he gave himself up to the rapture.

Very dimly, as from a great distance, he heard the woman locking up the shop and leaving. Rousing himself, he looked around him. He felt drained, but this was only to be expected. Doing the will of the High Ones had purged him of dross. His body was light, and his mind was as clear as a crystal and as sharp as the blade of his knife.

Brother Esto Sol Testis was still unconscious. Brother Non Extinguar felt for the bunch of keys in his pocket and secreted it in his own. Carefully, he placed the candlestick back on the altar and neatened what remained of the silken cords. Then he slipped quietly down the stairs, locking both the temple door and the downstairs door after him.

He reached his car without being seen, but then was unsure what to do next. He would have to wait until dark to move Brother Esto Sol Testis. There were too many people in town, and he could not risk being seen. For a moment, panic rose up in him and he wanted to run. But he forced himself to breathe slowly and rhythmically until he was calm again. From the pocket of his shirt he drew the card and looked at it. The Magician, symbol of his goal and his mission, his rightful inheritance, so clear and obvious if only the fools could read it. Allowing himself a short laugh, he started the car and drove home. He wanted to cleanse himself again, and to rest until dusk. The next part was going to be the hardest.

In the chill evening air he had returned once more to the temple. By now Brother Esto Sol Testis was conscious, though groggy, thanks be to the High Ones. Untying his feet, Brother Non Extinguar had made him walk across to the door, footsteps echoing dully on the wooden floor, and down the stairs to the waiting car. At first, scrambling furiously to his feet, he had tried to call out. The knife pricking into his neck had dissuaded him, however, and he had stumbled down the stairs on feet half numb from being bound for hours.

Disdaining the weakness of pity, Brother Non Extinguar had bundled him into the passenger seat of the car and driven—carefully, so as to arouse no suspicion—to the gardens. He had driven past the front entrance by the museum. A few people still wandered there, and he could not risk being seen by anyone. Besides, he had already determined there was a much shorter route to their destiny. A little further along, he turned in at the broad entrance that led to the sports grounds on the right and, on the left, rows of parking spaces, and then the little curved bridge over the stream. Carefully keeping to the shadows under the trees, he urged his prisoner on until they reached the Rose Garden. Five minutes it took to walk the pathway that wound left from the bridge, round behind the Information Centre and in front of the Victorian pillared portico of the Tropical Plant House. Then, to his right, he had seen the gap in the neatly trimmed hedge, its two dark yew trees standing guard on either side. The northern entrance to the Rose Garden. He had chosen this spot for its symbolism—or, rather, They had chosen it for him. He had forced Brother Esto Sol Testis round to the Eastern Entrance. Like the Sun, he would enter at the East. But he would not leave.

Once there, the rest had been easy. His well-honed ritual knife had done its job well, and so had the old butcher's saw he had bought specially from the same second-hand shop that had supplied the scythe. The mask he had made himself, copying carefully from the tarot card, Death, before burning it along with the others he would not need.

Severing the hand and the foot was messier than he had imagined it would be. But he had rejoiced, as They had, to see the lifeblood flowing out into the soil, to nurture it as its owner never had, despite all his glib talk about health and purity. After the blood had stopped flowing, he had hauled the body to the one and only obvious place for it—the sundial at the centre of the circular garden—savouring the symbolism, just as They surely did. He had picked the rose— the finest white bloom he could find—and placed it with infinite care beside the masked face. Finally, he had pulled the card from his pocket and, a final touch of divine irony, had secured it at the precise hour on the bronze face that signified sunrise. There. It was done.

He had returned to the car immediately, stripping off his outer layer of clothes and bundling them into the plastic bag he had brought, along with the saw. His knife he stabbed into the earth three times in ritual purification, placing it out of sight in the glove box. He had washed his hands and arms quickly in the running water of the stream, then driven home. Only when he had disposed of the plastic bag and its contents, and cleansed both himself and his knife, carefully placing it back in its leather sheath, did he allow himself to receive once more the bliss bestowed on him by his guide and protector for a job well done...

The candle on the altar flickered out. Opening his eyes, he realised the room was dark. On the floor before him lay the tarot deck. He picked it up and slowly opened it. Drawing out the cards, he shuffled through them, savouring the new smoothness of them until he found the one he wanted—the Magician in his red cloak, his white robe bound about with the ouroboros, symbol of eternity. Above his dark head shone the golden lemniscate, signifying infinity. There were his wand, directing universal energy to earth, and the sword, cup and pentacle, completing the elements with which he worked his magic. And all around him grew roses and lilies, symbolising passion and purity.

A quiver ran through him. With due reverence he placed the card on the altar. There he would consecrate it, as soon as They told him the time was right. Meanwhile, he would eat and rest. He was beginning to feel that slight dimming of the senses, that closing in and dulling of vision that was often the first sign of the descent into the pit. Oh, not yet, please! There was still work to do.

Resolutely stilling his mind, he stood up. There was his newspaper lying on the bed. He had bought it on his way home from work (Work! It was becoming more and more difficult to keep his mind on something so mundane, yet he must for at least a little while longer.), but had not read it yet.

He made himself tea and toast, and settled down to read the paper. Then he saw it. It was only a small advertisement, but for what it told him, it might just as well have been handwritten in finest black-letter script and illuminated in gold. It would mean waiting, but what did that matter? His heart soaring once more, he gave thanks to his Holy Guardian Angel for sending him just the opportunity he needed to complete the work.

CHAPTER TWENTY-TWO

Luke eased himself into his chair, placing his cigarette packet and lighter on its arm next to the heavy onyx ashtray that nobody but he used. Even Quincy was a non-smoker, claiming he needed his entire lung capacity for his work, thank you very much. Luke, who at the time had been nicotine-free for the distressingly lengthy interval of four hours, had responded with the tart comment that he hadn't realised being a shipping clerk required such a large lung capacity, regretting the remark as soon as he had made it. Laughing, Quincy had observed that the money in his bank account was ample compensation for any ignorant remarks people might care to make about his method of earning it. Luke had apologised, and they had come to an amicable understanding. Now, Quincy merely left the room when Luke lit up, and Luke refrained from disparaging remarks, even when in the grip of nicotine withdrawal.

At the moment, however, comfortably replete as far as nicotine was concerned, and relieved, as always, to have another programme recorded and ready for broadcast, he gave his attention to his mug of coffee, thoughtfully stirring in milk and sugar. He swallowed a mouthful, luxuriating in the rich combination of bitter and sweet. Then he turned to Joss. "You haven't been upsetting James again, have you?"

Joss bridled. "I did try and speak with him a couple of

times, if that's what you mean, and I must say he seemed even more anxious than usual, but he was already like it when I called, so you can't blame me. Anyway, what do you mean 'again'?"

Luke ignored her final query. "When he rang me earlier to say he wouldn't be here today, he sounded more than just anxious." Luke expertly tapped a cigarette from its packet and picked up his lighter. "From the way he sounded this morning, I don't think he'll be back on the team in a hurry."

Joss shrugged with the air of one reluctantly bowing to the inevitable. "He's obviously avoiding us. Which is a pity, because he almost certainly knows things that would help us in our enquiries."

"The question is," Luke said, releasing blue smoke from his lips in a thin stream, "what are we going to do about it?"

There was silence as they all thought about this. The late afternoon sun slanted through the french doors, its rays forming a pool of pale golden light at the base of a large bronze bowl that sat on the floor, apparently serving as a receptacle for unpaid bills. Outside, a plump orange cat made its lazy way across the leaf-strewn grass and through a narrow gap between the fronds of two ferns. By the time this vanishing act had been accomplished, however, nothing had presented itself to any of them. If James refused to confide in them, there was little, if anything, they could do to make him.

At length, Isabel voiced this self-evident fact, concluding, "Since we're not likely to get anything helpful from James, it seems to me our best bet is still to try and find out some more about the Brotherhood of the Flame."

"But how?" Luke demanded. "Let's face it, if James won't

tell us anything, we can be damned sure no-one else in the Brotherhood will, and presumably no-one outside it knows anything to tell."

"And what's more," said Joss, "I think it could be dangerous for us to try and find out directly. I mean it," she continued, seeing the looks Isabel and Luke gave her. "James was in quite a state when he told me he couldn't discuss anything with me. I believe he meant it, quite literally."

"What sort of state?" asked Geraldine, uncurling her long legs and stretching them out in front of her, then curling up again on the couch like a cat.

"As I said, I tried several times this week to get him to talk to me, but he won't. I even went round to his place, but he just kept saying he was terribly busy and he couldn't talk to anyone. He looked as if he hadn't slept for a month, and had spent the entire time in a state of abject terror."

"He probably has," Isabel said with feeling. "Just imagine all your colleagues being killed off, one by one, and knowing you were on the list, too, but not knowing where."

"Mmm." Joss nodded. "He was doing his best to hide it, but he really did look terrified."

"But James is always in a state of anxiety about something. It probably doesn't mean anything," said Luke hopefully. But he said it without conviction.

"Well," Joss said, "I don't intend to put it to the test. You go ahead if you like, but don't say I didn't warn you."

Luke shrugged, stubbing out his cigarette. His hair flopped over his forehead and he flicked it back with an irritable toss of his head.

Joss said, "Look, let's leave it for now, shall we? We don't seem to be getting anywhere, and I have to go soon anyway."

Luke nodded gloomily. "Much as I hate to admit it, I think you're right. For the moment at least, we seem to have reached an impasse."

But there was a stubborn set to his face as he stubbed out his cigarette and, for a long time after the others had left, he sat staring thoughtfully out through the french doors. Then he got up, pulled on his jacket, and went out.

* * * *

Isabel arrived home to the strains of Dominic's saxophone drifting lazily towards her through the open door. Declan came out to meet her. He was still limping badly, though he had repeatedly assured her it looked worse than it felt. She had invited him to the recording session that afternoon, but he had told her he had correspondence to deal with, insisting he'd never get it done while she was there to distract him.

"Finished your correspondence?" she asked, returning his kiss. "I trust Dominic wasn't too much of a distraction."

Declan grinned. "Not nearly as much as you would have been. How did your recording go?"

"Without a hitch, for a change, though there were only three of us there apart from Luke. Apparently James phoned Luke this morning to say he couldn't be there—again. He refused to talk to Joss when she called him, too. The general consensus is he's avoiding us."

"Because of the murders?"

"Presumably. Joss said he seemed frightened when she saw him the other day."

"Well, he would be, wouldn't he, if we're right about this Council of Seniors, or whatever it is they call themselves."

"Mmm. It looks as if you might be right about someone trying to do them all in."

At that moment, Dominic's saxophone fell silent, and his auburn head appeared round the bedroom door. "Hello, Mother. Did I hear someone mention a cup of tea?"

"No, dear," said Isabel, with a saccharine smile, "but your kind offer is appreciated." She glanced mischievously at Declan. "Isn't that right?"

"Don't ask me. I'm strictly neutral."

"Quite right, too," said Dominic. But he went to the kitchen and began to fill the kettle.

"I'm glad you're here," Isabel said, seating herself at the table. "I wanted to ask you something."

"By all means," said Dominic with condescending graciousness, spooning tea into the teapot.

"I seem to remember," Isabel said, "that you were at school with a boy called Trenwith."

Dominic placed three mugs on the table, then went to get milk and the teapot. Finally, he sat down and turned his large brown eyes on his mother. "You mean Clive? The one whose father's body was found in the Rose Garden?"

Isabel nodded, sipping the tea he had poured for her.

"What a freaky way to get killed!" enthused Dominic. "Whoever did it has real flair!"

"Whoever did it is seriously unbalanced," replied Isabel.

"That too," Dominic acknowledged, leaning back precariously in his chair to open a cupboard door and extract a packet of biscuits. He took several biscuits out, then offered the packet to Isabel and Declan. "What do you want to know about Clive for?" he asked, shooting Isabel a sharp glance.

"I don't. I just wondered if you'd ever met his father."

"Only briefly. Clive and I did music together for a year, and once or twice his father came to pick him up from school. In an amazing big black Jag. Clive said he'd brought it back from Britain after a business trip. He'd come gliding up the driveway, and the kids would say, 'Here comes Jonah in the whale'."

"What was he like?"

"Clive? He was okay. He was younger than me, so I only ever saw him at music. He played excellent piano, though—mostly classical."

"Actually," Isabel suppressed a smile, "I meant his father."

"Oh. He was strange. Very tall and thin, and always dressed in black. Phoebe used to go on about him looking like Heathcliff, but he always reminded me of a vampire." Dominic sat drinking his tea, a slight frown creasing his pale brow. Then he said, "Clive didn't actually live with his father. His mother had left him when Clive was quite a bit younger. Someone asked him why, once, and Clive said his mother had been scared about something his father was involved in, and she wanted to protect him and his sister. He was only about six when it happened, so he couldn't really remember much about it. But, for what it's worth, Clive didn't seem to like either of his parents much."

"Didn't like them, or didn't get on with them?"

Dominic took another biscuit and munched it thoughtfully. "Oh, he seemed to get on with his mother well enough, what little he saw of her. He just didn't like her much. Can't say I blame him, mind you, the few times I met her. She was like a Barbie doll from hell, all hair and make-up, and power dressing. She was always saying things like, 'Anyone can do anything if they really want to'. But she wouldn't let Clive or his sister do anything. They couldn't even get into the house unless she was at home, in case they made a mess. Honestly, their place was so neat you were scared to go to the toilet. And it was pink." Dominic's face registered his distaste.

"What, all of it?" Declan was intrigued.

"All of it," Dominic confirmed. "It must have been like living in some high-class brothel."

"Which you'd know all about, of course," Declan murmured.

Dominic blushed.

"What about his father?" asked Isabel, flashing Declan a glance of amused admiration. It took a lot to disconcert Dominic.

"Oh, he was different; but even worse, if that's possible. Clive's mother was just a bimbo with ambition. But his father..." Dominic paused, his brow wrinkled with the effort to find the right words. "Well, he gave me the creeps," he concluded with an involuntary shudder. "He gave Clive the creeps, too. He told us once his father was a black magician. We thought he was having us on, of course, but when I think about it now, I wouldn't be surprised at anything he was into."

"I'm beginning to think he may have been right," said Isabel thoughtfully.

Declan looked at her, startled. "Don't tell me you believe in black magic?"

"Depends what you mean. If you're talking about pacts with the devil, and black masses and the like, there are people who believe in that sort of thing. I'm certainly not one of them, and I doubt if Jonah Trenwith was, either, though his wife may have genuinely believed he was. The Brotherhood of the Flame seems to be based more or less on the Order of the Golden Dawn, and that was largely Rosicrucian and Kabbalistic. And the Rosicrucians were sort of vaguely Masonic, as well."

"What, funny handshakes and all that?"

Isabel laughed. "Possibly. But it was all really based on the alchemists' premise that man can transmute himself to a state of perfection, by means of secret knowledge to be passed on to those deemed worthy."

"What sort of secret knowledge?"

"If we all knew that," said Dominic, "it wouldn't be secret, would it?"

"Touché," Declan said with a grin.

"Actually," said Isabel, "a lot of the rituals have been published over the years, though how much is genuine is anybody's guess. Israel Regardie was in the Golden Dawn, and he published all of their rituals in a set of books at about the same time the order finally gave up the ghost, so to speak. Aleister Crowley published a lot of their material as well, in a magazine he produced called The Equinox. If I remember rightly, he published all their secret rites, in spite of his oath of secrecy—or quite likely because of it, knowing Crowley—and there was a court case where MacGregor Mathers, the head of the order, tried to stop publication, but Crowley won on an appeal."

"All very interesting, but what, if anything, does it tell us about Trenwith senior?" Declan asked.

"Probably nothing, as such. But let's assume for the moment that he was as ruthless as he sounds. Add that to his involvement with a group dedicated to the pursuit of power through secret knowledge, and what do you get?"

"A complete and utter bastard," Dominic said succinctly. "Which is exactly what Clive made him sound like. What's the Brotherhood of the Flame, anyway?"

Briefly, Isabel told him.

Dominic's lip curled disdainfully. "Pathetic! They sound like Rotarians on acid."

Declan gave a hoot of appreciative laughter.

"You're probably not far wrong," said Isabel through her own laughter. "Nevertheless, four people are dead, and there'll probably be more if something isn't done."

"Well." Dominic got to his feet. "I've got to be at Phoebe's in half an hour. Have fun."

"I take it," said Isabel, "I needn't expect to see you again in the near future?"

"Depends." Dominic's shoulders rose in an elegant shrug, and he was gone. Isabel gave an exasperated sigh.

Declan reached across and took her hand. "He'll be okay. I'm sure he can look after himself."

"Dominic? I'm not worried about him, infuriating though he is at times. It's these bloody murders. I'm beginning to wish we'd never got involved."

"You can always get uninvolved."

Isabel looked at him. "You don't really believe that, do you?"

Declan looked back, taking in the strong, intelligent face surrounded by its blaze of red hair, the dark grey eyes and pale, sun-flecked skin, the slightly stubborn set of her mouth. He felt her hand in his, strong and supple, grasping his own hand firmly, a metaphor for the woman herself. He smiled. "No, of course not."

He went to her chair and pulled her to her feet, drawing her close to him, folding his arms around her, kissing her hair, her face, her lips. Isabel's arms slid around his waist as she returned his kisses, losing herself little by little in the scent of his skin, and the warmth of his body against hers.

"Of course," she said at last, her eyes soft as they looked into his, "I might be able to manage it temporarily. But you'll have to help me."

"Isabel?"

"Mmm?" Isabel's voice sounded warm and languid against his shoulder.

"I've decided I'm not going back."

"What?" Her voice suddenly focussed, she pushed herself up on one arm and looked down at him. "What are you talking about?"

"I'm quitting my job."

"Are you sure that's what you want?"

Declan looked up at her. "Oh, yes," he said, "I'm sure." His mouth smiled lazily, but his eyes were dark and serious.

"It's not just because of me?"

"Not just. I used to love being a cop once, felt I was doing something useful, something important, but not for a long time now. I'm not entirely sure when the rot set in. I don't think I was even aware of it till I came to New Zealand and met you. Remember how you told me I might need a change of direction?" Isabel nodded. "Well, that brought everything into focus for me. Since then I've tried all the arguments I could think of for staying put, but somehow none of them seem convincing." He indicated his injured knee. "And now this has happened, there's really no choice any more."

"But they won't throw you out, will they, not at this stage of your career?"

"No, but I'm damned if I'm going to spend the rest of it sitting at a desk all day! And that's about all I'm fit for now."

Isabel was distressed at the note of bitterness in his voice. There were no words she could think of that would reassure him. Indeed, she could hardly blame him for feeling bitter. She lay back down beside him and pulled him close and began to stroke his hair.

When he finally raised his eyes to hers, they were wet with unshed tears. "Anyway," he said with a wry little smile, "I don't want to chase crims any more. I want to be Isabel Sinclair's partner in crime."

Isabel felt her heart jump and her throat contract. With pleasure? Fear? She wasn't sure. "You're not asking me to... to...?" She found she couldn't say the words. Maybe it was fear, after all.

"Is that want you want?" Declan's voice was very gentle.

"I don't think I... I mean I want to... but..." Oh, God! It wasn't just fear, it was abject terror!

It must have shown on her face, because Declan suddenly pulled her close and kissed her. "Oh, sweetheart, I didn't mean to scare you. I only want to be with you. I don't care how we do it. We don't even have to live together if that's what you prefer." He appeared to consider this last statement, adding with a crooked grin, "Mind you, you might have a bit of a job keeping me away."

Isabel covered her face with her hands while she attempted to deal with her confusion. At length she swallowed hard and said, "It's just that I've never been married before. Stephen didn't believe in it."

"No, I don't suppose he did." Declan's voice was ironic as he remembered what Isabel had told him about Dominic's brilliant but irresponsible father.

"And breaking up with him was so awful, I hate to think what it would have been like if we'd been married." Declan said nothing, allowing her to discover what she wanted. There was a long silence as Isabel struggled with her fears and desires. Declan waited. If he'd learnt anything useful from being a cop, it was how to curb his natural impatience. Which wasn't to say it was easy...

At last she looked into his eyes as though trying to read his soul. "Now you're back, I don't want to lose you again," she said simply. "So, if you're really sure about leaving your job, and you really want to live over here, I'd like you to come and live with me, please. If you want to, of course."

"*If* I...! Mother of God, Isabel, come here!"

Later, over pizza and whisky (it was all Isabel could find to celebrate with, and neither of them wanted to break the spell by going out), a practical problem occurred to Isabel. "If you aren't going to be a detective any more, what are you going to do?"

"I thought it was us Taureans who're supposed to be the practical ones," Declan replied with a grin, "but since you ask—I'm damned if I know." He scratched his head as if that might help the thought process. It didn't. "Maybe I should get you to do a tarot reading for me."

He hadn't meant it entirely seriously, but Isabel said, "I can't. It just doesn't work if I try and read for someone I'm close to."

Declan was basking in this last statement, which he knew

would not have been easy for Isabel to make, when she said, "I could always take you to see Tarot—I mean Terry. He's a friend of Martin's and Joss's, and he's very good. He helped us when we were investigating Bob Ferris. In fact," she added, as another thought struck her, "I wouldn't mind getting a reading myself. I haven't had one for ages, and I think it's time I did. I'll give Joss a call in the morning and get his phone number."

* * * *

The Rose Garden was no longer blocked off from public access, so clearly the police were satisfied they had found all they were likely to. Luke strolled between the two cypress trees flanking the nearest entrance, noticing for the first time that each entrance faced one of the cardinal points of the compass. There was no one else there. Presumably the inevitable curiosity of the public had by now also been largely satisfied. Wishing he had thought to investigate the site sooner, he crunched his way up the gravel path to stand before the sundial.

There was still a dark stain on its concrete base, though a surprisingly small one, Luke thought. Other than that, there was no sign of anything untoward. He looked around him. A few roses still clung with admirable, if misguided, tenacity to the branches of the well-tended bushes, buffeted by a raw, northerly wind. A number of bushes sported white blooms, and Luke found himself wondering which of them had provided the emblem of Death. Not for the first time he wished he had even a modicum of psychic ability. The subject had fascinated him since childhood, but so far he had been granted not the slightest hint of intuitive insight on any topic whatsoever. Today was no exception. Just as well he had long since given up expecting anything.

Among the many things he was not expecting was the arrival of two police officers. Looking up at the sound of their footfalls on the gravel, Luke wandered back the way he had arrived, as though his interest were no more than casual curiosity. Once beyond the hedge that marked the Rose Garden's boundary, however, he slipped behind the high, thick greenery and stood listening intently. However useless his psychic sense, the other five were more than adequate. Well, all right, he admitted to himself, taste and smell were probably impaired by years of smoking, but there was nothing wrong with his hearing.

After five or ten minutes, the two officers left the garden. Luke gratefully lit a cigarette and walked back to the sundial, reflecting that he had learned nothing new from their visit, and wasn't likely to. If anything, it seemed he and the others knew more than the police, who had yet, if the conversation on which he had just eavesdropped was anything to go by, to discover anything at all about the Magician tarot cards left with the victims. He gazed at the bronze face of the dial, its hand pointing eternally to twelve o'clock, unable to rid himself of the feeling there was something to be learned from the site of the latest murder, if only he had the ability to tap into it...

Suddenly decisive, he glanced at his watch. If he left straight away, he should just about get to Joss's before she left for work.

CHAPTER TWENTY-THREE

The massive house seemed to have aged since Isabel had seen it last, like a grand old lady finally bowing to the inevitable ravages of time. It almost seemed aware of the For Sale signs posted on its high, sagging brick fence. It was still, however, an imposing sight, standing at the end of the curved driveway lined with ragged trees, its twin towers guarding its porticoed entrance.

Terry, it appeared, had not changed at all. As he opened the door, Isabel saw the same tall, angular form, the greying ginger hair and shaggy beard, all dominated by his beaky nose. The same ink-stained hands reached out to greet her.

"Isabel! Lovely to see you again!" Isabel introduced Declan. "Come on in, both of you, and get warm. I'm holding court in the kitchen, as usual. Now Mother has finally had to go to hospital, I don't use the rest of the house much. As you can imagine, it costs a fortune to heat. That's why it's being sold, basically. Mother and I have both had to accept that she won't be coming back here, and I simply can't afford to live here any longer, much less the upkeep. The printing business isn't exactly in the forefront of this purported economic recovery." He gave a rueful grimace that embraced both sadness and a hint of bitterness. Perfectly justified, too, reflected Isabel, who had long ago been forced to acknowledge that modern society had scant regard for creativity. "Not at the level I operate at, anyway," Terry concluded, leading them through the grand, panelled hallway to the massive kitchen Isabel remembered.

On the long wooden table was a package wrapped in dark blue silk, which Isabel recognised as Terry's tarot deck, and beside it a brown earthenware teapot and a pottery milk-jug in a subtle shade of green. A cast-iron kettle steamed on the old-fashioned stove. Terry took the teapot to the stove and poured boiling water into it.

"You're the Australian detective, aren't you?" he asked Declan as he took three pottery mugs from a cupboard and set them on the table. "I remember hearing you on one of the programmes Luke Marriott made about that dreadful Bob Ferris chap."

"That's right," said Declan, his face deliberately deadpan, "I'm Mr Plod."

Terry's weather-beaten face broke into a huge grin. "They told you about that, did they?"

Declan nodded, grinning back, "But I'm a sucker for punishment."

"He must be," said Isabel. "He's coming to live with me."

"Congratulations, both of you." Terry carried the teapot carefully across to the table, then sat down and pulled the tarot deck towards him. "Don't tell me any more just yet, though. I don't want anything to influence the vibes." He opened the silk cloth and smoothed it out in front of him, revealing the fine silver embroidery Isabel recalled from her last visit. "Right, who's going first?"

"Declan, you can," said Isabel, "unless you want to see how it's done first."

Declan shrugged, indicating he had no particular

227

preference, so Terry handed him the cards. "Shuffle these," he said, "while I pour the tea."

"Is that all I have to do, just shuffle them?"

Terry nodded, making an expansive gesture with one hand. "No magic rituals or secret formulae. I realised years ago that was just hocus pocus to impress the client. So I dropped it."

"Me, too," Isabel agreed, gratefully accepting a mug of tea.

"No scones this time, I'm afraid," said Terry. "You caught me on the hop, rather. I've just finished the first big order I've had for months. And let's face it, big orders are not to be sneezed at. I've got some chocolate biscuits in the cupboard, though, if you'd like one."

"Not for me, thanks. We haven't long eaten."

"How long do I have to shuffle these?" asked Declan, then looked puzzled as the other two exchanged amused glances.

"Sorry," said Isabel. "We weren't really laughing at you. It's just that everyone asks that question. The answer is, you do it till you feel like stopping."

"If you have a particular question you want answered," Terry told him, "you can think about that while you're shuffling, but whatever's on your mind will probably come up anyway."

Placing the shuffled deck back on the cloth, Declan picked up his mug of tea, looking expectantly over its rim at Terry. Terry took the cards in his bony hands and began to lay them out. Isabel noticed he used the same layout he had used before, placing two cards in a central cross formation, then three in a row below this and three above. Since she had never seen this layout used by anyone else, or in any of the numerous books she had read on the subject, she suspected it was of Terry's own devising.

Turning her attention to the cards in the layout, she saw that the central cross was formed by the World, placed upright, and the Seven of Cups crosswise on top of it. Underneath, from left to right, were the Queen of Wands, the Tower and the Fool, while above were the Eight of Cups, the Four of Swords and the Empress.

"This is just to give us a general picture," said Terry, "then I'll do a more detailed reading. Now, let's see." He fell silent, gazing at the cards, his pale green eyes half closed. Finally he looked up at Declan, blinking. "End of an era," he said, pointing an index finger at the World card. "Some part of your life has come full cycle, so I'd guess you're wondering what to do next. No, don't tell me—" He waved a hand at Declan "—not yet. The Seven of Cups, crossing the World, confirms what I've just said. See, these rows of cups show you've got plenty of options, but for now they all seem to be hidden from you. Either that or you can't make up your mind. These three underneath show the recent past. First, the Queen of Wands." He grinned up at Declan, his eyes twinkling under their shaggy brows. "A rather fiery lady, probably with red hair."

Declan grinned back, wondering if the rest of the reading would be this good.

"Well, obviously," Terry went on, "you've already met her. The next card is the Tower. That's a major shake-up that's taken place in your life since you met her. Hmm." He glanced shrewdly at Declan. "I noticed when you came in that you're limping. That's a recent injury, I feel. But there's a lot more to it than that. I said a shake-up, but it feels more like a shakedown. No wonder you don't know what to do next—you're in the process of completely rearranging your life." He pointed to the Fool. "Well, you've already taken the plunge, whether you realise it or not."

Oh, I know it, thought Declan, glancing at Isabel. Her attention was on the layout, as though she, too, were interpreting the cards. He'd have to remember to ask her later. Whatever she'd said to the contrary, he had a feeling she was seeing just as much in them as Terry was.

Swallowing the remainder of his tea, Terry went on, "Ah, the Eight of Cups up here in the future suggests you'll be starting on a new pathway within the next few months. A new cycle of activity will begin, and you'll leave old attachments behind. Though I get the feeling there aren't too many of those. I'd say you've been a bit of a loner, though more through force of circumstances than inclination."

Too bloody true, Declan mused, with an ironic twist of his lips. Isabel, noticing it, reached out and squeezed his hand, receiving a smile of thanks. "What's this one?" he asked, indicating the next card in the layout. It showed a knight in armour, apparently dead, with four swords suspended above his recumbent body. "It looks a bit grim."

"Not so." Terry smiled. "He's merely resting between engagements."

"Is that what I'm supposed to do?"

"I'd never presume to tell you you're 'supposed' to do anything, old chap. What I feel, though, is that you're pretty battle-weary right now, and what you'd like to do is take a complete break to gather your resources for whatever you decide to do next. I feel you'll make a better decision if you allow yourself space to get used to all the changes that have taken place. Now, as for what you'll end up doing..." He

230

paused to gaze at the final card in the layout, the Empress, looking up suddenly to tell Declan, "I can't tell you what that will be." He grinned at the look of surprise on Declan's face, then pointed back at the Seven of Cups at the centre of the layout. "You'll probably take a while to make your mind up. But this lady, the Empress, represents creativity and a love of beauty." He looked up again, his eyes suddenly sharp. "You're not an artist, are you?"

Declan allowed himself a noncommittal shake of his head, still following Terry's instruction not to give anything away.

"Hmm. It's just that I had a flash just now of paintings, one in particular. I think it's one you have a special feeling for." Another pause. "Or perhaps you have a special feeling for paintings?"

"Both, I guess," said Declan.

Terry nodded. "Right. Well, maybe that's an area for you to consider. But one way or another, I see you surrounded by art and creativity."

He gathered up the cards, shuffling them back into the rest of the deck, then handing them to Declan. "Right, shuffle again and we'll have a more detailed look."

Declan shuffled. "I'm impressed already," he said.

Terry made a self-deprecating gesture. "We aim to please." He took the deck back from Declan, this time laying twelve cards out in a circle, starting at the top and working clockwise, finally laying a thirteenth card face down in the centre. "This," he said, indicating the top card, "is now, and each of the others represents a month of the year to come."

"And the thirteenth card?" Declan was intrigued.

Terry merely smiled, saying in a mock portentous voice, "All will be revealed."

This turned out to be an understatement of gigantic proportions. As Terry finally turned over the card at the centre of the circle, Declan's head was reeling. "I hope you can remember all this," he said to Isabel. "I doubt if I will."

"You will," she told him. "You'll remember all you need to, even if it's not straight away."

"That's right," added Terry. He tapped the side of his head with one finger. "It's all in there anyway, otherwise I couldn't read it for you." His hand swept out to encompass the circle of cards and the rest of the deck in a pile beside it. "After all, what are these, really, other than bits of coloured cardboard?"

The thirteenth card was the Magician. Declan gave an involuntary start, and Isabel drew in a sharp breath. Terry took all this in, but made no comment. "This," he said, "is you at the end of the process I've just described. By the time a year is up, you'll be in possession of yourself, and all the elements you need—" He indicated the magician's tools of wand, sword, cup and pentacle "—to do what you really want to do. And what's more, you'll know what it is. So, to sum up, I'd say give yourself a break, in every sense of the term, and when the time's right, you'll know what you want. And remember the paintings—they're important. And now—" He gathered all the cards together once more, then got to his feet "—I don't know about you two, but I need another cup of tea before I go on."

"Do you have any plans for after the house is sold?" Isabel asked, going to help Terry dry the mugs and the teapot.

Terry shrugged, pursing his lips and pushing out a long, sighing breath. "Not really. I suppose I could restore the old caravan. I had thought of going modern and converting it into a house-truck. But it would take a hell of a lot of work, and I'm not sure I can be bothered. Besides, I'd still need somewhere for the business. Still, this house should realise a tidy sum, even in the condition it's in. Mother and I came to an arrangement years ago about divvying up the proceeds, so I'll have enough to set myself up with something. It's not as if I need much."

It was a simple statement of fact, completely without self-pity, but Isabel was aware of an underlying loneliness and sense of loss. "I could do a reading for you, if you'd like it," she said on impulse.

Terry's face crinkled into a delighted smile. "I'd love that. Only not today. I'm going to visit Mother after this." Indicating the stack of cards on its embroidered cloth, he took the tea towel from Isabel's hands and hung it back on the handle of the old stove. "Thanks. You make a start on shuffling the cards while I pour the tea."

Within minutes the three of them were poring over a new layout. Not surprisingly, the card at the centre was the King of Swords, the card Isabel had come to identify with Declan, and which she had seen in her mind just prior to discovering his surprise arrival at her flat. Crossing this was the High Priestess, which she took to represent herself. Terry's comments confirmed this, Declan nodding vehemently when he spoke of 'inner wisdom'.

"Your recent past," said Terry, "shows upheavals, too, but perhaps more on an inner level." He pointed to the Queen of Swords, and next to it the Devil and the Ace of Cups. "The Queen of Swords is you as you were, facing life very competently, but on your own. Then you had all that Circle of Light business to contend with—that's the Devil, as you might expect—and after that came the beginning of something new, involving you spiritually and emotionally." He paused, glancing shrewdly from Isabel to Declan.

A slight smile tugged at one corner of Declan's mouth but he said nothing.

Isabel concentrated on the cards. Above the central cross were the Ten of Pentacles, the Eight of Wands and the Two of Cups.

"Ah," said Terry, rubbing his hands in delight, "just look at that! The Ten of Pentacles there is all about setting up a home or family. I think you might be moving house, too, but before that you'll be travelling. Not a long trip, but it has a good feeling about it. Yes, and after that the Two of Cups shows a partnership. Of course, I'm not necessarily saying it'll be a romantic partnership..." He threw a mischievous glance at Isabel and Declan, his green eyes sparkling.

Isabel felt her face turning red. Declan was having a similar problem, she noticed.

The twelve-month reading proved equally fascinating. She was interested to see what appeared to be a reference to the tarot murders, though, as was often the case with tarot readings, the card in question had application to at least two other areas of her life. At length Terry turned over the thirteenth card. It was the High Priestess again.

"Hmm," said Terry, thoughtfully stroking his beard, which sprang back with cheerful defiance the minute it escaped his fingers, "it seems you'll be continuing as a 'spiritual advisor', at least for the next year."

"Don't call me that," grimaced Isabel. "It makes me sound like those people you read about in magazines. You know, 'tarot reader to the stars'."

There was a snort of laughter from Declan. "I'll bet none of them are poor!"

Isabel gave him a look of disgust. "I'd rather keep my integrity, thanks very much."

"No wonder you haven't made your fortune. On the other hand," he added, so softly that only Isabel could hear him, "I guess it's one of the reasons I love you."

"No sign of a fortune, I'm afraid," Terry said with a smile. "Nevertheless, it looks like an interesting year, with a great deal of personal happiness for you. You can't say fairer than that, now, can you?"

"Indeed you can't." Impulsively, Isabel took his hand in both of hers and gave it a squeeze.

"Thank you so much, Terry."

Declan stood up, carefully unkinking his injured leg. He held out his hand to Terry. "Thanks, mate. It's been fascinating. I only hope I remember it all."

"Don't mention it. And, as Isabel said before, you'll remember whatever you need to."

Gathering the cards together, Terry began to wrap them once more in their silk cloth. As he did so, two cards fell from the deck to lie face down on the table. Isabel felt a prickling up her spine, and the sensation of slight breathlessness that for her often accompanied some psychic insight. It seemed Terry had felt something similar, as he turned the two cards over and laid them side by side on the scrubbed wooden tabletop, gazing at them intently. Isabel looked and saw the Magician and the Devil. The breathless feeling intensified. Then Terry began to speak. "This is not about either of you," he said, sounding slightly surprised, "though I think it affects you both. Someone you know is in great danger, I feel—a man, perhaps more a colleague than a friend. These two cards signify the source of the danger." He broke off, breathing deeply, and closing his eyes. When he opened them again they bore a look of concern. He pointed at the two cards. "I don't know who this person is, but he—I feel sure it is 'he'—is very, very confused. He thinks he's the Magician, but he's really the Devil. By which I mean," he added for Declan's benefit, seeing the bewilderment on his face, "that he operates from a state of ignorance and fear. He really has no idea what he's doing, and that's what makes him dangerous."

One hand resting lightly on the two cards in front of him, he fell silent again, staring unseeingly ahead of him. His voice, when at last he spoke, sounded unusually thin, as though filtered through a long funnel. "I'm in a big, dark room. It smells dusty, perhaps unused. No, it's used as a temple of some sort, though that wasn't its original purpose. There's an altar at one end, half black, half white, like two cubes put together, with symbols of some sort painted on them. I wish I could see it more clearly. Oh!" He swayed slightly, and Isabel moved involuntarily to support him, remembering just in time not to touch him, as he seemed to be in a trance. "There's been a death here, or—no, someone was injured. Oh, my God! He was killed, but not in the temple. I can feel fear, and anger... immense anger. And danger." His voice had sunk to a whisper.

There was a pause, for what seemed minutes, but was in reality a few seconds. When Terry spoke again, his voice sounded more like its normal hearty self. "I'm outside the building now, thank God. It feels much better. There's a shop with display shelves in the window. Damn, I can't make out what's on them. But I think the temple's next to it—or maybe upstairs. I get the feeling it's part of the same building, anyway." Apparently of their own volition, his eyes slowly opened. Rubbing one hand across them, Terry shook his head vigorously, then pushed the two cards back into the deck. "Whoo! I hope you two have some idea what that was all about, because I'm damned if I do."

"I think we might," said Isabel. "And thank you. I think you've just been very helpful."

"Thank God for that!" Terry spoke with feeling. "That sort of thing doesn't happen to me very often, I'm pleased to say, but when it does, it usually turns out to be important."

"Somehow," said Declan, "I don't think this is going to be an exception."

CHAPTER TWENTY-FOUR

"The problem is—" Declan leaned forward on Isabel's couch "—they can't just go arresting people on what they'd see as no more than a vague suspicion. As a matter of fact, sometimes even when they know for sure someone's guilty, they can't make an arrest because there isn't enough evidence to make it stick." Earlier that day, he had paid another visit to Constable Johnson. Johnson immediately took him to see the man in charge of the investigation, Inspector Colin Garfield, a solid, phlegmatic man of around fifty, whose square, steel-rimmed glasses, receding hair and quiet, almost grave manner, gave him an ineffectual air that was entirely deceptive.

While taking note of what Declan had told him of the panel's suspicions, Garfield had observed sadly that what they really needed was some good, solid evidence. They couldn't just go around searching private property on the off-chance. Those days were long gone. Unless there was a suspicion of drug abuse, he had added, raising his eyebrows in doubtful enquiry. Unfortunately, Declan had been unable to raise his hopes on that score.

"Like the Yorkshire Ripper," said Luke, with a sage nod of his head. For some reason, he was looking particularly smug today.

"Well, yeah. They had him in for questioning over and

over again before they finally nailed him; they just didn't have enough evidence to arrest him."

"Still," said Joss, "they are taking Leo Hart's death seriously now. I spoke to Simon Drawbridge this morning, and he's pleased about that, although he doesn't really expect it to amount to much. The trouble is, the only solid information that connects the murders is the tarot cards and, from what you've told us, Declan, there were no fingerprints on either of them."

"Well—" Declan tried to sound more hopeful than he felt "—at least the police are keeping an eye on things now. Most criminals slip up sooner or later, and when this bloke does, you can be sure they'll be onto him like a shot."

"I'm not so sure about that," Isabel said. "The thing is, he's probably not so much criminal in the usual sense as insane, or at least seriously unbalanced, so without knowing him, it's next to impossible to guess which way he's going to jump."

"Which leads us," said Declan, "back to motive. If we could figure that out, I reckon the rest would fall into place."

Joss nodded, pursing her lips thoughtfully. "I don't know how much help it'll be, but Luke and I have been doing a little investigating of our own."

Luke nodded, and took up the story. "After you all left on Wednesday, I felt totally discouraged. I kept thinking there must be something more we could do. So I went down to the scene of the latest crime. While I was there, a couple of cops turned up. Unfortunately, I didn't learn anything from them and, of course, I'm about as psychic as a lump of wood. But while I was looking at the sundial, I had an idea. I figured you two—" He nodded at Isabel and Declan "—probably had other things on your minds, so I went to see Joss."

Like a partner in a comic turn, Joss took over. "Luke was hoping I'd be able to pick something up psychically, so yesterday we both went down there."

"And did you? Pick something up, I mean?" queried Isabel.

"Not as much as we'd hoped, but there's still a definite 'atmosphere' there." Joss gave a slight grimace. The others waited as she strove for words to describe her experience. At last she went on, "I couldn't really see anything, which is unusual for me. But there were a lot of very strong and very mixed feelings—fear, panic, and a kind of cold fury. I walked around the garden for a bit, and round the outside of the hedge, too, and I came to the tentative conclusion that the murderer and his victim came in by the Eastern entrance—there's one for each of the four cardinal points—and that the death occurred in the garden part itself, then the body was dragged to the sundial. Whoever did it seemed inordinately pleased with himself. It was horrible—almost obscene." Joss shuddered at the memory. "Then I found myself looking at the face of the sundial, and particularly at the marking for eight o'clock in the morning. It was Luke who pointed out to me that at this time of year that's about sunrise."

"You don't suppose that's the time the murder was committed?" asked Isabel.

"It's possible, I suppose," Joss replied. "I couldn't tell what it was I was picking up, exactly. But the feeling I had was one of complete elation. It was stronger when I touched the spot, so I'd guess it's significant in some way."

Isabel suddenly let go of the curl she had been winding round her finger. "I know what it may be!" Three faces turned towards her. "The theme of the murder was Death, right?" They nodded. "Well on the Death card there's the sun on the horizon. People usually think it's setting, but actually it's rising. The card signifies rebirth—the dawn of a new day."

"Well, it's a thought," Joss said, "and for all I could pick up, you may be right, though as an avenue of enquiry, I'm not sure it leads us anywhere—not yet, at any rate—but I think we should definitely bear it in mind for future reference. In the meantime, I still think James, or someone in the Brotherhood, has a fair idea what's going on."

"Yes," agreed Isabel, "but let's face it, if James won't talk, the rest of the Brotherhood isn't likely to come forward to help us, much less the police. Quite the reverse, in fact. I think we're just going to have to find out for ourselves."

"What exactly," asked Joss with a sharp look, "did you have in mind?"

"I think we should start by having a look at their temple."

"But we don't have any idea where it is."

Isabel looked meaningfully at her friend. "Yes, we do. Terry told me and Declan yesterday. He described the inside of it—well, the altar anyway, and that sounded pretty distinctive—and he said it was next to, or above, a shop. Why don't we check the membership list again and see if there's anyone on it we recognise as a shop owner. Since we already know he owns a shop, we can start with Jonah Trenwith."

"He owns at least three shops that I know of," said Luke.

"Do you know where they are?" asked Joss, pulling a notepad and pen from her bag.

"There's the one in High Street, for a start. The others are both in suburban shopping malls. One's in Cashmere, but I'd have to check the phone book about the other one."

"It's not likely to be either of them, anyway," said Isabel, "because shopping malls don't tend to have anything upstairs other than more shops, or offices. Also, what Terry described sounded much older, more like a warehouse, perhaps."

"Okay." Joss made a note on her pad. "But there might be other Brotherhood members who own shops. You've still got the printout, haven't you, Isabel?"

"Yes." Isabel got to her feet and went to the door. "I meant to give it back to you at Luke's on Wednesday, but I forgot. Sorry."

She left the room, returning a moment later with the thick sheaf of papers. Joss removed the tray of empty coffee mugs to make room on the coffee table, carrying it out to the kitchen while Isabel leafed through the papers until she came to the membership list. Ten minutes later, they had perused the entire list, coming up with two names they recognised as being those of local shop owners.

"Of course," said Joss, "there could be others we haven't recognised."

"True," Isabel said, "but at least this gives us somewhere to start."

Declan looked at her. "I know I'm going to regret asking, but doing what, exactly?"

Isabel returned his look with a steady gaze. "Just looking," she said innocently, "that's all."

"I'll bet." He glanced at his watch, then stood up, wincing slightly at a twinge of pain in his knee. "It'll be dark soon, so if we're going to do it today, we'd better get a move on."

Eyes gleaming, Isabel jumped to her feet and gave his arm

a squeeze. Declan sighed, and cast her a long-suffering look, walking towards the door with an exaggerated limp.

Joss grinned at Luke. "Ain't love grand?"

* * * *

They were standing outside the narrow glass frontage of Demeter's Garden health shop peering in at the neat display of packaged foods, cosmetics, and vitamin supplements through the gathering gloom at the latter end of a typically bleak winter's day. It was almost six in the evening and the shop was closed, its glass-paned door locked securely, and protected by a heavy mesh outer door, also locked.

To the left of the shop was another door, of solid wood painted black, and beside it a laminated sign attached to the brick wall informed them that Jonah Trenwith, M.B.C.A., M.N.Z.C.A., had his clinic on the first floor, sandwiched between a second-hand bookshop on the ground floor and an accountant on the second. A small card stuck to the sign with sellotape further informed them the clinic was closed until further notice.

"Reckon they'll be waiting a while for him to open up again," Declan observed in laconic tones. He raised his eyes to two rows of grimy windows set into the high brick building above the ground-floor shops. "Wonder what's up there?"

"Warehouses mostly, I should think," Joss told him. "Some of the ones over the road there have been converted into apartments, but by the look of these, no-one's touched them in years."

"That's what Terry said at first about the one he saw,"

243

Isabel reminded her, "until he saw the altar."

Luke took a last puff at his cigarette before grinding it beneath his heel on the footpath. He indicated another black door on the other side of the health food shop. "That'll be the door that leads up to them," he said, "unless there's another entrance round the back." He began to walk along the footpath, but there was no telltale alleyway leading to the rear of the building, and no further doorways other than those that led to the row of ground-floor shops. "Yep," he announced, "this is it. Pity it's locked."

"What we need," said Joss to Declan, "is your Constable Johnson. Unless..." She regarded him shrewdly. "Surely you could pick the lock, couldn't you?"

Declan's mouth twitched slightly. "Is the Pope a Catholic?" he said. "Unless it's a deadlock—I never did make it to the advanced course." He looked at Isabel, his expression deliberately bland. "If I send you the airfare, you'll come and visit me in prison, won't you? Of course, I won't expect you to wait for me if they send me away for more than five years."

Correctly interpreting this as assent to commit breaking and entering, Isabel informed him, "It doesn't look like a deadlock, just a Yale."

"Oh, well, in that case it shouldn't be more than three years. I'll be out in eighteen months if I'm lucky. There is just one little snag though..."

"Yes?"

"I didn't bring my tools with me."

"Oh." Isabel's face fell. "I suppose that's that then."

Joss asked, "What sort of tools do you need? We might be able to improvise."

"Maybe a pocket knife with a small blade?" The others shook their heads. "Pair of tweezers?"

"Ah," replied Joss, "I think I can help you there." She dug into her bag and fished out a small cosmetic purse. "Yes, here you are."

"Thanks—I think." Declan took the tweezers and looked up and down the street. It was empty. Trying hard to look as though he were merely making a lawful entry, he approached the door. The others gathered helpfully around him, at once shielding him and scanning the street.

Moments later, there was a soft click and Declan was able to push open the door. "Don't forget to shut it behind you," he said as they all filed through after him, gazing up the narrow staircase to the small landing above. Before Luke closed the door, they had a brief glimpse of worn, greyish linoleum encasing the flight of stairs. By the time they reached the landing, their eyes had adjusted sufficiently to make out a door on either side of it. The one on the left opened into a small storeroom fitted with wide shelves on which boxes were piled. From a nail on the wall by the shelves hung two exercise books and a pen on pieces of string. Joss reached in and looked quickly through one of the books.

"Stock book," she informed them, "for the shop."

The other door had a sign attached to it, saying 'PRIVATE'. It was locked. Declan applied the tweezers once more, and soon had the door open. Once again, he reminded the others to close the door after them, and they gazed curiously around a large, long room with a high, beamed roof. In the gloom, the roof was shrouded in darkness, and it was impossible to make out the far end of the room clearly. It seemed to be hung with dark curtains. The other end, despite the only light being filtered through a row of small, painted-over windows set high in one brick wall, was instantly revealing.

Beneath a heavy-looking brass dish-shaped object hung by chains from one of the rafters, stood two cubes, about four feet along each edge, side by side. One was painted black, one white. Various symbols were inscribed on their sides, their colours counter-changed with that of the surface on which they found themselves. Several objects stood on the altar thus formed—a large, trident-shaped silver candlestick, a silver chalice, a carved wooden wand about eighteen inches long, a wicked-looking sword with an ornate hilt, a bronze disk with a pentagram embossed on its surface, a heavy flask made of blue glass, and two small silver bowls, both empty.

"Bingo!" exclaimed Luke. "Look at that, all the tools of the trade!"

While he and Joss and Isabel moved immediately for a closer examination of the altar and its accoutrements, Declan cast his eyes about the rest of the warehouse before moving to join them. As soon as they had finished their inspection, he pointed out a cupboard about the size of a small sideboard standing against the wall behind the altar. The wooden floor echoing beneath their feet, they went to join him as he bent to open its double doors.

Inside, two shelves ran its length. On the lower of these stood two more silver bowls, another blue glass flask, several packets whose labels declared them to contain church incense, neatly stacked boxes of long matches, and charcoal blocks similar to those used for lighting barbecues.

Joss glanced up at the brass object hanging above the

altar. "I wonder if they use that for their incense?" She turned her gaze back to the top shelf. A plastic bottle of kerosene stood there, along with a thin, unlabelled box. "What are these, I wonder?"

Luke lifted the lid to reveal to his puzzled gaze a number of thin, flat strips of what looked like plaited cotton.

"I think they're lamp wicks," Isabel told him, "but just look what I've found."

She unwrapped the black silk fabric from a flat, rectangular package. In it were three books, their black leather bindings unmarked. Carefully, she opened the top one. On the first page inside its marbled endplates, they saw, hand-written in graceful Italic script:

THE BOOK
of

THE BROTHERHOOD OF THE FLAME
Volume 1, A.D. 2001
Inscribed by
Brother Solem Fero, Adeptus Minor
Keeper of the Flame

"Looks like this is it!" Isabel exclaimed gleefully. "The official record. Funny sort of name, though, Solem Fero. It's Latin, isn't it? What does it mean?"

"I carry the Sun," Joss told her. "It's a Latin motto, by the look of it, you know, like they used in the Order of the Golden Dawn."

Isabel laughed. "Of course! How wonderfully pretentious."

"They also make great camouflage." Luke grinned. "Hang on, what was that?"

Isabel had been leafing through the pages. She turned

back to where Luke had indicated. It was a list in two columns. The first column was an alphabetical list of names, some of which were already familiar to them. Alongside these, in the other column, were more phrases in Latin.

"This is wonderful!" breathed Isabel. "It's a complete list of members, with all their secret names. We should make a note of these."

Joss reached into her bag. She was in the act of withdrawing her ever-present notepad when they heard a scrabbling sound from beneath them. They froze.

Declan was the first to react. "Someone," he whispered, "is unlocking the outside door. "Quick, we'd better try and find somewhere to hide."

Frantically, they looked about them.

"Down there." Declan pointed to the other end of the room. "I saw some curtains hanging there. Hopefully, there'll be room to hide behind them. If not, at least it's darker down there.

Bring those with you," he whispered to Isabel, indicating the books as he quietly closed the cupboard doors. "There's no time to wrap them up again. We'll just have to hope they don't go looking for them."

As silently as possible, and in varying stages of panic, the four of them hurried down the long room as footsteps grew louder on the stairs. Luckily, for some unfathomable reason, there was a space of about three feet between the heavy black curtains and a large, grimy double window that looked down onto a narrow courtyard at the rear of the row of shops. Another long, brick building stared blankly at them from its own dirt-encrusted windows across this tattered miniature wasteland. Crouching beside Declan on the dusty floor behind the curtains, the precious books balanced on her knees, Isabel listened as a key snicked open the lock of the door marked 'PRIVATE'.

CHAPTER TWENTY-FIVE

They heard several sets of footsteps resounding hollowly as they crossed the floor, then a number of thuds and scraping noises. To Isabel's horror, Declan opened the curtains a fraction and peered out. Turning back to them, he held up six fingers. Six of them. It must be a meeting of the Council, she surmised. They wouldn't have had time yet to elect anyone to replace Trenwith.

As though to confirm her hypothesis, they heard a harsh, authoritative voice. "Thank you all for coming at such short notice. Since this is a special meeting, I thought it best to meet here, on common territory. Our first order of business must, of course, be to select a new Senior for the Order, and then another Brother for the Council, to bring the number up to seven, as our rules oblige us. Are we all agreed?"

There were grunts and murmurs of assent.

Beckoning to Isabel, Declan moved back a little. Isabel slid forward to look through the gap in the curtains. As she did so, the books slid off her knees. Her heart thudded in sudden panic. Declan's hands shot out and caught them, lowering them gently to the floor. As soon as her pounding heart would let her, Isabel looked and saw six men, three sitting on stools, and three on chairs. She recognised James, as usual fiddling nervously with his tie. The speaker, who sat next to him, was a stocky, bullish man with close-cut grey hair. He obviously considered himself to be in charge of the proceedings, and his manner suggested this was what he was used to. The Colonel, Isabel thought, nodding to herself.

She felt a tap on her shoulder. Joss had edged forward for a look. Isabel moved back, and Joss peered through the peephole.

They heard James's voice, sounding anxious despite his professionally calm delivery. "Since we're all agreed on the order of business, may I suggest we use the same selection method as before—that is, we select our new Senior on the basis of the highest grade within the Brotherhood."

The voice that rose in response was high and nasal. Fortunately this meant it carried well. The four hidden listeners heard him say, "As the only one among us now to hold the grade of Adeptus Major, the position of Senior falls then to Brother Ferro Comite. Are we all agreed?"

There were more murmurs, presumably of assent, since they heard a scraping and shuffling of feet, then the grating voice they had first heard spoke again. "I accept the honour bestowed on me, with my assurance that I will do my utmost at all times to conduct myself as befits it." Further shuffling of feet, followed by a soft thud, indicated that the new Senior had resumed his seat.

Following this, there was a brief silence. Then the harsh voice of Brother Ferro Comite spoke again. "Now we must choose a new Council member. I suggest we each put forward the name, or names, of our choice, then discuss each one."

There was a slight cough, then another voice, strong, but well-modulated, spoke. "If I can make a suggestion, shouldn't we discuss the series of tragedies that has befallen the Brotherhood? I don't want to seem negative but, frankly, it's beginning to look as though selection to the Council is tantamount to a death warrant."

Luke's brow furrowed as he tried to think where he had heard that voice before. He shuffled forward to peer between the curtains as the new Senior's voice began to speak in reply, "I can appreciate your concern, Brother Lux e Tenebris. However, the Brotherhood must continue, and be seen to continue, regardless of outside events."

"The recent deaths," the well-modulated voice replied, "can scarcely be regarded as outside events. To begin with, they've touched the very centre of our order. And since two of them were murders—murders of a particularly gruesome kind, what's more, and both committed in a style of peculiar relevance to our teachings—surely we must assume they were done by one of us. Unless, of course, we are to believe some outsider has access to our teachings."

Luke stifled a gasp as he recognised the speaker. He had only met him in person once before, years ago at a training course for radio broadcasters, but how could he ever forget that quietly magnificent voice, particularly as its owner had gone on to greater things, first at several smaller stations around the country, then, having paid his dues in the provinces, as host of the prized morning slot on the city's highest rating commercial station. Brother Lux e Tenebris was none other than that very well-known radio personality, Julian Light. The cunning devil had used a play on his own name for his Brotherhood motto.

As Luke moved back from the curtain, it shifted slightly. It was too far away for any of the brothers to notice, but the movement must have stirred up some of the dust that lay thick on the floor. He felt a violent sneeze coming on. As the others looked on in horror, he clamped his fingers desperately onto his nose, eyes bulging. This measure was only partially successful, and the sneeze eventually escaped, thankfully reduced to a soft snort.

Declan, one eye to the gap in the curtains, saw the newly elected Senior raise his grey, bristly head and turn it slightly in their direction. But the bespectacled brother with the nasal voice had begun to speak, and he turned away again. Declan breathed a silent sigh of relief. As far as he was concerned, they could definitely do without having to explain their presence in the temple to half a dozen self-styled magicians.

"But our teachings on the tarot are hardly unique to us," Brother Solem Fero was saying. "The use of its symbols does not necessarily mean the murderer was one of our brothers."

"True," conceded the smooth-voiced darling of Nine to Noon with Julian. "However, who else would have any reason for doing away with what's beginning to look like the entire Council of the Brotherhood of the Flame? And who else would be likely to use a tarot theme for his victims? It's got to be one of us."

"In that case," came the far from dulcet tones of Brother Fero Comite, "what's his motive?"

Declan nodded at the others, his expression saying, 'We might be getting somewhere at last'. Joss pulled her notepad and pen from her jacket pocket and opened the notepad, holding it against her knee.

It was James's voice that responded, sounding even more worried than before. "I think I might know that."

"Yes?" Again the Senior's peremptory tone.

"Not long ago, at the autumn equinox, we held examinations for the grade of Practicus." Declan saw the others nodding. "There were three candidates, of whom one, Brother Gaudet Luce, passed, and the other two, Brothers Clariore Flammis and Non Extinguar, failed. Since grades are passed or failed by vote of the Council, might this not provide a motive?"

"Hmmm." The Senior spoke again. "You could be right, especially as both of the brothers we were obliged to fail tend to take things pretty seriously. Not," he hastened to add, "that I'm suggesting any of us should take the teachings lightly. In any case, we're still faced with the problem of discovering which of them, if either, it might be. And we can't make a move until we know." He paused, frowning, for a moment's reflection, then abruptly voiced his conclusion. "We need to consider this further. Perhaps a scrying, when the time is right. Brother Quaerens Lucem, would you find out the best time and let the rest of us know? Meanwhile, as time is running short, let's return to the outstanding business for this meeting. Any of you who have names to propose for our new Council member, please put them forward now. Brother Solem Fero will, as usual, record them."

James spoke again, sounding only a little tentative. "The helmet I found at the university..."

"Brother Nobilis Est Ira Leonis's helmet—yes?" The Senior's tone was impatient. Clearly, he was not a man with much tolerance for interruptions.

James continued, "I feel it may be a clue to the entire—situation."

"How? The connection seems tenuous, to say the least."

"Whoever left the helmet in the university library foyer almost certainly took it from Brother Nobilis, and since he would have had it with him when he died—he had his motor cycle with him at the time, remember?—it's reasonable to assume the person who took it was involved in his death. Otherwise, why take the helmet at all?"

"Why, indeed?" This was Brother Solem Fero, the Keeper of the Flame. "And why take it to the university, of all places?"

"I suspect it was simply a neutral place to leave it until he could get rid of it. Or maybe he thought it was a good place to 'lose' it, among hundreds of other helmets. What's more, it would have worked if I hadn't chanced to see it and recognise it."

It seemed the Senior could tolerate this diversion no longer. "What on earth has any of this to do with the murders of Brothers Dabunt Espera Rosas and Esto Sol Testis?" he exploded.

Quietly, if not entirely calmly, James explained. "Out of the two failed Practicus candidates, only Brother Non Extinguar would have reason to be at the university. He works there, as a technician in the Physics Department. That's what I've been trying to tell you. The helmet points to his possible implication in the death of Brother Nobilis Est Ira Leonis. What if that, too, was a murder? What if Brother Non Extinguar was responsible for the deaths of all of our Brothers on this Council? After all, the reason we failed him was that we sensed in him a certain lack of—stability."

"This is all speculation," the Senior's harsh voice broke in. "Naturally, we must take every possible step, both to find out the truth, and to protect ourselves and our homes and families. Brother Quaerens Lucem, new instructions. We meet tonight. Ten o'clock, here at the temple. Meanwhile, let's proceed with the remaining business."

The brothers put forward several names, though it was obvious they were merely going through the motions. Joss finished scribbling notes in her pad. Eventually, after a brief, and largely unintelligible discussion, a selection was made and duly recorded by the balding, scholarly-looking Brother Solem Fero. Fortunately for the four interlopers, growing ever more uncomfortable in the stuffy space behind the heavy curtains, the meeting broke up immediately after this.

There was a heart-stopping moment when The Keeper of the Flame appeared to be heading towards the cupboard behind the altar. Fortunately for Declan's peace of mind as he gazed out through his peephole, he was merely replacing his chair against the wall next to it. He shoved his notes into his pocket before leaving, presumably intending to update the records later, perhaps after the ten o'clock meeting. The four of them waited as the footsteps of the brothers receded down the stairs, until at last they heard the outer door being closed and locked, and the sounds of car engines roaring to life.

Luke and Joss got to their feet, brushing dust from their clothing. Isabel followed suit, picking up the Brotherhood records and their wrapping cloth from the floor, shaking out the cloth to get rid of the all-pervading dust. Then she noticed Declan had not moved, but was rubbing his knee and grimacing in obvious pain.

Quickly, she handed Joss the books and bent down to him. "Are you all right? Here, let me give you a hand."

"Thanks." Declan smiled thinly through his pain. "I seem

to have seized up." He took her hands and let her pull him to his feet. Pains shot through his knee like pellets from a shotgun. For a moment he felt dizzy and faint. He was glad to have Isabel to hold on to. Gradually, however, the pain subsided to the dull throb he had become more or less inured to. "Look, can we get on with this now?" he said at last to the others, his voice still showing strain. "It's getting late, and I could really use a shower and some food, not to mention some more of those bloody painkillers."

Consulting her watch, Joss suddenly looked at the others in horror. "I'd completely forgotten—I was supposed to be at work half an hour ago, and Martin doesn't even know where I am!"

"My, how time flies when you're having fun," observed Luke. "Tell them you've been working on a big story. After all, you may well be right."

For once, Joss was not amused. "Shut up, Luke. I'm not in the mood. Anyway, I'm not worried about work so much as Martin. He'll be frantic, especially if he's phoned work and I'm not there either. Look, I'm sorry, but I'll have to go." She handed her notepad to Isabel. "Here, take any notes you want, and I'll catch up with you later." Brushing furiously at her jacket and trousers, she hurriedly left.

"I think," said Luke, gazing at her retreating back, "we could all do with a drink. And I, for one, am dying for a cigarette."

"Sorry, Luke," said Isabel, "it'll have to wait. We can't risk taking these books away from here and, after all our trouble, we can't leave without at least getting that list of names and mottoes. Let's have a look." Rapidly, she flicked through the thin pages until she reached the list. "Ah, here we are," and began transferring the information into Joss's notepad.

While she did this, Luke and Declan each took one of the remaining volumes and began to leaf through them.

"This looks like an update," Luke said, "made at the beginning of the following year."

"There's another one here, too," said Declan. "Only three names in it, but their mottoes are there, too, so I guess we'd better get them down as well."

As quickly as she could, expecting at every moment the return of the Council members to prepare for their ritual, Isabel wrote down the names offered to her, until she had a list of some forty names and their corresponding mottoes.

"I wonder if there's anything else we should note?" she said, looking up at last.

Luke consulted his watch. "We've got just over two hours before they're due back," he indicated the volume from which Isabel had been copying, "but it could take days to go through everything in those."

With a thump that betrayed her frayed nerves, Isabel snapped the book shut. "Oh, for God's sake, let's go! I've had about as much as I can take for one day. Besides, what James said is probably more use to us than anything in here."

Declan, whose knee was again becoming seriously painful, waved his hand wearily at the leather-bound volumes. "I reckon we've probably achieved about as much as we're going to. For Christ's sake let's get out of here and go and have a drink."

"I second that," declared Luke with a loud sneeze. The dust was beginning to get the better of him, not to mention the nicotine withdrawal.

Isabel re-wrapped the cloth around the three volumes,

taking care to place them in the right order and to wrap them as nearly as possible to the way they'd been found.

Within minutes, the three of them had let themselves out into the dark, and thankfully empty, street.

Luke pulled his cigarette packet and lighter from his pocket, lighting a cigarette and drawing on it with obvious relish. "Right—" He grinned "—your place or mine?"

CHAPTER TWENTY-SIX

"I really thought I'd blown it, both literally and figuratively." Luke helped himself to more coffee, then leaned back contentedly in his big armchair. "Especially when that bloke with the crew-cut and the chainsaw voice turned his beady little eyes in our direction."

"Presumably," said Joss, "he's the one referred to in the minutes as the Colonel."

"He certainly looks the military type," Luke said.

"You mean the short hair and upright bearing?" There was a suggestion of irony in Joss's voice, which Luke did not miss.

He grinned. "No, I meant the macho aggression and general air of menace."

Joss laughed. "Shall we have a look at our notes, then, and see if our suspicions are confirmed? Did you remember to bring them?" Addressing herself to Isabel, Joss helped herself to another piece of Luke's supremely decadent chocolate sponge cake and took a luxurious bite.

In reply, Isabel pulled Joss's notepad from her bag and placed it on the polished top of Luke's table. "I wrote down the list of names and mottoes, including all the updates—there were three, if I remember rightly. And I jotted down what the three of us could remember afterwards of what they said about the failed candidates and so on. Mind you, what with having squatted in the dust and gloom of that temple for hours, listening to James and the others waffling on, it all became a bit of a blur."

"The whisky we bought on the way home won't have helped, either," Declan said with a twitch of his mouth. "Purely medicinal, of course," he added, for the benefit of Joss, who seemed about to remonstrate.

"But of course." Joss looked up from leafing through the notes, a twinkle in her blue eyes. "I trust you've all regained sufficient mental faculties to go through this list with me."

Luke, looking over her shoulder, noticed Leo Hart's name as Joss slowly turned the pages, and next to it his motto. "'Nobilis Est Ira Leonis'," he read out.

Isabel turned to Joss. "What does that mean?"

"The lion's anger is noble—something like that."

"Obviously chosen to fit his name," said Luke.

Joss flipped up the pages and they saw Richard Kleber's name, with the motto, 'Ex Flamma Lux'.

"Nearly all of them seem to have chosen mottoes involving light or flame," commented Declan. His education at Saint Pat's, by religious brothers of a very different kind, had left him with a surprisingly sound understanding of basic Latin—surprising, that is, in view of the fact that most of his Latin homework had been done by Kenny MacMahon, who ran a small but thriving specialist business based on the exchange of his intellect for the other boys' pocket money.

"Including James." There were hoots of laughter as Joss translated James's motto, 'Fulget Virtus – Virtue Shines Bright'.

"Trust James to have something sanctimonious as well as pretentious," chuckled Isabel.

"If you want pretentious, what about this one?" Joss said, pointing to the name above James's. 'Non Extinguar—I shall not be extinguished'. Good God!" the realisation suddenly hit her, "that's Hugh Murray, one of my tarot clients. And he's one of the candidates they failed for—what was it again?"

"The Practicus Grade," said Luke, "whatever that means."

"Practitioner," said Declan.

"As opposed to what?" Luke still looked puzzled.

"That must be what was on that CD Quincy wiped," Isabel told him with a grin. "It was one of the degrees, or grades, in the Golden Dawn. Let me see if I can remember them." She closed her eyes, her brow wrinkled slightly in concentration, and began to recite, "In the First Order there was Neophyte, Zelator, Theoricus, Practicus and Philosophus. Then, in the Second Order, the Adepts—Adeptus Minor, Major and Exemptus."

"I'm impressed!" said Luke. "Was that it?"

"No, there was one for each position on the Tree of Life of the Kabbalah. Above the Adepts there was a Third Order, supposedly of Secret Chiefs." Whatever the hell they are, thought Declan, but he remained silent as Isabel, her eyes still closed as though consulting some inner vision, continued. "Hmm, I know there were three of them, but I can't remember what they were." She opened her eyes again, blinking at the others. "Except the highest one was Ipsissimus. I remember that one because Aleister Crowley claimed he'd reached it, and of course no-one could say he hadn't, because how would they know, unless they were also one of the Secret Chiefs?"

There were nods from Joss and Luke, who were familiar through their reading with the flamboyant career of the self-styled Great Beast.

Declan, whose taste in esoterica did not run to nineteenth-century purported magicians, simply said, "So, our lot are using the same grades as this Golden Dawn. How does this help us?"

Isabel gave him a slightly sheepish smile. "I don't suppose it does, really. Sorry, I got a bit carried away." She turned to Joss. "What was the name of the other failed candidate?"

Joss flicked through her notes. "Um, Clariore Flammis was the motto they mentioned." She flipped back to the list. "His name is Robert Ingram, but that doesn't really help us much, either, does it?"

"No, but the addresses are all on the computer list."

Joss clapped one hand to the side of her head. "Of course they are! Damn! I forgot to bring it with me."

"It seems to me," said Luke, breathing a series of smoke rings into the air above his head, "that this Hugh Murray chap is a better bet."

"Yes," agreed Joss, "James certainly seemed to favour him, and his reasons for doing so were as good as anything we've come up with."

"His working at the university provides a possible link with Richard Kleber, too," said Isabel, "so we may as well start with him."

"I'll call you before I go to work, then, and give you both their addresses," said Joss. "But what exactly do you have in mind? We can hardly just knock on his door and say, 'Hello, we think you've murdered four men. Would you care to confirm this?'"

There was an edge of sarcasm to Declan's laconic voice as he said, "Since I seem to have found a new career as a burglar, why don't I just pick his lock, too?" Then, as he saw the delighted grins the others turned on him, "I was joking! Really! I didn't mean it!" He buried his head in his hands in not quite mock despair. "Oh, Mother of God! Me and my big mouth!"

* * * *

It was a tall, narrow, two-storeyed wooden house, one of a row of similar buildings overlooking the established trees and rolling grass of a park. Once grand houses for wealthy business or professional men and their families, all of them had long since been converted into apartments. Now they stood, down at heel but defiant, shabby porches and balconies declaring to the world at large that down on their luck they might be, but they still had standards.

Number 24 where, according to the computer printout, Hugh Murray lived, was at the end of the row, next to a block of new townhouses signalling the inevitable arrival in the neighbourhood of urban renewal. The house, however, stood its ground, elegant behind its low brick wall, despite peeling cream paint and an overgrown garden. Declan looked up at it, trying to imagine which window might be the one behind which Hugh Murray lived his apparently bizarre secret life.

Isabel followed his gaze, finding no clues there either. It had been decided that only the two of them would carry out this particular mission, as a delegation of four might arouse suspicion, from the neighbours if not Hugh himself. Obviously, Declan had to be one of them because of his expertise with locks (Joss had loaned him her tweezers, and he had brought along a small pocket knife and a piece of wire as well, though he was dubious, to say the least, about the entire exercise), and Isabel was the obvious choice as his partner.

As agreed, Joss had phoned the previous evening with the addresses of both their suspects. But they had decided to postpone their visit until next day, when Hugh would presumably be at work. With unexpected stubbornness, Declan had refused point blank to risk an encounter with their quarry and, despite Isabel's best efforts at presenting him with plausible scenarios, he had remained intransigent.

"I wonder which flat is his?" said Isabel, gazing at the faded green paint of the front door, set in the square porch behind its fat concrete pillars. There was no indication there, no board with cards in little frames.

Declan shrugged, pulling up the collar of his jacket against the cold gust of wind that suddenly rounded the corner of the house, having apparently lain in wait there for his arrival. He really must buy himself a decent coat, he told himself again, knowing as he did so that he probably wouldn't get round to it. To be lazy as well as sensitive was a definite pain in the proverbial. Still, there was one immediate solution, albeit only temporary. "Let's go inside," he suggested, "there might be something there."

They walked up wide concrete steps pitted with age, and opened the heavy door. A dark hallway greeted them, made narrow by a large staircase at one side, underneath which several old bicycles leaned wearily against a ramshackle pile of cardboard boxes. Propped up in the farthest, dingiest corner, was a faded blue and white canvas article that might once have been a sun umbrella.

Opposite the staircase, an ancient hall table looked about

to collapse beneath the weight of two dog-eared telephone books and a grubby green telephone. Isabel moved towards them. Unappealing though it looked, the telephone book might contain Hugh Murray's phone number—assuming he had his own telephone—and if so, his address would be there as well, including his flat number. Wrinkling her nose in distaste, she slid the stained volume from under the telephone and thumbed through its ragged pages. There was a wealth of additional material scrawled on them, but no entry for Hugh Murray in any shape or form.

"Damn! What do we do now?" Isabel replaced the book and turned to Declan.

He was narrowly saved from revealing his dearth of useful ideas by the appearance in the hallway of a tall, angular woman. She was wearing a fawn gabardine raincoat of uncertain vintage, and the green floral scarf she was tying around her thick, grey hair suggested she was on her way out to brave the vicious wind that undoubtedly still lay in ambush around some convenient corner of the house. She looked at them out of sharp, steel-grey eyes. "Were you looking for someone?"

"Oh, hello," said Isabel, rapidly concocting what she hoped was a plausible story. "I'm looking for my cousin, Hugh Murray. He gave me this address, but I'm afraid I've forgotten which flat he's in."

The woman's eyes narrowed thoughtfully. Isabel's felt an involuntary intake of breath as her chest tightened in anticipation. Would the woman see through her story? She certainly looked sharp enough. But the woman merely said, "Number five, upstairs," and walked past them.

"Thank you," said Isabel, with an inward sigh of relief.

Then, turning as she swung the door open, the woman said, "You won't find him there now, though. He'll be at work."

"Oh, of course. We'll have to come back later then. You don't happen to know what time he finishes?"

"He usually gets home around five," the woman replied. "He doesn't have many visitors, so I expect he'll be pleased to see you."

Positively thrilled, thought Isabel. She thanked the woman again, and she and Declan waited until they heard her footsteps clopping down the short path and out onto the pavement. Then they hurried up the staircase, past sagging wallpaper that looked as though it had been glued to the walls with shellac, past the little landing with its long, geometric-patterned, stained-glass window, to the first floor.

Here they were met by a wide hallway with doors off each side and, at its end, a stained-glass door that Isabel guessed probably led to a bathroom. The sagging wallpaper of the corridor had been painted a particularly unattractive shade of pink that reminded her of men's old-fashioned, long, woollen underwear. Whoever had perpetrated the crime had created this effect by denying the walls the final coat that might have eliminated the ugly, marled effect.

Each of the dark-stained doors was embellished with a metal number. Number five was the second on the left. Isabel and Declan stood before it, listening for sounds from behind the other doors. There were none.

"The place feels empty," whispered Isabel. Why she was whispering, she didn't quite know. For some reason, she had a knack for knowing whether a place was empty or inhabited, and she had learned to trust her intuition. Still, it would do no harm to err on the side of caution.

Declan nodded in reply, and pulled his 'tools' from his pocket. The original lock had been an old-fashioned mortise lock, but above it a newer Yale lock had been fitted. Although mortise locks were notoriously easy to pick, often simply responding to a different key, Declan sincerely hoped he wouldn't need to apply his skills to both locks. Fortunately, his fears proved unfounded, and within minutes they both slipped inside, closing the door quietly behind them.

Hugh Murray's flat was, in fact, one room, just large enough to contain a single bed, an armchair, and, under the high sash window, a small wooden table and chair which, from the books, papers and pens littering its surface, served principally as a desk. Isabel ran her gaze down the spines of a pile of half a dozen or so books. Among them she noticed a book by Paracelsus, another one about him, and Israel Regardie's massive tome on the Order of the Golden Dawn—an interesting insight into the current state of Hugh Murray's mind, she thought.

Along the left-hand wall, a green Formica bench held a tiny bench-top stove, with just enough room between it and the sink to prepare food or wash dishes. Above the bench, glass-doored cupboards held food and crockery, while beneath it were more cupboards and a small refrigerator.

The dingy walls of the room were virtually papered over with photo-copied enlargements of charts and pictures, many of which Isabel recognised as Kabbalistic or Rosicrucian. One showed a fearsome, Teutonic-looking man in a short tunic and boots, brandishing a sword above a large egg, while in another, a woman and a large serpent writhed together in a grave. There was the inevitable Kabbalistic Tree of Life, carefully coloured in the appropriate hues, and a number of smaller diagrams she did not recall having come across before.

But both her attention and Declan's were drawn to a large poster pinned to the wall at the end of the bed. It must have been enlarged from an actual tarot card, Isabel decided. It was the Magician from the Waite deck. Beneath it, against the wall, stood a small, low table covered with a dark red cloth. On this stood two white candles in plain brass candlesticks, a couple of small Indian brass dishes, empty, though one was stained black on the inside, a wooden incense holder with a stick of incense sticking out of it, a black-handled knife in a black leather sheath, and, propped up against one of the candlesticks, a new looking Magician card from the Waite deck. With a gasp, Isabel pointed at it.

Declan nodded. "Looks like we've found our boy all right." His hand reached for the knife, but he withdrew it again. "Better not touch anything. I don't fancy trying to explain to Inspector Garfield how my prints came to be there. Still..." He pulled his handkerchief from his pocket and picked up the knife with it. Carefully, he undid the sheath and withdrew the knife. Its narrow blade had been filed to a sharp point, "Fairly recently, by the look of it." Declan turned the knife over carefully, showing Isabel the shiny steel exposed by the rasping of a file. "No sign of blood, but." Not that he'd expected there would be. Everything about the killings showed a meticulous, possibly obsessive, mind at work. He made to replace the knife.

"What are those?" asked Isabel, pointing at the sheath.

Declan looked. Although the leather was dyed black on the outside, on the rough interior it was the pale brown of natural leather. Except for two darker smears, one on either side. "Blood. Well, maybe." Pulling the little pocket knife from his pocket, he carefully scraped off a fraction of the stained leather, then looked around for something to wrap it in.

"Here." Isabel gave him her own handkerchief and he tied the fragments in one corner. He pushed the knife back into its sheath and snapped the fastener shut before replacing it where he had found it. "I knew this would come in handy sooner or later," he observed, slipping the pocket knife back in his pocket. He glanced at his watch. "We've got about an hour and a half before he's due home."

"I'd like to be gone by half past four at the latest," said Isabel, "just to be on the safe side. So that's an hour. Let's see what else we can find."

She bent and lifted the red cloth cover of Hugh Murray's altar. Beneath it were a packet of incense sticks, two boxes of candles, several boxes of matches, a square box of church incense like the ones they had seen at the temple, and a number of little round cakes of charcoal lying loose in a plastic box. Straightening up again, Isabel looked around the room.

A small cabinet stood beside the bed, on top of it a radio-alarm clock, a metal lamp and two books. The top one was an old copy of the Selected Poetry of W.B. Yeats, Declan was interested to note. Whatever else, the guy had good taste in poetry. But what was that underneath it? Using his handkerchief again he picked up the Yeats to reveal another book with a shiny, black hard cover. He picked it up and turned it over. There was no title on either cover or spine. Opening the cover, he saw, written in black ink in a careful, but uneven, hand:

The Magical Journal of
Brother Non Extinguar
MAGICIAN

He held it out to Isabel. "Look at this!"

"Bloody hell!" Isabel felt a familiar prickling at the back of her neck, and realised she had been subconsciously half expecting it since they had arrived. Once again she had the feeling there was something here she ought to recognise. Pushing the feeling aside for the moment, she looked at Declan. "What else is in it?"

Declan turned the pages, carefully avoiding touching them directly. In the same hand were dated entries, beginning just prior to the previous December summer solstice, apparently the date on which the hapless brother's first failure to obtain the Practicus grade had occurred. His reaction, carefully noted, had been one of disappointment tempered by a resolve to study harder so as to pass at the next opportunity, namely, the autumn equinox. The following entries chronicled his efforts to this end, including the titles of books read, classes attended, and rituals attempted, along with his assessments of the results.

As they skimmed through the pages, Isabel gained the distinct impression of a mind becoming increasingly obsessed with the idea of being a practising magician, and increasingly frustrated with what the writer saw as deliberate attempts on the part of the Council of Seven to block his progress. Each piece of advice on the part of his instructors was seen as a personal criticism designed to hold him back from what he clearly saw as his rightful place in the Brotherhood.

At some point along the way, reference began to be made to rituals designed by Hugh himself to appeal to a higher authority—what he referred to as his Holy Guardian Angel, a concept clearly culled from one of the works of Aleister Crowley that he happened to be reading at the time.

Isabel and Declan exchanged glances.

"I was wondering how long it would be before Crowley reared his ugly shaven head," said Isabel.

"Is that who he got this Holy Guardian Angel idea from?"

Isabel nodded. "Probably. It's a concept from Enochian magic, and Crowley was really into that, among other things."

"What the hell is Enochian magic?"

"I don't know a lot about it, but it was a system devised—or received, according to him—by John Dee, at one time an official astrologer to Queen Elizabeth the First. It was based on an alphabet supposedly disclosed to him and his partner Edward Kelly by angels Kelly saw and heard in trance, and by means of which they communicated with Dee in their own language, Enochian."

Declan looked suitably dumbfounded. "Presumably it wasn't a real language?"

"Well, what little I've seen of it looks mostly unpronounceable. Apparently, though, it has complete inner consistency, including grammar and syntax, though not much of what they received was ever translated into English. As a matter of interest, John Dee already had an interest in codes—he'd written a book on them—so that may have influenced his interpretation of what Kelly came up with in his trances. But, anyway, the whole point of the exercise was supposedly to obtain guidance from one's Holy Guardian

Angel."

"And this is what our friend Hugh has been aiming at?"

"It certainly seems to be what he believes he's aiming at," Isabel said carefully.

Declan looked at her sharply. "Meaning...?"

"Meaning I think it's his way of justifying acts that are really the result of a combination of anger and frustration, and a fair sized dollop of self delusion. Look at how he describes his rituals, especially the effects they have on him." She pointed to a particularly lurid description, concluding with a grimace of distaste, "It reads like some sort of second-rate pornography."

Declan gave a snort of laughter. "I didn't know there was any other kind. But I see what you mean. Poor old Hugh. Maybe if he had a girlfriend, two innocent people—maybe four—might still be alive."

"I'm not so sure about that. I doubt if it's quite that simple. Look at this." Isabel had been leafing through the journal, her fingers tingling as though from a faint electric shock, though whatever it was her intuition was picking up remained tantalisingly beyond the reach of her conscious mind. Near the back of the book she had come to an entry dated the twenty-sixth of May.

It read, 'Met Brother N.E.I.L. while walking on Whitewash Head (sea and sky full of cleansing energy). Asked him why he had failed me yet again. He was, of course, surprised I knew. Then, like the others, he began to criticise, telling me I was not yet ready for the disciplines of Practicus. Heard voice of G.A. very clearly, telling me how angry He was, and knew I had to act. Brother N fell, pulling me down with him. He was much stronger than I expected, but in the end Right prevailed. Hit his head on rocks. Did not panic, like before, but awaited instructions. Received vision of the Fool, and knew what to do.

'N.B. Realising later the significance of the lamp and mountain in Brother E.F.L.'s death, I knew They must have planned that, too. There are no accidents, no coincidences, but only the Holy Will of the Great Ones, with which my will is now in tune.'

Declan let out a long, low whistle. "Holy Mother of God!"

"Well, something along those lines." Isabel gave a grim little smile, and turned more pages. "Look," she said at length, "here's an entry for the winter solstice. That's when Trenwith was killed."

It was a brief entry, but telling. 'Successfully completed removal of Brother E.S.T., according to Instructions. High Ones showed Their pleasure by granting Ecstasy beyond anything previously experienced. As with others, no-one suspects. Rituals obviously working. So much for their false theories!'

"The man's crazy!" exclaimed Declan.

Nodding agreement, Isabel turned to the final entry, dated just two days ago, and read, 'Brother F.V. now all that stands between me and completion of the Work, but I now know where and when this may be achieved. They have promised me it will be worth the necessary wait. All is ready for consecration of Sacred Instrument and Symbol, when time is right. If the rest of them have not got the message yet, they will before another week has passed. They will know then who is the Fool and who the Magician, for I shall be granted full communion with my Holy Guardian Angel, and all their petty grades will be irrelevant.'

"Damn." Isabel closed the book, taking care to keep Declan's handkerchief between it and her fingers. "There's still no indication of where or when he plans to do the deed."

"Presumably he's planning it within the next five days, but I wonder who the intended victim is?"

Isabel placed the book back on Hugh's bedside table, covering it once more with the tattered volume of poetry, and wiping her hands against her coat to rid herself of the tingling which had so far produced no information. She looked gravely at Declan. "Unless there's someone else in the Brotherhood with the initials F.V., it's got to be James. Somehow, even if he won't help us, we've got to try and make him realise he's in danger."

"Maybe we should drop by Joss's place when we leave here," Declan suggested. He looked at his watch. Almost half past four. "Which had better be now, I think."

Isabel nodded agreement, wishing they had had more time, and began to follow Declan to the door. Suddenly an idea came to her. She cast her gaze swiftly around the room, looking for a means to implement it. Before long, her eyes found what they sought. "Okay," she said, "let's go and see Joss. I can call Luke from there."

CHAPTER TWENTY-SEVEN

Joss took a deep breath and pressed the buzzer again. She knew James was at home, because she had waited, her yellow Fiat Bambina parked in a convenient side street, until she saw his car drive past. Hurrying to the corner on foot, she had been just in time to see the grey BMW pull into the garage adjoining James's neat brick townhouse. There had been no reply to her first ring, or her second, but now, it seemed, her persistence had paid off, as she heard footsteps coming towards her.

"Joss!" Surprise showed on James's face as well as in his voice. Joss fancied she saw a hint of fear there as well.

"Hello, James. Can I come in, please? It's important," she added, seeing hesitation cloud his smooth features.

For a moment it seemed James was about to demur, but then he smiled, albeit warily, and ushered Joss inside, leading her through a small entrance foyer and into a spacious living room decorated comfortably in shades of fawn and brown. James invited her to take a seat, but did not offer refreshments. Joss was amused to note that, even in his own home, James perched on the arm of a chair rather than relaxing into it.

Joss said nothing at first, trying to work out the best way to tell James what she had come to say. The visit from Isabel and Declan, and in particular what they had told her of the contents of Hugh Murray's journal, had convinced her of the need for urgent action. But now she was here, looking across at James's anxious face, she could think of no way to make it sound anything but melodramatic. Oh well... She let out the breath she had been holding and began.

"Look, I don't want to worry you unduly, James, and I don't quite know how to put this, but—we think your life may be in danger."

Something about the way James gasped at her words told Joss it was not so much what she had told him that astonished him, but the fact that she knew. Behind his worried frown she could sense his mind performing rapid calculations.

Finally, he said, "I very much fear you're right, Joss, though I have no idea how you reached the conclusion."

Joss gave a short, humourless laugh. "Let's just say we put two and two together. I wasn't sure until just now that we had the right answer."

James's answering laugh was also anything but cheerful. "The thing is," he said, looking dejected, "although I'm sure you're right, and I'm fairly certain I know who I'm in danger from, we—I mean I—haven't yet managed to find out what he's planning or when."

"I take it we're both referring to Hugh Murray? We have reason to believe he's planning to act within the next five days."

James gave another gasp, immediately covering his mouth with one hand as though to push it back. He gave Joss a look reminiscent of a sheep with its head caught in a fence, but said nothing. Her heart went out to him. It was obvious he desperately wanted to confide in her, but felt unable to do so.

"Look," she said kindly, "you really should go to the police. If we're right, he's already killed two people and may be responsible for the deaths of two others. Who knows how many more may die if he's not stopped?"

Before he could prevent himself, James shook his head and said, "Since you've just confirmed that Hugh is the murderer—" He gave an involuntary shudder at the word "— I'm quite certain I'm now the only one who need worry."

Joss leaned across and laid a hand on his arm. "Well, for goodness' sake be careful. After all, where are we going to find another tame psychologist for the panel?"

In spite of himself, James gave a wan smile. "You're very kind, Joss, and I do appreciate your concern, though I really can't discuss the matter with you, or with the police—at least, not in the way you mean. The matter will be dealt with, however, I can assure you of that."

But he didn't sound convinced, and neither was Joss. She thought back to the strange message James had asked Luke to broadcast, and was more certain than ever it had been aimed at Hugh. So if James had been suspicious of him that long ago, why hadn't he and his fellow brothers done something before now? Or perhaps James had been acting unilaterally. Briefly, she toyed with the idea of tackling him about it, but concluded this would be a fruitless exercise. Instead, she said, "I just hope you know what you're doing."

"It will be dealt with," James repeated. "I'm sorry, Joss, but I'm going to have to ask you to go. I have to—ah—leave myself in a few minutes."

Since there was no clock in the room, and he hadn't even pretended to consult his watch, Joss was sceptical. However, she got to her feet and allowed James to conduct her back to the front door. He was about to close it behind her when a thought occurred to her. She turned. "If we find out anything else," she said, "I'll let you know, if you like."

James appeared startled, and Joss had the impression her question had dragged his mind back from somewhere far away. "Oh, er, yes—yes, I'd appreciate that," he stammered, glancing nervously about him as though expecting an attack at any second.

With what she hoped was a reassuring smile, Joss took her leave.

Driving home, she reflected on James's assurances. She had no doubt they were sincerely given, but, for herself, she was more convinced than ever that he was in grave danger. If only they could discover where and when Hugh meant to strike. But they seemed to have exhausted all the normal lines of enquiry, and, for some reason, all their varied psychic abilities appeared to have deserted them.

* * * *

James ran a shaking hand across his dark hair. He closed his eyes and forced himself to take several slow, deep breaths, feeling his heart begin to beat more slowly. Straightening his tie with a mechanical motion, he moved to the sideboard and took out a bottle of his best brandy and seven balloon glasses. Setting these on a lacquered tray he brought from the kitchen, he carried them across to the coffee table. Nervously, he glanced about the room.

The tan velvet curtains were closed, the lamp on the table beside them casting a circle of soft radiance that gave them a golden sheen against the pale fawn of the walls. The two couches facing each other across the polished mahogany coffee table would give seating for six. He would need another chair. With a click of his tongue, he went to the dining alcove adjoining the kitchen, returning a moment later with a carved dining chair, which he placed at one end of the coffee table. He was about to pour himself a brandy to steady his ragged nerves, when the doorbell rang. With a feeling akin to guilt, James put the brandy bottle back on the tray and went to answer the door.

Brother Solem Fero stood there, along with Brother Quaerens Lucem, one of the newly appointed members to the Council of Seven. Thank God, thought James, it was not the new Senior who was first to arrive. He found the gruff ex-soldier intimidating at the best of times. The thought of dealing with him single-handed so soon after Joss's disquieting visit was little short of terrifying. By the time the Senior arrived, however, with Brother Perseverantia Vincit, the latest addition to the Council, he had managed, by means of brandy and light conversation, to regain much of his equilibrium, at least to all outward appearances.

James placed his brandy glass resolutely on the table and looked at the others. "Since I called this meeting," he said, "I've had some very disturbing news." Brother Ferro Comite looked sceptical, though perhaps no more so than usual. Taking a deep breath, James continued, "I have now received confirmation of my suspicion that Brother Non Extinguar was directly responsible for the deaths of Brothers Dabunt Espera Rosas and Esto Sol Testis, and almost certainly for that of Brother Nobilis Est Ira Leonis as well."

"What about Brother Ex Flamma Lux?" interrupted the

Senior gruffly.

"It seems he was involved in that as well, though I don't know for certain that he killed him. It may have been accidental. What is certain, however, is that all four of them died because they voted against Brother Non Extinguar's elevation to the grade of Practicus."

"So he's not out to get all of us, after all," Brother Lux E Tenebris commented with evident relief.

Feeling distinctly inadequate to the task of quelling the irrepressible Brother with a glance, James contented himself with pointedly ignoring him. "I," he said coldly, "am the only remaining Brother of those who failed him." Brother Lux E Tenebris said nothing, but looked gratifyingly chastened.

Brother Ferro Comite looked at him shrewdly. "I thought it might come to this," he said, "which is why I recommended Brother Perseverantia Vincit for the Council."

The Brother in question, a slightly younger version of Brother Ferro Comite himself, his dark hair cropped short above a pair of shrewd brown eyes, nodded briefly at his sponsor, then turned to James. "How did you come by this new information?"

His voice, curt and authoritative, with more than a hint of scepticism, must be a distinct asset when interviewing suspects, thought James, feeling at once both resentful and nervous. He thought quickly, then turned a bland face to Brother Perseverantia Vincit. "I—ah—I'm not at liberty to say. But I'm quite certain of it."

A frown crossed the brother's features, but was immediately superseded by a thoughtful look. "I haven't been dealing with the case," he said, "but I'll look into it and see what I can do."

For some reason, James was not reassured. "According to my information," he said, trying desperately to contain the panic he was feeling, "Brother Non Extinguar plans to act within the next five days. Since we have no way so far of knowing precisely when this will be, is there no way you can have him taken into custody immediately? Would it help if I made a formal statement?"

Brother Solem Fero nodded. "That does seem to be the most sensible thing to do. After all, no-one need know you're anything but a concerned citizen—as indeed you have every right to be if what you say is true. And surely the police are in the best position to protect you."

The Senior glared at him. "May I remind you that we also have power," he growled.

"Of course," Brother Solem Fero said placatingly. "I'm not disputing that, and naturally we must do everything we can to bring our erring brother to justice. But, as we all know, the Powers we serve are not averse to acting through—ah—mundane channels, where appropriate. That being the case, might it not be wise for Brother Fulget Virtus to make a statement, so that the police have enough information on which to act before yet another needless death can occur?"

Brother Perseverantia Vincit turned a stern gaze on him. "I'll see what I can do," he repeated in heavy tones. Having attained the rank of Assistant Commissioner, he was not in the habit of having his decisions questioned.

The Senior glanced swiftly from Brother Fulget Virtus's haunted face to Brother Perseverantia Vincit's implacable countenance. "Let us," he said, his voice expressing the full authority of his rank, "see what Brother Perseverantia can achieve within the next two days. That should leave us up to three days in which to act, should that still be necessary. In the meantime—" He turned to Brother Fulget Virtus "—you know what to do to protect yourself."

James nodded.

"Good." The Senior got to his feet, signalling the end of the meeting. "Brother Perseverantia Vincit, I'll be in touch with you first thing on Monday morning. Then, if necessary, we'll take whatever action seems appropriate." He was about to turn away when a thought struck him. "The next two days cover the weekend. Will that be a problem for you?" The Brother shook his bristly head. "Good. We'll leave it at that, then." He turned to James. "I'll be in touch, Brother."

As soon as the others had left, James went to the small guest bedroom in which he had created his personal temple. There was no time to waste. Although he now knew who his enemy was, and what he intended to do, he still had no idea when he planned to strike, or in what manner. Nevertheless, he could at least follow Brother Ferro Comite's suggestion and cast a sphere of protection around himself. He set about making his preparations, feeling himself become calmer as the familiar ritual took hold of him. Yet it was impossible to banish completely a dark sense of foreboding.

CHAPTER TWENTY -EIGHT

"Hey, not a problem!" Quincy shrugged his shoulders, turning his hands palms up to display strong, supple fingers. "I was staying home today, anyway, to wash my hair. It takes forever to dry, and I don't like using a hair dryer. They give you split ends." He seemed oblivious to any disparity between this statement and his frankly masculine appearance and voice, and the sleek, shiny hair he pushed back over his shoulder certainly showed no evidence of ill-treatment. "Now," he went on, "what is it you want me to work on?"

Isabel reached into her coat pocket and pulled out a tiny paper package. Placing it on Luke's coffee table, she pulled open the paper, taking care not to touch the object inside it. The others looked, and saw a thin silver ring, shaped to form a Celtic knot. The back of it had worn completely through.

"It was sitting on the mantelpiece," she explained. "I'm hoping it broke due to constant wear by Hugh Murray."

Quincy was about to comment when Joss said, "I'm surprised at you for letting her take it, Declan."

Declan gave her a wry look. "I'm the one who broke in, remember?"

"Won't he notice it's gone?"

Isabel shrugged. "If he does, he's not likely to suspect theft. There's so much stuff in his room, I dare say he's always losing things. And even if he does realise it was stolen, he's not going to know it was us, is he? He doesn't even know we exist. Anyway, I thought James's life was more important than a bit of broken jewellery."

Joss nodded. "When you put it like that..."

With an impatient flick of his hair, Luke broke in, "Do you two intend to sit around all day discussing the finer points of social ethics, or are you going to let Quincy do something practical about saving James's life?"

Laughing, Isabel said, "Sorry. Go ahead, Quincy. See what you can pick up."

Quincy gave an answering grin, and took the ring. "Do you want to know anything in particular, or shall I just do a general reading?"

"Just see what you get, first," suggested Isabel. "After all, it might not even be his ring."

Quincy nodded. Closing his eyes lightly, he held the ring between his hands, slowly rubbing them together in a circular motion. "This ring has been a lot of places," he said at last. "I'm getting a whole jumble of images—a table covered in books and papers, under a long, narrow window, what looks like a library, with rows of bookshelves, and long tables, a bench with racks of glass flasks and tubes and stuff—science equipment by the look of it—and a big, dark room that smells dusty and old... Wow, that's amazing!"

To the frustration of the others, he broke off to sit in silence, sliding the ring on and off his right index finger. A multitude of emotions flitted across his expressive face as he appeared to observe some inner scene, his eyes still closed. Bursting with impatience, the others waited. Finally, Quincy's face became calm once more, and he opened his eyes and began to speak.

"I was at some sort of ceremony. Lots of people in white robes, and some in red. Couldn't see any of their faces; they had these kind of hood things covering them. Then I was right in front of one of the guys in red, and he handed me something." Quincy paused for a deep breath while the others waited, holding theirs in anticipation. "It was a card— a tarot card. What's the one with the guy walking over the cliff? The Fool, isn't it?" The others nodded. "I thought so. Well, as soon as I saw it I felt angry like you wouldn't believe. Then the anger began to flow like a flame from a flame-thrower, and out of it came a whole stream of different images. Flames, that cliff I saw when I was reading off the motorbike helmet, the Hanged Man from the tarot, a sundial with a white rose beside it, and a tower, with someone falling off it. That's a tarot card, too, isn't it?" Isabel nodded, and Quincy opened his mouth to speak again.

Suddenly Joss gasped as she felt something like electricity pass up her spine. When she spoke, she sounded curiously breathless, as though she really had received an electric shock. "I think the Tower might be a prediction," she said. "All the other things you mentioned, Quincy, were images, either real or symbolic, of the deaths that have already happened. The Tower, as far as we know, isn't. And as soon as you mentioned it, I felt as though someone had stuck an electric cattle prod in the small of my back." She paused for a moment, passing a hand across her forehead before turning to Quincy. "I'd be interested to hear what you think, but I have a feeling there's going to be a real tower involved, only it isn't a tower at all. Oh, God, that doesn't make sense, does it?" She rubbed her brow again, frowning.

The others said nothing. Isabel and Luke knew from experience that Joss's clairvoyance had a habit of proving unnervingly accurate, regardless of how bizarre it might appear at the time. Luke picked up his cigarette packet, then, with a glance at Quincy, sighed and put it down again.

Quincy was turning the ring over between his fingers. "I'll see if I can pick up anything more about the tower," he announced, and closed his eyes again. For several minutes he said nothing, breathing deeply and rolling the ring between the palms of his hands, then, "I can feel a massive build-up of energy, anger, and excitement, and maybe a bit of fear as well. It's almost as if he's building it up on purpose, and it's going to be released in... Oh, shit! Hang on a minute."

He broke off, panting and struggling for breath. His thick hair fell about his shoulders in a dark cloud as he shook his head as though to clear it. Gradually his breathing returned to normal and he continued, "I think he's planning to release it somehow in the tower, but don't ask me what that means, because I haven't the faintest idea." He opened his eyes and gave one of his dazzling smiles. "It'll be at night, though, because whatever it is that happens in the tower, it's dark outside at the time. And whatever it is, he gets a real buzz out of it."

He grinned suddenly, showing white teeth, one of which was slightly—but very attractively, thought Joss—crooked. "Not unlike the lovely ladies who pay to see me—um—perform. Only this guy, I think he's strictly a DIY man—if you know what I mean." He gave Luke a poke in the ribs and a lewd wink. "And somehow, it's all mixed up with whatever it is he's planning to do in this tower." He turned to Joss, all humour gone. "From what you said about the other things I saw, I guess it must be another murder. Whoever this guy is, he's severely twisted."

"As a bloody corkscrew, by the sound of it!" Declan commented, shifting his leg slightly to ease the pain in his knee.

"That fits in with what Terry told me and Declan, though," said Isabel. "He said Hugh—only we didn't know it was Hugh at the time, of course—was very confused. He thinks he's the Magician, but in fact he's the Devil."

Holding his hands out in front of him, index fingers forming a cross, Quincy threw her a look of mock horror. "Not literally, I hope."

Isabel laughed, "No, in the tarot the Devil stands mainly for ignorance, and the harm it can do. Also for something frightening or unpleasant that has to be faced up to and dealt with."

"Both of which would appear to be particularly apposite here," Joss remarked.

Luke reached for his cigarettes and lighter. "If you've finished now, Quincy, I'm going to have a smoke. Otherwise you lot will have something really unpleasant to deal with before long."

"Yeah, I think that's about it for now." Quincy placed the ring back on its wrapping, flicking his hands and wiping them on his jeans as though to cleanse them. He turned to Isabel. "If you can leave the ring here, though, I'll see if I can get anything more from it later."

Isabel nodded assent.

Carefully wrapping the ring up again, Quincy stood up and stretched his arms above his head. "You go ahead and have your fix," he said to Luke. "I'll make us some coffee."

"So," Luke took in a lungful of smoke, closing his eyes ecstatically as he slowly breathed it out again, "what are we to make of all that?"

For a moment nobody spoke as they mulled over Quincy's reading. Joss sat leaning forward, elbows on her knees, her fair hair covering her face, apparently deep in thought. Declan carefully moved his leg again, wincing as pain shot through his injured knee. Her face full of sympathy, Isabel reached out a hand to him and Declan took it with a smile and gave it a squeeze. The last of the late afternoon sun streaming in through the french windows poured honey over everything in its path.

Sitting up suddenly, Joss said, "What Quincy told us ties in with what we already know, or have guessed but, apart from the tower, we don't seem to be any better off. What we really need to know is what and where this tower is, and when Hugh is planning to act."

"It would also help to know what he intends to do," added Luke, stubbing out the remains of his cigarette.

"Maybe Hugh doesn't know that himself yet," suggested Isabel.

"I think you're right about that." Quincy was making his way across to them carrying a tray of coffee mugs. Isabel moved the package containing Hugh's ring to one side, and he put the tray down on the coffee table before adding, "I couldn't get a damned thing about what it is he's got in mind, just all these feelings swirling round. Oh, and a brief flash of a guy in a long red robe, but not one of the ones I'd seen earlier. This one had a wand in his hand, and he was pointing it at the sky, with the other hand pointing towards the ground. That's the Magician in the tarot, isn't it?"

"Yes," Isabel replied thoughtfully, "it is, and it definitely ties in with what Terry told us, so I'm sure it's Hugh we're talking about. You know what I think?" The others shook their heads.

Declan slipped two of his capsules into his mouth and downed them gratefully with a mouthful of coffee.

Isabel smiled at him and took a sip of her own coffee. "I think Hugh sees what he's doing as some kind of magical operation, and he's the magician, though I shudder to think what the aim of it is. And I think the reason you couldn't pick up what he plans to do is that he doesn't exactly know himself yet."

"Of course!" Joss exclaimed. Four faces turned towards her. "He's waiting for instructions," she informed them.

"What's that supposed to mean?" said Luke, adding more sugar to his coffee.

Joss shrugged and shook her head. "Damned if I know, but that's what it is, I'd bet money on it."

Luke eyed her speculatively for a moment, before apparently changing his mind and turning to Quincy. "I don't suppose you've got anything further to add?"

"Right," agreed Quincy, "I haven't. Sorry."

"He wouldn't be working for somebody else, would he?" asked Declan.

"I don't think so," Joss said, after a moment's thought.

"No," Quincy added, "I'd say he's too much of a loner for that."

"Then who," said Luke, "is he receiving instructions from?"

"I didn't say he was receiving them," Joss pointed out. "I said he was waiting for them."

With an exaggerated sigh, Luke rolled his eyes upwards. "I give up." He pulled a cigarette from his packet and made a great show of placing it between his lips and lighting it.

"Why don't we leave it for now?" Declan suggested. "We just seem to be going round in circles. We can always meet again if anything further comes to light. Besides," he added, observing with gratification the nods from the others, "this bloody knee is giving me hell. I need a rest—and the kind ministrations of my guardian angel." He grinned at Isabel. Her response, however, was not quite what he was expecting.

With a sudden gasp, Isabel sat up straight, opened her grey eyes wide and stared back at him.

"Hey, I was only joking." Declan leaned towards her and put his hand on her arm. "I know it wasn't much of a joke, but..."

"No, no," Isabel broke in, waving his hand away, "it was what you said—guardian angel. That's who Hugh's waiting for instructions from!" She subsided again, rubbing her eyes.

"Of course! It was in his journal," Declan explained to Quincy, who was looking thoroughly bewildered.

"Ah. Makes sense, I guess," nodded Quincy, "though I'm not sure it helps any."

"It might," said Isabel. "I'd like to try a tarot reading. No, not now," she added, for the benefit of Declan, whose face had taken on a pained look. "I mean later."

"If you can leave it till tomorrow," said Joss, "we can do it together. I might be able to pick up something else myself."

"Good idea. But I've got a couple of clients in the morning, then I'm meeting Declan for lunch in town. Why don't we come over to your place after that?"

"Okay." Joss nodded, picking up her scarf and winding it

round her neck.

"Not that I mean to be rude or anything, but does that mean we can go home now?" Declan asked in a plaintive voice.

Isabel laughed, though not unkindly. She could see the weariness and strain in his face. "Come on." She reached out her hands to help him to his feet. "By the look of you, it's way past your bed-time, anyway."

A grin lit Declan's face and eyes. "If Hugh's been getting instructions like that, no wonder he's waiting for more."

Isabel turned to the others. "Honestly," she said through her laughter, "you can't take him anywhere!"

"Don't look at me," Joss retorted. "I'm on his side." She stood up and shrugged herself into her jacket, then turned to Quincy. "Thanks for your help. Give me a call if you get anything further."

"Sure. Not a problem." He gave another of his scintillating smiles.

CHAPTER TWENTY-NINE

When Declan arrived, the cafe was uncomfortably full. Threading his way between lunching business people, mothers with young children, and what looked like an outing of a branch of the Country Women's Institute—half a dozen or so middle-aged women in expensive-looking but eminently sensible outfits, arranging pots of tea and plates of sandwiches and cakes on two tables pushed together—he could see no sign of Isabel. Maybe she'd been delayed by her tarot clients. He dodged to avoid further damage to his leg as a harassed looking young woman with a small boy in a push-chair steamed past him towards the exit, and narrowly missed someone else's laden lunch tray. With a grunt of impatience, he decided to wait outside. Then he caught sight of a gleam of red hair. He made his way back through the crowd.

Isabel looked up, smiling, at his greeting, and pulled out a chair for him. "I thought I'd better reserve us a table. Did you have a profitable morning?"

"Yeah, sort of." Declan had been to have another chat with Constable Johnson and Inspector Garfield, largely to check on the preliminary results from the blood sample he'd handed in from Hugh's knife sheath, but also to see what else he might glean concerning developments on the 'tarot murders' case. "But can we talk about it over lunch? I'm starving!"

As Isabel finished pouring tea for herself (Declan had his usual strong coffee), she looked across at him. "So what did you find out?"

Declan sighed, "The preliminary results are through, but they don't really show anything. At least they do, but it's not exactly conclusive."

Isabel put her cup down with a clatter and gave Declan a look of mild exasperation. "So what exactly do they show?"

"The blood's human, which, on the face of it, confirms what we already know. But they can't tell if there are two blood groups or just one. The different types are all mixed up together. And, of course, they don't know Hugh's blood group, anyway. So we still don't know whether Hugh did the two murders with the knife, or just cut himself shaving."

"So they can't take him in?"

Pushing a hand through his hair, Declan shrugged, "Not yet. The forensic blokes reckon they'll need to do DNA tests to be sure of anything. They are working on it, but."

"How long do you think that'll take?"

"Hard to say. But they won't have results till well beyond the time frame we're working to. If it's any comfort to you, it does have top priority."

"I should think so, too!" Isabel tossed her head indignantly, sending her curls flying like sparks from a bonfire. "And it's not me that needs comforting—it's James's life that's at stake!"

Declan reached out and took her hands in his, looking into her angry eyes. "Sweetheart, *we* may know that, but I don't think the police have any psychics on the staff," he said gently.

"Well, maybe they should get some!" Isabel retorted, but her eyes softened under his steady gaze. "Not that it seems to be much use to us at the moment. I just hope someone will be able to do something before it's too late."

"Well, they're doing the best they can, and I guess that's all any of us can do. Meanwhile, we can continue our own enquiries. Talking of which, if you've finished, shall we go and see Joss now?"

Isabel nodded, and Declan let go of her hands. As they left the cafe, she patted her coat pocket to make sure she'd remembered her tarot cards. Joss had a deck, but Isabel preferred her own cards, worn though they were. She could feel the solid bulk of them wrapped in their black silk scarf, weighing down one corner of her pocket. And there was something else there, too.

"I'd completely forgotten! This came for you in today's mail." She drew out an airmail envelope, somewhat crumpled, and handed it to Declan.

He looked at the address, then at Isabel. "I've been waiting for this. Let's get in the car. I may need to sit down while I read it."

Hands clenched in a mixture of impatience and apprehension, Isabel waited as Declan read the two thin pages. She had already seen from the return address on the envelope that it was from a Chief Inspector Vodanovich in Brisbane. That was Declan's boss—the one he referred to as 'Voodoo'—so it must be about his job. Most likely they wanted him back early. She stared down at her hands, feeling suddenly bleak. Hearing the rustle of paper as Declan finished reading, she raised her eyes again, wanting, yet fearing, to know its contents.

Declan's face was devoid of expression as he returned her gaze, though his eyes had taken on a gleam of green. Then a smile fluttered at the corner of his mouth, slowly spreading across his face to become a full-fledged grin.

"I've done it!" he crowed. "Look!" He thrust the letter into Isabel's hands.

Smoothing out the pages, Isabel read:

'Your request has been carefully considered, taking into account both the circumstances involved, and the relatively short time remaining before your normal entitlement to retirement will be reached.

'It has been decided to allow you early retirement on basic pay, with the appropriate pension to commence at the date it would have commenced under normal circumstances.

'However, you will be expected back on duty in time for your medical check-up, at which time the above matters can be finalised.

'Please confirm your receipt and acceptance by letter as soon as possible.'

The second page contained a handwritten note:

'What the Chief is really trying to say is, he couldn't stand the thought of having you under his feet eight hours of every day. Never mind, Dekko, the rest of us are going to miss you. See you soon—and don't forget it's your shout! Cheers, Carol.'

Isabel gave the letter back to Declan. "Does that mean...?"

Declan nodded, and leaned across to kiss her. "Once I've got the medical and all the official stuff out of the way, I'm all yours."

* * * *

"You two look excessively smug. What have you been up to?" Joss led the way into the kitchen and began to clear away lunch remnants and newspapers.

Declan grinned. "I've just had my release papers from HQ in Brisbane—or near enough to it."

"He's still got to go back for his medical, and to sign papers and so on," Isabel put in, "but after that..."

"After that, I'm a free agent," Declan concluded.

"I hope you're not going to leave us in the lurch just when we may finally be getting somewhere with our friend Hugh Murray?"

"Not a chance!" Declan grinned happily at Isabel. "My life wouldn't be worth living." He sat down and bent to scratch behind Spock's ears, which had twitched hopefully at the sound of Joss unwrapping a packet of chocolate biscuits. Declan glanced up at Joss. "Talking of Hugh Murray, have you heard anything more from Quincy?"

"No, we'll just have to go with what we've already got."

"If we're able to pick up anything at all, that shouldn't be a problem, anyway," said Isabel, pulling her cards from her pocket and unwrapping them. "What do you think we should focus on?"

"Well." Joss bit thoughtfully into a chocolate macaroon. "Hugh, I suppose, and the Tower, since that's where it's all supposed to happen."

"Right." Isabel began shuffling through the cards. "Let's start with Hugh. I wonder what we should use to represent him? The Magician?"

Joss nodded. "That sounds appropriate."

Isabel found the card and placed it in the centre of the

black silk square before shuffling the other cards again. She laid out ten more cards in the familiar cross formation and gazed at them while sipping her coffee.

Declan watched Isabel and the cards by turns, while Joss sat with eyes half closed and apparently unfocussed. Her eyes snapped into focus, however, as Isabel began to speak. "The King of Pentacles here in the centre, that's probably James. He's hard working and successful, but unimaginative, wouldn't you say?"

"Sounds like James." Joss smiled, pointing to the Knight of Cups, which lay across the King. "I suppose that must be Hugh, then?"

"I think it must be." Isabel considered the card for a moment. "It's hard to say definitely without knowing him, but the Knight of Cups can be a bit of a dreamer, with a lot going on under the surface, and that sounds like our Hugh. The Chariot underneath them means the basis of the situation has to do with using willpower to overcome fear or difficulties, or to reach a goal. And there's always the risk of things getting out of control." Joss and Declan exchanged glances, while Isabel continued to gaze at the cards, a slight frown creasing her brow. "I get the feeling that for both of them it's a matter of trying to bend the situation to their will..."

"You mean they're both being stubborn?" Declan grinned.

Joss smiled, "We know only too well how stubborn James can be."

"Yes," Isabel said, "but it's more than that. It feels like they're both trying desperately to prove something, more to themselves than each other, but neither of them is in full control any longer—always assuming they ever were."

Again, she fell into a reflective silence, finally pointing to the card to the left of the central pair. "The Hierophant," she announced. "That's an odd one."

"What's a hierophant, anyway?" asked Declan. "That looks like the Pope to me."

Isabel laughed. "He usually is the Pope in the older decks," she explained to him. "A hierophant is basically a priest—someone qualified to interpret or transmit esoteric teachings. In this case I feel he represents the Brotherhood of the Flame."

"Why's he in the past then?" Joss asked.

"Well, let's face it, if the upper echelon keep getting killed off at the present rate, there won't be enough of them left to continue running the show." Isabel gave a sardonic laugh. "No, seriously, I think it relates to Hugh's own involvement with them. The Lovers, up there above him, suggests he may have to make a choice or a decision, one that'll be quite crucial for his future."

With a nod of his head, Declan indicated the card forming the right arm of the central cross. It showed a full moon between two towers, before which a dog and a wolf sat baying. In the foreground, a creature resembling a lobster was crawling up out of a pool onto a path that stretched away to vanish between distant hills. "I guess this must be his future, then. So what does it tell you?"

"It's all about dreams and fantasy," said Isabel, "and things hidden away in the subconscious. I get the feeling that's what Hugh is going to opt for, though it isn't at all what he needs. I can see him losing touch with reality altogether, if he hasn't already." She pointed towards the card at the bottom of four forming a column to the right of the cross. "Look, The Devil here shows how Hugh sees himself."

"As the Devil?" Declan looked at her quizzically.

"Well, obviously not literally. What it is, is delusions of grandeur, based on ignorance. It seems like some sort of nemesis—for Hugh, anyway—though I can't tell exactly what it'll be." She paused for a moment, gazing intently at the card. "No, whatever it is, is hidden for the time being. I suspect Hugh himself isn't aware of it yet. But the next one, which shows outside influences on him, that's straightforward enough."

"I'm so glad you think so," murmured Declan.

Joss had been sitting with her eyes closed, listening to Isabel's commentary. Now she opened them and gasped as she saw the Tower.

"What is it?" Isabel asked.

But Joss waved her query away and shook her head. "Go on. I'll tell you after you've finished."

Turning back to the Tower, Isabel went on, "I feel I want to read this literally, as the place Quincy saw, but also symbolically. Either way, it's where everything comes to a head for Hugh. In itself, that may not be a bad thing, as it could clear the air and allow him to face reality and learn from it." She indicated the card above the Tower. "I'm not sure he will, though. The Ace of Swords here shows he's hoping for great power, but I get the feeling he's way out of his depth, and if he actually gets what he wants, it could destroy him. It shows a real tendency to go to extremes."

Understatement of the year, thought Declan, watching as Isabel turned her attention to the final card, which showed a winged angel blowing a trumpet, and three grey human figures forming a family group rising from their respective coffins. Trust old Gabriel to be in on the act performing his trumpet voluntary. He always did manage to get all the interesting assignments. This irreverent supposition was confirmed by the card's title, 'Judgement'.

"Looks like Hugh's guardian angel is going to give him a talking to after all," he commented.

Isabel gave a snort of laughter. "You could say that. But one way or another, it seems he's going to get what's coming to him. I suppose he's largely brought it on himself, but..." Her voice drifted into silence as she cast her eyes over the layout "... there are so many major trumps in the reading that outside influences must also be important." She turned to her friend. "Now, Joss, you're obviously dying to tell us what you've got."

Joss's laugh was a trifle uneasy. "Not, perhaps, the best choice of phrase," she observed. "But I've been getting two things very strongly. First, I think you were right, Declan, about Hugh's guardian angel. Not literally," she added, seeing the look Declan gave her. "It's all inside his head. We already know he believes he's getting guidance from some angelic being, and I'm more convinced than ever that he sees the murders as some sort of divine task, through which he'll gain magical powers."

"The Ace of Swords," Isabel murmured.

With a nod, Joss continued, "The other thing I saw was the Tower, though not the one in the tarot. What I saw was the word, on what looked like a sign or a label—dark blue on white."

"So it looks like the Tower may be the name of a place, rather than an actual tower," said Declan. "At least that gives us something reasonably specific to look out for. Joss, do you have any maps or directories here? We could check them out."

"Only the telephone directory and a basic street map," said Joss, "but there are lots of others at work. I can check them this evening."

"Yes," said Isabel, gathering up her cards and patting them into a neat stack. "But we're no further ahead with the most important factor of all. We still don't know when Hugh plans to act."

"No-o." Joss rubbed her forehead thoughtfully with one forefinger. "Except it's going to be at night." She stopped suddenly, eyes widening in surprise at her own statement.

Declan gave her a sharp look. "What makes you think that?"

"It was when I saw the sign with 'Tower' on it. There was a light shining on it, and I'm sure it was at night. In fact, I'd swear to it."

CHAPTER THIRTY

The polished steel caught the gold of the leaping candle flame, holding it captive within the thin, sharp blade, where it transmuted the shining silver into gold. Slowly turning the knife in his hands, Hugh observed the effect with satisfaction.

For a moment he breathed in the scent of the incense burning before him on the altar, then slowly drew the blade through its intoxicating fumes. The purification of Air.

Again his eyes lingered lovingly on the gold dancing within the steel before passing the blade through the candle flame. The purification of Fire.

He dipped two fingers of his left hand—the side of the subconscious, the realm of intuition—into the small glass bowl and sprinkled water onto the knife blade. The purification of Water.

Finally, he dipped into the terracotta bowl, this time with his right hand, for right was the side of the conscious mind, the mind that planned and executed the dreams of the subconscious. He took three pinches of salt and mixed them with the water in the glass bowl. With his right forefinger, he drew a line of salt water along each side of the blade. The purification of Earth.

Grasping the knife firmly by its black handle, he looked down at the tarot card, already consecrated in similar fashion, lying at the centre of the altar. All had gone well. Now he could invoke the Guardians.

He rose to his feet, raising the knife above his head, feeling the power flow through him, then sweeping the blade in a slow arc to point towards the floor, murmuring, "As above, so below." He turned to face the east, direction of all beginnings. Then, holding the knife at arm's length in front of him, speaking firmly, and as loudly as he dared, since he knew most of the neighbouring tenants would be at home at this time in the evening, he began the invocation of the Guardians of the Four Directions.

Summoning each one in turn, waiting until he could sense the characteristics of each powerful Presence, he invoked their aid in his enterprise, making sure to command their continued presence as he left his room later and made his way to tonight's destination. It would not do to leave without the certainty of their protection. Too much was at stake.

At last, the circle was completed. He could feel its energy whirling about him, forming a cocoon of cold, blue fire, as he carefully placed the knife back in its sheath on the altar, then seated himself once more on the floor. A glance at his watch showed him there was still plenty of time. If he sat very quietly and allowed his mind to become still, surely he would sense once more the presence of his Holy Guardian Angel. Everything was ready now. Surely He would come near, now that His servant was so close to fulfilling the conditions...

* * * *

Throwing his jacket over the back of a chair, Declan lowered himself into it. He was exhausted. Isabel, showing a dismaying amount of energy, was bustling about putting the kettle on to boil and spooning tea into the pot. Her hair hung in corkscrews down one side, due to her habit of absentmindedly winding it round her fingers. Filled with a sudden desire to do the same with it himself, he said, "Come here a minute and sit with me."

"I won't be a moment. The kettle's almost boiled."

"I don't need tea, sweetheart. I need you."

Isabel threw him a smile that would have melted an iceberg, let alone his heart, but she poured boiling water into the teapot before going over and allowing Declan to pull her onto his knee and kiss her.

"Pity Quincy wasn't able to come up with anything more," she said at last, as Declan attempted to unravel her hair.

"Mmm. It's been a bit of a wasted effort all round—apart from your programme, of course."

They had spent the afternoon at Luke's place, Declan working his way through the assortment of directories and maps Joss had brought from work while the rest of them recorded the week's edition of The Psychic Connection. But no tower had come to light that seemed even remotely feasible as the scene of James's untimely demise. An hour and a half spent in the library afterwards hadn't turned up anything promising, either.

"No, the programme didn't go too badly," said Isabel, "though with Geraldine starting full-time work next month, if James doesn't start turning up a bit more often we'll have to look at getting someone else for the panel." James had once again excused himself, claiming he had some last-minute research to do for a public engagement. "You could scarcely even call it a panel, with just Luke and me and Joss.

Still," she conceded, "I suppose he does have other things on his mind at the moment."

"He's not the only one," murmured Declan, attempting to remove her coat and kiss her at the same time.

Extracting herself gently from his grasp, Isabel stood up and took off her coat, draping it over the back of a chair. She bent and kissed the tip of his nose. "I'll just go and pour the tea."

Declan heaved a sigh. "Just my luck to go and fall for a drug addict!"

"You can talk! How many cups of coffee did you have this afternoon while we were hard at work?"

"Yeah, well—" Declan's mouth twitched up at one side "—I have to keep my strength up somehow. I came here for a rest, and I've ended up working as hard as I would have back in Brisbane. Harder, I shouldn't wonder."

This was all too true, Isabel reflected as she carried two mugs of tea to the table. She sat next to Declan and leaned across to run her fingers down his cheek, feeling the tension there. "I'm sorry," she said softly. "Look, there doesn't seem to be anything more we can do for James right now, so why don't I just heat up a pizza for tea, and we can spend the evening relaxing. I'll give you a massage if you like." Declan's eyes told her he would, indeed. "And then," she continued recklessly, feeling breathless all of a sudden, "I might just let you have your wicked way with me."

Declan's hand tightened on hers. "I'll hold you to that," he murmured.

"Can you take this through?" Isabel handed Declan the plate of pizza slices. "There's still half a bottle of wine left from last night. I'll bring that." She reached up to close the cupboard door, then, with the bottle of wine in one hand and two stemmed glasses in the other, she followed Declan into the lounge.

The shrill of the telephone startled her, but she managed to save the glasses and set them down safely on the coffee table. "It's okay," she said to Declan, "I'll get it. Can you pour the wine? I won't be a moment."

Declan heard her voice out in the hall, sounding first surprised, then urgent. She had closed the door to keep the lounge warm, so he couldn't make out what she was saying. But when she returned, she looked tense and worried, and, he fancied, excited too.

"What's up?"

Without really seeing it, Isabel took the wine he offered, turning the glass between her fingers, but not drinking. "That was Joss. She's found the Tower."

"Yeah? Where?"

"It was in this morning's paper. She'd only just got round to reading it."

"I thought Joss practically wrote the thing."

"Not all of it. Not the Public Notices, anyway, and that's where it was."

"Where what was?" By now, Declan had completely forgotten both wine and food. Every instinct screamed at him that they were close to solving the puzzle.

Isabel put her glass down, then picked it up again and put it to her lips. At the last minute she put it back on the table and drew a deep breath. "It looks as though Joss may have been right yesterday," she announced. "James is giving a public lecture tonight."

That, thought Declan, accounts for the 'last-minute research'.

"It's at the College of Education," Isabel went on, with another intake of breath. "And guess where it's going to be?"

"This had better be good," Declan muttered, thinking with longing of his promised massage.

"Oh, it is, believe me. The room he's lecturing in is in the Tower Block."

"Holy Mother of God!" Without thinking, Declan picked up the nearest glass and gulped down a mouthful of wine, coughing as it burnt the back of his throat. Isabel thumped him unceremoniously on the back. It didn't help. Declan took hold of her hands before she could do any more damage. "If that's your idea of a massage..." he began.

But Isabel broke in, "Sorry, that'll have to wait. Joss has been trying to get hold of James, to warn him, but he's not at home or in his office at the university. She's going to try one more time, and if she can't get in touch with him, we're going to have to go to the lecture. It's the last in a series of three, so it's almost certain to be the place Hugh was referring to in his journal."

"Of course! The Tower! That's another one of your major trumps, isn't it?"

The phone rang again, and Isabel raced to answer it.

"That was Joss again. James is still not there."

"So, what's the plan now?"

"If we're right, there's no time to lose. Joss has already called Luke, and we're all going out there in his car. He'll be on his way now to pick Joss up from work, and then they're coming on here."

"What time does the lecture start?"

"Eight o'clock."

Declan looked at his watch, then up at Isabel. "And it's just after seven now. Hmm. How far is it from here to the College of Education?"

"About six kilometres, I think. Why?"

"If we hurry, we'll just about have time to polish off the pizza before we leave."

CHAPTER THIRTY-ONE

"That was it! You've just driven past." Joss pointed back to where a massive tree, a few lazy leaves still fluttering on its branches, stood sentinel at one corner of an expanse of tree-studded lawn.

"Damn!" Braking to a halt at the side of the road, Luke waited impatiently for a gap in the speeding traffic, then swung the car in a wide curve that took it neatly across the main road and into the short side street. Its entire length on the left-hand side seemed taken up with the grounds of the College of Education. On the right, expensive-looking town houses congregated chattily amidst well-tended gardens. Overhead, street lamps bent supercilious heads to inspect the street. Their light revealed no parking spaces, however. Both sides of the road were lined with cars.

"I wouldn't have expected James to be this popular," Isabel commented as Luke edged the car along.

"I dare say his isn't the only lecture," said Joss. "These days halls of learning can't afford to leave their facilities lying idle, even at night. Keep going, Luke. If that sign's anything to go by, there should be a parking lot round to the left there."

A parking space having finally been found, the four of them made their way, as quickly as the darkness and unfamiliar surroundings allowed, along the nearest path.

Tall flax bushes loomed along its borders like giant spiders, and, in small courtyards between buildings, sculptures crouched like beasts ready to spring. The air was chill and sharp with the promise of frost.

Shivering, Declan thrust his hands deeper into the pockets of his jacket. "Does anyone actually know where this Tower is?"

No-one did. Some metres ahead, double doors were visible. A small group of women emerged from the darkness to the right of them and went through them. Before it swung shut, they caught a glimpse of bright lighting and pale walls. The four of them hurried forward, hoping to find someone who could direct them. Pushing their way through the doors, they found themselves in an empty foyer with green felt covered notice boards taking up the walls on either side. It was soon apparent that no advertisement for James's lecture was among the profusion of notices pinned to them. There was no sign of the women they had followed in, or of anyone else.

"According to my watch," said Joss, looking about anxiously, "the lecture will be starting any minute now. I don't imagine Hugh will be stupid enough to make his move until after it's finished, but I had hoped to be able to warn James before it started."

With an impatient toss of her head, she turned to leave. The others followed. Just beyond the double doors, the path they had used converged with another at right angles to it, which was, in fact, a covered walkway leading in both directions.

"What we need," declared Joss, "is a sign."

"Give us a sign!" echoed Luke, looking upwards as though

311

some unseen power might grant his wish.

"Twit!" said Joss.

"Never underestimate the power of prayer." Declan's voice, sounding improbably sanctimonious, came from somewhere to their left. He was standing beside a pole from which a cluster of signs pointed in various directions.

In the light from a nearby window, Joss saw they were white with dark blue lettering. One, pointing towards a tall building at one end of the covered way, simply read, 'Tower'. A sharp tingle ran up her spine. "Down here," she said.

The others hurried behind her. A glass door at the end of the covered way gave onto a small foyer with two lifts facing the entrance. Quickly they pushed through the door and stood looking round. There was no-one in sight, and no indication of where the lecture might be.

Isabel felt a twinge of nervousness twist the tightening knot in her stomach. She glanced out through the glass front of the foyer, hoping to see someone who might be able to help them. Her gaze was met by a dark, primeval face staring malevolently back at her. She gave an involuntary start in the split second it took to realise it was carved into the trunk of a tree standing beside the doorway.

She felt Declan's hand on her arm. "You all right?"

Isabel nodded. "I wish we could find this wretched lecture. I just know something's going to happen. I can feel it, and it's making me nervous." She turned to Joss. "Didn't the ad in the paper say where it is?"

"It just said Room one-oh-four in the Tower Block. But without knowing what system they use here, we're not much the wiser."

"There don't seem to be any lecture rooms on this floor,"

said Luke. "I guess our best bet is to start on the next one up, and just keep going till we find it." He pushed the 'Up' button between the two lifts.

Joss nodded, noticing with annoyance that the lift was currently at the top floor. "Yes, I suppose you're right. But you'd think they'd have a map here somewhere, wouldn't you, or, at the very least, a poster or two advertising the lectures?"

She glanced around her impatiently, looking for the staircase she knew must be there somewhere. Her eyes picked up a crumpled ball of blue paper lying on the floor next to a metal waste bin against the wall to the left of the lifts. Automatically, she went to place it in the receptacle. Ah, there were the stairs, at the end of a short corridor. As she picked up the paper, a tingle ran through her hand, and her scalp prickled all over.

Quickly, she smoothed out its wrinkles to reveal a small photocopied poster advertising James's lecture series. As she swiftly perused its contents, her eyes lit up. "Aha! It is the first floor! Come on!"

With Joss leading the way, they streamed up the stairs. The first-floor landing gave them the choice of another flight of stairs or a corridor. The short corridor led to a foyer similar to the one on the ground floor. Again, there was no obvious indication of where to go. Isabel had the unnerving impression that someone—or something—was deliberately trying to impede their progress. Before she could voice her feeling, however, the sound of a woman's voice drifted out to them through an open door at the far end of the foyer. They hurried towards it. The clock on the wall between the lifts showed two minutes past eight.

The voice soon led them to Room 104, a small lecture theatre with rows of seats rising in an arc around a raised wooden platform. On it, two chairs flanked a central wooden lectern. As Joss and the others entered, they saw James seated in the chair furthest from the door, while a tall, slim woman in a navy-blue suit introduced him. Between sentences, she was making valiant attempts to prevent a paisley silk scarf from sliding from her shoulders to the floor.

Quickly, and as quietly as possible, they made their way to seats near the back of the room. They wanted the best view possible of the rest of the audience. James looked up. His face registered surprise as he recognised them. Swiftly suppressing it, he looked down again at his notes.

Isabel cast her eyes over the audience, but could see no tell-tale reaction. Not that she expected their backs to give much away. The knot in the pit of her stomach had been sending danger signals ever since she had seen the sign pointing to the Tower and, by now, she felt ill with apprehension and excitement. If only she could see a few faces. She glanced at Joss, sitting to her left. Joss's gaze was on James, and she seemed to be listening intently, though not to the woman on the dais, who had just finished her introduction, and was seating herself and stuffing her wayward scarf into her handbag, nor to James as he rose to begin his talk. Isabel recognised the look. Joss was not interested in what James had to say. Listening with her psychic faculties, she was hoping to pick up on Hugh.

Somewhat to her surprise, Isabel found James's talk on the psychological significance of dreams quite fascinating, and wished she had prepared herself to take notes. All too soon it was over, and James called for questions from the audience. Several hands went up. Isabel felt once more the familiar tightening in her stomach. She glanced at Joss, whose expression had now returned to normal.

"Couldn't pick up a thing," she whispered to Isabel. "If he's here, he's got the shutters well and truly closed."

"He's here all right," Isabel whispered back. "I can feel it. I just can't tell where."

Several frowns of annoyance were turned on them, so they both subsided into silence as James called for 'one last question.' Isabel turned to Declan with a rueful smile. He felt tense, geared for action, and the forced wait was all but intolerable. For all his years of experience, the sensation still came as a surprise. Like stage fright, he thought. Not that he'd ever experienced stage fright, but. He smiled back at Isabel and gave her hand a squeeze.

As question time came to an end, James retired once more to his seat, and the tall woman rose to thank him. To the sound of appreciative applause, she went to prop open the door, and the audience scuffled to its feet and began to straggle outside.

Luke turned to the others. "What do we do now?"

Joss glanced towards the front of the room, where James stood surrounded by an assortment of half a dozen or so people. "We can hardly tell him why we're here while he's surrounded by that lot," she said. "Let's wait outside, then nip back in as soon as they've all left."

"Praise be!" muttered Luke, with an exaggerated sigh of relief. "That'll give me time for a cigarette."

* * * *

The young man nodded his thanks, picked his scarf up from the seat where he had left it, and sauntered towards the door. Brother Fulget Virtus turned back and began to gather up his lecture notes from the lectern. For all his supposed insight into the human mind, he was clearly no match for a real magician. He had failed even to notice Brother Non Extinguar, seated in a corner at the back of the room.

Of course, he had made sure to arrive early—several hours early, in fact. His first task had been to check out the lecture room, waiting on the first floor landing, pretending to scrutinise the paintings on the wall and the display of books in the glass case there, glancing along the corridor from time to time (he hadn't wanted to appear too interested) until he was certain the last class of the day had left. It had taken him just minutes to work out the best place to sit. Finding the curtain-covered door that led out to the stairs at the back of the building had been a bonus.

Buoyed by this discovery, he had made his way to the cafeteria. He wanted to think, to have a clear picture in his mind of what he needed to achieve that night, and how he would achieve it. He had been finishing his coffee when his eyes, following the progress of a girl with long hair like shiny black satin, to a seat on the far side of the room, had come to rest on a small, photocopied poster on the wall above her head.

With a shock, he had recognised Brother Fulget Virtus's face, and realised the poster was advertising the date, time and place of his talk, a small map at the bottom showing the exact location. Again, the image of Brother Ferro Comite and the other Senior Brothers had invaded his mind, as it had frequently since that night when he had arrived home after work and realised someone had been in his room. Although nothing had been said or done, and none of them seemed to act any differently from usual, he had been unable to rid himself of the suspicion that they knew, and were watching him. What if they turned up tonight? For several terrifying moments, he had felt himself sliding towards the edge of the pit. Oh, God, no! Not that! Not now, when he was so close to success!

Frantically, he had invoked his Guardian and Guide, begging for a way out of his dilemma. It had taken some minutes to quell the panic that threatened to engulf him, but he finally succeeded in slowing his breathing and stilling the thumping of his heart. Then a solution had occurred to him. A map had been included on the poster because, without one, lecture rooms were so difficult to find in the ad hoc layout of the College. He, himself, only knew where to go because he had attended lectures here before. Chances were the Senior Brothers were unfamiliar with it. And the newspaper advertisement had only given the room number.

As soon as the girl had gone, he had strolled across very casually and removed the poster. For all anyone else would know, he might be one of the organisers of the talks. In his corduroy trousers, checked shirt and parka, he could easily have been a student at either the University or the College of Education.

He had dropped the screwed-up poster in the nearest waste bin. But it had occurred to him there must be more of them around the College. So the rest of the time available to him had been spent taking down every poster he could find and disposing of them. This had taken more time than he had expected, and eventually he had been forced to abandon his search, pausing only to tear down the poster on the wall by the lifts, crumple it, and fling it at the nearby waste bin before hurrying up the stairs to the first floor of the Tower Block.

When Brother Fulget Virtus had entered the room, nodding and chatting with a tall woman in a navy-blue suit, he was already in his chosen place, surrounded by the psychic cloak of invisibility whose technique he had perfected during the weeks spent waiting for this night. This night, when he would finally attain that... But no. Not yet. He still had work to do.

Gathering his cloak around him, he got to his feet and began, quickly and quietly, to move toward the dais. His body felt weightless, as though he were gliding just above the surface of the floor. In his jacket pocket, the handle of his knife felt hard and smooth. The power with which he had charged it tingled against his fingers, exciting him so that he found it difficult to breathe. But he dared not pause to calm himself fully. Any second now, Brother Fulget Virtus would turn round. He must trust in his Guides. They would surely not forsake him now, when he was so close to fulfilling his task. Their task. So close...

Throwing aside his psychic cloak, he silently uttered the words of power, and drew his knife from his pocket.

CHAPTER THIRTY-TWO

"That must be the last of them, surely." In the absence of an appropriate receptacle, Luke ground his cigarette butt guiltily into the floor of the corridor as a bespectacled young man wandered past them, winding a length of black woollen scarf about his neck as he went.

"I did a quick head count before we came out," Joss told him, "and I'm practically certain it is."

Luke slid the trampled butt surreptitiously to one side of the corridor with his foot and scuffed it against the wall, where it lay meekly to await the cleaners. "Right," he said, "let's get back in, then."

The room was empty.

"Where the hell is he?" Luke gazed helplessly towards the lectern.

"More to the point, where's Hugh?" Joss said tersely.

"We don't know for sure he was even here," said Declan, though his nerves were passing on messages from his brain telling him not to be so stupid.

Before any of the others could do the same, there was a thud and a scuffling sound from somewhere just overhead. In unison, their heads swivelled upwards.

"There must be another way out," Declan muttered, glancing swiftly about him. To the left of the low stage, he saw a heavy black curtain hanging against the wall. It was identical to the curtains drawn across the windows that lined the outside wall—they probably doubled as blackout curtains, just as the whiteboard at the front of the room could also be used as a film screen. But, unlike the others, this curtain reached down to the floor. And it wasn't against an outside wall, so a window was unlikely...

Beckoning the others after him, he raced to pull the curtain aside. His suspicions were confirmed. The door behind it lay slightly ajar. Beyond it, a short corridor led to a staircase, a continuation of the one they had encountered on the ground floor. Above them they could hear footsteps—more than one set, by the sound of them.

As they raced up the staircase, James's distinctive accent floated down to them, though it was impossible to make out his words. This was followed by a different voice. Being lighter, it carried better than James's deeper tones. "... to the top," they heard. "... just move." Its menace was unmistakable.

"How many floors are there?" panted Luke as they reached the second floor landing.

"Five." Joss was already part-way up the next flight.

Declan said nothing, but Isabel saw his face contort with pain as he limped toward the bottom of the stairs. "We're taking the lift," she said, grasping his arm firmly. "You two go on. We'll meet you at the top."

"Thanks a lot!" Luke muttered through gritted teeth as he scrambled after Joss.

* * * *

As he gathered up his lecture notes, straightening them

320

meticulously before returning them to their folder, James reviewed the evening. It had gone remarkably well, he felt, considering the state of his nerves. Despite Brother Per Severantia Vincit's assurances that he had the matter in hand, and despite his own protective operations, he had spent the week in a fever of foreboding. Several times, in fact, he had seriously considered calling the lecture off. In the end, however, his sense of duty had won out. Now, here he was at the end of another successful lecture series, and nothing untoward had happened. It seemed Brother P S V had, after all, been able to work some legal magic on his behalf.

Or maybe it was Joss and the other panellists. He had been surprised to see them here. When Joss had visited him at his apartment, he had desperately wanted to tell her of his fears. For all that she so often appeared to be ridiculing him, he believed she had been genuinely concerned for his safety. So maybe she'd gone to the police with her concerns, and her information had helped put Brother Non Extinguar out of action in time. Whatever, he hadn't appeared here tonight and, in a few minutes, James would be safely in his car and on his way to the comfort and security of his apartment. No First Order brother would be able to penetrate the circle of protection there, of that he was certain. Reassured, he slipped the neatened papers into the folder and clicked the clasp into place. Tucking the folder under one arm, he made to leave.

What was that? Had he heard something behind him? Rosemary had already left—she had to get her babysitter home by ten—so it couldn't be her. Besides, it was not so much a sound, as a feeling, as though someone close behind him had pulled aside a curtain, and he had felt the soft rush of air as the fabric moved. He had not had time to analyse the sensation sufficiently to react to it, when he felt something sharp push against the small of his back.

"Don't make a sound, Brother." Brother Non Extinguar's voice spoke softly against his ear. It sounded like a snake might sound if it could speak—smooth, and cold, and utterly without feeling. "This is a knife, and I assure you I know how to use it."

James felt sick with fear. He froze, as though that would somehow render him invisible. Unable even to swallow successfully, he doubted he could have made a sound.

"That's right, Brother. Just do exactly as I tell you. We're going to leave now. There's a door to our left, behind that curtain. You're going to open it, very quietly, and very quickly. Move now. I said move!"

The voice became fierce, and the knife jabbed hard against his ribs. James tried to swallow, but his throat seemed clamped together and would not do his bidding. He licked his lips. His tongue was thick and heavy, and tasted of terror. But the knife galvanised him into action, and he moved surprisingly quickly towards the door. He opened it and saw a short corridor with stairs rising to the right at its far end.

"Along there," urged Brother Non Extinguar's voice, his breath an obscene caress on James's neck, his knife accentuating his warning, "No, don't turn round. Just do as we tell you."

We? But before James could begin to speculate, the knife was urging him up the stairs, and it was all he could do to manipulate his body from step to step. At some stage in the nightmare—he was no longer certain which floor they were on—he thought he heard voices somewhere below him. He heard footsteps running along a corridor, changing tone abruptly as they began to climb the stairs. Someone was following them. It must be Joss and the others.

James forced himself to take a deep and ragged breath. He had to find a way of letting them know he was in trouble. "How far... are we... going?" he gasped, deliberately speaking as loudly as breathlessness and terror would allow.

"Keep your voice down!" hissed the reply in his right ear. "We're going to the top floor."

"Wouldn't it be... simpler to... take the lift?"

"No! We're going to the top, and we're going to walk." His voice sounded smooth, in the way polished steel is smooth. Again the knife blade jabbed into him, forcing him to walk faster, despite his aching legs and bursting heart. "Come on! No more talk, just move!"

After what seemed simultaneously an aeon and no time at all, they reached the top floor and made their way along the short corridor that led to the front of the building. Like the other floors, it had lifts on one side and windows on the other, with offices off the end near the corridor and lecture rooms off the other. James paused, gasping for breath, but the knife urged him forward towards the windows that reached from the ceiling to within half a metre of the floor. He found himself looking down to where light from some unseen source illuminated the roof of the covered walkway far below. The sky was black silk with diamond stars glinting on its surface.

For the first time, James saw his captor, his face reflected in the glass like a mask, white and angular with black cut-out eyes. Close beside it, he saw his own face, and the sight shocked him. He had never thought of himself as being particularly courageous, except, perhaps, in a moral sense. Neither had he considered himself a coward. But the face staring back at him showed an abject terror verging on the obscene, especially in one trained, as he was, to confront man's innermost demons. Could it be that he had simply ignored his own? Or was it, perhaps...? Disgusted, he shook his head and wrested it away. And came face to with the demon that was Brother Non Extinguar.

"What is it you want?" he croaked, his voice hoarse from exertion and fear.

"You have failed. You must be punished."

The voice that replied seemed disembodied, floating between them like a wraith, yet filled with barely contained force. James had experienced the effect before, and it had struck fear into him then, being one of the deciding factors in his decision not to become a clinical psychologist. Brother Non Extinguar was clearly mentally unbalanced—almost certainly psychotic. James felt panic squeezing him. He forced himself to breathe slowly, trying to cajole the right words out of his petrified throat.

"How – how do you feel I have failed?"

Brother Non Extinguar stared at him out of eyes as pale and as cold as a winter sky. James felt himself being sucked into them. He blinked abruptly.

"We do not have to explain our actions," Brother Non Extinguar's voice intoned. "We do what we will." An insane grin spread across his pale features, and with it, an abrupt change in his manner. When he spoke, his voice was filled with a horrid gaiety, like an evil child playing a cruel party game. "Turn around, Brother. That's right. Now!"

He grasped James's left arm with unexpected strength and twisted it up behind his back, forcing him to turn as directed. He slipped what felt like a loop of cord around his wrist and pulled it tight, quickly wrenching his right arm back and binding the two tightly together. James tried to cry out, but his lips made no sound. He saw his mouth opening and shutting in the dark glass of the window. It seemed completely unconnected with him, as though he were watching a television screen with the sound muted. There was a brief tearing sound, then Brother Non Extinguar's hands appeared in front of his face, and he saw a strip of wide silver duct tape being clamped across his mouth.

Brother Non Extinguar's voice in his ear was a ghastly parody of reassurance. "Not long now. Our task is almost done."

Reflected in the glass, James saw the glint of the knife blade as Brother Non Extinguar pulled it once more from his pocket.

* * * *

"Bloody leg!" Declan gave Isabel a look of gratitude as Luke and Joss disappeared up the stairs, and came to stand beside her as she pressed the lift button. He waved an arm at the metal doors. "This thing had better be working!"

A whirring sound and a soft thud answered him, and the doors slid open. As the lift sped upwards, he felt the slight dragging sensation as his body registered the change in gravity. It failed notably to curb the way his stomach was lurching in anticipation of what they might find on the top floor. In more ways than one, his stomach was way ahead of him.

"Shouldn't have had so much of that pizza," he muttered to himself.

Then suddenly the lift had bumped gently to a stop and the doors were sliding open. With a hand on Isabel's arm to warn her not to make a move just yet, Declan pressed the button to lock the doors open and glanced quickly around. There was no sign of Joss or Luke but, framed against one of the windows that took up most of the opposite wall, stood two figures. The window beside them was open, letting in the icy night air. Both had their backs to the lifts, but Declan and Isabel immediately recognised James. His reflection in the dark expanse of glass showed eyes wide with terror above a strip of silver tape that covered his mouth. An incongruous image rose in Declan's mind of the piles of 'true confessions' type magazines they'd found at the Brisbane luxury apartment of Walters and her sidekick Patterson. They'd been full of amateur pornographic photos, the anonymity of the subjects supposedly preserved by black rectangles placed across their eyes, though the effect had been merely to direct the attention elsewhere. Readers' girlfriends or wives most of them purported to be; or, in a sickening number of cases, children. With an effort, he managed to stifle the hysterical laughter that rose to displace his real feelings.

James's reflection all but obscured that of the man standing behind him. From the back, they could see wispy fair hair crowning a slight figure of about average height, clad in a dark blue anorak and grey corduroy trousers. It was impossible to see what, if anything, he was doing, but there was a peculiar tension about his body, sensed, rather than actually visible. Isabel felt a familiar tingling at the back of her head, and a tightening in her chest. It was more than just fear. Her psychic sense was trying to tell her something. Something she ought to have known all along. Something about that figure, tense as an arrow strung and poised for flight...

They heard footsteps on the stairs to their right. Joss appeared, closely followed by a panting Luke. The fair-haired figure swung round, and they saw the knife in his hand. Isabel recognised it by its black handle as the one they had seen at Hugh's flat. She also recognised Hugh. No wonder she had kept feeling she ought to know him. Briefly, she wondered whether he would remember her.

Confronted by Hugh's knife, Joss and Luke had stopped abruptly in their tracks. Like some bizarre tableau, they faced one another, each motionless, unwilling to make the first move. Very slowly, Hugh's eyes travelled from Luke and Joss to the open lift. They widened in recognition as they saw Isabel, a slight frown creasng his brow as though he couldn't quite fathom the significance of what he was seeing. Then a muffled sound emerged from behind James's gag as he saw, reflected in the windows, his fellow panellists and Declan.

Hugh rounded on him. "Silence!" he hissed, placing his knife once more against James's ribs. Lowering his head, James visibly subsided.

Staring at Hugh's reflection in the window, Isabel saw in the wide, wild eyes he turned on James not ordinary anger, but a kind of cold, mocking fury. She was reminded of a television interview she had seen with Charles Manson. But he had been safely behind bars at the time. Hugh was right there in front of them, with a knife in his hand.

Ignoring the rest of them, he continued to address James in a strangely disconnected voice. "Don't imagine you can escape punishment. She has chosen me to do Her Holy Will, and now that She is with me at last, I cannot fail Her."

James flinched, and made a strangled sound in his throat. As he spoke, Hugh motioned in Isabel's direction with his knife. With a gasp of horror, she realised the 'She' Hugh was referring to was her. She glanced at the others. Like her, they all seemed frozen in place.

Another sound from James turned her head in his direction. Hugh had pushed him to a kneeling position on the floor, and was standing over him. Apparently oblivious to those behind him, he pushed James's head forward, holding it in place as he raised his knife.

Suddenly released from paralysis, Isabel pushed aside Declan's restraining arm and stepped out of the lift.

"Hugh, no," she found herself saying, "you mustn't."

Hugh turned, disbelief on his face. "But... it's what You wanted. They failed me—me, Your chosen servant. I had to prove they were wrong. They had to be punished!" He paused for a moment, then a look of obscene eagerness spread over his features as he continued in a breathless rush, "The others weren't worthy, and neither is this one." He poked at James's kneeling form with one foot, his lip twisted in contempt. "They call themselves magicians, and think they can stand in judgement, but they haven't the wit to recognise true magic when it's right there in front of them. None of them heard your voice. But I did exactly as you told me, and now you've come to me, just as you promised. I must finish the task, so that you'll stay with me forever." His expression as he stared at her was a frightful travesty of desire and devotion.

Isabel took a slow breath, forcing herself to speak calmly as well as firmly. "No, Hugh. You've made a terrible mistake. Please don't make it any worse."

Behind her, she heard a sound. Keeping her gaze firmly locked on Hugh's, she signalled to the others to stay back with a slight movement of one hand, then stepped forward, holding her hand out towards him. She forced herself to speak firmly, desperately hoping for a tone Hugh would respond to. "Come, give me the knife."

CHAPTER THIRTY-THREE

Hugh gazed, rapt, at the tall figure before him. How beautiful She was, with that hair like flames, and her pale, yet vivid face. She could only be Brighid, Celtic Goddess of poets and smiths. He had never dared to hope for so much—a Goddess, one of the Old Ones, for his Holy Guardian Angel. He had always assumed his Guardian would be male. It had simply never occurred to him that the deep, soft voice that spoke to him was this beautiful creature. Though, of course, it made perfect sense. His ancestry was Scottish and Irish, so it was only natural he should be chosen to serve a Celtic deity. And he had always loved poetry and art...

But She seemed angry with him. Why? He had done everything exactly as She told him to, so how had he displeased Her? Perhaps he had misunderstood Her instructions. He must explain to Her again, then, so She would understand and stay with him. It would be unbearable if She left him now. He felt tears prickle behind his eyes. She was so beautiful! And she was all he had...

As he looked, she fixed her dark grey eyes on his and began to move towards him, one arm outstretched.

"Come," She was telling him, "give me the knife."

"But..." he heard his voice saying. He had no wish to disobey Her, but his mind was in turmoil. What was it She wanted...?

"Hugh, give me the knife." Her voice was low and soft, and infinitely kind, but Her words were unmistakably an order.

Confused, Hugh stared at the hand stretched out towards him. The fingers were long and slim, the skin pale and translucent. He was certain he could see a faint aura flowing around it like liquid light. Then he noticed something else. One of her fingers had something stuck to it—a small, pinkish rectangle, slightly darker than the skin it encased. He closed his eyes, but his mind felt fuzzy as it struggled to comprehend this phenomenon. What could it be? Why...?

Suddenly, he felt sick with realisation. His Goddess, his Brighid, his Holy Guardian Angel, had a sticking plaster on her finger!

Gasping, he opened his eyes and saw a woman with long red hair standing in front of him, wearing a green coat and a red tartan skirt. She was holding one hand out to him, saying, "Give me the knife, Hugh."

With mounting terror, he recognised her. She was that tarot reader he had gone to after... Oh, God! What if she had seen more than she told him? What if she knew everything? He looked down at his hand, puzzled to find his ritual knife there. He didn't remember bringing that with him. As he stared at it, struggling to comprehend, a muffled sound from behind him made him turn. Brother Fulget Virtus was kneeling on the floor, his hands tied behind his back with a white cord exactly like the ones used by the First Degree Brothers to tie their robes. Like the one he used. And there was a strip of duct tape across his mouth. Above it, his terrified eyes stared up at his captor.

His captor! Oh, God! God! What had he done?

He heard a low moan float out into the air before him, as the knife slid from his hand and clattered to the floor. Then the abyss engulfed him and sucked him into its black, greedy maw.

* * * *

As she saw the knife fall from Hugh's hand, Isabel felt relief surge through her. Then he began to move, and tension gripped her again. But instead of picking up the knife, he simply crumpled as though someone had deflated him. Silent tears trickled from his eyes as he lay in a heap on the grey linoleum floor. Despite all he had done, Isabel's heart went out to him. Swiftly, she crossed the floor and knelt beside him. He crept into her arms like a child, and lay there sobbing violently while she stroked his hair.

Released, suddenly, from their spell of immobility, the others went into action. Joss and Luke went to James and quickly untied his hands. Rubbing life back into them, James began gingerly to remove the duct tape from his mouth, wincing in pain as he did so. Declan picked up the knife Hugh had dropped, being careful not to erase any telltale finger-prints. Carefully, he wrapped it in his handkerchief and slid it into his jacket pocket. No doubt the forensic blokes would want a look at it later.

"I should have thought to call Garfield before we came here," he said, wondering how the hell they were going to get Hugh to the Police Station. Though, by the look of the poor bastard, he'd be better off in a hospital.

"If it's evidence you want," Luke said with a grin, "it's all here." He pulled his miniature digital recorder from his pocket and held it up.

Joss clicked her tongue at him and was about to say something when the clatter of footsteps sounded on the stairs. Moments later, Inspector Garfield's solid form appeared in the foyer, closely followed by Constable Johnson and three other constables, even younger looking than Johnson, if that was possible. Behind them hovered a drab looking man in his fifties, a large bunch of keys dangling from one hand, and a look of curiosity on his gnarled features.

"We ran into the caretaker on our way up here," Joss explained to Declan, "so we asked him to phone Inspector Garfield. We thought he might come in handy."

"Good thinking," said Declan, and went to explain the situation to Garfield.

When he saw the Inspector's face looking down at him, Hugh clutched at Isabel as though the Devil had come for him in person.

"It's all right, Hugh," she told him soothingly. "This is Inspector Garfield. He's here to help you."

She turned to the Inspector. "He's in pretty bad shape. I'm not sure he's back in touch with reality yet. I think he needs medical help."

James, who had managed to remove the tape and was fingering his lips as though to be certain they were still intact, looked up at these words. "I agree," he said with feeling, explaining to Garfield, "I have a degree in psychology. It's impossible to be certain without a detailed examination, of course, but he does seem to be exhibiting symptoms suggestive of either manic depression or schizophrenia. Then, of course, there's a syndrome that

333

combines symptoms of both. It's relatively rare, but in my opinion it would be well worthwhile considering the possibility..."

"Thank you, Sir," Garfield interrupted gravely. "I'll bear that in mind." He nodded at Johnson, who came across to help him. Together, they lifted the sobbing Hugh to his feet. At the sight of the handcuffs Johnson produced, he shrank back against Isabel, flailing his hands and moaning.

Isabel put a hand on his shoulder and looked steadily into his eyes. "Hugh," she said gently, "let the Constable put them on you. They're to keep you safe from harm until he can take you to get help."

Hugh's resistance seemed to collapse suddenly. He nodded, wiping his face on his sleeve, and allowed Isabel to hold his hands while Johnson clicked the cuffs into place.

As two constables led him away, Garfield went across to James, who was now standing by the open window, gazing dully at the covered walkway below, oblivious to the frosty air drifting through it. "Are you sure you're all right, Sir? We'll need a statement from you when you're feeling up to it, so if you'd like to come with me now, I'll get a doctor to have a look at you as well—just to make sure nothing's amiss."

James looked at him blankly for a moment, then stammered, "Oh, er, thank you, Inspector. Yes, yes, of course I'll come. But I have my car. I don't want to leave it here overnight. I'll—um—I'll need it in the morning."

"Well, Sir, I really don't think..." Garfield began.

Joss looked at James's bruised wrists and face, his dishevelled hair and clothes. He was clearly in no condition to drive, but he looked as though he'd burst into tears if the Inspector insisted. "I'll drive you, James," she said quickly, "if you think you can trust me with your car."

James smiled at her with heartfelt gratitude. "Thank you, Joss. I'd appreciate that."

Garfield nodded agreement, then went to where the caretaker was standing by the lift with the two remaining constables. "Thank you for your help, Sir. We'd appreciate it if you'd ensure no-one comes into the building until we've had a chance to do a thorough search. Don't worry, Sir, I'll square it with the Management first thing in the morning. If you'd like to take Constable Reeves and Constable Morrow to the room where the lecture was held..." The caretaker nodded eagerly. His job did not normally offer such excitement.

Declan had gone immediately to Isabel and put his arms around her. Now he looked at her, concern darkening his eyes. "Are you okay, sweetheart?"

Isabel nodded, and gave him a wan smile. "I'm all right. I could do with a cup of tea, though——good and strong."

From the lift, Garfield turned back to Declan. "I presume I can rely on you and your friends to join us at the Station before long. I'll need statements from all of you. I'm sure you'll appreciate how anxious I am to know exactly what's been going on, particularly as no-one saw fit to let me in on the secret while there was still time to prevent all this."

The gaze that encompassed them was filled with barely suppressed annoyance. Declan felt a wave of relief wash over him as he remembered how close he was to quitting it all. He sighed, and ran his fingers through his hair. "Right," he said, "We'll be along as soon as we can."

Garfield gave a curt nod and leaned across to press the lift button to take them down. As the lift doors closed, Declan noticed a small, flat object lying on the floor. He went to pick it up, and saw it was a tarot card—the Magician. He held it out to Isabel.

"This is like the card we saw at Hugh's apartment, isn't it?"

Isabel nodded. "I expect it's the same one. Probably fell from his pocket."

"Well," Luke began, "at least he didn't get the chance to leave it at the scene of the—" He broke off suddenly as he noticed James staring at the card in frightened fascination. "Sorry, James. Me and my big mouth."

James shook his head. "That's okay. I guess it's going to take me a while to get over it, but really, I can't thank you all enough for all you've done for me. I'm only too aware that you put yourselves in danger for my sake. If only I'd listened to you earlier, maybe—maybe other lives could have been saved as well."

He took the card from Declan and gazed at it in silence. "We were right all along," he said at last, speaking as though to himself. "Hugh wasn't ready for this. Whatever he may have believed to the contrary, the Fool was the right choice." Handing the card back to Declan, he moved wearily towards the lift.

Luke stared after him, shaking his head. "What the hell's that supposed to mean?" he muttered to the others.

"We'll probably never know," said Joss. "I don't imagine James is about to tell us. And don't you dare go asking him."

Her final remark was aimed at Luke, who was gazing at James's back in undisguised speculation. Luke grinned at her and shrugged, patting the tape recorder in his pocket. Even without a revelation from James, he reckoned he had the makings of another winning programme.

Declan had been contemplating the Magician card in his hand. In his mind he tried to see Hugh in the Magician's robes, wielding his wand with the Magician's sense of calm authority. But all he could see was Hugh's pale, stricken face as he crumpled to the ground and lay sobbing in Isabel's arms.

There was a soft whirring sound and the lift doors slid open. James stepped through and stood quietly waiting for the rest of them. With a sigh, Declan shoved the card into his pocket. His hand encountered Hugh's knife. He had forgotten to give it to Inspector Garfield.

"I reckon James was right, but," he said softly to Isabel.

Isabel nodded. "Let's hope he'll have the chance to find himself now."

Declan didn't trust himself to say any more, so he put his arm around her and held her very tightly for a moment. Then they went to join the others.

Vicious Circle

When a listener to `The Psychic Connection' radio programme is emotionally blackmailed by self-styled spiritual teacher Bob Ferris, resident panellists Joss Cherry and Isabel Sinclair decide to investigate. Meanwhile, the remains of a woman's body are found in a creek-bed in Queensland, Australia. Detective Sergeant Declan Kelly's search for Richard Forster, the last person to see her alive, leads him to communes in Queensland and New Zealand and the flesh-pots of Auckland's infamous Karangahape Road, until his trail meets that of the `Psychic Connection' panel. Their investigations culminate in a dramatic confrontation at the disused church where Ferris attempts to implement his bizarre plans to give birth to the New Aeon.

A Different Hunger

In Victorian London, when an ill-advised love affair sees young Rufus de Hunte challenged to an illegal duel, his father, to avoid the scandal this would bring, banishes him to New Zealand to become a remittance man. During the voyage Rufus meets the captivating Serafina Radzinska, travelling with Anton Springer, who may or may not be her father. Despite his uncertainty, Rufus finds himself falling in love with her - even after he discovers both she and Springer are vampires. When Rufus is badly beaten by the vicious Toby Fox, and seems certain to die, Serafina, who returns his love and fears losing him, turns him into a vampire. Rufus's horror and resentment threaten their love, but when they reach New Zealand and Serafina is captured by Viviana Alexandreu, an ancient and powerful vampire seeking revenge on Springer, Rufus must acknowledge his true feelings and find a way to rescue her and to end Viviana's insane vendetta once and for all.

Restitutions of the Blood

In 1890, when Alex Randall returns from university to his ancestral home of Shillington Hall, he finds his father remarried, less than a year after his mother's death. Dismay turns to anger when a son, Oliver, is born. Convinced the new Lady Randall means to steal his inheritance, Alex flees to London, where he meets and befriends Henri de Saint Clair, a charming, but enigmatic Frenchman. When Alex's friend Charles becomes involved in an illegal duel, and both parties are killed, Alex finds himself on the run from the law, and obliged to leave England. In Paris, he renews his friendship with the still strangely elusive Henri. After a series of misadventures that lead him to the very depths of Parisian society, Henri rescues Alex and restores him to health by means of a mysterious 'restorative' but, before long Alex's determination to discover the truth about his friend plunges him into a world darker - and more addictive - than anything he could have imagined.

About the Author

Lila Richards lives in one of the leafy suburbs of Christchurch, New Zealand, with two black cats. She works part-time as a sub-editor and proofreader for the New Zealand Meteorological Service. As well as writing, Lila reads eclectically, sews vintage clothes, and collects things, in particular old movies, owls, Egyptiana, and art deco paraphernalia. From time to time she enters the Middle Ages via the Society for Creative Anachronism (an international mediaeval re-creation group), where she transmogrifies into a ninth-century small-holder's widow living in the west of Ireland, and has attained the rank of Baroness.

www.ingramcontent.com/pod-product-compliance
Lightning Source LLC
Chambersburg PA
CBHW021530250626
47154CB00006BA/2051